The Beauty of Believing

Other books in the growing Faithgirlz!™ library

Bibles

The Faithgirlz! Bible

NIV Faithgirlz! Backpack Bible

Faithgirlz! Bible Studies

Secret Power of Love

Secret Power of Joy

Secret Power of Goodness

Secret Power of Grace

Fiction

The Good News Shoes

Riley Mae and the Rocker Shocker Trek (Book One)

Riley Mae and the Ready Eddy Rapids (Book Two)

Riley Mae and the Sole Fire Safari (Book Three)

From Sadie's Sketchbook

Shades of Truth (Book One)

Flickering Hope (Book Two)

Waves of Light (Book Three)

Brilliant Hues (Book Four)

Sophie's World Series

Meet Sophie (Book One)

Sophie Steps Up (Book Two)

Sophie and Friends (Book Three)

Sophie's Friendship Fiasco (Book Four)

Sophie Flakes Out (Book Five)

Sophie's Drama (Book Six)

The Lucy Series

Lucy Doesn't Wear Pink (Book One)

Lucy Out of Bounds (Book Two)

Lucy's Perfect Summer (Book Three)

Lucy Finds Her Way (Book Four)

The Girls of Harbor View

Girl Power (Book One)

Take Charge (Book Two)

Raising Faith (Book Three)

Secret Admirer (Book Four)

Boarding School Mysteries

Vanished (Book One)

Betrayed (Book Two)

Burned (Book Three)

Poisoned (Book Four)

Nonfiction

Faithgirlz Handbook

Faithgirlz Journal

Food, Faith, and Fun! Faithgirlz Cookbook

Real Girls of the Bible

My Beautiful Daughter

You! A Christian Girl's Guide to Growing Up

Girl Politics

Everybody Tells Me to Be Myself but I Don't Know Who I Am

Devotions for Girls Series

No Boys Allowed

What's a Girl to Do?

Girlz Rock

Chick Chat

Shine on, Girl!

Check out www.faithgirlz.com

faiThGirLz!™
the beauty of believing

The Beauty of Believing

365 Devotions that Will Change Your Life

Tasha Douglas
Mona Hodgson
Kristi Holl
Lois Walfrid Johnson
Allia Zobel Nolan
Nancy Rue

ZONDERkidz

ZONDERKIDZ

The Beauty of Believing

Requests for information should be addressed to:

Zonderkidz, 3900 *Sparks Dr. SE, Grand Rapids, Michigan 49546*

ISBN 978-0-310-73617-2

Content from:

- *My Beautiful Daughter*: 978-0-310-72643-2 Copyright © 2012 by Tasha Douglas
- *Real Girls of the Bible*: 978-0-310-73018-7 Copyright © 2008 by Mona Hodgson
- *Chick Chat*: 978-0-310-71143-8 Copyright © 2006 by Kristi Holl
- *Girlz Rock*: 978-0-310-70899-5 Copyright © 2005 by Kristi Holl
- *No Boys Allowed*: 978-0-310-70718-9 Copyright © 2004 by Michelle Medlock Adams—copyright/ Kristi Holl—author
- *Shine On, Girl*: 978-0-310-71144-5 Copyright © 2006 by Kristi Holl
- *Girl Talk*: 978-0-310-71449-1 Copyright © 2009 by Lois Walfrid Johnson
- *Whatever*: 978-0-310-72534-3 Copyright © 2012 by Allia Zobel Nolan
- *That Is So Me*: 978-0-310-71475-0 Copyright © 2010 by Nancy Rue

Cover design: Cindy Davis
Cover photography or illustration: Don Davis Photography
Interior design: David Conn

Printed in the United States of America

14 15 16 17 18 19 20 /DCI/ 19 18 17 16 15 14 13 12 11 10 9 8 7 6 5 4 3 2 1

Table of Contents

Section I — Growing Seeds of Faith

Let Your Christ-Light Shine

I've never been what you would call "model material." I wasn't voted Homecoming Queen or named "Cutest" for my high school yearbook. In fact, in middle school I probably would've been chosen "Most Awkward" if they'd had that category! And you know what? It was *hard* to be the tallest, the one with the most pimples, the one with the haircut most likely to be laughed about when all the Very Cool Girls were gathered in the bathroom. Nobody ever used "Nancy" and "beauty" in the same sentence, unless it was to say I wasn't one.

About grade nine, I started accepting that I wasn't headed for the Miss America Pageant, and I decided that the one thing I had going for me was being able to make people laugh. Since people like to laugh, they liked me. Then I discovered that I just automatically encouraged people and helped them see the good in themselves, so I did that more. Pretty soon, people who had problems (even the Very Cool Girls) were coming to me to vent. Eventually, I thought less and less about how not-so-cute I was next to the VCG's.

I didn't realize while all that was happening that God was behind it, that the changes in me were happening because I believed. I was simply showing the beauty within. My life pretty much revolved around the church and I prayed every day and hung out with other believing kids. But it still didn't occur to me until years later that it was all God's doing. I had the beauty of believing and I didn't even know it.

If I *had* known it, I could have avoided some mistakes, like sneaking the makeup my mom said I couldn't wear and hurting two really nice guys by secretly dating both of them at the same time because they both said I was cute (seventeen can be a very clueless age, just so you know). If I'd been even closer to God, I would have been aware that the beauty of Christ's light shining through is better than mascara and compliments. I hope what you're about to read will teach you the same thing.

—Nancy Rue

1

"And I am sure that God, who began the good work within you, will continue his work until it is finally finished on that day when Christ Jesus comes back again."

—Philippians 1:6 (NLT)

Under Construction

God is the master builder, in charge of constructing your life. He began his good work in you, and he will keep building your life until it is finally finished. Ephesians 2:10 says, "we are God's handiwork" or "masterpiece."

Masterpiece, huh? What about the days you're a rotten friend, a mouthy daughter, an insensitive sister? Are you still God's handiwork? Yes, without a doubt.

God is building a great work of art in your life, but many days you won't look, act, or feel like a masterpiece. It takes time. Like the buildings you see go up, the beautiful and sturdy ones aren't built in a day or a week or a month. Some days they don't look like a masterpiece at all—no one would guess how beautiful the finished work will be.

Your life is like that. Each of us is a "work in progress." God loves us just as much on the days we mess up as the days we shine for him. He knows our life is a learning process—and he sees the finished masterpiece he has in mind.

More to Explore: Philippians 1:9–11 and 3:13–14

Girl Talk: Do you feel like you are under construction? Can you see God working in your life?

God Talk: "Lord, thank you for never giving up on me. I want to keep working toward being a masterpiece for you. Amen."

From *No Boys Allowed* by Kristi Holl

2

"How can a young person stay on the path of purity? By living according to your word. I seek you with all my heart; do not let me stray from your commands."

—Psalm 119:9–10

The Ultimate Coach

Olympic skaters and gymnasts have their own coaches. These professionals are with them constantly, long before the big event, working them for hours every day to get them ready.

They have their athletes out there running and doing push-ups and lifting weights—things an audience will never see them do, but which are totally necessary if they're going to be in shape for competition.

Living your life isn't like preparing for some big event, because your events are happening all the time. But in order to be in shape for all the things that are going to come your way, you too need a Personal Trainer. Guess who?

God is there to train you to have great relationships, to serve him to the fullest, to make a difference in this world. Those are things other people will sit up and notice. But to do those things, God will put you through some things no one else may ever see. Things like praying long and hard, listening when it seems like the answers will never come, confessing with big tears on your face, obeying in little things nobody will think to praise you for.

Sign up for his training program, and you'll be ready for anything.

More to Explore: 1 Corinthians 12:27

Girl Talk: What is something that God is training you to do?

God Talk: "God, thank you for caring about me so much and for being my own personal life coach. Make me strong even when no one is watching. Amen."

From *That Is So Me* by Nancy Rue

"[God said,] 'What I want from you is your true thanks; I want your promises fulfilled. I want you to trust me in your times of trouble, so I can rescue you and you can give me glory.'"

—Psalm 50:14 (TLB)

Think "Thanks"

Whatever the circumstances, no matter what, we should always have "Thank you, God" on our minds. After all, the Almighty has given us our life, parents, BFFs, our health, our pets. We can see, hear, speak, smell, taste, and feel. We live in a beautiful world full of beautiful creatures and landscapes.

Jesus continually thanked his Father for everything. That tells us how important an attitude of gratitude must be.

Okay, but what if we get an "F" on our finals, or don't make the cheerleading team, or our parents divorce? We can't be expected to think *Gee, thanks, God* for that.

Well, actually, you can—and should. Life is tough at times, but there is at least a hint of good in every situation that you can be grateful for. The Bible says, "Give thanks in all circumstances: for this is God's will for you in Christ Jesus" (1 Thessalonians 5:18). When we do this, we're saying to God that we believe he's a loving Father who has a plan for us. And though we might not understand what it's all about, *he* does. We can trust that God will use even the hard stuff for good before all is said and done.

More To Explore: Psalm 106:1 and Ephesians 5:19–20

Girl Talk: Jesus healed ten lepers. But only one returned to thank him. When God does something spectacular in your life, do you say, "Thank you?"

God Talk: "Dear God, remind me not to complain about what I don't have and focus instead on thanking you for what I do have. Amen."

From *Whatever: Livin' the True, Noble, Totally Excellent Life* by Allia Zobel Nolan

4

"Do not nurse hatred in your heart for any of your relatives."
—Leviticus 19:17 (NLT)

Be Heart Smart

Your relatives might do things that you hate. Even so, don't think about it all the time. The more you meditate on it—the more you replay the incidents in your mind—the more hate will grow.

Riley knew about hate. Although she spoke politely when face-to-face with her grandmother, her real feelings were another matter. "She's ruining my life!" she told her mom. Grandma had gambled away her savings and then moved in with Riley's family. Riley had to give up her bedroom and crowd in with her little sister. Grandma snapped at Riley about everything: her clothes, her friends, her music, her manners. She even complained that Riley's room was too hot in the afternoon for her nap. "Then give me back my room and go home!" Riley yelled, finally snapping too. Riley—and her parents—were horrified at what she'd said. But Riley had been nursing hatred in her heart for months. It was bound to come out

What could Riley have done instead? What can you do if you have such negative feelings about someone? "When you stand praying, if you hold anything against anyone, forgive them, so that your Father in heaven may forgive you your sins" (Mark 11:25–26 NIV).

More To Explore: 1 John 2:9

Girl Talk: Do you have to hide your real feelings about someone close to you? Have you asked God to help you get rid of those awful feelings?

God Talk: "Lord, I'm having a really hard time with _____ right now. Please take away my anger and hate toward this person. Show me ways to be kind. Amen."

From *Shine On, Girl!* by Kristi Holl

5

"For the Lord God is a sun and shield; the Lord bestows favor and honor; no good thing does he withhold from those whose walk is blameless."

—Psalm 84:11

Owning Up

It was a beautiful summer day, and Dakota was outside playing baseball with some of the boys in the neighborhood. Her dad had asked her not to play in the street, but there wasn't a lot of traffic this time of day, so she decided it was ok.

Mick was pitching, and Dakota knew he'd give her his fastest ball. Taking a firm grip on the bat, she waited. Sure enough, there it came—a little low, but right over the plate.

Dakota swung and connected. A fly popped off to the right. Then *C-R-A-A-A-S-S-H!* The sound of broken glass shattered the air.

Dakota looked around and felt sick. Sure enough, it was Mrs. O'Rourke's window.

One moment everyone stared at the house. The next instant every kid scattered in a different direction. Every kid, that is, except Dakota. Everything within her wanted to run. At the same time, something held her there. Finally, Dakota crossed the street, her feet dragging. Dreading what she was about to do, Dakota climbed the steps and rang the bell.

"I'm sorry," she said when Mrs. O'Rourke answered the door. She wanted to blame the other kids and say that it wasn't her fault. But only four words came out. "I broke your window."

"I know." Mrs. O'Rourke surprised her. "Just before the ball hit, I saw you out another window."

Full of misery, Dakota apologized again.

"I forgive you," Mrs. O'Rourke answered quietly. "I respect you for coming to talk with me. I know that was hard to do."

Suddenly Dakota's gaze found the older woman's eyes. Something Dakota saw there drew her to Mrs. O'Rourke. *Why have I always thought she's crabby?*

Aloud she asked, "What can I do to pay for the window?"

Mrs. O'Rourke swung the screen door farther open. "Why don't you come in? We'll talk about it."

Dakota drew a deep breath. For some strange reason, she almost felt as if she had a new friend.

More to Explore: Philippians 1:27

Girl Talk: Can you think of a time when you did something wrong but made the right choice? What helped you do that?

God Talk: "God, thank you that you always forgive me when I mess up. Please give me the courage to confess my mistakes to other people as well. I love you. Amen."

From *Girl Talk* by Lois Walfrid Johnson

6

"For he satisfies the thirsty and fills the hungry with good things."

—Psalm 107:9 (NLT)

How Hungry Are You?

Would your body be happy with one meal per week? No! In fact, many people eat much more than three times a day to feel satisfied. Your spirit needs feeding too, and the Bible contains our spiritual food. Sitting in church for one hour per week feeds your soul as much as one meal per week would feed your body. You can become depressed, anxious, fearful, critical, and impatient—all signs of a starving and malnourished soul.

Set aside some time to be quiet with God every day. Start out small, if this is new to you. Five or ten minutes of Bible reading, plus five or ten minutes of prayer is fine to start. Making it a habit is your first goal.

Suppose you just don't feel hungry for God's Word. Most days you don't even think of reading your Bible or praying. Then pray and ask God to increase your spiritual hunger and thirst. He delights to answer prayers like that! When we're hungry and thirsty enough, we'll go to the source of our food and eat till full.

So dig into God's Word first thing every morning and eat your fill. It satisfies!

More to Explore: John 6:35 and Matthew 5:6

Girl Talk: Do you have that spiritual hunger for God's Word? Do you want to be filled by God?

God Talk: "Thank you, Lord, for giving me food to sustain my physical body. Please increase my spiritual appetite, so that I may grow closer to you. Amen."

From *No Boys Allowed* by Kristi Holl

7

"Turn from your sins and turn to God, because the Kingdom of Heaven is near . . . Prove by the way you live that you have really turned from your sins and turned to God."

—Matthew 3:2, 8 (NLT)

Change from the Heart

In the verse above, John the Baptist was preaching about repentance. Repenting is not only changing your mind—it's a total turnaround of your life. It involves turning *from* sin and turning *to* God.

You may find a younger brother or sister very annoying. He hogs the TV after school. She wolfs down all the good snacks and then eavesdrops on your phone calls. Usually, before the night is over, you've swatted a sibling at least once. Your brother or sister runs screaming to your mom, who in turn scolds you. "I'm sorry," you always mumble. Sometimes you truly *are* sorry. One night, though, your mom says, "I don't want another apology, honey. If you're sorry, then show it. Stop hitting."

You need to do more than say you're sorry. If you really regret your behavior, you'll change. However, repentance doesn't start with altering one's behavior. For change to last, it must begin with a change of heart. And what is the reaction in heaven when a sinner repents? "I say to you that likewise there will be more joy in heaven over one sinner who repents than over ninety-nine just persons who need no repentance" (Luke 15:7 NKJV).

More to Explore: Ezekiel 18:30–32; 33:1

Girl Talk: Do you apologize just so someone will stop being mad at you? Or do you truly intend to change your behavior?

God Talk: "God, I can't change myself. I've already tried! Please change me from the inside out. Amen."

From *Chick Chat* by Kristi Holl

"Does the clay say to the potter, 'What are you making?'"

—Isaiah 45:9

The Perfect Potter

Imagine you're making a snake out of Play-Doh, and it suddenly looks up at you, opens its big clay mouth, and says, "What do you think you're doing? I don't want to be a snake. I want to be an elephant."

Obviously that isn't going to happen, which is exactly the point of this verse. God is like a Great Potter, creating each person just the way he wants him or her to be. As his creations, we don't get to say, "I want to be something else!" But we try it anyway. Have you ever heard yourself say...

- I wish I were more ________________.
- I wish I weren't so ________________.
- If I were more like ________________, things would be better.

The first step in discovering your one-of-a-kind-ness is accepting that you are made by God to be exactly who God wants you to be. He decided who you are and will be, and eventually he'll reveal that plan to you—one wad of clay at a time.

More to Explore: Psalm 139:14

Girl Talk: What are some things about you that make you different from everyone you know?

God Talk: "Jesus, you knew exactly what you were doing when you created me. Help me to love the person that I am—every part of it. Amen."

From *That Is So Me* by Nancy Rue

9

"Let us then approach God's throne of grace with confidence, so that we may receive mercy and find grace to help us in our time of need."

—Hebrews 4:16

Hannah's Promise

The book of 1 Samuel tells the story of Hannah and her husband Elkanah. Elkanah, like many other men of his time, had another wife. This other wife, Peninnah, had given birth to many children, but Hannah had no kids of her own. Back then, people placed a lot of importance on having children, and Peninnah loved to rub this in Hannah's face.

Every year Hannah and her family traveled to worship in the temple in Shiloh. On those trips, it was especially hard for Hannah to avoid Peninnah's insults. Peninnah's meanness hurt Hannah so much she'd cry and not eat. One year, standing in the temple, Hannah cried out silently in her heart: "O Lord Almighty, if you'll see your servant's misery and give me a son, I'll give him to the Lord for all the days of his life."

Eli the priest noticed her praying and weeping. He saw that her lips moved, but she didn't speak. Eli said to her, "How long will you keep on getting drunk?"

"I'm not drunk," Hannah said. "I'm sad. I have been pouring out my soul to the Lord."

"May the God of Israel give you what you have asked of him," Eli said. After this, Hannah's face was no longer downcast.

The next morning, Hannah and Elkanah and the rest of his family traveled back home. Soon, Hannah became pregnant and had a son she named Samuel, which means "asked of God" in Hebrew. And just as Hannah promised, when her son was about three years old, she took Samuel back to the temple at Shiloh where he grew in stature and in favor with God.

Often, God works in different ways from what we expect. Hannah knew that. Like Hannah, you can take your sadness to God and cry out to him. You can trust him to answer your cry, even if it's not the answer you expect. He knows what's best for you.

More to Explore: Hebrews 5:7

Girl Talk: Have you ever prayed to God with your tears?

God Talk: "Lord God, you have proven yourself faithful and trustworthy. Please give me the grace to trust you. Help me to pray out of a deep love for you. Amen."

From *Real Girls of the Bible* by Mona Hodgson

10

"The battle is the Lord's."

—1 Samuel 17:47

Reaching Goals: Lean on God

Just before the battle with Goliath in 1 Samuel 17, David announced to one and all that he expected God to win this battle for him. David was well aware that in his own strength, he was no match at all for Goliath. Yes, David had to step up to the battle line himself. He also totally depended on God to save him.

Because of different personalities, many believers go to extremes. Sarah sits back, does nothing but pray, and says she's "just trusting the Lord" to give her good grades. (No, she's not. She's being lazy.) Wendy works hard from dawn to dusk, rarely prays, and believes she will succeed someday in the music field based on her own talent. (No, she won't. She's arrogant and thinks she doesn't need God's help for anything.) Be careful that you don't fall into error either way.

Successfully reaching your goals depends on two things that might, at first, seem like opposites. You need to do the necessary work, praying each step of the way. But you also need to understand that it is God who will give you the power to succeed. To reach your goals, find the balance.

Do plan, be persistent, and be confident. Then, leaning on God, take action—for the battle is the Lord's.

More to Explore: Psalm 44:6–7 and Zechariah 4:6

Girl Talk: How often do you pray for God's guidance? Do you sit back and wait, or do you work and prepare?

God Talk: "Lord, I believe my goal of ________ is from you. Help me to be prepared to finish it. Amen."

From *Girlz Rock* by Kristi Holl

"Don't let anyone look down on you because you are young, but set an example for the believers in speech, in conduct, in love, in faith and in purity."

—1 Timothy 4:12

Act Your Age!

Timothy was quite young when Paul wrote him this letter. People weren't taking Timothy seriously. Paul told him not to let anyone think less of him because he was young. So instead, Timothy chose to set an example. He showed the believers how grown up he was by how he lived, how he loved people, his faith, and his sexual purity.

Adults watch the actions of some youths—their drinking, violence, foul language, and drugs—and, without thinking, judge all kids as being alike. Here, Paul is giving you a guaranteed, sure-fire way to get the adults in your life to treat you with respect. If you set a good example of Christian conduct in what you say, in how you love and treat people, and in your spiritual walk—you'll definitely get adult attention (the kind you want!).

Age and maturity don't mean the same thing. Old people can be mature or very immature. Young people can be either one too. It's your choice. Whatever you choose, you will be known for your behavior and respected (or not) because of it.

More to Explore: 1 Peter 5:3

Girl Talk: Do you ever feel passed over because you are young? Do you know that you can do as much for God as anybody else?

God Talk: "Lord, I want to do great things for you. Help me to find out what you want me to do with my life. Thank you for your guidance. Amen."

From *No Boys Allowed* by Kristi Holl

12

"He made known to us the mystery of his will . . . to bring unity to all things in heaven and on earth together under Christ."

—Ephesians 1:9–10

Growing Up God's Girl

I bet you've been asked this question—probably by some grown-up who was trying to have a conversation with you and couldn't think of anything else to ask: What do you want to be when you grow up?

If you were five or six at the time, you probably had an answer all ready—firefighter, doctor, astronaut, rock star. And if asked a week later, you had a different answer—ballet dancer, zoo keeper, ice skater, depending on what you saw on TV in between.

These days it might be a little harder to discuss that. Who has time to think about what you'll be doing a bajillion years from now?

There's one specific thing you CAN know now, because it's what God has planned for each one of us. He wants every single one of us to belong to Jesus Christ. That's why he sent Jesus, and why Jesus appointed apostles to spread his message, and why Jesus will return when God has everybody gathered together. So next time a grown-up asks what you're going to do with the rest of your life, you can tell her: I've already started. I'm a Christ-follower.

There's no mystery about that.

More to Explore: Micah 6:8 and Jeremiah 29:11

Girl Talk: What can you do to be a Christ-follower *today*, before you grow up?

God Talk: "Jesus, you have a plan for my future. Help me to remember that you also have a plan for me for *right now*, and that's following you. Amen."

From *That Is So Me* by Nancy Rue

13

"Let's march into his presence singing praises, lifting the rafters with our hymns! . . . Because God is the best, High King over all the gods."

—Psalm 95:2, 3 (MSG)

A Joyful Noise

Johanna went to her Gran's new house for Easter. She had never been to the local church and didn't know what to expect.

The service was lively and filled with music. The youth choir, backed by two killer guitars, a piano, and drum, led the congregation in some classic and newer songs. Everyone was totally into it. Johanna, who always thought her voice was lame, finally joined in too. When she left the church, she felt a sense of joy she couldn't quite explain.

The Bible says, "Sing to the Lord, all the world! Worship the Lord with joy; come before him with happy songs!" (Psalm 100:1, 2 TEV)

It doesn't say: those with voices like Taylor Swift sing to the Lord; all others forget about it. It doesn't say: sing to the Lord, but don't sing too loud; otherwise, people sitting next to you will think you're weird.

God has done some pretty cool things for us, and, along with everything else that sings his praises—the birds, trees, mountains, and hills—we should too. Whether our voice is sweet as a songbird or more like a squeaky mouse, the Lord hears it all. And to his ears, there's nothing lovelier.

More To Explore: James 5:13

Girl Talk: When do you feel the most free to sing and be yourself? Try to remember that feeling and bring it with you when you go to church.

God Talk: "Mighty Lord, remind me I'm not in a singing contest at church. I'm there to give you praise! Amen."

From *Whatever: Livin' the True, Noble, Totally Excellent Life* by Allia Zobel Nolan

14

"For our struggle is not against flesh and blood, but against the rulers, against the authorities, against the powers of this dark world and against the spiritual forces of evil in the heavenly realms. Therefore put on the full armor of God, so that when the day of evil comes, you may be able to stand your ground, and after you have done everything, to stand."

—Ephesians 6:12–13

The Battle for Beauty

Have you ever unintentionally become involved in a fight when you were just minding your own business? News flash, faithgirl. It's happening to you now. As God's daughter, you are involved in a conflict that you didn't ask to be a part of. But—so you don't end up right smack dab in the middle of a warzone asking yourself, "Wow. What just happened?—here's some help!

What happened is you inherited an enemy. You are now engaged in a battle because you belong to Jesus Christ. Jesus, the Lion of the Tribe of Judah, has an enemy called Satan. Because he hates Jesus Christ, Satan goes after all Jesus' friends—including you. So you must "Be alert and of sober mind" (1 Peter 5:8).

Yes, there is a battle for the beauty of believing. Not only are you a darling daughter, you are also a well-equipped soldier in an intense spiritual fight. The fight found you, because you are God's child. Are you ready to rumble?

What can you do to resist evil right now? Obey the commands of Jesus Christ, faithgirl, trusting God to protect you from the evil one.

More To Explore: Ephesians 6:18

Girl Talk: Can you name all the weapons in Ephesians 6 God gives you for withstanding the fight?

God Talk: "Father, thank you for giving us victory over the enemy! When the battle gets tough, be my shield and my protection!"

From *My Beautiful Daughter* by Tasha Douglas

"Stop judging others, and you will not be judged. For others will treat you as you treat them. Whatever measure you use in judging others, it will be used to measure how you are judged."
—Matthew 7:1–2 (NLT)

What Glasses Are You Wearing?

Stop forming negative opinions about other people. Then people won't form negative opinions about you. Whatever standard you use to compare people will be the same standard others use to judge you.

It's almost instinctive to form opinions about others: their clothing and hair, the way they walk. Judging is a pride issue. We judge someone as inferior so we can feel superior. Everything we observe gives us a chance to judge—or show mercy. If you're kind in your judgments of others, it's like wearing pink-tinted sunglasses that color everything rosy. Judging harshly is using a magnifying glass to focus on someone's faults to make them even bigger.

If you have a judging habit, catch yourself when you form a negative opinion about someone else's looks or actions. Then replace it with something positive, out loud, if possible. The more consistently you replace judgmental thoughts with positive ones, the quicker you'll break the habit.

No one likes to be judged. Choose to form positive opinions about people. Then watch how they'll look at *you* through rose-colored glasses.

More to Explore: James 4:11–12 and Luke 6:37

Girl Talk: Do you have a habit of judging others? Would you rather be looked at under a microscope or through rose-colored glasses?

God Talk: "God, I am so thankful that you are a merciful judge. Help me to see the positive in others as you see the positive in me. Thank you. Amen."

From *No Boys Allowed* by Kristi Holl

16

"Who may climb the mountain of the Lord? Who may stand in his holy place? Only those who . . . do not worship idols."

—Psalm 24:3–4

Me? Worship Idols?

There are certain standards you must meet before you approach God. If you want the Lord to hear your prayers, then you must not worship idols. God wants to be first in your life.

Morgan had heard about idol worship, but she thought that couldn't have anything to do with her. It was about bowing down to stone statues or worshiping things carved out of wood, wasn't it? Not necessarily. Morgan actually had an idol herself. His name was Chad. She thought about him day and night. She daydreamed about him instead of finishing her homework. When she dressed for school, she only wondered, *Will Chad like this outfit?*

An idol doesn't have to be made of stone or wood or gold. An idol can be anyone who is adored blindly and excessively. When your feelings about another person totally absorb you, you've allowed that person to become an idol. When your intentions are to please him first and above all others, he's taken God's place in your life.

It's okay to like boys. But it's *not* good or healthy to make a boy into an idol. The only person who belongs in first place in your life is the Lord.

More to Explore: Acts 14:11–15 and Exodus 20:3

Girl Talk: Who is the most important person to you? Does their opinion of you matter more to you than God's opinion?

God Talk: "Lord, sometimes I put others ahead of you. Help me to keep you first in my life, no matter who else is important to me. Amen."

From *Chick Chat* by Kristi Holl

17

"Keep your eyes open, hold tight to your convictions, give it all you've got, be resolute and love without stopping."
—1 Corinthians 16:13 (MSG)

You Gotta Be You

Look," Avery said to her BFF, "I didn't know what the video was about when Stacey asked me. I can't back out now."

"I did," Emily said. "I just told her I don't do R movies."

"And she probably thinks you're dork of the day," Avery said and walked off.

If you're an authentic Christian, this means you're true to God, to his Word, and to your beliefs. Simply put, you don't become a people pleaser at the expense of your faith. You don't say you believe one thing one minute, then act like you don't the next.

Jesus was awesome at this. He aligned his will with God's and didn't waver. He didn't stop eating with sinners because people whispered behind his back. He didn't take up a sword because people wanted a military leader. He didn't lie about who he was to save his life.

Jesus was the real thing through and through.

You can be that way too. But it's going to take courage. You need to be one strong cookie to be "God's Girl," instead of "At-the-Mercy-of-Anybody's-Whim-Because-She-Wants-to-Be-Liked-Girl." But don't worry. God is there to help you.

More To Explore: 2 Corinthians 1:15–22

Girl Talk: Do you "stick to your guns" when it comes to your beliefs? Or do you go back and forth depending on who you're talking to?

God Talk: "Jesus, people always knew where you stood—with your Father—in everything you did. I want to be true to myself by being true to you. Amen."

From *Whatever: Livin' the True, Noble, Totally Excellent Life* by Allia Zobel Nolan

18

"'In your anger do not sin': Do not let the sun go down while you are still angry."

—Ephesians 4:26

Put Out the Fire!

Brianna was angry. She loaned her new bike to her best friend, who promised to take extra good care of it. It was returned bent and crumpled. Her best friend had left the bike in her driveway, where her dad backed his truck over it. The frame was bent, and the red paint was scratched. Even though her friend offered to get it fixed, Brianna was furious. She wanted to call her friend names and scream at her. Instead she bit her tongue. For an hour, Brianna ranted and raved to herself about her irresponsible friend. When she calmed down, she knew she had a decision to make. Would she punish her friend by venting her anger or giving her the silent treatment? Or would she forgive her and drop it? Brianna called her friend, made arrangements to get the bike fixed, talked about school for a few minutes, then hung up. She still hated that her bike was damaged, but she was glad she'd kept her friend.

Christians don't lose their emotions when they get saved, but you don't have to continue giving in to a bad temper. Ask God to change you from the inside out. He will!

More To Explore: Proverbs 14:29

Girl Talk: Has anger ever gotten the best of you? What could you have done instead of giving in to your anger?

God Talk: "Lord, I know I don't always handle anger well. Please help me not to give in to my anger. I want to stay calm and forgiving, like you. Amen."

From *Shine On, Girl!* by Kristi Holl

"No discipline seems pleasant at the time, but painful. Later on, however, it produces a harvest of righteousness and peace for those who have been trained by it."

—Hebrews 12:11

God Uses Problems to Direct You

We don't enjoy discipline while it's happening—it's painful! Being trained in self-control is hard! But afterward, you will earn great rewards.

Morgan knew she'd overeaten all summer, but it wasn't until she bought new school clothes that she realized how much weight she'd gained. Not being able to buy the cute clothes she saw was hard enough, but returning to school was worse. Girls in gym class raced circles around her. A girl from her class last year said she hardly recognized Morgan—and Morgan knew she referred to her new chipmunk cheeks.

Discipline often comes in the form of problems we want to hide from. We often fail to see how God is trying to use *those very problems* to help us learn more about ourselves. He may want to turn you in a different direction or motivate you to make a change in your life. The weight comments and being left in the dust in gym class were painful for Morgan. However, they motivated her to take better care of her body, which is the temple of the Holy Spirit.

Developing self-control is hard, but remember the rewards! Stay focused on the prize you'll receive at the end.

More to Explore: Hebrews 12:5–6 and 2 Corinthians 4:17

Girl Talk: How do you handle being disciplined? Can you understand why you need to be corrected from time to time?

God Talk: "Lord, being corrected is not my favorite thing. Please help me to remember that you discipline me because you want what is best for me. Amen."

From *Girlz Rock* by Kristi Holl

20

"To humans being belong the plans of the heart, but from the Lord comes the proper answer of the tongue."

—Proverbs 16:1

Making Plans

We use our minds to think and plan and get organized. That's an important function of our brains. But if those plans are to work out, God must give us the ability to express those ideas and the strength to achieve those goals.

Has this ever happened to you? You plot and plan how to convince your parents to increase your allowance and allow you to stay up later on weekends. You have all your arguments organized. You've even written them down. But when you start talking, you grow so frustrated at their questions that you can't remember any of your well-planned ideas. You blow up and run from the room. Later that night, you reread your list of convincing reasons, but take time to talk to God before talking to your parents. "Lord, please give me your words to say," you pray. Your second talk with your parents will go much better!

It's good to make plans and think about your goals, but always remember that God is still in control. He knows what's best and how plans will—or won't—work out. If you're a follower of Jesus, then it is up to him to lead the way.

Be organized. Make plans. Then give the plans to God to bring about.

More to Explore: Exodus 4:11–12

Girl Talk: Are you organized with your homework, your jobs, and your spare time? Do you make plans? Do you depend on God's wisdom to carry them out?

God Talk: "Lord, I'm glad you're in control, even when I make all kinds of plans. Only you can make them work. Amen."

From *Chick Chat* by Kristi Holl

"We cannot stop telling about the wonderful things we have seen Jesus do and heard him say."

—Acts 4:20 (TLB)

An Expert Witness

Ava had it in for JayCee. She called her a geek because JayCee loved math and made fun of the fact that she was a Christian.

"So, where was your God on 9/11?" she jeered, "Out to lunch, like you?"

"Let's talk about it," JayCee said, but Ava walked off. Then the unthinkable happened: Ava was failing in math. So the teacher asked JayCee to be her study partner.

Working with JayCee closely and seeing her live out her faith in little ways left an impression on Ava. She still made fun of JayCee every chance she got. But three months later, she asked her if she could drop in on youth group to "check out this Jesus dude."

Jesus told us to "Go into all the world and preach the Good News to everyone, everywhere." (Mark 16:15 NLT). There are dozens of ways we can do that. Like JayCee, we can witness without words—spread the Good News by showing rather than telling. Some girls may roll their eyes when you say Jesus wants us to treat others how we want to be treated. But if they *see* you do it ... they just might ask you about it.

More To Explore: Matthew 28:19

Girl Talk: Who are some people in your life who need to know God? How could you share the love of Jesus with them?

God Talk: "Jesus, please send your Spirit to help me spread the Word about you everywhere. Amen."

From *Whatever: Livin' the True, Noble, Totally Excellent Life* by Allia Zobel Nolan

22

"Do not lie to one another, since you laid aside the old self with its evil practices."

—Colossians 3:9 (NASB)

Nothing But the Truth

Kylie paused the movie when the phone rang. "Hello?" She rolled her eyes when she heard it was Darla, the boring girl who lived two doors down. "Sorry, but I can't go to the pool," Kylie said. "I'm doing chores for my mom." She felt a twinge of guilt when she hung up, but lying seemed better than going to the pool with Darla or telling her she was boring.

Most of us think of ourselves as honest people, yet studies show that some of those who identify themselves as believers lie many times each day. Why do we do it, when we know that lying is wrong? Sometimes we don't want to be held responsible, so we hide behind made-up excuses. Or we lie to avoid discipline. Or we want to look good to someone else.

Why is telling the truth so important in loving others? Because telling the truth builds trust, and lies destroy trust. If you love someone, you will tell them the truth. Telling the truth takes courage and confidence, but God's Word is clear: do not lie.

More to Explore: Leviticus 19:11 and Zechariah 8:16

Girl Talk: Think of the last time you told a little white lie. Do you think it solved the problem, or did it make the problem last longer?

God Talk: "Lord, sometimes little lies seem to solve problems for me. Please help me to remember that the truth spoken in love is so much better than lies. Amen."

From *Shine On, Girl!* by Kristi Holl

"Peter said to Jesus, 'Lord, it is good for us to be here. If you wish, I will put up three shelters.' "

—Matthew 17:4

Baby Steps

You can fix macaroni and cheese out of a box and make a mean peanut butter and jelly sandwich. Think you're ready to cook a whole meal by yourself for the entire family?

Once you get a taste of something, it's easy to think you're ready for the whole enchilada, but most big skills take time to learn, and that's especially true of spiritual things.

Peter didn't know that yet when Jesus chose him, along with James and John, to go up a high mountain with him. There, they saw him glow with godliness as he talked to Moses and Elijah (long since dead). Jesus picked Peter because he was learning and growing, and Jesus knew he could trust him. But when he saw the three spirits together, Peter showed that he didn't totally understand it. He wanted to put up tents for them! What a silly idea!

And that's okay. Faith is a journey, and who better than Peter to show us that, because he's so very much like us. Keep stumbling along. Every experience with God brings you closer to understanding.

More to Explore: James 1:4 and John 13:1–11

Girl Talk: Sometimes it's hard to know how to live close to God. Even grown-ups don't have it all figured out. What questions do you still have about what it means to follow Jesus?

God Talk: "Jesus, I'm like Peter in a lot of ways. Sometimes I don't get all this spiritual stuff. Help me to keep growing closer to you. Amen."

From *That Is So Me* by Nancy Rue

24

"Merely hearing God's law is a waste of your time if you don't do what he commands. Doing, not hearing, is what makes the difference with God."

—Romans 2:13 (MSG)

Are You All Talk and No Do?

Maybe you know a girl in Sunday school who listens attentively. Yet at school, she acts stuck-up, tells dirty jokes, and behaves totally differently. What's going on? According to Romans, she's wasting her time at church because the words are going in one ear and out the other. Unless it changes your attitude and behavior—unless you actually DO what the Bible says—your church attendance won't make any difference to God.

Are you that person yourself? Maybe you're not phony. Maybe you fully intend to do what God's Word says, like forgiving that person who gossiped about you, or being patient with your little brother. You haven't done it *yet* because it's too hard or you don't have time. Be careful that you aren't proud of all your Bible knowledge, but then fail to put it into practice. So what if you can recite whole books of the Bible from memory, if you don't obey any of it? God would prefer that you know only three verses, if you actually put them into practice.

Be a doer of the Word, and not a hearer only.

More to Explore: James 1:22

Girl Talk: Do you know what God's Word says, but aren't following it? How hard do you try to put God's Word into practice?

God Talk: "Lord, I know I don't always do what I say I do. Please help me to do what you want me to do, not just read about it. Amen."

From *No Boys Allowed* by Kristi Holl

25

"Whoever corrects a mocker invites insults; whoever rebukes the wicked incurs abuse. Do not rebuke mockers or they will hate you; rebuke the wise and they will love you."

—Proverbs 9:7–8

Becoming Wiser and Wiser

If you try to correct someone who jeers and sneers and treats people with contempt, you'll probably receive rude, nasty remarks for your effort. Correct a wise person, though, and she'll love you.

Lisa babysat for the Wilson family's three small children. When Mrs. Wilson arrived home early one day, Lisa was on the phone with a girlfriend and hadn't even realized that the youngest napping child had crawled out of bed and gone outside. When Mrs. Wilson asked her to not take personal calls anymore while babysitting, Lisa erupted. She slammed down the phone and scowled at Mrs. Wilson. That was the end of her babysitting job! The new babysitter, Samantha, needed correction too. She fed the children too many sweets. Her response when corrected? "I'm sorry, Mrs. Wilson. I'll do better from now on." And she did.

"Whoever loves discipline loves knowledge, but whoever hates correction is stupid" (Proverbs 12:1). That's pretty blunt—but it's true. If you want to be wiser, you'll listen to correction and take the discipline. It's stupid to make the same mistakes—and pay for them—over and over again.

More to Explore: Proverbs 15:12

Girl Talk: If you were a horse, what kind of bit would you need in your mouth? Do you respond to simple directions, or do you have to be forced into obedience?

God Talk: "Jesus, it's embarrassing to be corrected, and sometimes it hurts. Help me to listen to correction and learn from it. Amen."

From *Chick Chat* by Kristi Holl

26

" [Jesus said,] 'Well done, good and faithful servant! You have been faithful with a few things; I will put you in charge of many things.' "

—Matthew 25:21

The Big Choice

Trish-ah-a-a-a-a-a!" came a little voice from the bedroom.

"Hang on," Trisha said into her cell. She was babysitting at the Robinson's again. Whenever Trisha was having the most fun talking with a friend, Emmy wanted her attention.

"I'll be there soon," Trisha shouted to Emmy.

For a few moments, everything was quiet. Trisha slid into a more comfortable position and started texting. Soon, she forgot about the little girl she was babysitting.

Trisha was just about to check on her when the Robinson's phone rang. By now, Trisha was texting back and forth between two friends. She couldn't just leave them hanging!

For an instant, Trisha looked at the Robinson's phone. *It's just someone wanting to sell something,* she decided. Pushing the ringing phone out of her mind, she went back to texting.

Suddenly, a loud crash broke into her conversation. Filled with panic, Trisha jumped up and ran for Emmy's bedroom. As she raced down the hallway, Trisha noticed the door to the master bedroom was partly open. She tried to push it the rest of the way, but the door wouldn't move. Looking down, Trisha discovered the reason. A large piece from a glass lamp had spun across the hardwood floor. Other pieces lay all around one side of the bed.

Emmy sat on that bed, only a few feet above most of the broken glass.

"Emmy!" Trisha snapped. "You're supposed to be in bed. What are you doing in here?"

Emmy pushed back into a pillow and huddled there. "You didn't come when I called." Tears welled up in Emmy's eyes and slid down her cheeks. "I want my mommy."

Trisha looked at Emmy, then at the floor. *I'm in big trouble*, she thought. *What am I going to tell her mom and dad?*

An instant later an even worse thought struck Trisha. *Emmy must have pushed the lamp off the bedside table. What if she'd been on the floor and* pulled *it off?* It wasn't hard to imagine the little girl all cut up from flying glass.

That's when Trisha realized she'd made a big mistake. Emmy's parents had trusted her with the safety of their daughter, and Trisha hadn't been responsible. When we become followers of Jesus, he also gives us a lot of responsibility. Can you be trusted with it?

More To Explore: Romans 12:5–8

Girl Talk: Do you ever babysit? What kind of babysitter do you think God wants you to be?

God Talk: "God, please help me to use my gifts well. Help me to be a girl people can count on. Amen."

From *Girl Talk* by Lois Walfrid Johnson

27

"A good man brings good things out of the good stored up in his heart, and an evil man brings evil things out of the evil stored up in his heart. For the mouth speaks what the heart is full of."

—Luke 6:45

The Heart of the Matter

Whatever is truly in your heart will come out in your words and actions. You can't pretend for long. If you have a heart full of good, you'll produce good deeds and say good things. If evil words and actions flow from a person, it's because she has evil stored in her heart instead.

When your little brother chatters nonstop on the way to school, do you say, "That sounds interesting," or "Shut up, twerp"? When a gossip session at lunch is tearing down a teacher, do you join in or find something positive to say? Whatever comes out of your mouth reveals the condition of your heart.

There shouldn't be a mixture—some good, some bad—coming out of our mouths. However, oftentimes there is. Read Psalm 51, and confess whatever needs confessing. "Create in me a pure heart, O God, and renew a steadfast spirit within me" (v. 10). Your mouth is like a barometer of your heart, measuring and revealing its condition, so pay attention to your words.

More to Explore: Psalm 37:30–31

Girl Talk: Do you watch the words that come out of your mouth? What situations are the hardest for you?

God Talk: "Lord, I have good intentions, but I don't always say nice things. Please help me to think before I speak. I want to say what you would say. Amen."

From *Girlz Rock* by Kristi Holl

"Whatever you do, whether in word or deed, do it all in the name of the Lord Jesus, giving thanks to God the Father though him."

—Colossians 3:17

Martha's Sister Trouble

Martha owned a house in Bethany where Jesus often went to teach, rest, and receive nourishment. During one of Jesus' visits, Martha was working hard to prepare a good meal for Jesus and his disciples. Her sister Mary, on the other hand, was in with the men, sitting at Jesus' feet like she had nothing else to do. The harder Martha worked, the more frustrated with Mary she became. Finally, Martha stomped into the room where Jesus and the others sat. She went straight to the Lord to complain.

"Lord," Martha said, "don't you care that my sister has left me to do the work all by myself? Tell her to help me."

Martha wanted Jesus to take her side and fix the problem by telling Mary to get off her lazy fanny and get to work. But she learned that the Lord doesn't always give the answer we want or expect.

"Martha, Martha," Jesus answered, "you're worried and upset about many things, but only one thing is needed. Mary has chosen what is better, and it won't be taken away from her."

As it turned out, Martha didn't have sister trouble; she had Martha trouble. It wasn't wrong for her to show her love for Jesus by cooking a nice meal for him. But Martha had a bad attitude. She was more upset that Mary wasn't working than she was happy to be helping Jesus. She had failed to focus on who it was she wanted to serve.

Mary had chosen to take advantage of the time Jesus spent in their house to learn from him. This was a good thing and the right choice for her. Instead of worrying about her sister, Martha should've lost the bitter attitude and served Jesus with joy. As Martha learned, God cares more about the state of your heart than he does about your outward actions.

More to Explore: Mark 12:30

Girl Talk: Do you always have a good attitude when you're doing your chores or attending your little brother's soccer game? How could your heart be more joyful?

God Talk: "Thank you, God, for your patience. Even when I'm frustrated or lonely, angry or confused, guilty or afraid, happy or sad, you meet me where I am. Help me to have a happy servant's heart when I'm doing something nice for other people — even when I don't want to. Amen."

From *Real Girls of the Bible* by Mona Hodgson

"Neither do I condemn you," Jesus declared. "Go now and leave your life of sin."

—John 8:11

All Sin Erased

Wow. A *life* of sin. It's one thing to make a mistake once in a while, even once a day–but to live a whole life around a bad thing, yikes.

That's the way it was with a woman some important men brought to Jesus. She'd been caught doing something very wrong, which she had evidently been doing repeatedly for some time. Under the law of Moses, she should have been stoned to death.

Mind you, the teachers and Pharisees didn't really care whether the woman was punished. They were just trying to trap Jesus, because he'd been talking about forgiveness and love instead of law. If he said to let her go, he'd be going against the law. If he said to go ahead and stone her, he'd be going against what he'd been teaching. These leaders thought they were so clever.

Jesus turned that around on them. He said, "If any of you is without sin, let him be the first to throw a stone at her."

Is it any surprise that they all dropped their stones and went away pouting?

More to Explore: 1 John 1:9

Girl Talk: Is there something in your life that you know is wrong but you find yourself doing again and again? Whatever it is, take it to God.

God Talk: "Lord, it seems like I keep making the same mistake over and over again. Please forgive me for ________________. Take away this bad pattern. I know that you have the power to help me walk away, and you will never stop loving me. Amen."

From *That Is So Me* by Nancy Rue

30

"Then Peter came to Jesus and asked, 'Lord, how many times shall I forgive my brother or sister who sins against me? Up to seven times?' Jesus answered, 'I tell you, not seven times, but seventy-seven times.' "

—Matthew 18:21–22

Forgive *How* Many Times?

Peter shows what we all feel at times. While we love the mercy and forgiveness God gives us on a daily basis, we resent having to forgive other people, especially when they do the same thing over and over. Does Jesus mean we have to forgive seventy-seven times—and then we can clobber the offender? No, he's making a point: we need to forgive over and over, just as God forgives us daily. Forgiveness is a gift given to those who don't deserve it.

Every day, people do things that hurt us. Your forgetful grandmother thought your birthday was next month and missed it today. Your best friend has to cancel your movie date to do her homework. A bully at school calls you a mean name.

Galatians 6:2 (AMP) says we need to "bear (endure, carry) one another's burdens and troublesome moral faults." It's easier to endure other people's faults when we realize how many we have ourselves. Instead of becoming bitter, be gentle and quick to forgive.

Give the gift of forgiveness to someone you know today.

More to Explore: Luke 17:3–4

Girl Talk: Have you been hurt by someone you care about? How are you dealing with it? Have you forgiven that person?

God Talk: "Thank you for forgiving all my sins, Lord. Help me to be a forgiving person too. Amen."

From *No Boys Allowed* by Kristi Holl

31

"The good soil represents those who hear and accept God's message and produce a huge harvest—thirty, sixty, or even a hundred times as much as had been planted."

—Mark 4:20 (NLT)

Cultivate Your Faith

When you plant garden seeds, you don't expect much of a crop from dry, rocky ground or a patch full of weeds. But good soil—black soil full of minerals—will produce up to a hundred times the amount of seed that was planted. In the same way, people with good hearts, ready to receive God's Word and act on it, will also produce an abundant harvest.

God has given you special talents and abilities that he wants you to use. Do you love to run fast? Do you have a good singing voice or an ability to play the flute well? Can you write poetry or paint watercolors? God wants you to enjoy the gifts and talents, but also use them to bring joy to others and glory and praise to God. Is your life producing such a harvest? It can!

If you don't like your harvest, check your soil. Is it full of weeds (like resentment, laziness, or jealousy)? Is your soil dry and hard from lack of water (from ignoring reading your Bible)? If your soil needs attention, be a good farmer. Plant it with seeds of obedience to God's Word—then wait for that bumper-crop harvest!

More to Explore: Luke 8:15

Girl Talk: Are you using your talents to the best of your ability?

God Talk: "Lord, I want to use my talents for you. Please help me to honor you in all I do. I want to give you a bumper crop! Amen."

From *Girlz Rock* by Kristi Holl

32

"Those who are kind benefit themselves, but the cruel bring ruin on themselves."

—Proverbs 11:17

Payback

Amber's grandma had fallen and broken her arm. Grandma loved a clean house, and Amber knew she'd appreciate having someone clean it for her. With her cast, it was too hard for Grandma to drag the vacuum around or scrub out the tub. To be honest, Amber wished she didn't have to spend her Saturday cleaning Grandma's house. However, because she cared, she went anyway. Several hours later, with the house sparkling, Grandma and Amber sat in the porch swing, eating ice cream and laughing about things Amber had done when she was younger. Grandma also shared some stories about her own childhood, things that surprised Amber. By the time Amber had to leave, she hated to go. The joy and laughter far outweighed the energy she'd spent cleaning.

When you give to someone in need—whether it's your money, your time, or your talents—you are planting a seed. If you give just a little, the blessings you get back will be little as well. If you give a lot, the harvest of gratitude, joy, and peace will be huge. Be generous—scatter your seed far and wide! Then enjoy your crop of blessings.

More To Explore: Galatians 6:7

Girl Talk: Who could use some help from you right now? Make a plan to help them.

God Talk: "Jesus, sometimes I get so involved in my life that I forget about others. Help me find ways to give to other people. I want to be a blessing to them and to you. Amen."

From *Shine On, Girl!* by Kristi Holl

"All who are skilled among you are to come and make everything the Lord has commanded."

— Exodus 35:10

Building the Church

After God led the Israelites out of Egypt, God wanted them to recognize that *he* was making all the good things happen for them, and that meant they needed to worship him. Because they were such a clueless bunch, he gave them specific instructions for how to do that, starting with the *place* where they were to gather on the Sabbath.

God was still leading the Israelites to the Promised Land, a trip that was going to take forty years, so their place of worship—their tabernacle—had to be sort of portable. But that didn't mean it should be tacky or thrown together. God knew it would mean a lot more to the people if they each had a part in building it. He had a job for each of them.

This project was to be done only by those who were willing. God still expects us to take part in building his church, whether it's babysitting in the nursery or making cheer-up cards for the old folks or singing in the kids' choir—not because we have to, but because we're willing to share our skills and ourselves.

That's actually the fun part. With so many "right things to do," it's great to have one that is pure joy, all the way.

More to Explore: Romans 12:4–5

Girl Talk: What's one little thing you can do for *your* church? What about for your family or group of friends?

God Talk: "Jesus, thank you for giving me talents and skills that I can use to serve others. Show me how I can use my gifts to help my church. Amen."

From *That Is So Me* by Nancy Rue

34

"But the Lord said to me, 'Tell them, "Do not go up and fight, because I will not be with you. You will be defeated by your enemies."' So I told you, but you would not listen."

—Deuteronomy 1:42–43

Divine Defeat

The Lord told the Israelites to go into the Promised Land and defeat those who lived there, but they were scared and refused. Later, the Israelites changed their minds, but God warned them it was too late. They disobeyed and went to fight anyway—and were defeated. God used defeat to get the attention of the stubborn Israelites. Today, God still gets our attention by allowing us to experience defeat.

Hannah's family was having problems, and the tension made her edgy. She swallowed the anxiety, but it erupted later as anger at her best friend. She even mouthed off to her reading teacher when she didn't have her assignment done. Hannah was allowed to experience defeat. Her best friend refused to come over on the weekend. She also spent time after school in the reading room. As she finished her overdue assignment, she prayed, "Lord, are you trying to tell me something?"

Are things going badly in certain areas of your life? It may be that God is trying to get your attention to move you back on the path to joyful, peaceful living. Listen up!

More to Explore: Isaiah 59:1–2

Girl Talk: What are you having trouble with right now? Could God be trying to get your attention about something?

God Talk: "Jesus, I want to take an honest look at my life and not blame my problems on others. Help me to listen to your words of wisdom. Amen."

From *Chick Chat* by Kristi Holl

35

"But seek first his kingdom and his righteousness, and all these things will be given to you as well."

—Matthew 6:33

First Things First

God's Word says that if we will make living for the Lord our *first* concern, he will *give* us all we need from day to day. Stop chasing after material possessions. Focus on the kingdom of God, and let the things chase you!

For example, do you wish you had more friends? Instead of working hard to impress people or buy friendship with flattery or gifts, seek God instead. Ask him how you can meet someone else's need for friendship, how you can show his love to people. As you focus on living for God, he will provide you with friends. And they will be true, loyal friends—not the fickle kind you can buy.

Or do you wish you had more money to buy things you need? Then do things God's way. First, give some money away to a person who needs it. God will then provide for your own needs, often in a way you least expect it.

Put first things first. Live your life to be pleasing to the Lord, and don't worry about getting things. Make living for God the main thing, and he will see that you have everything you need.

More to Explore: Matthew 13:44–46 and Psalm 34:9–10

Girl Talk: What is at the top of your priority list? Where do you put God on your list?

God Talk: "Lord, I know I have lots of things on my mind that really don't matter. Please help me to put you first in my life! Amen."

From *No Boys Allowed* by Kristi Holl

36

"Then the King will say to those on his right, 'Come, you who are blessed by my Father, inherit the Kingdom prepared for you from the creation of the world. For I was hungry, and you fed me. I was thirsty, and you gave me a drink. I was a stranger, and you invited me into your home."

—Matthew 25:34–36 (NLT)

Mind Your Mission

Have you ever received a list of things to do? Jesus Christ had a list of things Father God assigned him to do too. Jesus said, "The Spirit of the Lord is on me, because he has anointed me to proclaim good news to the poor. He has sent me to proclaim freedom for the prisoners and recovery of sight for the blind, to set the oppressed free, to proclaim the year of the Lord's favor" (Luke 4:18–19). Now that's what you call good work!

Are you ready to get in on the action? With some help from the adults in your life, you can serve right now, faithgirl! And please don't say, "But I'm too young." Girls like you can be the most compassionate and generous people in the world. Your energy is amazing! And though there is plenty of work to be done, there are not as many people willing to do it. Today, you can begin to change the world. Ask Father God how.

More To Explore: 1 Peter 4:10

Girl Talk: What Bible characters started serving God in their youth? How old was Esther? What about Daniel and his friends? Samuel?

God Talk: "Father, thank you for choosing me to work with your son Jesus Christ! Show me the gifts and talents you have given me to help fulfill your mission! Amen."

From *My Beautiful Daughter* by Tasha Douglas

"Many, Lord my God, are the wonders you have done, the things you planned for us. None can compare with you; were I to speak and tell of your deeds, they would be too many to declare."
—Psalm 40:5

Oh, I Get It!

Think about the last mystery movie you saw or book you read. Was there a place in it where you said, maybe even out loud, "Oh, I get it!" It was probably the moment when enough things had happened that you could look back and figure out what was going to come next.

Your life is kind of like a mystery—at times you can look back and see why certain things had to happen. Maybe you didn't want to move from your old school, but in your new one you found a best friend you never would have met otherwise. When it seems like none of your prayers are being answered and God couldn't possibly have a plan in the middle of the chaos of your life, take a few minutes to look back at what's happened so far. There might be tons of "Oh, I get it!" moments to declare.

More to Explore: Proverbs 19:21 and Genesis 45:1–8

Girl Talk: What are you struggling with right now? What are some ways that good might come out of the situation—even if they're a long ways down the road?

God Talk: "God, sometimes I get upset when bad things happen because I don't understand why you would let them happen. Help me to trust you. Show me—'Oh, I get it!' moments from the past, so I can see how you work out things that seem bad for good. Amen."

From *That Is So Me* by Nancy Rue

38

"Some sat in darkness and deepest gloom, miserable prisoners in chains. They rebelled against the words of God, scorning the counsel of the Most High."

—Psalm 107:10–11 (NLT)

Afraid of the Dark

What a frightening picture! Prisoners in chains, sitting in terrible dread and depression. They decided to reject the words of God, his advice and guidance, and do what they pleased instead. The end result was miserable despair—a result they chose for themselves.

People who are afraid of the dark keep all the lights on so they feel safe. Would it make sense, if you're afraid of the dark, to turn *off* the lights at midnight, then sit in pitch blackness? Of course not, but that's what some people do. They invite darkness and misery into their lives by living in rebellion of God's Word. By rejecting godly advice and counsel, they become prisoners in chains. They are prisoners to hatred or an out of control appetite. If they have accepted Jesus as Savior, they'll still go to heaven. But they won't enjoy their days on earth much!

Are you now stuck with a problem that has you in despair? If so, don't hesitate another minute. Flip on that light switch. Go to God, confess, and let him help you burst those chains.

More to Explore: Isaiah 9:2 and Matthew 4:16

Girl Talk: Do you feel in the dark because of a problem that keeps bothering you? Confess it to God, and turn the light on!

God Talk: "Lord, I am really struggling with ______________. I confess to you that I don't want to do it again. Please set me free from this darkness. Amen."

From *No Boys Allowed* by Kristi Holl

39

"Strip yourselves of your former nature [put off and discard your old unrenewed self] which characterized your previous manner of life."

—Ephesians 4:22 (AMP)

Change Your Clothes!

Stop being the kind of person you were before you accepted Christ as your Savior. Your old lifestyle—the rebellious words and actions—should be a thing of the past. Like a piece of clothing that has shrunk, it doesn't fit who you are anymore.

How do you make the change from what you were to what you want to be? Step one: Discard your old manner of life. Step two: "Be constantly renewed in the spirit of your mind [having a fresh mental and spiritual attitude]" (Ephesians 4:23 AMP). This renewing happens when you read and study God's Word and listen to good Bible teaching. It's vital! Step three: "Put on the new nature (the regenerate self) created in God's image, [Godlike] in true righteousness and holiness" (Ephesians 4:24 AMP). You are a new creature since you were born again, and your life should reflect this. "Put on" that new life—and wear it proudly!

More To Explore: Hebrews 12:1

Girl Talk: How often do you read God's Word? How do you carve out time to study the Bible? If this area is lacking, start with two to three days a week and build from there.

God Talk: "Lord, I have accepted you as my Savior and want you to be first in my life. Day by day, give me the strength to be a new person. Thank you. Amen."

From *Shine On, Girl!* by Kristi Holl

40

"All hard work brings a profit, but mere talk leads only to poverty."

—Proverbs 14:23

Talk Is Cheap

If you work hard at anything, there will be a benefit. It might be money or health or a sense of satisfaction. Idle chatter, however, won't get you anywhere. Mere talk means little.

You talk all summer about getting fit so you can play basketball in middle school. You read about healthy eating plans and check online fitness websites for training schedules. You plan to be in top shape before tryouts because you've heard there's a running test you'll have to pass. Unfortunately, you never progress beyond talking about it. Putting it into practice looks like hard work. You still go to basketball tryouts in the fall, but you drop out halfway through the required half-mile run.

Talk is cheap. It's time to stop being a person who only talks about what she is going to do; it's time to put plans into action. It is time to stop talking about having a deeper relationship with God and start praying more and spending more time in God's Word. We must go beyond knowing what to do and get to a place where we finally do it.

Put those idle words into action—and start reaping the rewards.

More to Explore: Ecclesiastes 5:3 and Proverbs 28:19

Girl Talk: What things do you talk about doing—but haven't started or completed yet? Can you take a step today to move from idle chatter to action?

God Talk: "Lord, I want to be a person who keeps her word. Help me be someone who doesn't just talk, but puts things into action. Amen."

From *Chick Chat* by Kristi Holl

"'Do not lay a hand on the boy,' he said. 'Do not do anything to him. Now I know that you fear God, because you have not withheld from me your son, your only son."

—Genesis 22:12

Making Sacrifices

God said to Abraham, "Take your son, your only son, Isaac, whom you love, and go to the region of Moriah. Sacrifice him there as a burnt offering."

What? God wanted him to set fire to his precious son on an altar, like he would a lamb or a calf? *Seriously?*

You may be thinking, "Hasn't Abraham proven himself enough? Wasn't it kind of cruel of God to put him through this?" But just as always, Abraham did exactly as he was told. It's hard not to imagine the tears of sadness pouring down Abraham's face when he bound his son and put him on the altar and raised the knife. Or the tears of relief when God stopped his hand and provided a ram to use instead.

That's the kind of obedience that separates the people who say they believe in God and want to serve him, and the people who really do. God no longer asks his children to go this far, but he can ask a lot. Are you ready for that?

More to Explore: Psalm 128:1 and 2 John 1:6

Girl Talk: What could you let go of this week that would make God smile? Your turn in the front seat? The brownie in your lunch?

God Talk: "God, thank you for providing a ram for Abraham and for sacrificing *your* son on the cross so that my sins could be forgiven. If you ever ask me to make big—or little—sacrifices for my faith, give me the courage to do that. Amen."

From *That Is So Me* by Nancy Rue

42

"If we say we have no sin, we are only fooling ourselves and refusing to accept the truth. But if we confess our sins to [God], he is faithful and just to forgive us and to cleanse us from every wrong."

—1 John 1:8–9 (NLT)

Heavenly Soap

No one but God is perfect, but sometimes we fool ourselves into thinking we're not so bad. After all, we don't steal or tell big lies or cheat like *some* people we know.

Maybe you didn't steal or cheat today, but God is interested in your attitudes and thoughts as well as your behavior. Did you tell a classmate, "Pretty outfit" while you were thinking, "Ugly rag"? Did you shove your little brother out of the way when he stood in front of the refrigerator? These things fall short of the standard Christians should live up to.

You're not alone. We all fall short sometimes. Thankfully, God has provided a way to wash that dirt from our hearts and spirits. Be humble. Admit where you fell short, and specifically name the sins you want forgiveness for. Then trust God that you are totally forgiven.

We bathe because we've had contact with dirt in our world and need to be washed. Take time to confess your sins daily too, and go to bed at night with both body and spirit squeaky clean.

More to Explore: Jeremiah 2:22

Girl Talk: What sin do you have pressing on your heart right now? Have you asked God's forgiveness for that sin?

God Talk: "Lord, I know I fail your expectations every day. Please forgive me for ____________. Thank you for always being ready to forgive. Amen."

From *No Boys Allowed* by Kristi Holl

43

"Children, obey your parents in the Lord, for this is right. 'Honor your father and mother'—which is the first commandment with a promise—'so that it may go well with you and that you may enjoy long life on the earth.' "

—Ephesians 6:1–3

Honoring Parents

There are many commandments, but the first one with a promise attached is aimed at kids. Children are to honor their fathers and mothers. That means to show respect and obey them. And the promise? That you'll live a long and successful life.

Sophia's mom died when she was only five years old, and when Sophia was eight, her dad remarried. Sophia liked Susan, her stepmother, except when she told her to do her homework or wash supper dishes. "You're not my real mom," Sophia said, "so you can't tell me what to do." When she complained to her best friend, Taylor, about it, Taylor only laughed. "You wouldn't like washing dishes even if Susan was your real mom." Sophia admitted Taylor was right. Even if her real mom were still alive, she wouldn't want to do her homework or chores.

It's not about whether you like doing what your parents ask. It's about being obedient because you love God. It might seem unfair at times, especially if you have a cranky parent, but the Lord is pleased when you're obedient in everything, no matter what. God will richly reward you for obeying when it's hard.

More To Explore: Proverbs 6:20–22

Girl Talk: How easy is it for you to obey your parents? Is there anything about your attitude that should change?

God Talk: "Lord, I know you want me to obey and respect my mom and dad. Please help me keep the right attitude toward them. Amen."

From *Shine On, Girl!* by Kristi Holl

44

"A good name is more desirable than great riches; to be esteemed is better than silver or gold."

—Proverbs 22:1

Vashti's Stand

The book of Esther tells the story of the powerful King Xerxes and his queen, Vashti. In the third year of his reign, Xerxes gave a seven-day banquet in the palace garden. This was an incredibly fancy party. Servants served wine in goblets of gold, and the guests sat on gold and silver couches. Because it was improper in Persian culture for men and women to be entertained in the same place, Queen Vashti hosted the women in the palace.

On the last day of the banquet, the king was drunk and commanded his eunuchs to go and bring the queen to him. He wanted to put Vashti on display like a trophy. The king's men crashed Vashti's party and delivered the king's message to her.

What would she do?

He was the king and he usually treated her very well. Vashti did enjoy a lot of nice things and special privileges because of her position as queen. But Vashti chose to tell the king, "No way." She refused to parade around in front of a bunch of drunken men.

Vashti's refusal wounded King Xerxes' pride, and he threw a fit. He decided to kick Vashti out of the palace. Vashti lost her crown, her position in society, her home, and all the nice things that came with it. But she didn't lose her values. Vashti left the palace with her self-respect intact.

How important are material things to you? Do you value the latest fashions, designer electronics, and iffy friendships more than your godly character? Are they more important to you than your faith in God and making decisions that please him?

Are you willing, like Vashti, to give up temporary and material things to do the right thing?

More to Explore: 1 Peter 3:3–4

Girl Talk: Even though she was beautiful, Vashti understood that the way she looked was not the most important thing about her. Have you ever been tempted to believe your value comes from the way you look?

God Talk: "God, thank you that you care more about inner beauty than outer beauty. Help me to remember that my godly character is more important than all the clothes and accessories in the world. Amen."

From *Real Girls of the Bible* by Mona Hodgson

45

"Two things have I heard: 'Power belongs to you, God, and with you, Lord, is unfailing love.'"

—Psalm 62:11–12

Walking the Tightrope

Have you figured this one out yet?

You're supposed to be nice to people, but you shouldn't let them walk all over you. You're supposed to include the kids nobody else wants to hang out with, but sometimes those are the kids who get in trouble, and that's bad for you.

It's like walking a tightrope sometimes. It requires way more balance than most of us have. Fortunately, God is your Personal Balance.

God asks us to love our neighbors as much as we love ourselves, but sometimes loving somebody means you have to do something that person isn't going to like. For example, your best friend is amazing, but she's gotten pretty bossy lately. You have to tell her you're tired of being pushed around and you'd like to get back on even terms again.

The right thing seems pretty clear—until you're in the middle of the situation. Just get quiet and ask God how you can be both loving and strong. Somebody might wonder why you're standing there with your eyes closed. If anybody asks, just say you're trying to get your balance.

More to Explore: Ephesians 4:2–3

Girl Talk: Is there a place in your life where you are losing your balance? How do you sometimes struggle to be both loving and strong?

God Talk: "Jesus, show me the right balance between loving people and standing up for myself. Help me to remember to ask you for help when I need it. Amen."

From *That Is So Me* by Nancy Rue

"Finally, I confessed all my sins to you and stopped trying to hide them. I said to myself, 'I will confess my rebellion to the Lord.' And you forgave me! All my guilt is gone."

—Psalm 32:5 (NLT)

What Are You Hiding?

We often do things with our sins other than confess them. We make excuses for ourselves. ("I shouldn't have smarted off to my mom, but I'm just so tired.") We cover it up. (We hide a new shirt in the back of the closet, the one we bought instead of the school book we needed.) We "forget" the sin. (After gossiping about our friend, we cover the guilty feeling by quickly focusing on a TV show.) Do the sins go away, along with the consequences? No. Your mom is still mad. You still need that book for class. Your friend is hurt when the gossip gets back to her.

When you carry around unconfessed sin, it's like hiding some forbidden food in your room. It's "out of sight, out of mind" for a while—until it spoils and starts to stink. Sin doesn't stay hidden forever either.

So 'fess up! It will remove the guilt from your conscience, give you peace in your heart, and spark a determination not to do that thing again.

More to Explore: 2 Samuel 24:10 and Psalm 86:5

Girl Talk: Do you have sin that is hidden away in your heart? Tell it all to God and ask for forgiveness.

God Talk: "Lord, I have done something I'm not proud of, and I need to confess it to you. I'm so sorry I ____________. Thank you for forgiving me every time I ask. Amen."

From *No Boys Allowed* by Kristi Holl

47

"I am God, and there is no other; I am God, and there is none like me . . . What I have said, that will I bring about; what I have planned, that I will do."

—Isaiah 46:9, 11

Do You Promise?

God is totally trustworthy. If he says he will do something, you can count on it getting done. He isn't like a human being. He always tells the truth, and whatever he promises to do, he *will* do!

Believers should imitate God and also be trustworthy.

Brianna thought of herself as dependable and honest, but was she really? Let's see. If she had a babysitting job, but a friend asked her to a movie, she called the family and said she'd forgotten about some previous plans. Then she went to the movie. If her dad asked where she went after school, Brianna said she stopped at the library. (She did stop there, but only to drop off some overdue books before heading to the mall.) Was Brianna truly honest and dependable? Or was she just fooling herself?

God is 100 percent honest. He never deceives, and he can be depended on. If we are followers of Jesus, we must strive to be honest and dependable at all times too.

More to Explore: Isaiah 45:5–6

Girl Talk: Are you always honest? Can you be honest with your friends without being cruel or hurting their feelings? Is it ever right to tell a "white lie"?

God Talk: "Lord, I want to be a girl my friends and family can count on. Help me to keep my word, no matter how hard it is sometimes. Amen."

From *Chick Chat* by Kristi Holl

48

"The faithless will be fully repaid for their ways, and the good rewarded for theirs."

—Proverbs 14:14

Going Backward?

People who follow God for a while but later return to their old ways of sinful living are sometimes referred to as "backsliders." A backslider's life is eventually filled with negative consequences.

Megan was sad when her friend Tia stopped coming to youth group, where they had both sung with the praise band. Megan continued to sing on youth night, and eventually the band was asked to perform in church. Months later, the group made a music CD. And Tia? The crowd she hung out with preferred parties to church, and one night Tia was injured in a car accident. The driver was underage and drunk. Tia would be in therapy for months to regain the use of her legs.

What happened to Tia was largely the result of her own actions. Actions have consequences, either positive or negative. If a farmer plants weed seeds in his field, she will harvest only a worthless crop of weeds. Sinful living has its own consequences—although God will use those consequences as ways to help us mature.

So pull out the weeds in your life. Plant healthy seeds in their place. Then get ready for a harvest of blessings!

More To Explore: Mark 4:3–20

Girl Talk: What weeds are choking out good decisions in your life? Ask God to help you get rid of those weeds.

God Talk: "Lord, there are some things in my life that are choking my walk with you. Please help me get rid of them and plant healthy, godly activities in their place. Amen."

From *Shine On, Girl!* by Kristi Holl

49

"Those who know your name trust in you, for you, Lord, have never forsaken those who seek you."

—Psalm 9:10

Falling In Trust with God

Have you ever played the "Trust Fall" game? You know, the one where you stand on a chair and fall backwards, trusting that your four or five friends standing below will catch you before you hit the floor? Trusting God can be a little like playing this game.

Trust means talking to God, telling him we know he's with us, and then believing he can help us through anything—even though we can't see him. As Christians, it's how we live. We're " … sure of the things we hope for," and "certain of the things we cannot see" (Hebrews 11:1 TEV). For us, it's not "seeing is believing" but "believing is seeing."

One word explains how we can do this: Jesus. He's proof positive that the Father exists, because he, himself, is the Father's reflection. Jesus confirmed that when he said: "Anyone who has seen me has seen the Father!" (John 14:9 TLB). The fact that the Father would send Jesus, his only son, to die on the cross for our sins is also proof positive the Father loves us—a whole lot.

More To Explore: Psalm 31:14

Girl Talk: Are there any worries in your life that you need to trust God with? Pray about them and turn them over to God.

God Talk: "Dearest Jesus, when I don't understand things that are happening, and I'm afraid, help me to trust you. Amen."

From *Whatever: Livin' the True, Noble, Totally Excellent Life* by Allia Zobel Nolan

"Go from your country, your people and your father's household to the land I will show you."

—Genesis 12:1

Have a Little Faith

Abram and his wife, Sarai, were living in Mesopotamia when God told Abram he wanted him to set off on a pilgrimage to a better land where he (God) would be honored. You might think, "Hey, a road trip—I'm there!"

But travel was rough in those days. People had to carry everything they owned with them, including tents to live in, and there were dangers along the way, from wild animals to desert robbers. And God didn't spell out for Abram exactly where he was going to end up. He just said, "I will make you into a great nation, and I will bless you ... and all peoples on earth will be blessed through you." All of it came true, over many centuries, but Abram couldn't know that. All he had was God's word. That was the thing about Abram—he never questioned God. If God said do it, he just went for it.

Could you be quicker to obey God when you know how to behave? When it comes to the authority of God, it's a good idea to be like Abram and move now, ask questions later.

More to Explore: Hebrews 11:9–12

Girl Talk: Have you ever left a place or situation in order to follow God? Maybe you've gone home when friends decided to send ugly emails. Or maybe you chose to walk out of the bathroom when gossip started.

God Talk: "God, I know that obeying you is the right thing to do, even when it's hard. Help me to trust you like Abram trusted you. Amen."

From *That Is So Me* by Nancy Rue

51

"Do you not know that in a race all the runners run, but only one gets the prize? Run in such a way as to get the prize."
—1 Corinthians 9:24

Running for Your Life

Believers are like runners in a race. In order to finish well, runners have to focus on the finish line. Heaven is the finish line for believers. If you want to live a life that counts, that has purpose, you need to live today while keeping the future in mind at all times.

June had accepted Christ as her Savior two summers before at church camp. For more than a year, she read her Bible daily, talked to her friends about Jesus, faithfully attended Sunday school, and was careful to choose godly friends. When she went to middle school in sixth grade, things changed. She got busy with new friends, ball games, movies, and shopping. She wasn't doing anything wrong, but she had lost her focus. She stopped reading her Bible and praying. She stopped growing spiritually.

To be sure that you finish the race with strength, do what the athletes do. Set goals for your spiritual growth, write them down, and keep track of the progress you make. Know that progress takes time, but keep at it.

Keep your eyes on Jesus, and go for the gold!

More to Explore: Philippians 3:14

Girl Talk: Do you get caught up in what's cool, what's fun? How well do you keep your focus on God and what he has to teach you?

God Talk: "Lord, help me remember that I *always* need to focus on you, not just some of the time. I want to put you first! Thank you. Amen."

From *Girlz Rock* by Kristi Holl

52

"A rebuke goes deeper into one who has understanding than a hundred blows into a fool."

—Proverbs 17:10 (NASB)

Caught in the Act

Suppose you've agreed to see a movie with your friend on Friday night, and she's looking forward to it. Then, on Wednesday, a popular girl in your class invites you to a party—also for Friday night. You happily accept the invitation, then call your friend and tell her you have to babysit on Friday, but that you can go to the movie on Saturday instead. It works! When you hang up and turn around, your dad is standing there. From his disapproving look, you realize that he's heard the whole thing. "Come with me," he says quietly.

For a few minutes he talks about honesty and what it means to be a loyal friend. He was disappointed to hear you lie to your friend, but he doesn't tell you what to do. Instead, he leaves the decision up to you. Up in your room, you sink onto your bed. You know your dad is right. You truly want to be a person who can be counted on to keep her word.

Don't be a person who has to be corrected severely before learning from her mistakes. Be wise instead. "Instruct the wise and they will be wiser still; teach the righteous and they will add to their learning" (Proverbs 9:9).

More to Explore: Proverbs 13:1

Girl Talk: How do you respond when a parent or a teacher corrects you? Are you a wise girl or a foolish one?

God Talk: "Lord, I know I need correction sometimes. Help me to listen to it with an open mind and heart. Amen."

From *Chick Chat* by Kristi Holl

53

"Caleb interrupted, called for silence before Moses, and said, 'Let's go up and take the land—now. We can do it.'"

—Numbers 13:30 (MSG)

Be a Possibilitarian

The "Making a Difference" Club recommendations were due. But when LeeAnne suggested helping with the inner city reading program, everyone shot her down.

"Look," April said, "those kids don't want to learn to read. And they could start trouble. It's a bad idea, LeeAnne. Let's just have a can collection, like we always do."

But LeeAnne wouldn't let it go. She insisted, "Guys, this is our ministry. And we've dedicated our work to Jesus, so he'll help us. We can *really* make a difference teaching kids to read."

Sometimes, we just have to take a stand. We have to become a Possibilitarian. We have to speak up, go against peer pressure, and ignore the naysayers who tell us "It can't be done," or "Let's do something easier." That's the kind of attitude God admires and blesses.

Both Joshua and his friend, Caleb, had that mindset. When Moses sent them and ten others to check out Jericho, these two were the only ones who returned with a good report. Everyone else said, "The men are like giants; we'll get slaughtered. We're not going." But Caleb saw the possibilities because he knew that with God's help anything is possible.

More To Explore: Joshua 2:9–11 and Philippians 4:13

Girl Talk: Have you ever spoken your mind when everyone else thought differently? How did that make you feel?

God Talk: "Dearest Jesus, even if it means going against the crowd, I want to be a Possibilitarian for you. Please help me to do that. Amen."

From *Whatever: Livin' the True, Noble, Totally Excellent Life* by Allia Zobel Nolan

"A heart at peace gives life to the body, but envy rots the bones."

—Proverbs 14:30

The Green-Eyed Monster

A peaceful heart is relaxed and easy, not tense and fearful. This peace of mind and heart will actually give you a longer, healthier life. But envy and jealousy gnaw at you, deep inside. The Bible says it can even rot your bones!

Jealousy is sneaky. It's natural to compare ourselves to others or want what someone else has. But when that comparison makes us unhappy, we're probably feeling jealous. Try to be happy for them instead. Can you compliment them on an outstanding performance or their pretty outfit? Taking positive action is a quick way to kill that green-eyed monster.

The Bible says in James 3:16 that where you have envy (which is another word for jealousy), you will find disorder and every evil practice. Not good! The sooner you tackle these emotions, the easier they are to defeat. God wants you to have a heart filled with peace. A heart at peace is a heart focused on God. So the next time you feel jealous, ask God to help you put jealousy in its place—out of your life!

More to Explore: James 3:13–18

Girl Talk: Are you jealous of someone? Be honest with yourself, but more importantly, be honest with God. He will help you overcome jealousy.

God Talk: "Jesus, I am really jealous of ________________. I know that I shouldn't be, but I am. Forgive me. Please help me to love this person like you do. Thank you for all the good things in my life. Help me to focus on all the blessings I already have instead of envying the blessings of others. Amen."

From *No Boys Allowed* by Kristi Holl

55

"The Spirit himself testifies with our spirit that we are God's children. Now if we are children, then we are heirs—heirs of God and co-heirs with Christ, if indeed we share in his sufferings in order that we may also share in his glory."

—Romans 8:16–17

A Darling Daughter

The beauty of believing means you are a darling, cherished daughter of the heavenly Father whose heart is set on loving you. God's desire is to love you so well that you are drawn to loving God with your whole heart and trusting him with your life. Today, God is saying to you "I've never quit loving you and never will. Expect love, love, and more love!" (Jeremiah 31:2–6, MSG).

Experiencing the lavish love of God requires a lifetime. As you continue growing in faith, you'll learn to receive the special way God shows you the magnitude of his love. With each passing day, you'll understand Father God's love more and more as you see all the wonderful things God does for you.

Though fully understanding just how wide and long and high and deep the love of Christ is takes time, you can bask in this love that surpasses human knowledge today, faithgirl. Trust that God has chosen and adopted you as a special daughter; and God delights to do good things on your behalf.

More To Explore: 1 John 4:19

Girl Talk: What are some of the ways you think God shows love for you?

God Talk: "Father God, thank you for your love. It is bigger than I can imagine. Open my heart to receive it so that I will love you and others just as you love me."

From *My Beautiful Daughter* by Tasha Douglas

"She said, Yes, Lord, yet even the little pups eat the crumbs that fall from their masters' table. Then Jesus answered her, O woman, great is your faith! . . . And her daughter was cured from that moment."

—Matthew 15:27–28 (AMP)

True Grit

Girls who give up if they don't get what they want right away can't expect a lot of success in anything, really. On the other hand, everyone admires a girl with persistence, who keeps going even when the path is difficult.

Jesus met a woman like that. She was a bold, Canaanite mother with four strikes against her: she was a pagan, a foreigner, a woman alone pestering a group of male strangers (and not in her inside voice, for sure), and she had a demon-possessed daughter whom she insisted Jesus heal.

Jesus' answer? "[He] didn't say a word to her" (Matthew 15:23 TEV). It was as though he wanted more from this woman and knew his silence would bring it out. And when he did speak and seemed to say "no," she didn't walk away angry or depressed. She did the opposite: "she came and, kneeling, worshipped him and kept praying, 'Lord help me!'" (Matthew 15:25 AMP).

What about us? Are we willing to be that persistent? To keep praying and knocking on God's door, boldly asking his help? If we are, our Lord will surely take care of our needs. BTW, Jesus doesn't mind if we pester him; in fact, he kind of likes it.

More To Explore: Luke 18:1–8

Girl Talk: Have you ever been persistent in prayer? What for?

God Talk: "Jesus, sometimes when I pray, and the answer doesn't come quickly enough, I lose heart. Help me to trust you and keep praying. Amen."

From *Whatever: Livin' the True, Noble, Totally Excellent Life* by Allia Zobel Nolan

57

"They pulled their boats up on shore, left everything and followed him."

—Luke 5:11

Giving It Up to God

Have you and your friends ever talked about what possessions you would grab if your house were on fire and you had to get out fast? No matter what you imagine taking with you, it's hard to think about leaving the rest behind.

What if you were called to something that required you to take absolutely nothing that you owned with you? What if you had to drop everything and go? Leave your family and friends? Simply stop your life and start a new one?

Okay, so maybe you can't even picture it, but Simon Peter, James, and John didn't have time to think about it. When Jesus said, "Guys, don't be afraid. I want you to help me gather people instead of fish," they went with him. Nothing else mattered.

Right now, while you're still growing and learning, God won't ask you to drop everything—school (which you might not mind!), family (which you just couldn't do), friends (which—well, don't even go there). But he might ask you to abandon something so you can be closer to him. Will you be like Simon Peter and simply do that little thing?

More to Explore: Philippians 3:7–9

Girl Talk: Are there things in your life you could let go of in order to better follow Jesus? Maybe it's a bad habit, a negative attitude, or an activity that's crowding your schedule. Give it up for God.

God Talk: "Jesus, please show me if there are things in my life I need to let go of in order to make more space for you. Give me the courage to do that. Amen."

From *That Is So Me* by Nancy Rue

"Hope deferred makes the heart sick, but when dreams come true, there is life and joy."

—Proverbs 13:12 (NLT)

Sick at Heart

When your dreams are postponed to a later time, your heart becomes discouraged and disappointed. But when those dreams come true, you're filled with new life and energy.

You know firsthand about disappointment. You moved to a new school when your dad, who's in the U.S. Air Force, was transferred again. Each day you pray for God to bring a special friend into your life. Every night you cry yourself to sleep because no one seems to reach out. You keep praying. Then one day, you notice the Drama Club's sign-up sheet on the bulletin board. You love art and think you could paint scenery. After school, you meet with the stage crew. Both Sierra and Jenna are friendly to you, and the three of you walk home together afterward. That night, your disappointment is gone. In its place is a new joy at having your prayer answered.

We don't always receive what we hope for right away. Just because your answer seems delayed, don't get discouraged and give up praying. Some things just take time.

Keep praying, keep your hope alive—and look forward to a heart filled with joy.

More to Explore: Psalm 69:3 and Proverbs 13:19

Girl Talk: What things are you hoping for that haven't happened yet? Are you still praying for them?

God Talk: "Lord, thank you for putting dreams in my heart. Help me to keep praying—and be patient—while I wait for my dreams to come true. Amen."

From *Chick Chat* by Kristi Holl

59

"Then He said to His disciples, 'The harvest truly is plentiful, but the laborers are few.'"

—Matthew 9:37 (NKJV)

Help Wanted!

Even if a farmer's bumper crop of corn is ripe and the fields are full, he won't have a harvest to sell unless plenty of workers run the machinery and get the crop to market. Jesus called the hurting people to whom he preached to a huge harvest, ready for picking. Many people needed a Savior, but few people were willing to teach others the good news.

Are there people in your neighborhood, among your relatives—even at home—who don't know Jesus? This includes those you really like and those you don't like. Every soul is precious to Christ—the meanest kid in your grade as well as the kindest one. Jesus said they are like scattered sheep without a Good Shepherd.

Telling people about Jesus often makes us uncomfortable. Will they put you down or think you're crazy? They might. But it's also possible they will consider you the best friend they've ever had for sharing this good news with them. Don't put it off. Jesus said the harvest is ready NOW.

Pray and ask God if there is someone today he wants you to speak to. Ask God to give that person a heart to listen and to give you boldness to share. Help *is* wanted—you!

More to Explore: Luke 10:2

Girl Talk: Is there someone in your class or family that you would like to talk to about Jesus?

God Talk: "Lord, I know it's important to tell your good news. I want to be courageous and talk to ______________ about you. Please help me to find the best way to tell them. Amen."

From *No Boys Allowed* by Kristi Holl

"One thing I do know. I was blind but now I see!"
—John 9:25 (NIV)

Can't Argue with That!

When Jesus healed the blind man, the religious leaders refused to believe the man. They claimed Jesus was a sinner and had no power to perform miracles. The formerly blind man said he knew only one thing: he'd been blind, but since Jesus touched him, he could see!

You may have heard for years in Sunday school class that you should share Jesus with your unsaved friends. You want to, but for some reason you just can't. You may not feel smart enough. Or you get tongue-tied easily. But one day in the restroom, you find a girl sobbing her heart out. You discover that this girl's dad has left his family. Your own dad died two years before in a car accident. Without thinking or being nervous, you simply talk to the hurting girl. You tell her how Jesus was your best friend when your dad died. Simply describing what your life was like before and after knowing Jesus can comfort someone's wounded heart.

The healed blind man did the same thing. No matter how the Pharisees argued, they couldn't debate one basic fact: *the blind man could now see*. That was his testimony. The same is true today. People simply can't argue against the truth of your experience with Jesus.

More to Explore: Luke 7:21–22

Girl Talk: Have you ever shared your experience with Jesus with an unsaved friend or family member? How did that go?

God Talk: "Lord, thank you for being the best friend I ever had. Help me to be bold in telling others about you. They need you too. Amen."

From *Chick Chat* by Kristi Holl

61

"Fools find no pleasure in understanding but delight in airing their own opinions."

—Proverbs 18:2

Hot Air

Some people (the Bible calls them fools) would rather tell their own views to anyone who will listen than understand the truth. The fool's happiness is in listening to her own voice—not in understanding a matter. Often there is no truth to her opinions—just guesses and rumors—and when the truth comes out, she appears foolish.

Destiny met such a person when she befriended the new girl, Peni, who came to church. Destiny invited her to their youth group and over to her house to meet her friends from school. It wasn't long before Destiny regretted knowing Peni. No matter what the group did, Peni dominated. She had strong opinions about everything, which she voiced loudly. Half the time she didn't know what she was talking about. If Destiny questioned anything Peni said, Peni invented "facts" to support her opinions. She only ended up looking more foolish—and causing people to avoid her. Destiny talked to Peni, explaining kindly how her behavior was driving people away. Peni got angry, stormed off, and found another group of girls to air her opinions to.

Don't be a girl who just talks to hear herself talk. Find out the truth and understand a situation before giving an opinion. And if you don't understand a situation, silence is always golden!

More to Explore: Ecclesiastes 10:3

Girl Talk: Do you have pushy opinions about everything? Do you know someone who does? How do you deal with that person?

God Talk: "Lord, I like having my opinions matter, but help me remember that listening is even more important. Amen."

From *Shine On, Girl!* by Kristi Holl

62

"When Jesus saw their faith, he said to the paralyzed man, 'Son, your sins are forgiven.'"

—Mark 2:5

Medicine for Your Soul

You might remember this story from Sunday school. A man couldn't walk—he might even have been more paralyzed than that, we don't know for sure—and his friends lowered him through Peter's roof so he could be healed by Jesus. By forgiving the man's sins first, Jesus showed that it's more important for our spirits to be healed than our bodies.

It's very much okay to want to be relieved of pain and scary doctors. Go ahead and pray for that kind of healing, because God wants to hear that from you. Just don't forget to ask for spiritual health and forgiveness too. Carrying around guilt can make you feel sick in another way that's just as bad. Would you rather be in bed with a sore throat, a popsicle, and a mom waiting on you hand and foot, or walk around knowing you've done something wrong and any minute now someone is going to find out? Just something to think about.

More to Explore: Proverbs 17:22

Girl Talk: What was it like the last time you recovered from being sick or hurt? How did it feel to be well again? That was God at work. What was it like the last time you got something off your chest and were forgiven? How did it feel to be forgiven? That was God at work.

God Talk: "Lord, help me to remember to take care of my body *and* my soul. I know that the health of both are important to you. Amen."

From *That Is So Me* by Nancy Rue

63

"[A wife of noble character] speaks with wisdom, and faithful instruction is on her tongue."

—Proverbs 31:26

Abigail's Appeal

In the desert of Maon, west of the Dead Sea, there lived a woman named Abigail. Her husband, Nabal, was one of the richest ranchers in the area, but he was very foolish.

One day, David and a big group of his soldiers camped out on Nabal's property. They were hungry and went to Nabal to ask for some food. But Nabal spat in the face of David's messenger. "Who is this David? Why should I share with him?" he said, and he refused to give them anything to eat.

Nabal's response made David very angry, because David and his men had risked their lives to defend Nabal's flocks from harm. He was ready to kill Nabal and all the men of this household for the insults.

When Abigail got word of her husband's foolishness, she wasted no time. Abigail ordered tons of presents for David to be loaded onto donkeys. Then Abigail climbed onto her own donkey and headed toward David and his men. She begged David to change his mind and spare her husband. David, impressed by Abigail's gifts and concern, agreed.

Abigail took control of a dangerous situation and acted according to her faith in God. It took courage to go out to meet David, humility to plead with him, and wisdom to say what she said to the future king of Israel. Her wisdom kept David from sinning. God used Abigail to save many lives.

When you're in the middle of difficult circumstances—a friend betrays you or a parent is too busy for you or your teacher doesn't understand you—you're the one who chooses your reaction and response. Like Abigail, you can place your trust in God and choose to develop a godly character—one of humility, generosity, understanding, wisdom, and calm judgment.

More to Explore: Proverbs 9:10

Girl Talk: Have you ever been stuck in a bad situation that wasn't your fault? Did you act wisely to fix the problem or did you complain and pout?

God Talk: "Dear Jesus, thank you for being my peacekeeper. Help me to recognize danger and act wisely according to your will. Amen."

From *Real Girls of the Bible* by Mona Hodgson

64

"Work hard and cheerfully at whatever you do, as though you were working for the Lord rather than for people."

—Colossians 3:23 (NLT)

Get a New Boss

Whatever job you have before you—washing dishes, babysitting for the neighbors, mowing the lawn—do it with excellence and without grumbling. Your employer may pay you, but the Lord is really your boss. Work just as hard for your employer as you would if Jesus were standing next to you, watching.

When you babysit, do you play with the children, or do you plunk them down in front of the TV so you can text your friends? When doing yard work for a customer, do you work hard when he's around, but when he leaves, sit in the shade and drink soda? Work hard and cheerfully, remembering that your true boss is there beside you.

Perhaps, though, your problem is the opposite. Even when you do an excellent job, some people are impossible to please. A cranky critic will find fault with some tiny thing, even if ninety-nine percent of your work is superb. In cases like this, remember that you're working for a new boss—the Lord—and not for this judgmental person. Keep doing an excellent job, but remember that your worth and value are not in what you do, but in who you are as belonging to Christ.

More to Explore: Ephesians 6:5–7

Girl Talk: Have you done any paying or non-paying jobs lately? Do you feel proud of your work? Does it make a difference that God is always watching your efforts?

God Talk: "Jesus, I thank you for the jobs you send my way. Help me to do them with a cheerful heart. Amen."

From *No Boys Allowed* by Kristi Holl

"Let your eyes look straight ahead; fix your gaze directly before you . . . Do not turn to the right or the left; keep your foot from evil."

—Proverbs 4:25, 27

Focus!

If you want to be successful in anything, you must learn to focus. Keep your eyes trained on where you want to go. Don't be looking to the right or the left. Look straight ahead and focus on the finish line.

Have you ever ridden a horse? A horse can become skittish and nervous when you ride him along country roads. He swings his head from side to side, watches cars coming and going, and jumps when he spots little animals scurrying in the fields. After you put blinders on the horse, though, he settles right down. With leather eye-patches sewn to the sides of his halter, a horse is prevented from seeing things on either side. Distractions no longer bother him. He faces forward, and you both enjoy your ride much more.

Do you ever resemble such a horse? Maybe you're learning to play the saxophone. Or you're working and saving for a bike. What happens when other interesting things catch your attention? Do you get sidetracked and forget your goal? Instead, keep moving forward toward your goal and turn your eyes away from worthless things. How can you stay steady and focused? You pray for help. Often.

More to Explore: Joshua 1:7

Girl Talk: Do you have trouble completing projects or tasks? Do you find yourself being distracted by other things? What can you do about it?

God Talk: "Lord, I know I get scatterbrained sometimes. Help me to concentrate better. Keep me looking straight ahead. Amen."

From *Chick Chat* by Kristi Holl

66

"Moses said to the people, 'Do not be afraid. God has come to test you, so that the fear of God will be with you to keep you from sinning.'"

—Exodus 20:20

Making the Grade

Tests. Nobody likes 'em. But they're a fact of life. Teachers use them to find out how much we've learned and whether the stuff we've been taught is sticking. God uses them to strengthen our trust, check our obedience, and see how our faith holds up when things get hairy.

Take Noah. While everyone around him hinted that he had stayed out in the sun too long, Noah obeyed God, and then "by his faith … was made right in God's sight." (Hebrews 11:7 NLT). In other words, Noah aced his exams.

Then there were Joseph, Moses, Joshua, David, Daniel, Job, Jonah, Mary, Joseph, Peter, Paul—honor students all.

How'd they do it? The Bible says by "faith." When they faced trials, they didn't think, *This is too hard. I can't do it.* Instead, they thought, *I don't know where this is leading, but I do know God is loving, powerful, and trustworthy. So I'm with him.*

That's a good study plan for us to follow. If we "live by faith, not by sight," (2 Corinthians 5:7), we'll be ready to trust God unconditionally—even if our BFF ditches us, we break a leg in soccer, or some other nasty thing comes our way.

More To Explore: Daniel 3:8–30 and 2 Timothy 2:13

Girl Talk: Do you feel like you're being tested in any way right now?

God Talk: "Dear God, help me to trust that your love will see me through any trial or problem. Amen."

From *Whatever: Livin' the True, Noble, Totally Excellent Life* by Allia Zobel Nolan

"All those who exalt themselves will be humbled."

—Luke 18:14

Nobody Wins the Comparison Game

God wants you to know that you were worth creating. He loves you so much and didn't make a single mistake with you! But when we remember this, we have to be careful that we don't fall into the "I was more worth creating than *she* was" trap.

It might come out something like, "Well, I may not be as pretty as she is, but I'm WAY smarter." It doesn't take a brain surgeon to figure out that's just a way to make yourself feel better when some drop-dead gorgeous girl walks in and everybody goes, "Ooo!" If it gets to be a habit, you actually start believing you're a better person than everyone else.

Jesus told a story about a Pharisee who prayed, "Thank you that I'm not a loser like other people. I do everything right," and a tax collector who prayed, "God, have mercy on me, a sinner." God, Jesus said, would look much more kindly on the second man, who was honest about himself.

You don't need to beat your chest like that tax collector did, but do look at yourself as you really are. Both the good stuff and the stuff that still needs work are worthy before God.

More to Explore: Romans 12:3 and 1 Corinthians 12:4

Girl Talk: What are some things you like about yourself and are proud of? What are some things you know you still need to work on?

God Talk: "Jesus, I know that you made me exactly the way you want me to be. But help me to never think that I am better than any other girl. Nobody is perfect, including me. Amen."

From *That Is So Me* by Nancy Rue

68

"The man said, 'The woman you put here with me—she gave me some fruit from the tree, and I ate it.' Then the Lord God said to the woman, 'What is this you have done?' The woman said, 'The serpent deceived me, and I ate.'"

—Genesis 3:12–13

Who? Me?

In the Garden of Eden, Adam and Eve could eat the fruit from any tree they liked—except one. But Eve disobeyed God's command and ate the forbidden fruit. Adam also ate it. When God confronted them, Adam blamed both God and the woman for his own sin. ("It was *the woman* that *you* gave me who brought me the fruit.") Eve had her own excuse, and she blamed the serpent. ("*He* tricked me.")

You might find yourself making excuses for your problems too. The game of "poor me" and "it's your fault" got started in the Garden of Eden. To this day, people blame their problems on others. They blame their parents, their teachers, and the world in order to shift the responsibility. Some people prefer to believe that something else is controlling the outcome of their lives. However, we must stop blaming others and study our own behavior instead. Take personal responsibility for change. Then you can turn around and head in the direction of God's good plan for your life.

More To Explore: Genesis 3:6

Girl Talk: Think about a recent problem you had. Where did you place the blame? Did you put the responsibility in the right place?

God Talk: "Lord, it's so easy to blame others when things go wrong. Help me to take responsibility when it's my fault. Thank you for loving me no matter what I do. Amen."

From *Shine On, Girl!* by Kristi Holl

"God blesses the people who patiently endure testing. Afterward they will receive the crown of life that God has promised to those who love him."

—James 1:12 (NLT)

Victory Prize

In biblical times, wreaths or "crowns" were placed on the heads of victorious athletes. You may be an athlete, but you may not feel victorious! You may be exhausted. When you join the track team, you dream of getting in shape and winning a ribbon at the first meet. However, a week into the season you want to quit. Your shins hurt. Your thighs ache. Your lungs burn. Your big toes are bruised. And yet, you want that ribbon. So you take a deep breath and head out to run those laps.

Ribbons aren't given simply for entering the race. Diplomas aren't given just for starting high school. Starting isn't difficult. You also need to *patiently endure* a testing time before receiving the award. Awards are given to those who "keep on keeping on" when they'd rather quit—plus they strive to finish the job with a good attitude.

If you're a follower of Jesus, you have the power of God inside you. You can't overcome problems by yourself, but the Holy Spirit working through you can!

More to Explore: James 1:2–4 and 1 Corinthians 9:25

Girl Talk: What trial or test are you facing right now? A relationship test at school or home? A health issue? Do you grumble and complain—or do you still have the joy of the Lord?

God Talk: "Lord, I can't win without your help, but help me to also do my part to be patient and endure. I won't quit! Amen."

From *Chick Chat* by Kristi Holl

70

"[Jesus said,] 'Go home to your own people and tell them how much the Lord has done for you, and how he has had mercy on you.'"

—Mark 5:19

Gone Skiing

Whitney had never been cross country skiing before, so when Shawna invited her to come on their family outing, Whitney was more than a little nervous.

But Shawna's parents were patient and told her exactly what to do. It wasn't long before Whitney felt at home on skis. By the time she started getting tired, Whitney decided skiing was the most fun she'd ever had.

When she rounded a bend, she saw Shawna's parents at the side of the trail. They'd brushed snow off a picnic table, and now Mrs. Sullivan took food from her backpack. "Winter picnic!" she called.

Whitney took off her skis and dropped onto the bench. As she saw the apples and sandwiches, her stomach growled. But just as she reached out, ready to dive in, every head bowed. Every head except Whitney's. As Shawna and her parents began praying, Whitney felt uncomfortable. *What a strange thing to do!* Yet it seemed to mean something to them. Whitney closed her eyes so they wouldn't catch her staring. *Is that what makes them different?*

After lunch, when everyone started skiing again, Whitney said to Shawna, "Something about your family is different. You're so nice to each other."

Shawna laughed, then her eyes grew serious. "We haven't always been that way."

"What happened?"

"First Mom became a Christian. Then I did. Then we prayed for Dad. We prayed a lo-o-o-ng time."

As they followed the ski trail, Whitney was quiet, thinking about it. When twilight fell on the woods, they stopped skiing. The next morning when they started again, Whitney still watched Shawna and her mom and dad. *I wish my family could be like them.*

Deep inside Whitney a thought started to take shape. All day her longing grew. She wanted something more in her life. She wanted more for her family.

Just like Shawna, you and your family can be an example of God's love to friends who spend time with you. Being a daughter of God makes you different — in a good way. Can your friends see that?

More to Explore: Philippians 4:9

Girl Talk: What do you think Whitney told her family when she went home?

God Talk: "Jesus, often I'm too scared to tell other people about you. Yet I believe you want me to speak up. In your name, I ask for all the power of your Holy Spirit to help me. Thanks, Jesus!"

From *Girl Talk* by Lois Walfrid Johnson

71

"The Lord does not look at the things people look at. People look at the outward appearance, but the Lord looks at the heart."

—1 Samuel 16:7

Leah's Rival

All her life, Leah lived in the shadow of her younger sister, Rachel. Rachel was pretty. Leah was plain and had weak eyes—and no glasses. She also had a father, Laban, who was a selfish and tricky man.

One day, Jacob, the son of Isaac, showed up at Laban's well. When he saw Rachel, he fell madly in love with her. "I'll work for you for seven years in return for your younger daughter, Rachel," he told Laban.

Laban agreed, and seven years later he hosted a big wedding feast. But that night Laban tricked Jacob and made him marry Leah instead. Jacob had to work another seven years for Laban before he could also marry Rachel, the woman he really loved.

The Bible says Jacob loved Rachel more than Leah. Leah had been forced to marry a man who pushed her aside for her pretty little sister. Leah must've felt inferior, unwanted, and jealous. She thought that maybe if she gave birth to many sons, Jacob would love her. But Jacob still loved Rachel best.

Finally, Leah gave birth to her fourth son and named him Judah, meaning "praised." She decided she was done trying to earn Jacob's affection. She was going to praise the Lord instead. Leah had been manipulated by her father and upstaged by her sister. But Leah didn't choose bitterness. Instead she was thankful for her children. With each son God gave Leah, she grew in inner beauty. And in the end, God chose for his son Jesus to be born from the line of Leah, not Rachel.

Like Leah, you may compete with someone in your life. Maybe it's a sibling, cousin, or friend. Do you sometimes feel jealous of other girls and the attention they get? Remember, God loves you because you're you. No one else's approval is more important.

More to Explore: Lamentations 3:24 and Proverbs 27:4

Girl Talk: Have you ever felt jealous of a friend or a sibling? How did that affect your friendship?

God Talk: "Lord God, I'm so glad you love me for who I am. That's what matters most. Help me not to compare myself to the people around me or be jealous of other girls I meet. Amen."

From *Real Girls of the Bible* by Mona Hodgson

72

"Whatever is true, whatever is noble, whatever is right, whatever is pure, whatever is lovely, whatever is admirable — if anything is excellent or praiseworthy — think about such things."
— Philippians 4:8

Whatever!

Your mind is the control center for your whole body, so feed it great food! What makes a great "mind meal"? Think about what is real and true and worth depending on. Think about people with high moral qualities who deserve honor.

We make choices every day. Should we watch that video with our friends, even though the language and morals are bad? What about the books and magazines you choose, or the music you listen to? Are you feeding your mind with excellent images and words?

Thinking great thoughts also helps us control our feelings. Look hard for something good in a bad situation, and think about that instead. Maybe your friend canceled your shopping trip, but now you have time to read that great book. Maybe in gym you got paired with the new girl instead of your best friend, so choose to be glad for a chance to make a new friend. *Your thoughts control your feelings.*

More to Explore: Proverbs 23:7 and Matthew 5:6–9

Girl Talk: If you think mean thoughts, how do you feel? If you forgive someone, how does that make you feel? Which one feels better?

God Talk: "Lord, I thank you for giving me a choice in what I do. Please help me to make the right choices, to do what is pure and excellent. Amen."

From *No Boys Allowed* by Kristi Holl

73

[Jesus said,] "If you forgive anyone's sins, their sins are forgiven; if you do not forgive them, they are not forgiven."
—John 20:23

A Pitcher's Problem

Jennie gripped the metal mesh with her fingers and kicked the fence. *What's happening to me, anyway?* she asked herself. Only last week she had played great, but today it was like she had totally forgotten how to throw a softball.

To make matters worse, she had overheard her friends Tara and Linnea gossiping about all her mistakes after the game. *Or my used-to-be friends!* Jennie thought angrily.

The next time her team played, Jennie was still mad, and it showed in her game. She tried to stay calm, but she threw the softball wildly from the pitcher's mound. Jennie wasn't surprised when the coach pulled her out. Nor was she surprised to see Tara take her place. Jennie's anger flared up again, this time like a forest fire.

She felt desperate. Lately Jennie hadn't prayed much, but she started now. Even so, her prayers didn't seem to get off the ground. Something seemed to stand in the way between her and God.

The second inning passed. Then the third. Jennie still sat on the bench. By the beginning of the fourth, she started sorting out her choices. One word dropped into her mind.

Forgive? You gotta be kidding, God.

Through the rest of the inning, Jennie kept coming back to that one word: *Forgive!*

But, God, they were the ones being mean!

Suddenly Jennie knew what choice to make. Eyes wide open, she stared ahead, praying silently. She used only seven words: "Jesus, in your name I forgive them."

In the next moment, Jennie felt the weight she'd carried all week drop off her back. "Yaaaay!" she called out the next time something went right. But it was more than a cheer for the Cardinals. She was cheering herself on.

More to Explore: John 15:16–17

Girl Talk: After she forgave Tara and Linnea, Jennie felt she no longer carried a heavy weight. You may forgive someone and not "feel" any different. Yet your prayer of forgiveness still counts. How do you know?

God Talk: "Jesus, when someone hurts me, I want to hate that person. Yet even on the cross you prayed, 'Father, forgive them, for they do not know what they are doing.' Because of what you did, I forgive the person who hurt me. Take away my bitter and angry feelings."

From *Girl Talk* by Lois Walfrid Johnson

"Do not be deceived: God cannot be mocked. A man reaps what he sows."

—Galatians 6:7

A Bounty of Blessings

Don't be misled. Remember that you can't ignore God's laws and get away with it. You always harvest *what* you plant. (You plant corn—you harvest corn.) You always harvest *more* than you plant or sow. (You plant a bushel of corn, and you reap hundreds of bushels back.) You always harvest *later* than you sow. (You plant corn, you wait during the growing season, and you reap during the harvest season.) The same is true of your actions—your seeds—no matter what kind.

This principle works both positively and negatively. Those determined to do whatever they please, no matter what God's Word says, can count on reaping a negative harvest of problems and destruction. For those living a godly lifestyle, it is a promise of reward and blessings, and an encouragement to persist in doing what's right.

What kinds of things can you sow as seed? Money you give away can be a seed you plant, but anything you do for someone else's good is a seed you sow. It might be a smile, an encouraging word, making time to listen, praying for someone, or doing a favor for your mom.

Your future lies in the generous seeds you plant today.

More to Explore: 1 Corinthians 9:6 and Hosea 10:12–13

Girl Talk: Think about the past day or two. What do you think you've been sowing? Were you encouraging and helpful? Or were you sulking and backstabbing?

God Talk: "Lord, I want to plant the right seeds for those around me. Please help me to rely on you and to do the right thing in everything I do. Amen."

From *Girlz Rock* by Kristi Holl

75

"Whatever is good and perfect comes to us from God above."
—James 1:17 (NLT)

Perfect Gifts

God is good and perfect himself, and every good thing and perfect gift given to us comes from him.

We have all been given good things. Jasmine loves her new cocker spaniel. Hannah loves making apple pies with her grandmother. Ava loves her new baby sister. Kayla loves having a day off without homework. Sophie is grateful for her new jeans. Jordan loves her dad's sense of humor. Gabby loves sitting by the lake on vacation. Each girl is grateful for a different good gift, but each gift ultimately comes from the same source: God above.

Every day, we have so many things to be thankful for, so many good gifts in our lives. Do we deserve any of it? No. In fact, even though we were born sinful, God chose to offer his very best gift to each of us. "The wages of sin is death, but the gift of God is eternal life in Christ Jesus our Lord" (Romans 6:23). When you accept that gift—when Jesus becomes your Savior—it blesses both the giver (God) and the receiver (you)! Every day, God showers us with wonderful gifts. What should be our response? "Praise the Lord! Oh, give thanks to the Lord, for He is good!" (Psalm 106:1 NKJV).

More To Explore: Matthew 7:11

Girl Talk: What has God blessed you with lately? Write God a letter right now and thank him.

God Talk: "Lord, you have given me so much. I want to thank you for ______________. It means so much to me. You're awesome! Amen."

From *Shine On, Girl!* by Kristi Holl

"Solid food is for the mature, who by constant use have trained themselves to distinguish good from evil."

—Hebrews 5:14

Practice, Practice, Practice

Think about something you've learned to do well or are working on. Maybe it's dribbling a soccer ball. A dance move. A new piece on the piano. Long division. How did you get it right? Did you read a book about it? Have somebody tell you how to do it? Watch someone else do it? Those things might have helped. But didn't you master that skill by *practicing*?

It's impossible to get really good at step-ball-change without putting on your tap shoes. Nobody ever played in a recital without hours at the keyboard first. It's the same with learning to do good. You can read the Bible, listen to sermons, and hang out with good-doing people all you want, but you won't even begin to bring out the goodness in yourself unless you practice.

It's tough. There are no "goodness scales" to pound out, no worksheets to sweat over. You just have to "be good" again and again. Make the right choice even if it isn't the popular choice. Create safe, healthy, fun situations to replace hazardous-to-your-health ones that put people down.

You'll make mistakes. Just start over and try again. It's the only way to train yourself. God's right there, coaching you.

More to Explore: 1 Corinthians 9:24–27

Girl Talk: What is one little thing you could do right now to practice "doing good"? Get out there and do it!

God Talk: "Lord, thank you for being my 'goodness' coach. Show me all the little ways I can practice doing good today and in the future. Amen."

From *That Is So Me* by Nancy Rue

77

"Each one should test their own actions."

—Galatians 6:4

Can You Pass the Test?

Suppose you're having more and more trouble getting your homework done in the evenings. It shows up on your report card with a big dip in grades. "But it's not my fault!" you tell your parents. You share a room with your teenage sister, making it too noisy in your room to study. And the Internet's down at home, so you can't do research for your papers. And anyway, you just don't *get* math. Even so, you know that your low grade isn't the best you could have done. Instead of laying blame elsewhere, examine your own actions.

You hate to admit it—even to yourself—but your study habits have slipped badly. You used to tackle your homework before supper, but now you spend that time playing computer games. You used to study at the quiet kitchen table, but now you study on your bed, next to your sister's stereo and constantly ringing phone. You have to admit it. After analyzing your own actions, you know the cause of your lower grades: your own behavior.

That's good news! When we test and examine our actions, we can usually find areas for improvement, places where a change could make a big difference. Take some time out now and examine your life, then make those positive changes.

More to Explore: 1 Corinthians 11:28

Girl Talk: What things in your life are you happy with? What would you like to do better? Examine and analyze your actions. Do you see areas for improvement?

God Talk: "God, help me to do excellent work in everything I do. Instead of blaming others, help me to be responsible. Amen."

From *Chick Chat* by Kristi Holl

True Beauty

What is beauty?

The answer depends on who you ask. TV advertisers might hang a beauty sign on a particular height, size, color of eyes or skin or hair. Others might say beauty has more to do with a girl's character qualities. Anger, jealousy, lying — I think we can agree that those aren't beautiful traits, but compassion, love, and honesty are.

When I was invited to participate in this devotional, the title — *The Beauty of Believing* — captured my attention. The phrase made me consider my definition of beauty, to think about how what you and I believe creates true beauty.

"Your beauty should not come from outward adornment, such as elaborate hairstyles and the wearing of gold jewelry or fine clothes. Rather, it should be that of your inner self, the unfading beauty of a gentle and quiet spirit, which is of great worth in God's sight" (1 Peter 3:3 – 4).

Scripture isn't telling us to refrain from wearing bracelets, toe rings, and bangles. Those can be fun expressions of who you and I are as a person, but those outward adornments aren't a true expression of beauty. A *gentle and quiet spirit* is born of a confidence in God's unfailing love for us. Placing our faith in God brings peace, even during exams, in the middle of a stormy relationship, or when we're bent at a graveside.

I pray for you to have the beauty of believing that God cares for you, that you can call his name — Jesus — and he'll be there with you. Always. Your God. That's beautiful!

— Mona Hodgson

78

"Imitate those who through faith and patience inherit what has been promised."

—Hebrews 6:12

Promise to Be Patient

The Bible is full of promises for the believer, promises for peace, joy, love, friendship, rewarding work, and much more. It takes two things for these promises to come true. The first ingredient is faith: believing God's Word. The second ingredient is patience.

Jillian's best friend was moving away. They'd been best friends and next-door neighbors for five years, and Jillian was brokenhearted at the news. She claimed Psalm 147:3: "[God] heals the heartbroken and bandages their wounds" (MSG). She truly believed God would do that for her, but when a week went by and she still felt sad, she decided the promise didn't work. Jillian was wrong. The promise is sure, and God's Word can be counted on. Jillian had faith—but she was missing the ingredient of patience.

Patience is the ability to stay steady during the challenging storms of life. You usually have to wait a length of time before you receive your promise. It's like planting a seed (your faith), then waiting for the harvest to appear.

Are you waiting for a promise of God in your life? Then practice both faith and patience. It's a winning combination.

More to Explore: Romans 2:7

Girl Talk: How's your patience level? Can you stick things out, or do you want things done right away?

God Talk: "Lord, it's so hard to be patient. I really do want to wait for your perfect timing. Please help me stay calm and know you are taking care of everything. Amen."

From *Girlz Rock* by Kristi Holl

"Blessed are the pure in heart, for they will see God."
—Matthew 5:8

Squeaky Clean

Pure in heart?" you may be saying. "I guess *I* won't be seeing God!" Okay, so none of us is totally "pure" inside. The stuff going on around us—gossiping girls, annoying boys, teachers having bad days—makes it pretty hard to constantly think, feel, do, and say lovely things.

Jesus is saying you can only come close to that in two ways.

One, you have to work on it. Deliberately turn away from gossip, even when it's really juicy and could get you a lot of attention. Patch up a quarrel, even though you KNOW you're right and it kills you to give in. When you do that, you see a little bit of what God is like, because God is always pure that way. Doing the absolute right thing makes you purer in heart.

And two, Jesus says, let God work in you. Pray for purity. Make space inside yourself for God. Pay attention. He knows you can't do it all by yourself and he doesn't expect you to. Let him purify you. It's such a blessing.

More to Explore: Psalm 28:6

Girl Talk: What's one thing you could do today to clean up your heart a little bit?

God Talk: "Lord, you know my heart better than anyone else, even better than me. Show me the areas I need to work on. Amen."

From *That Is So Me* by Nancy Rue

80

"Jesus Christ is the same yesterday and today and forever."
—Hebrews 13:8 (NASB)

Jesus Never Goes Out of Style

Fashion trends change so quickly that sometimes they're over before you've had the latest layered haircut or bought the coolest shoes or found that mini handbag in fake leather. Movies that are popular this year will be in the sale bin next year. The world is constantly shifting, but one person never changes: Jesus. He's the same today as he's always been, and he'll be that way forever.

The more you read the Word of God, the more things you find out about Jesus. He's the Good Shepherd guiding and protecting us; he's the Great Physician healing us; he's our Rock to stand firmly upon; he's the Way, the Truth, and the Life. He loves children and wants them to come to him. He's the Bread of Life. He always has been. He always will be.

Not all the people in our lives can be counted on like that. Friends move away or find new best friends. Favorite teachers and pastors retire. Sometimes parents leave, or a grandparent dies. In a world that is constantly changing, be thankful that Jesus is the same today as he always was—and that you can count on him for all your tomorrows. He has promised to never leave you, and (unlike people sometimes) he always tells the truth.

More to Explore: James 1:17

Girl Talk: Have you had changes happen to your body? How do you feel about these changes?

God Talk: "Lord, I know there will be changes all through my lifetime. Help me to look to you when changes come. Thank you for never changing. I love you. Amen."

From *No Boys Allowed* by Kristi Holl

"Don't you know that your bodies are temples of the Holy Spirit? The Spirit is in you. You have received him from God. You do not belong to yourselves. Christ has paid the price for you. So use your bodies in a way that honors God."

—1 Corinthians 6:19–20 (NIrV)

Future Love

Abby's parents were fighting. Again. She slipped out of the house and ran over to see her neighbor Shannon. Shannon was eighteen and had always seemed like an older sister to Abby. Whenever things got too tough at home, Abby escaped and went there.

Shannon gave Abby some cookies and sat down with her at the kitchen table.

Abby leaned forward. "Shannon, when I see your mom and dad together, they have a good time. They act like they love each other."

"They do," Shannon said.

Abby looked down at the kitchen floor. "For you, it's easy," she said. "You've watched your mom and dad all your life. You can try to be like them. But what about me? What if I end up with someone who treats me just as badly as my dad treats my mom?"

"That doesn't have to be the case." Shannon's green eyes were deep and serious. "I've learned a lot of good ideas from my mom and dad. But you can learn from them too. They aren't perfect any more than anyone else, but try to remember what you like."

"But—" Abby didn't know how to say it. She tried again. "How will I know what to look for?"

Shannon thought for a moment. "Well, the most important thing is that my mom and dad are Christians. That doesn't always mean a marriage is good, but it helps. Mom and Dad pray together, and when they disagree about something, they ask Jesus to help them know what to do. I want to marry a

Christian too. Someone who feels as strongly about their faith as I do. And I want someone who respects me."

Abby thought of another question. "How will I know if I really love someone?"

"He'll be someone you think a lot of." Shannon's ideas tumbled out. "You'll respect him and like the way he acts. You should be able to talk with him, even about hard things. You have fun together, even if it's just taking a walk. You miss him when he's gone, and you like doing nice things for him."

When Abby finally left Shannon's house, she had a lot to think about. As she crawled into bed, she prayed for her mom and dad. Then, for the first time, she prayed about whom she might someday marry.

More to Explore: 1 Corinthians 13

Girl Talk: What are some of the character qualities you want to find in the people you choose for your closest friends?

God Talk: "Jesus, help me to recognize the character qualities that are important in my special friends. If you want me to get married someday, I ask in your name, Jesus, for someone with the good qualities that are important both to you and to me. Amen."

From *Girl Talk* by Lois Walfrid Johnson

"Before a word is on my tongue you, Lord, know it completely."
—Psalm 139:4

In His Hands

What have you planned lately? Your birthday party? A sleepover with friends? A way to keep your little brother from reading your diary? To make sure it was going to work out, you had to have all the information beforehand. For a party, for instance, you needed to know how much money you had to spend, how many friends you could invite, and how much chaos your mom was willing to put up with.

God has a plan for your whole life, which means he has to know absolutely everything about you. Everything—like:

- what you can do without so much as a thought (your natural strengths).
- what you have to work at (your challenges).
- how you get along with people (and don't!).
- what scares you.
- what makes you totally jazzed.

There isn't anything about you that God doesn't know. Since God is the only one who knows you that well—even your parents don't know your innermost thoughts all the time, right?—only God can set up a life for you. In fact, it's already done: "All the days ordained for me were written in your book before one of them came to be" (Psalm 139:16).

More To Explore: Proverbs 16:9

Girl Talk: What are three things that nobody—or almost nobody—knows about you? God knows those things!

God Talk: "God, thank you that you know me inside-out and have a perfect plan for my life. I can't wait to see what it is! Amen."

From *That Is So Me* by Nancy Rue

83

"Since ancient times no one has heard, no ear has perceived, no eye has seen any God besides you, who acts on behalf of those who wait for him."

—Isaiah 64:4

Worth Waiting For

There's no god like our God! Since the world began, no one has ever heard of (and no one has ever seen) a God like ours, who works for those who wait for him!

Stephanie's parents had separated, but not yet divorced. They were trying to work out their problems, but Stephanie feared that things were going from bad to worse. She helped out at home with her little sister and cleaning the apartment, and she prayed every night for her parents to be reunited. The eleven months she waited—praying every night and expecting God to work a miracle—were the longest months of her life. Yet she continued to look forward to her family being restored. At the end of eleven long months, when her parents were back together, did Stephanie think that waiting on God had been worth it? You bet!

Believers wait and expect God to go to work for them, to make things happen that only God can make happen. Whatever you're facing, pray and wait for God to act. He won't let you down.

More To Explore: Isaiah 40:31

Girl Talk: When was the last time you waited for God to do something? Did you wait for it to happen or did you try to "help" because it seemed to take too long?

God Talk: "Lord, I know your timing is perfect. Sometimes it's really hard for me to wait. Please give me patience as I wait for you. Amen."

From *Shine On, Girl!* by Kristi Holl

"They will have no fear of bad news; their hearts are steadfast, trusting in the Lord."

—Psalm 112:7

Unshakable Trust

Some people have no anxiety about coming danger or receiving bad news. Their minds and emotions are steady, firm, unwavering, and unshakable. How do they attain this wonderful state of being? By trusting in the Lord, relying on him, putting their faith in him, and obeying his commands.

We all receive bad news sometimes. That's part of life. It might be fairly minor, like your friend can't go to the movie with you after all. It might be more serious, like getting an F on a test or your report card. Or the bad news can be extremely painful, like the death of a favorite grandparent or your parents' divorce. We find it very easy to get upset at bad news, crying and lashing out at people, or becoming severely depressed. Instead, we are to have a calm, "steadfast heart" that trusts in the Lord.

A heart with unshakable faith is needed so we can stop, pray for wisdom, and sit back and allow God to work. God will handle those problems that we don't have the ability to control. Always remember that the bad news you receive does NOT take God by surprise. He's ready to help you get through it calmly, so that you come out on the other side even stronger.

More to Explore: John 14:1

Girl Talk: When you get bad news, how do you feel? What do you usually do?

God Talk: "Lord, when bad things happen, I am not usually calm. Please help me stay calm and have firm faith in you. Amen."

From *Girlz Rock* by Kristi Holl

85

"Blessed are the poor in spirit, for theirs is the kingdom of heaven."

—Matthew 5:3

Rich in Love

You probably get what "poor" means. It's not how you feel when your mom says she can't afford that iPod you're dying for. Real poverty is having to do without the things the body needs. Very poor people don't have enough to eat, may not have shelter, or are low on clothes to protect them from the weather.

"Poor in spirit" is being without the things that make the heart glad, like hope and joy and love. You may have been poor in spirit yourself when you had a fight with a friend, or felt left out at school, or needed time with your mom when she was too busy. And yet Jesus says you are blessed when you're totally bummed out. You're filled with God at times like that. How can that be?

God never says he "can't afford" to give you what your spirit needs. He is in fact the only one who can. That's a blessing.

More to Explore: Psalm 116:7–8

Girl Talk: Have you ever felt "poor in spirit"? Did you feel any different after praying about it?

God Talk: "Jesus, some days I just feel down. I feel disappointed or unloved or sad. Help me to remember that you are with me even in those dark times. Thank you for never leaving me. Amen."

From *That Is So Me* by Nancy Rue

"Now to him who is able to do immeasurably more than all we ask or imagine, according to his power that is at work within us . . ."

—Ephesians 3:20

Beyond Our Dreams

If you are a believer, God's mighty power is working in you. By his power, he is able to accomplish more than we would ever dare to ask or hope.

Maybe you're having terrible trouble understanding your subjects in school. You read the same paragraphs over and over but can't understand the meaning. Your grades go from A's to D's. "Dear Lord, please help me," you pray every night. "I don't want to flunk fifth grade." One day, a young woman visits your school and gives you some tests. She discovers that an accident the year before, when you hit her head, has left you with a learning disability. The young woman offers to teach you some special ways to read and learn. Within six months, your grades are as high as before the accident.

Sometimes when we pray for God's help, we hope for just enough help to get by. Yet "no eye has seen, no ear has heard, and no mind has imagined what God has prepared for those who love him" (1 Corinthians 2:9 NLT). God doesn't just want us to have a life in which we barely survive. He wants us to grow stronger and thrive. So pray—and expect answers beyond your wildest dreams!

More To Explore: 1 Timothy 1:14

Girl Talk: How do you pray? Do you pray for just a little help, hoping that God will answer? Or do you pray for the best that God can give you?

God Talk: "Lord, help me to trust in your power and ask for it when I need it. Amen."

From *Shine On, Girl!* by Kristi Holl

87

"Even though I walk through the darkest valley, I will fear no evil, for you are with me; your rod and your staff, they comfort me."

—Psalm 23:4

No Fear!

The rod and staff were sticks used by shepherds for counting, guiding, rescuing, and protecting their sheep. The Bible says that we are sheep, and Jesus is the Good Shepherd. He is close beside us, to protect and comfort us.

We all need protection sometimes. You may not understand why girls at your middle school torment you. You're positive you've never said or done anything to them. They may not physically hurt you, but they terrify you just the same.

What have you focused on recently? If we focus on the fearful situation, it will appear impossible to overcome. Focusing on God's promises, on the other hand, gives us strength and lessens the fear. Start with these: "The Lord is with me; I will not be afraid. What can mere mortals do to me?" (Psalm 118:6). "Though I walk in the midst of trouble, you preserve my life" (Psalm 138:7).

No matter what you're going through right now, your response can be, "I will *not* fear!" Speak it out loud forcefully several times. Focus on God's power, and you'll feel the comfort of God promises.

More to Explore: Psalms 27:1–3; 46:1–3

Girl Talk: What things cause you fear? How do you feel when you focus on the problem? Do your feelings change when you concentrate on God's promises?

God Talk: "Lord, you haven't given me a spirit of fear. I trust you. Please help me to trust you even more. Amen."

From *Chick Chat* by Kristi Holl

"Blessed are the meek, for they will inherit the earth."
—Matthew 5:5

Most Happy to Be Me!

Which of these would you LOVE to be voted as?

- Cutest
- Most Talented
- Most Likely to Succeed
- Most Popular

How cool would it be to have your picture above that title in the yearbook? Actually, it might be cool for a while, until everybody forgot about it and went on to the next thing.

Jesus says that you're more God-filled when you're just happy to be who you are. There's nothing wrong with being drop-dead gorgeous or American-Idol talented or the girl everyone wants to be around. But you don't have to be that in order to be filled with God. You just have to be you. Then you will be:

- Miss Peaceful, who isn't always worried about what other people think of you.
- Happy Girl, because you're free to be.
- Way Loved, because people adore and respect you for being just yourself.

That's the inheritance God the Father wants you to have.

More to Explore: Galatians 1:10; Psalm 23:6

Girl Talk: Do you think the most popular (or smartest or prettiest) girl you know always feels like she's at the top? Do you think it's hard for her to do and be what it takes to stay there?

God Talk: "God, I know that the titles we get here on earth don't matter. Thank you for giving me the one title that does last: Loved by God! Amen."

From *That Is So Me* by Nancy Rue

89

"Whether you turn to the right or to the left, your ears will hear a voice behind you, saying, 'This is the way; walk in it.'"
—Isaiah 30:21

Following the Paths of Righteousness

God promises to lead us and guide us when we don't know what to do. If we are truly listening, we'll hear that "still small voice" inside giving us sure directions.

Jill just found out that her friend Merissa copied her math homework and turned it in as her own. What should she do? Kyla has permission to sign up for one activity in the summer, but she loves both swimming and softball. Which one should she choose?

We all need to make decisions—big and little—many times each day. How do we know the right choices to make? The key is your relationship with God. The closer you are to him, the easier you will hear his voice and direction.

Hearing God clearly requires that we give up what *we* want and are willing to do what *he* wants. It takes time and calls for reading the Bible, patience, and prayer. If you're willing to do these things consistently, you'll find it much easier to hear God's voice when you need guidance.

More to Explore: Psalms 143:8; 32:8

Girl Talk: Do you have times when you just don't know what to do? Who do you turn to first? Is it God? Your mom? Your friend?

God Talk: "God, I have times when I don't know what to do. Please guide me and show me what to do. You want what is best for me, and I thank you so much for that! Amen."

From *Girlz Rock* by Kristi Holl

90

"It is God who works in you to will and to act in order to fulfill his good purpose."

—Philippians 2:13

The Power Source

Alexis had great intentions for her summer job babysitting three small neighborhood children. Their mom didn't want them watching much TV, but instead to play at the park, go swimming, and go to the library for story time. When Alexis accepted the job, it sounded like fun! Imagine getting paid to go to the pool! It was a shock to discover how much hard work was involved in "playing" with kids. At the pool, Alexis didn't lay out with her friends—she entertained for endless hours in the baby pool. At the library, Alexis didn't browse through shelves of novels—she tried to keep the baby from eating the board books and screaming. At the park, she never sat down—she pushed two kids on the swings while keeping the baby from eating sand. "I quit," Alexis finally told their mom. "I haven't got the strength."

Instead of leaning on her own strength, Alexis needed to ask God to work through her. Once she prayed, God gave Alexis the desire to do an excellent job babysitting, along with the energy to do the work. Trust in God for the power to do the job—and do it well.

More To Explore: Hebrews 13:20–21

Girl Talk: Are you trying to do a job that has exhausted you? Are you trying to do the job in your own strength? If you're doing what God wants, ask him for help. He'll give it!

God Talk: "Lord, I want to do great things for you. Please give me the motivation and energy to do everything you want me to do. Amen."

From *Shine On, Girl!* by Kristi Holl

91

"The light shines in the darkness, and the darkness has not overcome it."

—John 1:5

No Longer Dark

Mei Ling flicked off the light and took a running leap into bed. Outside, the November wind blew around the corner of the house. A wavering light filled the room. Eerie sounds sent shivers through her whole body.

Shadows danced on the walls, growing long in corners and melting down into the stairway outside her door. Feeling scared and alone, Mei Ling huddled under the blankets.

Minutes later, her dad came into her room to say good-night. He gently pulled the blankets off her head. "Something wrong, Mei Ling? Can I help?"

Afraid to admit her fear of the dark, she shook her head. But Dad guessed. "Are you afraid of the wind and the dark?"

This time, Mei Ling nodded.

"All of us have times when we're afraid," Dad told her. "What counts is what we do about it—like choosing to face the reason, for instance."

Going over to the door, he flicked the light switch. The bright light reached into the corners, and every shadow melted. As Mei Ling looked around the room, her fear vanished.

"Now watch." Dad turned off the light and went to the window. "I can close the blinds if you want." When he did, the room became dark with no dancing shadows. "But there's something we're missing."

When Mei Ling joined him at the window, Dad pulled the blinds back up. Bare branches, stripped of leaves, moved back and forth—first blocking the streetlight, then letting the light shine through. As Mei Ling watched, the light kept changing. Now she understood the sound she heard—branches tapping against the side of the house.

"What happened when I opened the blinds again?" Dad asked.

"I saw what made me afraid. The branches moving back and forth. Touching the side of the house."

"Are you afraid now?"

Mei Ling shook her head. "I know what the shadows are. I don't have any reason to be afraid."

Dad smiled. "And what do you see instead?"

"The wildness of the November wind."

Dad smiled and picked up the Bible next to her bed. "Let's read Psalm 121 tonight." Once more he turned on the light.

Mei Ling began reading. Her voice grew stronger when she reached the third and fourth verses. "He who watches over you won't get tired. In fact, he who watches over Israel won't get tired or go to sleep."

When Dad turned off the light and left, Mei Ling snuggled down under the blankets. This time she pulled them only as high as her shoulders. *It's not so bad when I face things*, she thought.

Drowsiness settled around her as she repeated the verses from Psalm 121 that meant the most to her. Then she turned the words into a prayer. *He who watches over me won't get tired. He won't get tired or go to sleep.*

Moments later, Mei Ling fell asleep.

More to Explore: Isaiah 43:1–3

Girl Talk: What makes you afraid? Try to remember when these things started making you scared and why.

God Talk: "Jesus, thank you that you are with me always, even when I am afraid. Help me remember to turn to you when I get scared. Amen."

From *Girl Talk* by Lois Walfrid Johnson

92

"Blessed are the merciful, for they will be shown mercy."
—Matthew 5:7

Practice Mercy

Mercy sounds like something that happens in court. The judge shows mercy for the criminal and only puts him in jail for ten years instead of for twenty—that kind of thing. We think of it as a big deal that only happens to adults.

You've experienced mercy yourself, though. What about that time you really messed up and your parents decided not to ground you for the rest of your life? Or the time your sister promised she wouldn't tell on you for something you SO did?

You even show mercy. It's what you do when you care so much about a friend, you forgive her for hurting your feelings. Or when your little brother flushes your math homework down the toilet, and you don't flush him down with it. God doesn't miss the mercy you show because he invented it. He likes it—so much that he has mercy on you when you need his forgiveness. It's nice how that works out, isn't it? It makes it definitely worth it to cut that homework-flushing little brother some slack.

More to Explore: Ephesians 2:4–5

Girl Talk: When was the last time you showed mercy to someone? When is the last time someone showed mercy to you?

God Talk: "God, thank you that you are willing to show mercy to me over and over again. Help me also to always have mercy on those who hurt me. Amen."

From *That Is So Me* by Nancy Rue

93

"What is the price of five sparrows? A couple of pennies? Yet God does not forget a single one of them. And the very hairs on your head are all numbered. So don't be afraid; you are more valuable to him than a whole flock of sparrows."

—Luke 12:6–7 (NLT)

Million Dollar Hair

If God cares for small birds that are worth only a couple pennies, then imagine how much more he cares for you. He watches over you so closely that he even knows how many hairs you have on your head.

You don't ever need to be afraid. God says you are *valuable*: of great worth, precious, and priceless! Get outside for a minute. Watch the birds overhead as they glide on the breeze without a care in the world. They aren't worried about where their next worm is coming from! If God provides every need for the birds, how much more will he take care of you?

Thinking deeply about this truth can help when you feel sad and lonely, when you think no one notices you. If he is concerned enough to count every hair on your head, then God is even more concerned about your nightmares, that fight with your friend, your dream of being a nurse, and yes, even your frizzy hair.

More to Explore: Luke 12:22–31

Girl Talk: Have you ever felt lonely, even if you're around family or friends? Take a walk in a park or look through a nature magazine to remind yourself that God takes care of everything in this world, including you!

God Talk: "Lord, I'm feeling all alone today. I don't know why I'm so valuable to you, but I thank you for your unfailing love. Please help me remember how much you care for me. Amen."

From *Girlz Rock* by Kristi Holl

94

"The Lord said to Jacob, 'Go back to the land of your fathers and to your relatives, and I will be with you.'"

—Genesis 31:3

Safe in God's Hands

The Bible tells the story of a man named Jacob, the grandson of Abraham. He followed God as his guide, but many times God's intentions must have seemed like a mystery to him.

He married the woman of his dreams, Rachel, but only after his father-in-law, Laban, tricked him into marrying her older sister, Leah, first. Laban, whom Jacob worked for, was always trying to cheat him, and Laban's sons spread rumors that Jacob used their dad to become wealthy.

Jacob could have decided God didn't like him anymore and tried to go it on his own, but he continued to follow God's guidance. God finally said, "I have seen all that Laban has been doing to you. Now leave this land at once and go back to your native land." Then God went to *Laban* in a dream and told him to "be careful not to say anything to Jacob, either good or bad" (Genesis 31:24).

This story makes clear an important truth for all of us: Listen to God and do what he says, even if it's scary. God will take care of the details you have no control over. It's sort of a relief, isn't it?

More to Explore: Proverbs 3:5–6

Girl Talk: God never said that following him would be easy. Have you ever had to do anything difficult because of your faith in Jesus?

God Talk: "Jesus, thank you that you hold me safely in your hands, even when life is tough. Help me to always listen for your voice. Amen."

From *That Is So Me* by Nancy Rue

"Do not be afraid, for I have ransomed you. I have called you by name; you are mine. When you go through deep waters and great trouble, I will be with you. When you go through rivers of difficulty, you will not drown! When you walk through the fire of oppression, you will not be burned up; the flames will not consume you."

—Isaiah 43:1–2 (NLT)

A Friend in Times of Trouble

If you have accepted Jesus as your Savior, you don't need to be afraid anymore. God has saved and reclaimed you. Now you belong to him. Even when troubles seem too big to survive, God will walk you through them. You won't drown in your difficulty. You won't be destroyed, no matter how hard it gets sometimes.

Even when you forget to pray, God never leaves you. When you fail in your tests and trials, he never leaves you. Although you may not feel God's presence, he never leaves you. He's there to walk alongside as you go through fiery trials. Life can sometimes hand us some very deep rivers of trouble. You may be adjusting to a new stepfamily. Your health—or someone you love—may be in serious danger. You may have a family member fighting in the military. You may live in a city where serious crime happens daily. Is God still there, walking beside you? YES!

More to Explore: Exodus 33:17

Girl Talk: Do you ever feel alone when things aren't going right? Have you talked to God about what's happening?

God Talk: "Jesus, you know what I'm going through. Please give me your peace and hope. I need you to get through this. Thank you. Amen."

From *Girlz Rock* by Kristi Holl

96

"But I trust in you, Lord; I say, 'You are my God.' My times are in your hands; deliver me from the hands of my enemies, from those who pursue me."

—Psalm 31:14–15

A Royal Gift for Jochebed

Picture this: You're a Hebrew girl. You and your people are slaves in Egypt, which is a foreign land. You get married and have a daughter and two sons. One of your sons isn't even old enough to roll over yet. Now imagine that the pharaoh in Egypt orders all Hebrew baby boys be killed. He doesn't want any more Israelites around who could grow up and fight him. Pharaoh tells his people to throw all the boys born to Hebrew women into the Nile.

The tiny bundle in your quivering arms—your son—is a Hebrew baby boy.

That was real life for Jochebed.

Jochebed's daughter Miriam and son Aaron both kept quiet about their new baby brother. But the baby was growing and making more noise. Jochebed wouldn't be able to hide him from Pharaoh and his people much longer.

So one day, Jochebed wove a basket out of papyrus and coated it with tar and pitch to waterproof it. She kissed her baby boy's soft cheek, tucked him into the basket, and clutched it as she walked. Praying, Jochebed asked God to protect her son's life. And then she set the basket in the reeds along the bank of the Nile River and told her daughter Miriam to watch.

Jochebed's walk home must have been tough. Her baby was too little to take care of himself, but this was the only way she could think to save him. Would God provide a way for her son to live?

At home, while Jochebed cooked over the fire, she continued to pray for her baby. Then she heard Miriam's shouts.

"Mama, Mama, hurry. Come quick."

Frightened, Jochebed hurried back to the Nile river. Nearby, she saw the pharaoh's daughter holding the baby.

Pharaoh's daughter named the baby Moses and paid Jochebed to take him home and nurse him until he was old enough to live in the palace. God saved Moses from certain death. And he provided a way for Jochebed to be close to her son and care for him until he was older.

Behind the scenes, God worked out his plan for Jochebed, Moses, Aaron, and Miriam. God does the same thing for you. You may not always see God or hear him or even feel him at work in your life, but God is there. And like Jochebed, you can trust God to work through your circumstances for his purposes, which are always best.

More to Explore: Exodus 2:1 – 10

Girl Talk: How might God be working behind the scenes in your life?

God Talk: "Dear God, thank you for being with me always. You know what's best in every circumstance. You're faithful to provide what I need. Help me to trust you always. Amen."

From *Real Girls of the Bible* by Mona Hodgson

97

"Jabez cried out to the God of Israel, 'Oh, that you would bless me and enlarge my territory!' . . . And God granted his request."

—1 Chronicles 4:10

The Price of Blessing

We all want to be blessed. Jabez was no different. One thing he asked God for was "enlarged territory." That can mean more land, but it can also mean having more power or a more important job.

Rachel wanted the most important role in the musical her middle school planned to perform. She wanted to play the lead singer, Maria, in *The Sound of Music*. She worked hard before tryouts, learning lines and music. When the auditions were over, she nearly fainted with joy when her name was listed beside "Maria Von Trapp." Soon, however, Rachel realized the honor came with many added responsibilities. She worked longer hours. She attended individual rehearsals with the vocal and drama teachers. After practicing many nights till nine o'clock, she still had all her homework to do. When God answers a prayer for more blessings, people are thrilled! (At least for a while.) Soon they realize that blessings also carry new responsibilities. So don't pray for the blessing if you're not ready for the added responsibility.

But if you're ready and have done a heart check-up on your motives, go ahead and ask! God loves to bless his children.

More To Explore: Matthew 7:7–11

Girl Talk: What do you want to be blessed with? Have you confessed all lingering sin, so that God is free to work?

God Talk: "Lord, I thank you for all the good things you have already given me. Please bless me now with ______________. Thank you for your continued loving presence. Amen."

From *Shine On, Girl!* by Kristi Holl

"I write these things to you who believe in the name of the Son of God so that you may know that you have eternal life."
—1 John 5:13

All My Problems?

Emily's church had brought a busload of middle school kids to hear a well-known Christian singer. Emily and her friend Rachel followed José, the youth leader, and his wife, Maria, into the auditorium. Seats were filling up fast.

Soon the concert began. The music was great. Often the audience clapped along, stomped their feet, and called out. After a number of songs, the singer started telling how he had come to know Jesus.

"Accept Jesus, and all your problems will be over," the singer said.

Emily felt confused. *I've already invited Jesus into my life. But I still have problems. Is there something I didn't do right?*

All around Emily, kids began standing up and going forward. One minute Emily wanted to join them; the next she felt as if her feet wouldn't move. *Should I go forward again?* she wondered. *Didn't I really accept Jesus?*

On the ride back to church, Emily found an empty seat next to Maria. She wanted to talk about how she was feeling, but she wasn't quite sure where to begin. "Maria, the singer said that if I became a Christian, all my problems would be over. But they aren't!"

"Are you confused?" Maria asked. "I'm glad you told me. The singer didn't explain that very well. He should have said, 'If you accept Jesus, he'll be *with you* in your problems.'"

Whew! Emily felt as if a heavy bag of books had fallen off her back.

"Have you found that's true since you asked Jesus to be your Savior?"

Emily thought about it for a moment and nodded. "He explained it in a different way—the singer, I mean."

"Did you wonder if you needed to go forward again?" Maria asked.

Emily nodded.

"Sometimes that happens. Different speakers use different ways to explain how to receive salvation. But when José and I prayed with you a few months ago, you told Jesus you were sorry for your sins and asked forgiveness. You asked him to be your Savior and Lord. When you did that, you became a Christian."

"But—" Emily hesitated. "Sometimes I'm not sure. Sometimes I don't *feel* like I'm a Christian."

"If you believed what you were saying when you prayed that prayer, you *are* a Christian," Maria told her. "You can't depend on your feelings. You have to go by what God promises."

Digging in a pocket of her jacket, Maria pulled out a small Bible. When she found the right place, she turned the Bible toward Emily. "Read this."

Emily looked down and started reading. "I write these things to you who believe in the name of the Son of God so that you may *know* that you have eternal life ..." In Maria's Bible the word *know* was underlined.

Emily took a deep breath, then let it out. All around her, the bus was noisy, but deep inside Emily, there was something steady and quiet.

More to Explore: Romans 10:9

Girl Talk: What did Maria mean when she said, "You can't depend on your feelings. You have to go by what God promises."

God Talk: "Thank you, Jesus, that through your death on the cross, you give me salvation and eternal life, beginning right now. Amen."

From *Girl Talk* by Lois Walfrid Johnson

"Your name will no longer be Jacob, but Israel, because you have struggled with God and with humans and have overcome."

—Genesis 32:28

Wrestling with God

Going back to his homeland, Jacob was going to have to face his brother Esau whom he hadn't spoken to in years. Jacob was afraid Esau would kill his whole family. Following God's guidance, though, he sent some livestock ahead with his servants as a gift for Esau.

But wouldn't you know, when he was alone in camp that night, some guy jumped him and started wrestling with him. Jacob had been fighting people all his life, first Esau, and then Laban, and now some stranger. Jacob kept on even after the guy knocked Jacob's hip out of joint. Finally, Jacob said he would only let go if the guy would bless him. That's when the man revealed that he was God himself, in the form of an angel!

What did that mean for Jacob? Jacob could be afraid and struggle, but God would always be stronger than he was. You might be scared and fight God sometimes, too, but he'll always be strong for you. So ask God to bless you, even when you've been wrestling with him. You can expect to *be* blessed when you let God be your guide.

More To Explore: Deuteronomy 31:6

Girl Talk: Have you ever "wrestled" with God? Tell him about those things in your life that you just don't understand.

God Talk: "God, I don't always understand why certain things happen, and sometimes I even fight you about it. Thank you that you bless me, even when I'm scared and confused. Amen."

From *That Is So Me* by Nancy Rue

100

"The Lord caused the Egyptians to look favorably on the Israelites, and they gave the Israelites whatever they asked for."
—Exodus 12:36 (NLT)

God Bless You!

When it was time for the Israelites to leave their slavery behind in Egypt, God did a marvelous thing for them. He caused their former owners, the Egyptians, to like the slaves so much that they gave the slaves whatever they wanted to take with them!

You wish *your* enemy would do that! You're sick of being picked on at school. You have no idea why Jason, the class clown, has singled you out, but he's made fun of you all year. You tried ignoring him, as your teacher suggested. You stood up to him and demanded that he stop it, as your dad suggested. You're tempted to call him names back. Finally, you give up and do what you should have done in the first place: you pray. You ask God to change Jason's heart and cause him to be friendly to you. Every time he picks on you, you pray again. Slowly, over a matter of weeks, Jason stops making fun of you. One day, when you drop your books, you're astounded when Jason stops and picks them up for you.

God can change the hearts of people. Live an obedient life. Pray for your enemies. Then relax and let God make it happen in his time.

More To Explore: Daniel 1:9

Girl Talk: Is there someone in your life you just can't seem to please? What things have you tried? Have you asked God for help?

God Talk: "Lord, I don't know what to do about ______. Please show me the way to respond to this person. Amen."

From *Shine On, Girl!* by Kristi Holl

"The King [Jesus] will reply, 'What I'm about to tell you is true. Anything you did for one of the least important of these brothers of mine, you did for me.' dec63 "

—Matthew 25:40 (NIrV)

Secrets of the Heart

Jill's favorite aunt Mickey called on a Friday morning to ask if she could drop by and spend the night on her way down south. She had an unexpected work trip. Jill was the only one home, but she was sure it would be alright with her mom. Only later did she find out that both her mom and her older sister Sabrina had dates for the night.

When Jill finally heard a car door slam around 8 o'clock, she ran down the stairs and out the door. She threw herself into Mickey's arms.

"Hey, there! Good to see you!" Mickey held Jill out for a long look. "Wow! What a lovely grown-up person you've become!"

Jill smiled. Mickey hadn't changed. Her eyes were warm and caring.

Jill and Mickey went to a country inn for dinner, and it was fun being in such a nice place. It was even more fun to talk, just the two of them. But when they were having dessert, Jill thought about how both her mom and sister were out on dates. "Mickey," she asked, "do you ever feel sad that you're not married?"

"Sometimes. But I'm not sorry about it," Mickey said. "Some people feel sorry for me, but that's their problem."

"How come? I mean, why haven't you gotten married?"

"So far, I haven't felt that God put me together with the right man. It's much better *not* to marry than to marry the wrong person."

"But do you ever feel like you're—" Jill stopped.

"Like I'm not cute or worth being with?" Mickey grinned, but her eyes were serious. "You know, Jill, it can be really fun to find the right person at the right time. But it isn't *all* there is to life."

Mickey set down her iced tea. "I don't want to spend my life looking around every corner for a man. If God wants me to marry, he'll show me who the person should be. But if he *doesn't* want me to marry, that's okay. It's okay to *not* get married. I have a full life," Mickey went on. "Because I don't have a family, there are ways in which I'm free to help other people. But you see, if I'm married or not married, I'm a whole person. I'm a person valued by God."

"Do you ever get lonely?" Jill asked.

"Sure," Mickey told her. "Times like that I try to reach out to others — to see if there's a way I can help them. Times like that I come and see you."

Jill grinned. "And take me out for supper."

More to Explore: 1 Corinthians 13

Girl Talk: What are some good things about being single?

God Talk: "Jesus, help me to remember that I am a whole person, valued by God, even when I feel lonely or forgotten. Amen."

From *Girl Talk* by Lois Walfrid Johnson

"Let our lives lovingly express truth [in all things, speaking truly, dealing truly, living truly]. Enfolded in love, let us grow up in every way and in all things."

—Ephesians 4:15 (AMP)

Nothing but the Truth

Believers should have a truthful and loving way of dealing with others. But don't express the truth in a harsh way. Day by day, and year by year, let Jesus make you more and more like him.

Maybe you have two friends. They both tell you the truth, but one feels warm and caring, while the other girl's "truth" cuts deep. When you all try out for the track team, Friend #1 says to you, "You're a natural for long-distance running. You hardly broke a sweat running the mile!" Friend #2 also speaks the truth: "You know, your short legs are stubby, so don't even think about hurdles. You'll fall flat on your face." Both girls spoke the truth, but only one spoke the truth in love.

Believers who are growing in their faith speak words of truth, but in a loving manner. They aren't brutal, then claim, "I'm just telling the truth. Don't be so touchy." True Christian love is open and genuine, not two-faced and phony. A growing Christian backs up her loving words with action. Let love guide you—in your thoughts, words, and actions.

More To Explore: Psalm 32:2

Girl Talk: How do you speak the truth? Are you loving or brutal? The next time you speak the truth, let it be gentle, and follow it up with action.

God Talk: "Lord, I want to grow in my relationship with you. Please help me be always truthful, but also always kind and gentle. Amen."

From *Shine On, Girl!* by Kristi Holl

103

"We live by faith, not by sight."

—2 Corinthians 5:7

Faith in His Word

We base our actions and our lives on what we believe, not what we can see with our eyes or experience with our senses. Instead of magnifying our circumstances, we should focus on the truth in God's Word.

Your homework is so hard you can't do it? Truth: "I can do all this through him who gives me strength" (Philippians 4:13). God's Word says you can lean on his strength and power to get the job done.

Your conversations with that angry person always end up in fights? Truth: "A gentle answer turns away wrath, but a harsh word stirs up anger" (Proverbs 15:1). God's Word says if you answer him with a gentle answer, it will turn aside his anger.

Are you going to believe what you see with your eyes and experience with your emotions? Or are you going to believe what God says in his Word? Remember, "God is not a man, that he should lie" (Numbers 23:19 KJV). His Word is the absolute truth.

Your problems may not disappear overnight. God may seem slow in coming to the rescue, but he uses the waiting time to stretch your faith and encourage you to be steady in prayer. "We fix our eyes not on what is seen, but on what is unseen, since what is seen is temporary, but what is unseen is eternal" (2 Corinthians 4:18).

More To Explore: Romans 8:24–25

Girl Talk: How often do you let your feelings rule your actions?

God Talk: "Lord, I let my feelings get the better of me sometimes. Please help me to go to you first. I want my actions to reflect you. Thank you. Amen."

From *Girlz Rock* by Kristi Holl

"You, Bethlehem . . . though you are small among the clans of Judah, out of you will come for me one who will be ruler over Israel."

—Micah 5:2

Promises for the Small

Have you ever seen one of those t-shirts that says, 'WHERE IN THE WORLD IS ______?' and has the name of some itty-bitty place that doesn't even have a Wal-Mart? Like Bucksnort, Tennessee?

That was the attitude people back in Old Testament times had about Bethlehem. It was one of the smallest, puniest villages in Israel. But God promised that the One he was sending to save his poor, outcast people would come from that little bend-in-the-road place.

Far away to the East, some magi believed they saw a message in the stars. They arrived in Jerusalem and asked around, "Where is the one who has been born king of the Jews?" Now, there was already a king in Jerusalem, a very bad dude named Herod, who was freaked out at the suggestion that somebody else was going to kick him off the throne. In a panic, he called his advisors and asked them where this king, this Christ, was to be born. "In Bethlehem in Judea," they replied, "for this is what the prophet has written." Little did Herod know that Jesus Christ had already been born there. God had kept his promise.

More To Explore: Joshua 21:45

Girl Talk: Think about a grown-up who does a lot to take care of you, like your mom or dad. What promises do you think they've made to themselves to keep you safe and happy?

God Talk: "Lord, thank you that you always keep your promises! And thank you that you kept your promise to send your Son into the world. Amen."

From *That Is So Me* by Nancy Rue

105

"Stand firm, and you will win life."

—Luke 21:19

Solid as Rock

Michelle's sixth-grade year was one long trial after another. In church camp the summer before, she was challenged to be bolder in her faith. So she decided to "come out of hiding." Until now, she never mentioned church at school. Michelle just tried to be nice and blend in. She never had to defend her faith—because no one knew she had any. Then in sixth grade, she wore her cross necklace and "What Would Jesus Do?" T-shirt. She got noticed—and teased. When Michelle took stands on issues, she was often alone. But this was her attitude throughout: "I remain confident of this: I will see the goodness of the Lord in the land of the living. Wait for the Lord; be strong and take heart and wait for the Lord" (Psalm 27:13–14). She put her trust in God and focused on him instead of those who ridiculed her.

Eventually, two girls told Michelle they were Christians too, and Michelle made two excellent friends. "And so after waiting patiently, Abraham received what was promised" (Hebrews 6:15). Standing firm through tests and trials will also see the promises of God become reality in your own life.

More To Explore: Psalm 40:1

Girl Talk: Have you had any trying times lately? What do you think God might be trying to teach you?

God Talk: "Lord, doing the right thing is not always popular. Please help me to be patient and stay focused on you. I know that with you beside me, I can't go wrong. Amen."

From *Shine On, Girl!* by Kristi Holl

"Blessed are those who mourn, for they will be comforted."
—Matthew 5:4

From Sad Tears to Happy Tears

Think about the last time you were so upset you thought you'd *never* feel better. Did your friends ditch you? Did your grandpa die? Did your parents get a divorce? Even things nobody else thinks are a big deal can leave you feeling that way—anything from getting an F on a quiz to hurting the feelings of somebody you really love. Grieving is like an elephant sitting on your chest, squeezing out your hope.

Maybe somebody came along who said or did just the right thing to give you hope that maybe you *would* get over it. A new friend appeared. Your mom shared her grief and a plate of cookies with you. Your dad promised he would always be there for you. You could breathe again.

That's why those who mourn are blessed—because they will be comforted by God, who knows all the right things to do and say. That feeling of hope in the future is worth the fear you had that it was lost forever. Every time God comforts you, you will feel a little safer, knowing that nothing can happen that will take away hope forever. And that's a blessing.

More to Explore: 2 Corinthians 1:3–4

Girl Talk: Think about a time when you were really sad about something. What did someone do to comfort you? Now imagine God doing that for you every time your heart hurts.

God Talk: "Jesus, some days I just feel down. I feel disappointed or unloved or sad. Help me to remember that you are with me even in those dark times. Amen."

From *That Is So Me* by Nancy Rue

107

"Commit to the Lord whatever you do, and he will establish your plans."

—Proverbs 16:3

Success God's Way

You're in sixth-grade band, and for your fund-raiser, you have to sell at least ten boxes of candy. There's only one problem: you hurry home every day to care for your mom, who's recovering from surgery. You also watch your little sister and cook supper. There's no time to go door-to-door selling candy. Two days before the deadline, you've sold only one box—to your dad. "Lord, I trust you to show me what to do," you pray. On Sunday, two ladies from church visit your mom, and when they leave, one lady asks about the candy by the front door. You explain about the fund-raiser, and the lady buys two boxes. That night, about an hour before bedtime, the doorbell rings again. Four people from church stand there. "We understand you're selling candy," one of the men says. "Do you have any left?" You nod, too surprised to speak.

"Take delight in the Lord, and he will give you the desires of your heart. Commit your way to the Lord; trust in him and he will do this" (Psalm 37:4–5). God wants to plant his desires for you in your heart, so that he can fulfill them. He will make a way for you to succeed, even where there seems to be no way.

More To Explore: Philippians 1:6

Girl Talk: Have you ever been given a job that seemed impossible? How hard did you try to do the job?

God Talk: "Lord, when things seem impossible, please remind me to call on you first. Only with your help can I do it. Thank you. Amen."

From *Shine On, Girl!* by Kristi Holl

"May your roots go down deep into the soil of God's marvelous love; and may you be able to feel and understand, as all God's children should, how long, how wide, how deep, and how high his love really is; and to experience this love for yourselves."

— Ephesians 3:17, 18 (TLB)

God's Love: First, Free, Forever

You could spend your whole lifetime, and ten bazillion, gazillion lifetimes, thinking about God's love, and still have more to think about. For now, though, let's check out these three big points:

God loved us first. He tagged you way before you even were "you," before your parents met, before Adam and Eve ate the apple. "Long before he laid down earth's foundations," the Bible says, "he had us in mind, had settled on us as the focus of his love" (Ephesians 1:4 MSG).

God's love is free. We can't buy it. We can't earn it. It's not based on whether we wear Hollister, or whether we're on the dance team, or how good we are. There are no strings attached.

God's love is forever — the only kind that will last and last. It won't break. It won't spoil. You can't lose it. As Paul says, "nothing can separate us from his love: neither life nor death, neither angels nor other heavenly rulers or powers, neither the present nor the future, neither the world above nor the world below" (Romans 8:38 – 39 TEV).

More To Explore: Deuteronomy 10:17

Girl Talk: How does it feel to know that you are so loved by God?

God Talk: "Jesus, there has never been a time when you didn't love me. There will never be a time when you don't. I love you too. Amen."

From *Whatever: Livin' the True, Noble, Totally Excellent Life*
by Allia Zobel Nolan

109

"Now I am coming to You; I say these things while I am still in the world, so that My joy may be made full and complete and perfect in them [that they may experience My delight fulfilled in them, that My enjoyment may be perfected in their own souls, that they may have My gladness within them, filling their hearts]."

—John 17:13 (AMP)

I've Got the Joy, Joy, Joy...

Jesus is talking here to his Father, God, about his disciples. (That's you too!) Jesus said he taught his followers how to live so they could be happy. Jesus wants you to have "gladness" filling your heart and joy flooding your soul.

Some days are easy to feel joy. Your homework gets an A. Your hair behaves. Your little brother is staying overnight with a friend. But what about the days you fall in the mud, you forget your homework, and you're grounded for mouthing your mom? Can you have joy on those days? Believe it or not, yes, you can. Your joy comes from the Lord, not from your circumstances.

One reason Jesus wants you to be filled with joy is that he loves you. Another reason is that joy makes you strong! And the stronger you are, the less tempted you will be to think angry thoughts or say mean things.

Understand this: *it is God's will for you to enjoy life!*

More To Explore: John 15:9–11 and Romans 14:16–18

Girl Talk: Who gets the credit when you have good days? Who do you usually blame for the bad days? How can you remember to have joy every day?

God Talk: "Lord, I want to be filled with joy. I want to love my life on good days and bad. Thank you. Amen."

From *Girlz Rock* by Kristi Holl

"I will pour out my Spirit on all people . . . Even on my servants, both men and women, I will pour out my Spirit in those days."
—Joel 2:28–29

Fire of Faith!

The disciples could believe in Jesus because – hello! – he was right there with them. But we don't see Jesus in the flesh or hear him talking to us like a person. We can't follow him around to watch him turn a kid's lunch into a whole banquet. And yet we know he still lives, in us, through us, around us. What's that about?

It's about the Holy Spirit, another thing God promised through a prophet. He said he would pour out his spirit on ALL people. That was a huge promise back then, because there were strict rules about who was better than whom. But God promised he would allow his Spirit to pour over absolutely everyone, so that all could be forgiven and comforted.

Many, many years later, after Jesus had gone back up to heaven, great tongues of fire rested on the disciples and "all of them were filled with the Holy Spirit" (Acts 2:4). When people wanted to know what was going on (*were the disciples drunk?* they wondered), Peter reminded them of God's promise in Joel's prophecy. The promise is still there. For you. For everyone.

More To Explore: 2 Corinthians 3:17–18

Girl Talk: The Holy Spirit works in many ways. Ask an adult you trust how the Holy Spirit has moved and whispered in their life.

God Talk: "God, thank you that you sent the Holy Spirit to be with me in everything I do. It feels wonderful to know that you are all around me, all the time. Amen."

From *That Is So Me* by Nancy Rue

111

"I have hidden your word in my heart that I might not sin against you."

—Psalm 119:11

What Are You Eating?

Whatever is saved or stored in your heart will guide and direct your life. So it's important to feed your heart with God's Word.

Suppose your mom remarries, and when the two families are combined, you have to share your bedroom with a younger stepsister. The little girl irritates you with her nonstop chatter. Your mom begs you to be patient, and you do feel guilty when you snap at your stepsister and make her cry. Yet, you can't gain control over your tongue. Your feelings always take over.

Then you hear at Sunday school that memorizing God's Word can keep you from acting on those impulses. You're doubtful, but you try it anyway. You memorize verses about the tongue: "She opens her mouth with wisdom, and on her tongue is the law of kindness" (Proverbs 31:26 NKJV). "May God, who gives this patience and encouragement, help you live in complete harmony with each other" (Romans 15:5 NLT). Gradually, things change with your stepsister. When you're tempted to speak sharply to her, God's Word comes up out of your heart. Then you can take a deep breath, smile, and answer in a more gentle manner. Before long, you discover that you actually like your stepsister (and yourself!) much better.

More To Explore: Psalm 37:31 and Proverbs 2:10–11

Girl Talk: What things are you tempted to do that you know are wrong? Have you worked to change your heart by changing what you feed your mind?

God Talk: "Lord, you know the problems I have. Help me to change my heart by storing your Word there. Amen."

From *Chick Chat* by Kristi Holl

"Abram believed the Lord, and he credited it to him as righteousness."

—Genesis 15:6

Believing God

Because Abram believed the promises God gave to him, God said Abram was a righteous man. To be righteous means to honor God and live your life according to his will. When Abram believed God's promises, it honored God. God responded by declaring him righteous because of his belief.

Jamie had a hard time believing anyone. She'd heard her older brother declare he never took drugs—then watched him be arrested for drug abuse. Her dad had promised he'd be there forever—just a month before he walked out without an explanation. So when her mom promised one weekend that she'd take Saturday off and go with Jamie to an amusement park, Jamie muttered, "Yeah, I'll believe that when I see it." Her mom was hurt that Jamie didn't believe her. It didn't seem fair. She hadn't done anything to lose Jamie's confidence or make Jamie distrust her.

Even more so, God deserves our trust for being our all-loving Creator and Giver of good gifts, and he wants us to believe him. "Without faith it is impossible to please God, because anyone who comes to him must believe that he exists and that he rewards those who earnestly seek him" (Hebrews 11:6). You don't just have faith (or trust) by itself. You have faith IN something or someone. The proper and most reliable place to put our faith is in God.

People will let you down. Sometimes it's on purpose, like when they make promises they don't intend to keep. Most often, people don't mean to disappoint you—they're just imperfect human beings. Put your trust in God instead of people. He will never let you down.

More To Explore: Hebrews 11:1

Girl Talk: Which people in your family do you trust? Do you find it hard to keep trusting? Do you have faith that God will never let you down?

God Talk: "Lord, sometimes it is hard for me to trust others. Help me to remember that you can always be trusted and that you will never let me down. Thank you. Amen."

From *Shine On, Girl!* by Kristi Holl

"For his Holy Spirit speaks to us deep in our hearts and tells us that we really are God's children. And since we are his children, we will share his treasures—for all God gives to his Son Jesus is now ours too."

—Romans 8:16–17 (NLT)

The Daughter of the King

When we accept Jesus, something wonderful happens. We go from ordinary girl to adopted child of God—from everyday commoner to royal princess and co-heir to the throne.

How cool is that? Still, our role as princess will be way different than the ones we see in the movies—you know, where the girl prances around the palace in a pink puffy dress giving orders. As daughters of the King, instead of demanding everything our hearts desire, we'll have to give up this world's stuff, so we can inherit the treasures of the next world.

We'll also have to forfeit behaviors that are inappropriate for the daughter of the King to do (cursing, lying, gossiping.) And instead of the popularity and applause that usually accompanies nobility, we can expect to suffer some slings (being mocked or dissed for our beliefs) and arrows (being rejected by girls who think we're Goody Two-shoes).

But the Bible says if we suffer with Jesus, we will also share in his glory. Think of it: As his princess-daughters, we'll be able to live for all eternity among the royals of heaven—God and all the saints!

More To Explore: 1 Corinthians 2:9

Girl Talk: How does knowing that you are a daughter of the King change the way you look at yourself?

God Talk: "Heavenly Father, thank you for making me your princess-daughter. Help me to act in ways that always make you proud. Amen."

From *Whatever: Livin' the True, Noble, Totally Excellent Life*
by Allia Zobel Nolan

114

"As the Father has loved me, so have I loved you. Now remain in my love."

—John 15:9

Living in Love

Jesus said that he loves you just as God, the Father, loves him. Just as much, and in the same way. Imagine that! So it's important that you continue to rest and live in that everlasting, bountiful love.

Sometimes it's hard to believe God can love us that much. After all, we all do things that we know are wrong and for which we need forgiveness. Maybe you cheated and turned in a book report that you actually wrote last year. Perhaps you pretend to like your stepmother, but you secretly hate her. When you're so imperfect, can God still love you? YES! Or maybe your family is breaking up, or your health is breaking down. Does God still love you, no matter what is happening in your life? YES!

Sometimes we need reminders that God loves us. Say it out loud: "God loves me, and I can trust him. God loves me, and I can trust him." If you have trouble believing that God really cares about you, repeat that to yourself several times every day for a month. Get it down deep inside you.

More to Explore: John 15:10–11 and Romans 5:6–8

Girl Talk: Do you have days when you think that God can't possibly love you? Would it help you to remind yourself daily that God does love you?

God Talk: "Jesus, I know you love me so much that I can't understand it. Sometimes, I can't even believe it. Please help me to remember every day that you love me. Thank you for your love that never ends. Amen."

From *Girlz Rock* by Kristi Holl

"Cursed is the ground because of you; through painful toil you will eat food from it all the days of your life."

—Genesis 3:17

Work at It

After Adam and Eve ate the forbidden fruit, God could have just wiped them out and started over with a new pair. Instead, he had mercy on them.

That doesn't mean he let them off. He kicked them out of the perfect Garden, but he didn't destroy them. He loved them too much. Just like any good parent, he taught them the consequences of being disobedient. Since then, people have had to work for their food, and work hard, with all kinds of obstacles ("thorns and thistles," v. 18) coming up to get in the way.

But there was still hope in what God did. He said we *would* eat the food we have to work hard for. It might be "painful toil" sometimes, but we are still allowed to be an important part of God's creation. Now that's a God ya gotta love.

Close your eyes and think for a few minutes about the work God has you doing these days—besides "getting an education" and "helping around the house." Maybe being nice to that girl everybody else teases? Not whining about your lack of a cell phone? Ask God to give you a hand with it. He wants to help you with your work.

More to Explore: Ecclesiastes 3:12–13

Girl Talk: Do you ever see things that remind you evil still exists in this world? Have you ever stopped to pray about it?

God Talk: "Lord, thank you that you give humans the opportunity to work for you. Show me what work you'd like me to do. Amen."

From *That Is So Me* by Nancy Rue

116

"Be strong and courageous, and do the work. Do not be afraid or discouraged, for the Lord God, my God, is with you. He will not fail you or forsake you."

—1 Chronicles 28:20

Press On with Courage

Sometimes the job God asks us to do looks enormous. The size of a task—if stared at long enough—can cause fear or discouragement to grip the heart. But if we remember that God—the Creator of the whole universe—is with us, then fear loses its power.

Katie had prayed a long time before she took the job as junior counselor at summer camp. But when she arrived, she found she was in charge of six homesick little girls. They cried, wouldn't talk, and wanted to leave. Katie stepped outside the cabin, gazed up at the stars, and prayed hard. She was scared at the size of her job. However, a couple of minutes into her prayer, a peace settled over Katie's heart. She knew God was with her. He wouldn't fail her or leave her on her own. She went back inside the cabin, got the lonely girls into sleeping bags, and chose this verse for their bedtime devotions: "Be strong in the Lord and in the power of His might" (Ephesians 6:10 NKJV).

No matter how big your task is, take heart. God won't leave you to handle it alone.

More to Explore: Joshua 1:9

Girl Talk: Are you facing a job or a challenge that seems too big for you? Do you need courage and strength from God to keep moving ahead?

God Talk: "Lord, help me remember that I'm never alone. Give me your courage to finish my work. Amen."

From *Chick Chat* by Kristi Holl

"I have fought the good fight, I have finished the race, I have kept the faith."

—2 Timothy 4:7

Feeling His Glory

Jennifer bent down and checked her shoelaces. As she went through her warm-ups, the spring sunshine lit her face.

Jen the runner. Jen the track star. Jen, wanting with all her heart to be a champion athlete.

But that was then. Her old school. The one where she knew everyone, and everyone knew her. Once, her friends would have come alongside the track, giving high fives, cheering her on. Yes, that was then.

Now, deep inside, Jen felt lonely. *Can I run like I did when I had friends surrounding me?*

Looking around the field, Jen saw the long white lines someone had sprayed on the grass that morning. Everything was ready for the school field day. Yet her thoughts weren't on the hundred-meter dash. Instead, she noticed Mona, a classmate who would run against her. *I wish I could laugh and feel sure of myself the way she seems to do.*

Two months before, after Jen's family spent a lot of time praying about it, her dad bought a restaurant in town. He believed God wanted them here. Jen had to admit that she thought so too, but it was hard being the new kid in town.

Then, Jen remembered a song her dad had played on the piano the night before. Trying to work up her courage, she hummed softly to herself. *In my life, Lord, be glorified. Be glorified.*

As Jen walked over to the starting line, she prayed. *Whether I win or lose I want to honor you, Lord.* Lifting her head, Jen smiled. Yes, that was what mattered most. Honoring God. Even more than winning. Even more than fitting in at her new school. Today she was going to honor God by running to the best of her ability. After all, God was the one who gave her the ability to run. And she wanted to thank him for it.

Like Jen, you can honor God by appreciating the good things he's given you. Maybe he made you a great artist. Paint a picture! Maybe you're awesome at basketball. Shoot some hoops for Jesus! God loves to watch you try your best. It's another way you can worship him.

More to Explore: Hebrews 12:1

Girl Talk: What are some things you love to do? How does it make you feel to know that you can honor God just by enjoying them?

God Talk: "God, thank you for giving me the ability to do ____________. Help me to do it with an attitude of worship. Amen."

From *Girl Talk* by Lois Walfrid Johnson

118

"You remain the same, and your years will never end."
—Psalm 102:27

Never-Ending Lord

Grace had seen too many things come to an end in the past year. She wished she could have even two months in a row without changes. Her mom had left the family to pursue an acting career in California. Soon after the divorce, her dad remarried a woman with two little kids. They moved to a bigger home in another part of town, so Grace changed schools. They'd stopped going to church, and Grace missed her youth group. She felt like her former life had been wiped out. Would anything ever be the same again?

There is one thing that never changes—and that's God. In a world that is sometimes overwhelming with its changes, it's important to remember that Jesus is the Rock that never moves. Anyone who lives by Jesus' words is "like a man building a house, who dug deep and laid the foundation on the rock. And when the flood arose, the stream beat vehemently against that house, and could not shake it, for it was founded on the rock" (Luke 6:48 NKJV). Sometimes changes come so rapidly that it feels like a flood. But if you build your life on the Rock, you'll weather the storm and still be standing!

More To Explore: Psalm 18:2

Girl Talk: Have you ever felt flooded by changes? Did you know that God will always be your shelter in that flood?

God Talk: "Lord, sometimes I feel knocked over by all these changes in my life—my body, my friends, school. Please help me remember that you never change, and that you will always be there to support me. Amen."

From *Shine On, Girl!* by Kristi Holl

119

"Blessed are those who hunger and thirst for righteousness, for they will be filled."

—Matthew 5:6

Hungry for the Truth

What are you in the mood for right now? Domino's Pizza? Ben and Jerry's Ice Cream? Your mom's double chocolate brownies? Let your mouth water. Can you almost taste and smell it? Getting pretty hungry?

Now imagine being that eager to understand what God wants you to do. Think of wanting to do the right thing so much you can almost taste it. Maybe you do feel that way. There might be something you'd give a lot to be able to change—like being nicer to your sister or treating that handicapped girl more like a friend. You've tried on your own and you just can't do it, and you SO want to because you love God.

Letting God come in to work that change in you will be like finally biting into that cheese-dripping slice with pepperoni or taking the first lick from that double cone. However close you feel to God right now (even if it's, uh, like you're in a separate universe), go to a quiet place, get still, and ask God to bring you closer. Ask the way you beg your mom to stop at Baskin-Robbins—only times one hundred. The asking might make you feel like God's nearer all by itself.

More to Explore: Isaiah 55:1–2

Girl Talk: Do you feel hungry for God? What do you think it means to thirst for Words of life?

God Talk: "Dear Jesus, I don't always feel close to you. But I *want* to so badly! Keep that hunger alive in me so that I continue seeking you. Amen."

From *That Is So Me* by Nancy Rue

"Hear me, my God, as I voice my complaint."

—Psalm 64:1

Telling All

You know from many years of Sunday school that believers are supposed to "do everything without grumbling or arguing" (Philippians 2:14). And yet, some days you feel so frustrated that you're ready to explode. Sometimes it's little things like your sister drinking all the orange juice. Sometimes it's big things like getting a bad grade on a test. You bottle up your feelings, pretending things are great. When you pray, you feel like a phony.

But you don't need to feel this way! God is the one person to whom you can always tell the absolute truth. If it weren't all right to be totally honest with God, would David have written these psalms? "O Lord, hear me as I pray; pay attention to my groaning" (Psalm 5:1 NLT). "I pour out before him my complaint; before him I tell my trouble" (Psalm 142:2). Being totally honest with God about your feelings is good. It isn't the same as grumbling about your life to everyone you meet. It's just sharing your feelings with him so you can sort them out together—and he can help you in each situation. Talk to God. He cares.

More To Explore: Psalm 130:1–2

Girl Talk: When you pray, what do you talk to God about? Is it on-the-surface stuff, like "Help me pass my test tomorrow"? Or is it heartfelt, like "I'm so mad at Mom. Why can't she understand me?" How can you "go deeper" in your prayers?

God Talk: "Lord, I want to be able to talk to you about anything. Please help me remember that it's okay to share everything with you. Amen."

From *Shine On, Girl!* by Kristi Holl

121

"I pray that out of his glorious riches he may strengthen you with power through his Spirit in your inner being, so that Christ may dwell in your hearts through faith."

—Ephesians 3:16–17

Strength from Within

Kylie ate a whole box of cookies, after promising herself she'd just eat two. She was so tired of trying to lose the weight her doctor suggested. Amber was disappointed too, but in her mom. She'd promised *again* to make it to her soccer game, but when Amber scored the winning goal, her mom wasn't there to see it—*again*. Amber felt like quitting.

What can these girls do for strength when their own has run out? As believers, they can pray for help. "In the day when I cried out, You answered me, and made me bold with strength in my soul" (Psalm 138:3 NKJV).

Whenever we experience a disappointment, we need inner strength and encouragement. God—out of his unlimited resources—gives us that strength to endure with a good attitude. As you trust in God more and more, Jesus will be more and more "at home" in your heart. When that happens, your disappointments won't seem like such a big deal because you'll know you're not alone. Even more than God wants to remove your pain or uncomfortable circumstances, he wants to use them first to help you grow.

More To Explore: Isaiah 40:29–31

Girl Talk: Think about the last time you were disappointed. Did you dwell on how bad things were for you? Did you ask God for help and encouragement?

God Talk: "Lord, sometimes I feel too weak to keep going every day. Please help me to remember that you will give me all the strength I need. Amen."

From *Girlz Rock* by Kristi Holl

"The Israelites were unfaithful in regard to the devoted things."
—Joshua 7:1

Admitting Your Mistakes

After Moses died, God put Joshua in charge. Joshua was devoted to God and did everything God told him. But did the people keep God's commandments about how the moving tabernacle was to be handled? You guessed it. NO.

This time it seemed like God wasn't going to give them a second chance. The Israelite army went up against a weaker army and got beaten. Joshua fell facedown in front of the ark and wailed, "Now everybody's going to think we're a bunch of losers, and they'll all be out to get us."

God told Joshua to stand up and face the truth. The Israelites were defeated because somebody had stolen stuff from the tabernacle of God and were using it for themselves. What did they expect?

If you want another try—if you don't want to be defeated by your own sin—you have to admit you were wrong and do what God wants you to do. As long as you do that, God will turn your mistakes around. He wants to do that for you.

More To Explore: Proverbs 28:13

Girl Talk: Have you ever seen someone make a mistake that affected the whole group? What happened when they admitted they messed up?

God Talk: "God, when I make a mistake, help me to admit that I am wrong. Thank you that you want to give me second chances. Amen."

From *That Is So Me* by Nancy Rue

123

"This is the confidence we have in approaching God: that if we ask anything according to his will, he hears us. And if we know that he hears us—whatever we ask—we know that we have what we asked of him."

—1 John 5:14–15

Asking and Receiving

Gabby had always had a hot temper. She hated being told what to do—by her parents, her teachers, her older brother, her youth pastor. She didn't really mean to, but argumentative words flew out of her mouth before she thought about it, and she was tired of the consequences. Then she read a verse in the Bible: "Everyone should be quick to listen, slow to speak and slow to become angry" (James 1:19). Gabby correctly figured that if God wanted her to be slow to speak, God would give her the power.

We can be sure that God will listen to us whenever we ask him for anything in agreement with his own plan. And how can we know what that is? We can find God's will in his Word. It's spelled out for us in his commands and needs to be "stored" in our minds and hearts. Then, since we positively know he is listening when we make our requests, we can be sure that he'll give us what we ask for.

More To Explore: Jeremiah 29:12–13

Girl Talk: Are you reading the Bible regularly? What have you read recently that makes you think, *God's trying to tell me something?*

God Talk: "Lord, thank you for giving me the Bible. I can always look for true answers there and know how to pray according to your will. Amen."

From *Shine On, Girl!* by Kristi Holl

"Everyone born of God overcomes the world. This is the victory that has overcome the world, even our faith. Who is it that overcomes the world? Only the one who believes that Jesus is the Son of God."

—1 John 5:4–5

Victory!

Are you fighting a battle? Maybe you're a believer, but always blame your red hair and Irish ancestry for your terrible temper. After exploding at people, you laugh it off. "After all, I'm a hotheaded Irishman!" Lately, though, it isn't funny. You lost two good friends after letting your anger spew on them. Then you were kicked off the basketball team for yelling at the coach and the referee. If you don't overcome your hot temper soon, you won't have any friends left. It's time to fight back—and win. So you try, but find it much harder than you expected.

We feel so weak and small, so how can we defeat the enemies inside us plus those around us in the world? Can we really be overcomers? *Yes*, because we're not doing the fighting. It's Jesus *in* us—fighting the war for us. "You, dear children, are from God and have overcome them, because the one who is in you is greater than the one who is in the world" (1 John 4:4). And what should our attitude be? "But thanks be to God, who gives us the victory through our Lord Jesus Christ" (1 Corinthians 15:57 NKJV).

More to Explore: John 16:33

Girl Talk: What habits or temptations do you have trouble fighting? Have you tried letting Jesus defeat them *for* you?

God Talk: "Lord, I want to be someone who can defeat the enemies in my life. Thank you for fighting the battles for me. Amen."

From *Chick Chat* by Kristi Holl

125

"Those the Father has given me will come to me, and I will never reject them."

—John 6:37 (NLT)

Acceptance Guaranteed

Jesus said he would never reject or push away anyone who trusted in him. He knows we aren't perfect, but he approves of us and accepts us and lives in us! No matter who on this earth rejects you, Jesus will never reject you.

We all want the acceptance and approval of friends and family members. Rejection is one of the hardest, most painful things we have to endure in this life. Classmates may reject us because we look different, act different, have an accent, or have little money. Family members may treat us almost as if we're invisible.

The worst rejection, however, is when we reject ourselves. We decide that because someone else doesn't like us or accept us that there must be something wrong with us. We become afraid to express ourselves because we fear the rejection of others. What will they think of us? Will they laugh and point fingers? Will they talk behind our backs?

Jesus accepts you just the way you are. He knew you weren't perfect when he saved you. He knows you have weaknesses and that you make mistakes. Even so, he will never reject you. Nothing can ever come between you and God's love for you.

More To Explore: Matthew 11:28 and John 17:12

Girl Talk: Have you ever felt rejected by someone? What did that feel like?

God Talk: "Lord, when I'm rejected by someone, I feel so unworthy. I know you love me no matter what. Please help me remember that you care for me and that I'm worth a lot to you! Thank you! Amen."

From *Girlz Rock* by Kristi Holl

126

"Go in the strength you have."

—Judges 6:14

Use What You Have

The Israelites were doing so much bad stuff, God handed them over to their enemies, the Midianites—not a nice group of people. Naturally they cried out to God, so he sent them a prophet to explain all over AGAIN what they needed to do and be.

That prophet was Gideon, and he was truly bummed out. The angel of the Lord said to him, "The Lord is with you, mighty warrior" (Judges 6:12). Gideon said, "If the Lord is with us, why has all this happened to us?" It seems obvious to us why, but God told Gideon to go with the strength he had, and he would strike down those evil Midianites. He said he'd be with him.

After the Israelites had strayed from God a million times, God was still willing to give them one more chance, through Gideon, who was from the weakest clan and was the smallest and youngest guy in his family.

You, hopefully, don't have to do battle with large bands of enemies, although it may seem like it at times. When those times come, God wants you to use whatever you have, and he will be with you, giving you that one more chance.

More To Explore: 2 Corinthians 3:4–5

Girl Talk: Do you ever feel like Gideon—the weakest and youngest? What gifts has God blessed you with?

God Talk: "God, thank you that you are always with me, even in the face of enemies. I know that what you have given me will always be enough to do your will. Amen."

From *That Is So Me* by Nancy Rue

127

"So do not fear, for I am with you; do not be dismayed, for I am your God. I will strengthen you and help you; I will uphold you with my righteous right hand."

—Isaiah 41:10

Loneliness

Suppose your parents divorce, and you have to move to a new school district. The first day of school may be a lonely experience. In fact, the whole first month you might feel invisible. Your classmates already have best friends to hang with. You've never felt so lonely. When you finally tell your mom about it, she says, "I wish I could go with you to school and be your best friend, but I can't. However, I know someone who *will* go with you." She helps you understand that God will help you and give you strength and *never* leave you alone.

One way to fight loneliness (or any other problem) is to make the Bible verses personal to *you*. Say them out loud. You might say today's verse like this: "I do not fear, for God is with me; I am not dismayed, for he is my God. He will strengthen me and help me. He will hold me up with his righteous right hand." Making the verses personal and speaking them aloud will increase your trust in God. It can give you a peace and reassurance you never had before.

Even when you feel lonely, you're not alone. God is right there—holding tight to your hand as he holds you up.

More to Explore: Matthew 28:20 and John 14:27

Girl Talk: Do you ever feel lonely, even in a group at school or with your family at home? Do you think Jesus ever felt lonely? What did he do about it?

God Talk: "Lord, sometimes I'm really lonely. Help me to remember to reach for your hand because you're always there. Amen."

From *Chick Chat* by Kristi Holl

"[There is] one Lord, one faith, one baptism."
—Ephesians 4:5 (AMP)

I Am THE Way

Society today teaches that there are many ways to God. It is popular to believe that all religions are basically alike and that "all roads lead to God." Not true! There is only one Lord—Jesus.

Maybe you've gone to church and Sunday school all your life. Then you go to middle school. Your literature teacher talks about "the Man upstairs," and your drama coach talks about a Higher Power. Both teacher and coach feel there are many spiritual paths a person might take to find a relationship with God. The coach explains that it is like a wagon wheel. God is the center of the wheel, and the spokes are different religions. She says people can travel any "spoke" (or path) they want to, and eventually they'll all be with God forever. While that kind of talk sounds soothing to many, it's 100 percent false.

There is only one way to God. "Jesus said ... 'I am the way, the truth, and the life. No one comes to the Father except through Me'" (John 14:6 NKJV). That's pretty strong—and very clear-cut. Don't be fooled by the devil or led away from God. Jesus is the Way—and the only way!

More To Explore: Philippians 2:5–11 and Acts 4:12

Girl Talk: Has anyone ever tried to convince you that there are many ways to get to heaven? How did you respond to them?

God Talk: "Lord, when people try to tell me false things about you, I want to be ready. Please give me the right words to tell them about the true way: Jesus. Amen."

From *Shine On, Girl!* by Kristi Holl

129

"See, I will create new heavens and a new earth. The former things will not be remembered, nor will they come to mind."
—Isaiah 65:17

New Beginnings

Have you ever asked someone to forgive you, and she did? But then she reminded you every chance she got what it was you did that she had to forgive you for? How much did you hate that? Maybe you've been on the other side of that too. You TOLD someone you forgave her, but you couldn't seem to resist the chance to bring it up every now and then. Why do we do that?

Our Father doesn't hold a grudge or expect you to carry guilt inside you for the rest of your life over every mistake you've made. It's over, and you are free to go on living tomorrow better than you have today. And if you make a mistake tomorrow—which you surely will because you're a human being—you can go to God without feeling as if you've already had all your chances.

It's sort of hard to believe, but you CAN believe it, and to show it, simply celebrate it. Every time you go to God for a new start, rejoice with a grin, because God loves you enough to forget your past. It just doesn't get any better than that.

More To Explore: Psalm 103:12

Girl Talk: When was the very last time you went to God and said, "I am SO sorry I did that, Father"? If it's been a while, do it now!

God Talk: "Jesus, thank you that you forgive me every time I do something wrong. Help me to always forgive others just as willingly as you forgive me. Amen."

From *That Is So Me* by Nancy Rue

"You need to persevere so that when you have done the will of God, you will receive what he has promised."

—Hebrews 10:36

Promises Worth Waiting For

TV shows, movies, and magazines cry, "Get it now!" It might be an instant meal, instant beauty, or instant wealth. God's Word says the opposite. He gives a promise or principle and tells you how to obtain it. After you've done what God said, there might be a waiting period before the promise appears. God uses that waiting period to "grow you up" spiritually, developing character qualities that will benefit you all your life.

What things has God promised to give believers? Everything from love and peace to eternal life. He also gives us wise principles to live by. For example, if you need money, check out these ideas: "A generous person will prosper; whoever refreshes others will be refreshed" (Proverbs 11:25). And "all hard work brings a profit, but mere talk leads only to poverty" (Proverbs 14:23). Your part? Work hard and be generous. Practicing these principles over time can turn your circumstances around.

Being patient is *not* the ability to sit calmly and do nothing, waiting for something to happen. Patient perseverance, the kind needed to receive God's promises, is very active. It is the ability to hang tough when it gets hard. Instead, "rest in the Lord, and wait patiently for Him" (Psalm 37:7 NKJV). Your promise is on its way!

More To Explore: Matthew 21:28–31

Girl Talk: Is it hard for you to wait for something you want or need? Do you talk to God about it?

God Talk: "Lord, it's hard for me to be patient. Help me to remember that my answer is on its way. Amen."

From *Girlz Rock* by Kristi Holl

131

"When I am afraid, I put my trust in you. In God, whose word I praise—in God I trust."

—Psalm 56:3–4

Your Personal Protector

Worries and fears can whisper in your head. It's completely normal to feel anxious when you're having trouble with a subject at school or when your best friend isn't acting so much like a friend. It's also normal to get upset when you hear about crimes on the news or your parents having a (loud) disagreement. God made us with a built-in system for alerting us to danger. It's that dry mouth, sweaty palms, butterflies-in-the-stomach feeling you get that spurs you on to either run away or fight back.

It helps to go to someone you feel safe with and talk it out or just get a hug, but that someone might not always be available—like if you wake up frightened in the middle of the night or you're staring, frozen, at your math test in the middle of class.

God is always, always there as your Personal Protector. You can close your eyes and breathe him slowly in, calm yourself in the knowledge that he is right inside you with protection from your fears. Nothing can come between you and him, not even your worst nightmare!

More To Explore: Philippians 4:6–7

Girl Talk: What are your biggest fears? What do you worry about? Take some time to pray with God about them.

God Talk: "God, sometimes I get scared about ______________. Help me to trust you with my fears. Amen."

From *That Is So Me* by Nancy Rue

"Your eyes saw my body even before it was formed. You planned how many days I would live. You wrote down the number of them in your book before I had lived through even one of them."
—Psalm 139:16 (NIrV)

Year-Round Love

As the kids at school talked, Joanna wanted to put her hands over her ears. She wished she could shut out the sound of their words. Their voices sounded like hammers pounding on steel.

"Your mom dropped you on a doorstep," said one of the girls.

"She didn't want you," added another.

The minute Joanna could get away, she took off for home. By the time she was out of sight from the kids, she could no longer hold back her tears. As they streamed down her cheeks, Joanna broke into a run. When she reached the front door, she was panting.

Joanna stopped long enough to take a deep breath, then quietly slipped inside. *Maybe I can get to my bedroom without anyone seeing me.*

But the little Christmas bells on the door gave her away. As she tiptoed toward the steps, Mom came into the hall.

"Joanna! What's going on?"

Joanna kept moving, but as she passed under the light, Mom stopped her. "What's the matter?" she asked gently.

Joanna wondered if her cheeks were streaked from crying. "Nothing," she said.

But Mom put an arm around her shoulder. "Dad's home, and we've been putting up the tree. Come and see."

Knowing there was no escape, Joanna walked slowly into the family room. The tree was beautiful and the tallest she could remember. Partway up a step ladder, Dad was putting a star at the top of the tree. When he saw Joanna, he climbed down to give her a hug.

"Have a hard day?" he asked.

Joanna shrugged. She didn't want to say what was wrong. But as Dad gave her another hug, the words tumbled out.

"The kids at school said I was adopted."

Joanna saw the look that passed between Mom and Dad, but it was Dad who spoke first.

"You know that. We've talked about it lots of times. Why is it bothering you now?"

"One of the kids said my mother dropped me on a doorstep—"

Joanna's shoulders began to shake. "She said my own mother didn't want me! I wasn't worth anything, not even to her. I'm just—just—"

Joanna broke off and plopped into Dad's big chair. "I am totally nothing!" she wailed.

Dad sat down on the floor, cross-legged, in front of her. As Mom pulled up a chair beside her, Joanna's sobs increased. She needed to know someone loved her. But she didn't know how to say it or how to ask all the things she wanted to know.

More to Explore: 1 John 4:10

Girl Talk: Do you ever have days when you just don't feel loved and wanted?

God Talk: "Jesus, I choose to look to you in everything that happens to me. Help me know deep down inside how much you love me. Thank you that even in the moment I was conceived, you saw and cared about me. Amen."

From *Girl Talk* by Lois Walfrid Johnson

"I will praise the Lord, who counsels me; even at night my heart instructs me . . . You make known to me the path of life."

—Psalm 16:7, 11

The Teacher for Tough Times

Wouldn't it be great to have your own personal tutor who was at your beck and call 24/7? If you were having trouble with long division, you could just turn and say, "Could I get a little help here, please?" That's probably not going to happen—unless your daddy gets a giant promotion! But when it comes to the other things in life that you need help with, you do have a Personal Teacher. That would be, of course, God.

Difficulties with anger or lying or temptation—God can help you handle that. Tough times with a teacher, a coach, a babysitter—God knows all about tough times. There isn't anything God doesn't have an answer for.

It takes some practice to rely on God for individual instruction. It means figuring out what's bothering you, which God can help you with, then finding that quiet place and taking the time to be with God and talk it out. And listening—through the Bible, through wise people, through acting on what you think God is telling you and seeing how it works.

Go to God, the best Teacher, first, because he will often lead you to just the right people at just the right time. All you have to do is ask.

More To Explore: Psalm 32:8

Girl Talk: What traits make a good teacher?

God Talk: "God, thank you that you are the best teacher I could ever ask for. Help me to listen and learn from you in everything I do. Amen."

From *That Is So Me* by Nancy Rue

134

"You should behave instead like God's very own children, adopted into his family—calling him 'Father, dear Father.'"

—Romans 8:15 (NLT)

Who Am I?

If you've accepted Jesus as your Savior, then you've been adopted into God's own family. You've been taken in as a member, with all the rights of any other son or daughter. And you have the privilege and honor to call God your very own Father.

If you have days when you don't feel special or loved or important, remember who you are in Christ:

- I am Christ's friend. (John 15:15)
- I am chosen by Jesus to bear good fruit for him. (John 15:16)
- I am a temple, or home, for God. His Spirit lives in me. (1 Corinthians 3:16; 6:19)
- I am a new person. (2 Corinthians 5:17)
- I am God's workmanship (or handiwork), created in Christ to do his work. (Ephesians 2:10)
- I am chosen of God, holy, and dearly loved. (Colossians 3:12)

Memorize one or more of these verses. Then, when you're in a situation that makes you feel like a nobody, speak those verses right out loud.

More To Explore: Ephesians 1:4–5

Girl Talk: Do you ever feel ignored or unloved? What verse will you memorize now for help later?

God Talk: "Lord, sometimes I feel like no one loves me. Please help me remember that you always love me, that I am important to you. Thank you for loving me. Amen."

From *Girlz Rock* by Kristi Holl

"Then will the eyes of the blind be opened."

—Isaiah 35:5

It's All In the Details

Which is a more comforting promise to hear?

- "I promise we'll do some fun things during your spring break."
- "I promise that during your spring break we'll go to the movies Tuesday and to the lake on Saturday."

That second one is way more reassuring that certain things are going to happen.

The suffering people of Israel wanted details too. So God didn't just say, "It's going to be all right." He gave very particular ways in which he was going to make things better. He said Immanuel (Jesus) would:

- strengthen feeble hands (Isaiah 35:3).
- steady weak knees (v. 3).
- strengthen fearful hearts (v. 4).
- open blind eyes (v. 5).
- unstop deaf ears (v. 5).

And they all happened! God still heals today. No, not everyone who is blind gets to see again, and not every deaf person suddenly has miraculous hearing. But everyone—everyone—can be close to God and feel his comfort and his love. That's the best healing of all.

More To Explore: Isaiah 43:25

Girl Talk: Do you have any needs for healing? Maybe not in your body, but in your heart?

God Talk: "God, thank you that I can always feel comfort from your love. Please bring healing for ____________. Amen."

From *That Is So Me* by Nancy Rue

136

"I the Lord do not change."

—Malachi 3:6

No Variation

Mia and Lori were best friends all through grade school, and Mia assumed they always would be. But when they started going to a middle school that blended four elementary schools, things changed. Lori wanted to include new girls in everything they did. Then Mia found out that Lori was going to movies and shopping with them—but not inviting her along. Most times when Mia invited Lori to spend the night, Lori referred vaguely to "other plans." Plans that no longer included Mia. It was hard for Mia to admit that things had changed with Lori, and changed drastically. Accepting the change was painful.

People do change, and sometimes people will let us down. They're human, not perfect. No matter how many people change, remember that God is always constant. No matter where you live, no matter what you're going through—God never changes. You can bet your life on it, and you can settle down and rest. "Jesus Christ is the same yesterday and today and forever" (Hebrews 13:8). If you're a follower of Jesus, your inner life can also be stable and solid and unchanging. No matter what.

More To Explore: Hebrews 3:8

Girl Talk: What has changed for you in the last few months? Was it a welcome change, or are you still adjusting? Have you asked God to help you through it?

God Talk: "Lord, just when I think I have my life under control, something changes. Please help me to go with the flow and rely on you and your unchanging love and security. Amen."

From *Shine On, Girl!* by Kristi Holl

"From that time on Jesus began to explain to his disciples that he must go to Jerusalem and suffer many things . . . and on the third day be raised to life."

—Matthew 16:21

Hard Beginnings, Happy Endings

Some things can be hard to hear and accept.

"Honey, I'm sorry, but Grandpa is going to die."

"We have to move. Daddy has a new job."

You want to cry, throw a fit, and demand that things change right NOW! Can you imagine how the disciples felt when Jesus told them he was going to be killed? Peter, for one, wasn't having it. He took Jesus aside and said, "No way! I'm not going to let this happen to you!" Jesus wasn't having *that.* He knew it was going to be hard on them, but it had to be. It was what God had promised.

God "promised" to have his son killed? That doesn't sound like much of a promise! It's definitely the hard-to-hear kind. But God had also promised that the glory of the Lord would be revealed. Jesus was going to come back from the dead. And sure enough, on the third day after he was killed, an angel said to the women who went to his tomb, "Do not be afraid ... he has risen, *just as he said*" (Matthew 28:5–6).

The tough promises can have very happy endings.

More To Explore: Psalm 119:50

Girl Talk: Is there something tough you need to say to anyone that you've been putting off?

God Talk: "God, thank you that you sent your Son and that he rose from the grave, just as you said he would. Amen."

From *That Is So Me* by Nancy Rue

138

"If you keep my commands, you will remain in my love, just as I have kept my Father's commands and remain in his love."
—John 15:10

If

We are to follow Jesus' example. Just as he was obedient to his Father, we are to obey Jesus. Obedience and love go hand in hand. And what a promise is attached to this obedience! We will live in Jesus' love in the same way that he rests in God's love.

Jesus made it very plain. "If you love me, keep my commands" (John 14:15). Don't tell Jesus (or others) that you love the Lord if you're not willing to do what he tells you to do. "Whoever has my commands and keeps them is the one who loves me. The one who loves me will be loved by my Father, and I too will love them and show myself to them" (John 14:21). When you obey the Lord, he pours out such love on you. As you grow in this love, something wonderful happens. Obedience becomes a habit—and a joy!

More To Explore: 1 John 2:5–6

Girl Talk: How often do you say that you love God, even though you're not doing what he asks? What is one thing that you know he wants you to do, but you're having trouble obeying?

God Talk: "Lord, I want to better prove my love for you by obeying your desires for me. Please help me follow you every day. Amen."

From *Shine On, Girl!* by Kristi Holl

"I am the resurrection and the life. The one who believes in me will live, even though they die."

—John 11:25

Alive? Forever!

Has anyone you loved died? Maybe a precious grandparent or a pet you treasured? It's so hard because that person or furry companion is never coming back. But what if the one who has passed on *did* return?

Jesus had three friends who were brother and sisters to each other: Mary, Martha, and Lazarus. He loved them like family. While Jesus was out of town, Lazarus got very sick, and Mary and Martha sent for Jesus, knowing how he healed people. Instead of hurrying back, he told his disciples that Lazarus' illness wasn't going to end in death and this would be a good chance to show who God was.

But Lazarus died, and by the time Jesus got there, he'd been in his tomb for four days. He told them to take him to the tomb and roll away the stone. Jesus simply said, "Lazarus, come out!" (John 11:43). And Lazarus walked out, still wrapped up in the burial cloths, looking a little like a mummy.

What was that all about? Jesus showed that God even has power over death. He assured them that we'll all leave this earth, but he is the coming-back-to-life after our time here is over. A life that goes on forever with him.

More To Explore: Revelation 21:4

Girl Talk: Has anyone that you loved died? How would it make you feel to see them again?

God Talk: "Jesus, thank you that you have power over death. I'm so happy that even when someone dies here on earth, they get to live with you forever in heaven! Amen."

From *That Is So Me* by Nancy Rue

140

"The Samaritan woman said to him, 'You are a Jew and I am a Samaritan woman. How can you ask me for a drink?' (For Jews do not associate with Samaritans.)"

—John 4:9

Are You Talking to Me?

The Samaritan woman drawing water at the well was surprised when Jesus asked her for a drink. At that time, Jews refused to associate with Samaritans. Also, women were usually ignored. But Jesus didn't consider her "beneath" him.

You learn about prejudice when your family moves. You never felt out of place while living in Texas, but when your family relocates to a small town in Minnesota, you're the only Hispanic student in your school. Most kids ignore you. A few call you names. Being the target of discrimination and bigotry is more hurtful than you ever would have guessed. Two years later, your family moves back to Texas. You absolutely love being "home," but you've changed. From now on, you're careful to never make another prejudiced comment.

Certain people believe they are worth more than others. God's Word, however, has strong words for such people: "Do not think of yourself more highly than you ought, but rather think of yourself with sober judgment, in accordance with the faith God has distributed to each of you" (Romans 12:3).

More To Explore: Acts 10:28

Girl Talk: Have you ever treated someone differently because of how they looked? Are you sometimes treated differently because of the way you look? How does that feel?

God Talk: "Lord, I don't want to treat others differently or badly. It's hard not to follow the crowd, but I know I can follow you instead—with your help. Amen."

From *Shine On, Girl!* by Kristi Holl

"I know that you can do all things; no plan of yours can be thwarted."

—Job 42:2

The Big Picture

Have you ever made a plan, done all the work required to make it happen—and then it turned out to be a mess? Who *hasn't* had that happen! There are so many things that can go wrong with any plan, and sometimes it seems like *all* of them do. That isn't always true, thankfully. And it's never true with God's plan.

"Wait a minute," you may be thinking. "A lot of bad stuff happens. Is that part of God's plan?" That is a very tough question. When things that we consider to be bad happen, we only know that:

- people have the freedom to act as they will, so sometimes they'll try to mess up God's plan.
- God knows the WHOLE plan for the WHOLE world, and we don't. What we consider to be "bad" may be a necessary part of the BIG PLAN.
- God is always there to help us through the bad, hard things.
- if we listen to him and follow what we hear, nothing can thwart God's plan for US. Like it says in Isaiah 14:24: "The Lord Almighty has sworn, 'Surely, as I have planned, so it will be, and as I have purposed, so it will happen.'"

More To Explore: Isaiah 55:9

Girl Talk: Have you ever had something bad happen in your life but couldn't figure out why? God loves to hear your questions.

God Talk: "God, thank you that you have a plan for me and for the whole world. Help me to remember that even when hard stuff happens. Amen."

From *That Is So Me* by Nancy Rue

142

"The sisters sent word to Jesus, 'Lord, the one you love is sick.' When he heard this, Jesus said, 'This sickness will not end in death. No, it is for God's glory so that God's Son may be glorified through it.'"

—John 11:3–4

Dealing with Disappointment

Remember the story of Martha, Mary, and Lazarus? Mary and Martha were terribly disappointed and hurt when Jesus didn't hurry to their home and heal their brother. They had no idea that God was planning something even greater than healing Lazarus.

We all are disappointed at times by those we love. But we need to remember that God knows more about every situation than we do. It's like we're standing on a street corner, watching a parade. We can only see the float or band that's right in front of us. But God is like the TV cameraman high up on the corner of the roof who looks down and can see the whole parade: beginning, middle, and end. Mary and Martha could only see that their brother had died. But Jesus knew the ending—that he was going to raise Lazarus from the dead and display God's power.

The next time you're disappointed, trust that God knows more about the situation than you do. He has a much better plan in mind!

More To Explore: Zechariah 9:12

Girl Talk: Who has disappointed you in the recent past? Did you rely on yourself or on God to cheer up?

God Talk: "Lord, sometimes I feel hurt by the way others treat me. Help me to let go of my hurt feelings and to rely on you for my happiness. Amen."

From *Girlz Rock* by Kristi Holl

[Jesus said,] "I will never send away anyone who comes to me."
—John 6:37 (NIrV)

Jasmine's Special Friend

Jasmine felt nervous as she entered the long hallway. Since moving to a new school, she had dreaded Monday mornings. It seemed everyone had plenty to talk about. Everyone had a special friend. Everyone belonged to a group.

Everyone, that is, except me.

Already, a cluster of girls had formed around Dena's locker. Jasmine knew they'd be talking about all that had happened that weekend. As she pushed back her brown hair, she wished she could join them. At the same time, Jasmine felt afraid to walk past the girls. They all acted very sure of themselves, and they all made her feel left out.

Trying to comfort herself, Jasmine remembered how great she had looked as she started for school that morning. *Maybe someone will notice my new jacket. Maybe they'll think I'm worth having in their group.*

Trying to look more confident than she felt, Jasmine drew a deep breath. *If I smile, they'll have to smile back.* But even as the thought came, Jasmine started feeling shaky inside.

As she drew close to the girls, Kacie looked up. Jasmine stopped. "Hi, Kacie!"

For a moment, Jasmine thought Kacie would answer. Instead, she raised her chin and turned back to the others. The other girls laughed.

Feeling the hot blush of embarrassment rush to her face, Jasmine wanted to run. Instead, she felt frozen to the spot. *Are they laughing at me? Or just making sure I feel left out?*

Either way, Jasmine knew it made no difference. Instead of going to her locker, she headed for the bathroom.

To her relief, it was empty. Dropping her books on a ledge, Jasmine went to the mirror. Her new jacket didn't seem nice anymore. Feeling the material, Jasmine tried to believe it was still important. It wasn't. Instead, the mirror reflected the tears in her brown eyes.

Jasmine blinked the tears away, but her lips trembled. *I'm not going to cry,* she promised herself. But tears streamed down her cheeks. The loneliness she felt was too deep. *It's no use. They'll never accept me. I'll never be part of their clique.*

It wasn't the first time Jasmine prayed about it, but now she meant every word. *Jesus, they make me feel worthless. Awful. I need friends. I forgive them for the lousy way they act. But what can I do?*

In the next two days nothing seemed different. Would God ever answer her prayer? Did he even hear what she'd asked?

Then, before school on the third day Jasmine headed for her locker. As she passed Dena and her friends, all the girls ignored her. But at that moment an idea dropped into Jasmine's mind.

Keep your eyes and ears open. Look for kids who think and believe the way you do.

Jasmine gasped with surprise. Then she smiled. Was this God's answer?

More to Explore: John 3:15

Girl Talk: Can you think of a time when you were shut out of a group? How did it feel?

God Talk: "Jesus, I don't like feeling lonely and left out. But I forgive the kids who make me feel that way. I'm glad that you have called me a friend and will never turn me away. Amen."

From *Girl Talk* by Lois Walfrid Johnson

"This kind can come out only by prayer."

—Mark 9:29

Power Trip

Jesus didn't come just to heal, but to give the ability to others to be healers. Can you even imagine being one of the people Jesus trusted with that? What a rush, huh? You put your hands on people who are crippled or mentally confused and just like that, they can walk and think like everyone else. After a few times, do you think you'd start to get pretty proud of your sweet self? That might be what happened with the disciples.

A man had brought his son to them, because he was having foam-at-the-mouth seizures. But the disciples couldn't drive out the spirit. Why not? After Jesus drove out the spirit for the boy, he explained to the disciples that they had forgotten to pray, to call on God's power to do the healing. They didn't remember where their ability to heal came from.

Whenever we need healing or we want to help someone else get better, we need to call on God. If we have trouble believing that God's going to come through, we can do as the boy's father did and say, "Help me overcome my unbelief." God will do that.

More To Explore: Ephesians 1:18–21

Girl Talk: Think of someone you know who is suffering in some way. Is there something you can do to relieve a little of the suffering? Before you take part in their healing, pray by calling on the power of God.

God Talk: "God, you are an amazing healer of both the body and the heart. Help me to always rely on your power. And if I ever don't trust you, help me overcome my unbelief! Amen."

From *That Is So Me* by Nancy Rue

145

"The goat chosen by lot as the scapegoat shall be presented alive before the Lord to be used for making atonement by sending it into the wilderness as a scapegoat."

—Leviticus 16:10

Scapegoat

Gabby wanted to buy a mountain bike and had earned $40 toward it so far. Mr. Brown, who owned the local bike store, was saving the bike for her. This week she would make her first small payment. Sighing, she told her friend, "At this rate, I'll never get to take the bike home!" That Saturday when she went to make her first payment, Mr. Brown wheeled the bike out and handed it over to her. Gabby was puzzled. "What's this? Even after my payment, I will still owe you $110." Mr. Brown showed her the sales ticket. In bright red ink, he'd written, PAID IN FULL. "Your parents came in and paid it off. They said they were proud of all your help around home." Gabby grinned.

In the Old Testament, a person's sin debt had to be paid every year in the form of a goat sent into the wilderness—a scapegoat. But when Christ died on the cross, he wrote PAID IN FULL across your sins. He canceled the record that contained the charges against us. Salvation is a free gift to us—but it cost Jesus his life. Thank him today for being your scapegoat—and carrying away your sins forever.

More To Explore: Isaiah 53:6

Girl Talk: Do you have any debts? How would it feel to have someone pay them off?

God Talk: "Lord, thank you for being my scapegoat. I can't imagine how it felt, but I'm so grateful you died for me. Amen."

From *Shine On, Girl!* by Kristi Holl

"The Lord replied, 'My Presence will go with you, and I will give you rest.'"

—Exodus 33:14

Never Alone

Moses was nervous about leading the Israelites into the Promised Land, but God told Moses not to worry. Why? Even though it would be a huge job, God promised to go with him. God himself would travel with Moses, and he would give Moses the rest he needed.

If you're a follower of Jesus, you can be just as confident as Moses was when he led his people to the Promised Land. Jesus gives you this promise: "And surely I am with you always, to the very end of the age" (Matthew 28:20). Not only will Jesus be with you every step of the way along your journey, but he will provide refreshment for your weary body, mind, and emotions. "Then Jesus said, 'Come to me, all of you who are weary and carry heavy burdens, and I will give you rest'" (Matthew 11:28 NLT).

Just as God promised Moses, Jesus promises to be with you, guide you, and give you rest.

More to Explore: Deuteronomy 31:7–8

Girl Talk: Is God with you right now? How do you know? Can you always feel his presence?

God Talk: "Lord, thank you for always staying with me. Help me remember that I'm never alone. Amen."

From *Chick Chat* by Kristi Holl

147

"The thief comes only to steal and kill and destroy; I have come that they may have life, and have it to the full."

—John 10:10

Living the Good Life

Satan (the thief) is interested only in himself. He wants to steal (our health, our work, our peace) and to kill (our joy, our bodies) and to destroy (our families and friendships). Jesus came for the opposite reason: to give us an abundant, joy-filled life—a life overflowing with blessings.

Like the route for any journey or trip, life is always changing. It will be hard to enjoy your life until you understand that. Relationships are always changing—either growing or dying. Your body is growing at a rapid rate. (Just look at your baby pictures to see how you've changed!) Your schoolwork changes from year to year, getting harder. No matter how good your life is right now (or how hard), it will pass. Then you'll be in a new phase to enjoy.

This time next year you'll be very different in some ways. Just don't struggle so hard trying to get to the next place that you fail to enjoy where you are right now. It's good to have goals (earning that grade, learning that ballet step, making a new friend). But remember that Jesus died so you would have a joyful, abundant life TODAY too.

More To Explore: Luke 19:10

Girl Talk: Are you enjoying your life as it is today, or are you wishing for things that will happen in the future? What things are you enjoying today?

God Talk: "Lord, I look forward to a lot of things in my life. Help me to enjoy today and what is happening now. Amen."

From *Girlz Rock* by Kristi Holl

"Peace I leave with you; my peace I give you. I do not give to you as the world gives. Do not let your hearts be troubled and do not be afraid."

—John 14:27

The Promise of Peace

Okay, let's just admit that we've all thought about this: if salvation doesn't make life on earth perfect, or at least easy, and if you're still going to be faced with temptation, even though you're saved, and if people are going to give you a hard time about it ... uh, why, again, do you want it? There's the life-after-death thing, but you aren't really thinking about dying right now, when living is hard enough in this unpeaceful world where:

- kids fight on the playground.
- kids are mean to each other on the bus.
- boys make fun of girls.
- girls say boys are gross.
- teachers get sick of it and tell everybody to shut up.

And that's just in school. We haven't even started on what goes on at home, on the playing fields, even in church. But Jesus said to his disciples, who were asking the same question, "I give you peace as a gift to carry inside and the knowledge that nothing can separate you from me." Don't be afraid. It's always here, no matter what the world may throw at you.

More To Explore: 2 Thessalonians 3:16

Girl Talk: Celebrate peace today! Spread it around. Stop an argument. Ease a worry. Bring peace to as many people as you can.

God Talk: "Jesus, you left us with amazing peace so that even when life gets rough, we won't be afraid. Help me to spread this peace to everyone I meet. Amen."

From *That Is So Me* by Nancy Rue

149

"The Lord is gracious and compassionate, slow to anger and rich in love."

—Psalm 145:8

True Riches

Hannah felt like a failure. She was a quitter, and she hated that quality in herself. She set big goals and worked hard at them—until things got hard. For her social studies project on Texas, she planned to build an oil well that showed actual drilling. Halfway through, she got discouraged and quit, settling for a C instead of an A. She went out for the junior track team, but four days into practice she had blisters, and her legs hurt so badly she quit. And now she'd done it again. She'd started a paper route, but hated getting up at 5:00 a.m. every day. Within a week, she quit. She felt guilty, and she wanted to talk to God about it, but she was afraid. Surely God was mad at her for dropping out again.

Hannah didn't know the Lord as well as she thought. He wasn't shaking his finger at her in anger. God isn't like that. Instead, the Lord picks us up, dusts us off, and gives us encouragement to try again. "The Lord is merciful and gracious; he is slow to get angry and full of unfailing love" (Psalm 103:8 NLT). Don't be afraid to go to your heavenly Father with your failures. He loves you. He'll help you start over as many times as it takes.

More To Explore: Psalm 86:5

Girl Talk: When you set out to do something, how successful are you? How hard do you work?

God Talk: "Lord, I don't want to be a quitter. Please be with me as I work. I want to work hard and make you proud. Amen."

From *Shine On, Girl!* by Kristi Holl

"Father, forgive them, for they do not know what they are doing."

—Luke 23:34

Forgiveness—No Matter What

It's not hard to forgive the little things. Like when your best friend tells you that you have a booger coming out of your nose, right in front of a bunch of boys. It makes you mad for a while, but you can forgive and even forget and move on.

But what about those times when somebody does something really major to you or to someone you love? A careless driver hits your dog with his car. A group of girls makes your life miserable at school. It's really hard to say, "I forgive you."

It's hard because you're human. Fortunately, God isn't. He forgives even the worst sins.

And it has never been worse than people nailing Jesus to a cross and letting him die there in pain and shame. Doing that to the Son of God—it's just hard to imagine God forgiving that.

Jesus looked down at the people who had spit on him and beaten him up and said, "Father, forgive them. They do not know what they are doing." It wasn't that they didn't realize they were hurting him. They just didn't know he was really God. That's how God forgives even the worst—because he understands us. Isn't that the best?

More To Explore: Psalm 103:10–14

Girl Talk: Is there someone you are having a hard time forgiving? Remember how quickly Jesus forgave and follow his example.

God Talk: "God, I'm glad that you understand me. You know that I'm human, and I often mess up. But you are always willing to forgive me. Thank you for that. Amen."

From *That Is So Me* by Nancy Rue

A Beautiful Masterpiece

Michelangelo is a famous artist who painted the ceiling of the Sistine Chapel in Rome. He also carved beautiful lifelike statues, including angels and a famous statue of David. Someone once asked him how he was able to sculpt real-looking people from blocks of hard marble. *"Every block of stone has a statue inside it, and it is the task of the sculptor to discover it,"* he said. *"I saw the angel in the marble and carved until I set him free."*

Inside every believer is a beautiful person waiting to be set free too. That beautiful life is sometimes hidden beneath our hard outer shell, the outside part that the world sees. But spending time in God's Word does for us what Michelangelo did for the blocks of marble. Today we may feel like a gray chunk of stone, but if we are followers of Jesus, there is a beautiful believer inside. As you study God's Word and believe the truth you read there, your beauty will begin to shine forth.

There truly *is* beauty in believing. It happens when you stop looking at life's circumstances, and you focus on God instead.

The Faithgirlz verse is all about this idea: "So we fix our eyes not on what is seen, but on what is unseen. For what is seen is temporary, but what is unseen is eternal" (2 Corinthians 4:18).

Where does the "gray stone" that encloses us (and hides our beauty) come from? Mostly it comes from lies you believe about yourself. You might believe a lie that says, "Nobody loves me." Or maybe you believe the lie that says you're never going to have a good life. But when you study God's Word, you discover the truth: "I have loved you with an everlasting love" (Jeremiah

31:3 NKJV) and "For I know the plans I have for you," says the Lord. "They are plans for good and not for disaster, to give you a future and a hope" (Jeremiah 29:11 NLT).

As you believe these truths, bit by bit the gray stone chips away. Each chip is a wrong idea you've believed about yourself or God or the world. As the lies fall away, and as you hold close to the truths you are learning, the real you—a truly *beautiful* spirit—will be revealed.

We have to choose whom to believe. If we believe people's opinions that say we need to be rich and famous and look like a supermodel to be beautiful, we'll be filled with despair. Just remember: "Man looks at the outward appearance, but the Lord looks at the heart" (1 Samuel 16:7 NASB). God knows that true beauty resides in the heart, and believing him will let that beauty shine out where it can be seen—and where it will touch the lives of others.

Your part is to believe. "For we walk by faith, not by sight" (2 Corinthians 5:7 NKJV). As you trust more and more in God's promises in the Bible, your true beautiful self will emerge more and more. It's true that sometimes the chipping away of past beliefs and behaviors is painful. But you won't miss a single thing that God carved away and took out of your life. And when the Holy Spirit's work is finished, you'll be standing there, radiant and joyful.

Beauty isn't outside. It's inside, just waiting to come out. It's for every girl who trusts in God's Word.

—Kristi Holl

"I have told you these things, so that in me you may have peace. In this world you will have trouble. But take heart! I have overcome the world."

—John 16:33

When Trouble Comes

Trouble comes in all shapes and sizes. You might be experiencing growing pains in your legs at night or have asthma. You might have people problems: your best friend moved or the bully in gym class stole your shoes. You might have money troubles sometimes: you can't afford to join your friends at the water park, or your family's been evicted from your apartment for not paying the rent.

Sometimes people are told that if they just accept Jesus as their Savior, all their problems will be over. The Bible clearly teaches that is not so. Jesus told his disciples that they *would* have troubles, but not to be discouraged by them. God uses the trials and tests in our lives to teach us valuable things, like patience and endurance and the power of prayer. We wouldn't develop these necessary qualities if life were smooth all the time. However, we can have peace in the middle of the trouble. We can be sure that God has everything under control. So take heart and have courage!

More To Explore: Ephesians 2:13–14

Girl Talk: When you talk to God about your problems, do you ask them to be taken away? Or do you ask God to help you through them?

God Talk: "Lord, it is tough to get through problems. Please give me patience and peace as I give my troubles to you. Thank you for always being with me. Amen."

From *Girlz Rock* by Kristi Holl

152

"God, who gives life to the dead and calls into being that which does not exist."

—Romans 4:17 (NASB)

Get Your Faith Eyes in Focus

God does miracles. When he said, "Let there be light," the sun, moon, and stars were formed. And God can call things into existence for you too. What do you need that you don't have right now? A best friend? A new flute to replace a broken one? What things would you like to have? A place on the track team? A new dress that's not in your budget? Pray and ask God for what you need. Philippians 4:19 promises that God will supply everything you need (but not necessarily everything you *want*). God knows what would be the best for you in every situation.

Use your God-given imagination for seeing the good things God can do in your life instead of the bad things you fear might happen. This is not a magic potion or using mind control to get what you want. What you imagine affects what you do. If you imagine yourself stumbling and falling in a race, you are much more likely to do that. If you focus on running swiftly and surefooted, you are more likely to succeed. Your thinking determines your feelings about situations, and your feelings determine your actions.

Use your God-given imagination to see yourself as God sees you!

More To Explore: Luke 7:11–16

Girl Talk: Do you spend a lot of time thinking about things you don't have? Have you tried asking God what he wants for you?

God Talk: "God, thank you that you know what is best for me. Help me to see myself as you see me so that I can pray for the things that I really need. Amen."

From *No Boys Allowed* by Kristi Holl

"My grace is sufficient for you, for my power is made perfect in weakness."

—2 Corinthians 12:9

Weakness Wins

"Weak" is the opposite of "strong," right? Just like "hot" is the opposite of "cold," and "adults talking about insurance" is the opposite of "interesting."

That's usually true. But when it comes to God, sometimes he sees us the strongest when we admit we're the weakest. Here's what that looks like.

Let's say you don't have much trouble resisting temptation. Nobody can talk you into lying or cheating or talking about Susie behind her back. It's so easy for you, you hardly even consider where your strength comes from. And then a new girl moves to your school, a girl who can play soccer like Mia Hamm. She scores more goals in the first game than you have all season—and suddenly it isn't so easy to keep from pointing out that her dribbling is sloppy or she commits fouls nobody else sees. You've found your weakness.

What do you have to do to avoid becoming what you always thought you were too good to be? You have no choice. You have to turn to God, who—hello!—gave you that strength in the first place. Now you can really be strong because you know you can't do it without God's help.

More To Explore: Romans 8:26

Girl Talk: Are you a little out of shape in some places? What are your weaknesses?

God Talk: "God, I know I'm weak in some areas. Thank you that when I am weak I can turn to you for help. Amen."

From *That Is So Me* by Nancy Rue

154

"Cast your cares on the Lord and he will sustain you; he will never let the righteous be shaken."

—Psalm 55:22

Holding Hands

Throw your troubles on the Lord. Let go of them. Release the weight of the worries you carry around. God will take care of you. He won't allow his followers to slip, fall, or fail.

Worries come in all shapes and sizes, and they can be heavy. Your burden might be divorced parents, hating the way you look, a crabby grandparent who lives with you, money worries, or living in a dangerous neighborhood. Whatever the problem that causes you to stumble, the solution is the same. "The steps of the godly are directed by the Lord. He delights in every detail of their lives. Though they stumble, they will not fall, for the Lord holds them by the hand" (Psalm 37:23–24 NLT). Think of a small child holding on to her daddy's hand. She trips over a rock, but Daddy's hand grips hers tight so she doesn't fall. That's how your heavenly Father holds you. Hold on to God, and let him carry your worries.

More To Explore: 1 Peter 5:7

Girl Talk: What troubles or worries are getting to you right now? How do you handle them? Have you asked God to hold your hand and get you through it?

God Talk: "Lord, I'm having a hard time with ______. Please help me get through it and stay strong. I know you can get me through anything. Thank you. Amen."

From *Shine On, Girl!* by Kristi Holl

"A cheerful heart is good medicine, but a broken spirit saps a person's strength."

—Proverbs 17:22 (NLT)

Laughter, the Best Medicine

Modern doctors are now learning what the Bible has known all along. A lively, high-spirited, joyful heart is good for your health, just like medicine. By contrast, a subdued, weakened spirit drains a person's strength, leaving him exhausted and weak. Believe it or not, the choice is yours!

When you receive bad news—a poor grade on a test, your friend is moving—you have two choices. You can cry and get depressed and eat a box of chocolates. Or you can smile, choose cheerful, uplifting words to share, and help transform a bad situation into a hopeful one.

Being cheerful is a choice. Most of us have known people who didn't have much to be cheerful about, but chose to be upbeat and happy anyway. They've learned a great secret. They know being cheerful will help keep them strong.

As one preacher put it, "If you have the joy of the Lord, notify your face." In other words, smile! Proverbs 15:13 says a joyful, glad heart should produce a cheerful, happy face. Stand in front of the mirror, crack a big smile, and feel the immediate inner change.

More To Explore: Proverbs 15:30 and Psalm 126:2–3

Girl Talk: Have you ever wanted to gripe about something but said something positive instead? How does that make you feel?

God Talk: "Lord, I know things can't always go my way. Help me to smile in all things and look to you for comfort and relief. Thank you for always being here with me. Amen."

From *No Boys Allowed* by Kristi Holl

156

"We are hard pressed on every side, but not crushed; perplexed, but not in despair; persecuted, but not abandoned; struck down, but not destroyed."

— 2 Corinthians 4:8 – 9

A Hope-Full Existence

Life can be very hard sometimes, but if you belong to Christ, you always have a sure hope. You may feel pressured, but you won't be broken. Situations may leave you bewildered and confused, but never without hope. You may be suffering, but you are never deserted or left behind. You may feel struck down temporarily, but you will never be ruined.

Some years are easy, and some years you face very fiery trials. Do you ever feel confused by the suffering you experience? It's normal to wonder why it has to be that way and how it's all going to work out.

Just don't be fooled into thinking you'll be destroyed by it. You always have hope because Jesus lives in you! This isn't the kind of hope you find in the world, like "I hope I get asked to that party," or "I hope it doesn't rain." That kind of hope is flimsy, wishful thinking. The kind of hope *you* have is rock-solid. God is "the God of hope" (Romans 15:13)! That's why you never have to worry, no matter what you're going through at this moment.

More To Explore: 2 Corinthians 6:4 – 10 and Romans 5:3 – 5

Girl Talk: Are you going through any trials right now? Do you worry that God doesn't care, or do you talk to God about your problems?

God Talk: "Lord, I have a rough time to get through. Help me to rely on you, knowing that I always have hope in you. Thank you for your everlasting love. Amen."

From *Girlz Rock* by Kristi Holl

"You have searched me, Lord, and you know me. You know when I sit and when I rise; you perceive my thoughts from afar."
—Psalm 139:1–2

Hagar's Desert Revelation

God promised Abram and Sarai that they would have a baby, even in their old age. Sarai could hardly believe this announcement, so she decided to take matters into her own hands. She decided that her servant Hagar, who was younger, would have a child for Abram.

Because Hagar was Sarai's servant, Hagar didn't have much say in the matter. The Bible doesn't tell us what Hagar's feelings were at that point, but it does say that after Hagar became pregnant with Abram's son, Sarai mistreated her, and Hagar began to hate Sarai. Pregnant and alone, Hagar ran away into the desert.

An angel of the Lord found Hagar near a spring. "Hagar, servant of Sarai," he said, "where have you come from and where are you going?"

"I'm running away from Sarai," Hagar said.

"Go back and obey her," the angel of the Lord said. "I'll increase your offspring. There will be too many to count. You'll have a son. Name him Ishmael, for the Lord has heard of your suffering."

Then Hagar said, "You're the God who sees me. Now I've seen the One who sees me."

Hagar returned to Abram and Sarai's home and had a son. She named him Ishmael just as the Lord had said.

Fourteen years later, Sarai, whose name had been changed to Sarah, gave birth to Isaac. Now that Sarah had a child of her own, she again wanted Hagar and Ishmael to leave her home.

God told Abram, now known as Abraham, to let Hagar and Ishmael go as part of God's plan. Early the next morning, Abraham gave Hagar some food, an animal-skin canteen full of water, and then sent them back into the desert. When the water ran out, Hagar left her son under a bush, sat nearby, and cried.

God called to Hagar from heaven. "What's the matter, Hagar? Don't be afraid. God hears the boy crying. Lift the boy and take his hand. I'll make him into a great nation."

Hagar and Ishmael were out in the middle of nowhere, and God heard their cries, just as he hears your cries and sees your tears today. When God opened Hagar's eyes, she saw a well of water. She filled the skin with water and gave Ishmael a drink.

More To Explore: Deuteronomy 7:9

Girl Talk: God always keeps his promises. What are some other promises in the Bible that God has for you?

God Talk: "Dear heavenly Father, thank you for knowing me and loving me. Thank you for being a friend who is always with me. Amen."

From *Real Girls of the Bible* by Mona Hodgson

"If anyone slaps you on the right cheek, turn to them the other cheek also."

—Matthew 5:39

Saving Face

Before you get all huffy at the idea of standing there letting somebody smack your face twice, understand exactly what Jesus was talking about.

More people are right-handed than left-handed, so Jesus was referring to a righty. If a right-handed person slaps a person facing him or her on the right cheek, the slapper has to do it with the back of his or her hand, not the palm. In Jesus' day, a backhanded slap was meant more to insult than to physically harm.

So—if someone insults you, Jesus said, don't insult her back—even if the best come-back ever springs right to your tongue. Instead, just look her right in the eye, not in a "bring it on" way, but with a gaze that clearly says, "You didn't hurt me with that; you can't hurt me."

She may keep on. That's okay. It's better to be insulted twice than to get into a big fight where somebody is really going to get hurt. If she can't get to you, she won't be back for more. Turn away from her, and take your cheek with you.

More To Explore: James 1:19–20

Girl Talk: How do you respond when someone insults you?

God Talk: "God, help me to turn the other cheek when girls are mean to me. I want to be an example of your love to them. Amen."

From *That Is So Me* by Nancy Rue

159

"Yet I am always with you; you hold me by my right hand."
— Psalm 73:23

In His Grip

Sometimes — at school, at home, at a friend's sleepover — we are hit with the fearful thought: "I don't belong here, and I don't fit in." We aren't alone, but we feel lonely just the same. At times like these, remember that you still belong to God. He always accepts you. In fact, he's holding on to your hand so you can't get lost and are never alone.

Being lonely can make you depressed and dismayed, but help is on the way! "Don't be afraid, for I am with you. Do not be dismayed, for I am your God. I will strengthen you. I will help you. I will uphold you with my victorious right hand" (Isaiah 41:10 NLT). Sometimes God will fill your heart with so much love that your loneliness just disappears. You can't explain it; it just melts away. Sometimes he sends people to you — in person, on the phone, through e-mail or a text message — to meet your need for company. He will meet your need in different ways at different times.

No matter what happens, remember that you're not alone. You always belong to God. He has your hand firmly in his grasp, and he will never let go.

More To Explore: Psalm 139:7 – 12

Girl Talk: Have you felt lonely in the past week? What can you do when you feel this way?

God Talk: "Lord, I am feeling really alone right now. I know you are always there. Please help me to remember I can always call on you. Amen."

From *No Boys Allowed* by Kristi Holl

"When I am in distress, I call to you, because you answer me."
—Psalm 86:7

A Direct Line to God

When we spot trouble—crimes, fires, car accidents—we call 9–1–1 for emergency help. In the same manner, you have a hotline to heaven. God's phone line is never busy, you never get put on hold, and you never get his voicemail. You can talk to God anytime—day or night.

If you need help, try these "Emergency Numbers":

- When you're in danger, call Psalm 91.
- When you're lonely and fearful, call Psalm 23.
- When you need peace and rest, call Matthew 11:28–30.
- When you need courage for a task, call Joshua 1.
- If your wallet and piggy bank are empty, call Psalm 37.
- When feeling sadness or sorrow, call John 14.
- When you need forgiveness, call Psalm 51.
- If you're worried, call Matthew 6:25–34.

We all need help sometimes. You can always pray, and you can go to God's Word. God promises to meet your needs. So give God a call!

More To Explore: Philippians 4:19

Girl Talk: Now that you know you can talk to God about anything, who can help you find answers in the Bible? Who can support you as you work on getting closer to God?

God Talk: "Lord, thank you for the Bible and for loved ones who can help me. Thank you for always being there for me. I love you! Amen."

From *Girlz Rock* by Kristi Holl

161

"Be strong and courageous. Do not be terrified; do not be discouraged, for the Lord your God will be with you wherever you go."

—Joshua 1:9

Mega Courage

Suppose you wave good-bye to your mom and follow the stewardess into the plane. Hopefully your legs will hold you up till you find your seat. You're flying—alone—to spend the summer with your dad and his new wife in Colorado. You've never been so scared in your life. What if Crissy, your new stepmom, doesn't like you? What if you hate the town, the house, your room? You buckle your seat belt and blink back tears.

While taxiing to the runway, you dig in your backpack. What's that? You pull out a small package with your mom's handwriting on it: "Read this if you're afraid." It's a tiny pink Bible. In it is a card with verses. You read eagerly: "The Lord is my light and my salvation—whom shall I fear? The Lord is the stronghold of my life—of whom shall I be afraid?" (Psalm 27:1); and "I am with you and will watch over you wherever you go" (Genesis 28:15). Many times during the flight—and during the summer—you read God's Word for courage. Your strength increases as you grow to believe that God's in total control of everything you face. You can have that confidence every day!

More to Explore: Joshua 1:6–7

Girl Talk: What things frighten you? Do you believe God is in total control of those scary situations?

God Talk: "Lord, thank you that I can get my courage and strength from you. Help me to always remember that. Amen."

From *Chick Chat* by Kristi Holl

"They are like a man building a house, who dug down deep and laid the foundation on rock. When a flood came, the torrent struck that house but could not shake it, because it was well built."

—Luke 6:48

How's Your Foundation?

A firm foundation is critical when building things. Suppose you're helping your brother build a toy house with blocks. Without a broad base at the bottom, the blocks on top soon topple over. Or when cheerleading teams build pyramids, the strongest members make up the bottom row. Then the lighter-weight members will be safely held up. When a new house is built, cement provides a solid foundation.

You want the same kind of solid foundation in your own life. How do you acquire it? By studying God's Word, then applying it to the situations in your life. If you do that on a consistent basis, you can avoid many of the storms by wise actions. If you don't bother, "you ignored my advice and rejected the correction I offered," then "calamity overcomes you like a storm, you are engulfed by trouble, and anguish and distress overwhelm you" (Proverbs 1:25, 27 NLT).

Some storms come into every girl's life though, even when you do everything right. When they come, make sure there aren't any leaks in your foundation, then ride out the storm. When it's over, you'll still be standing!

More To Explore: 2 Timothy 2:1

Girl Talk: Are you facing serious problems in your life today? Does your foundation ever feel ready to collapse?

God Talk: "Lord, I don't want a flimsy foundation. I want to build my foundation upon your Word. Please help me to do that, Lord. I love you. Amen."

From *No Boys Allowed* by Kristi Holl

163

"You intended to harm me, but God intended it for good to accomplish what is now being done, the saving of many lives."
—Genesis 50:20

God Uses Problems to Protect You

As far as Joseph was concerned, God turned into good what his brothers meant for evil. Joseph's brothers, out of jealousy, sold him into slavery. But their betrayal was used by God to put Joseph in a place of power in Egypt. God brought Joseph to that high position, so he could save the lives of many people during a famine when there was a severe shortage of food. In his position, Joseph saved the lives of the Israelites (including his brothers), the Egyptians, and all the nations that came to Egypt to buy food. God brought good out of the evil. He still works like this in the lives of believers.

God used a painful problem (Joseph's being sold into slavery) to save Joseph and many others from a worse problem: death during a famine. So when you face a problem or a disappointment, take time to pray. Ask God if he is perhaps trying to protect you from serious pain in the future. Then give him your thanks and praise!

More To Explore: Proverbs 2:8

Girl Talk: When you look back at past problems, did God do you a favor by allowing some trouble into your life? Can you see any results now that you couldn't see then?

God Talk: "Lord, I sometimes don't understand why you send problems my way. Please help me to know whether you are trying to protect me. Thank you for your perfect wisdom in my life. Amen."

From *Girlz Rock* by Kristi Holl

"The Lord said to Moses, 'Is there any limit to my power? Now you will see whether or not my word comes true!' "

—Numbers 11:23 (NLT)

All Powerful

The Israelites complained to Moses about the manna God provided for them to eat each day. They were tired of it and wanted meat, so God said he would send meat. Moses doubted that God could find enough meat to feed several million hungry people. God's response? "Stand back and watch my word come true. My power is unlimited."

When circumstances look impossible, it's a great opportunity for God to show his strength. God made promises to his people, and he keeps his word. "God is not a man, that he should lie. He is not a human, that he should change his mind. Has he ever spoken and failed to act? Has he ever promised and not carried it through?" (Numbers 23:19 NLT). So lean on the Lord. Nothing is too hard for him!

More To Explore: Genesis 18:14

Girl Talk: What things in your life look impossible to you right now? Have you asked God to show you his power? How do you think that might help?

God Talk: "Lord, help me remember that you always keep your promises. Please be with me through everything today. Thank you for your love and power. Amen."

From *Shine On, Girl!* by Kristi Holl

165

"Jesus said, 'I will not leave you as orphans. I will come to you.'"

—John 14:18

Hugs and Tears

All afternoon, the sand had been warm. Bright sunlight touched the Wisconsin lake with a thousand sparkles. It had been fun meeting new friends at Bible camp, but tomorrow it would all end.

As she went into the cabin to change out of her swimsuit, Ashley heard a muffled sound from the back room. Was someone crying?

Moving quietly, Ashley followed the sobs to the bedroom. There she found Mia lying face down, weeping into her pillow. Ashley stopped, edged away, and then stepped back. *What should I do? Pretend I don't see her? Sneak away?*

Though they were in the same cabin, Mia came from another church. Ashley had just met her this week. Yet Mia's sobs shook the bed.

"Hey, what's wrong?" Ashley asked, stepping forward. She knew that Mia's dad had cancer, and she wondered if that was the cause of the tears.

As Mia looked up, her shoulders stopped shaking. "I am so scared." Mia spoke between sniffs. "This week has been perfect. I don't want to go home. It's awful watching Daddy get sicker every day." Her words ended in a sob, and she stopped, drew a deep breath. "I'm scared he's going to die."

"Oh, Mia, I'm so sorry!" Reaching forward, Ashley gave her a hug.

When Mia finally spoke again, her words were muffled. "Before I came, Mom said she wanted me to go and have a good time. Daddy said the same thing. He said, 'Mia, you need time with friends. You need time to know that whatever happens to me, God will be with you.'"

Mia's voice broke. "But I can't see God. What will I do if I can't see my Daddy? What will I do if I can't talk to him? What will I do if he's not there when I go to bed at night? When I wake up in the morning?"

Tears welled up in Ashley's eyes. As they ran down her cheeks, she brushed them aside. But the tears kept coming. She didn't know what to say, so she gave Mia another hug.

Finally, Ashley said, "My parents are divorced. It's different from what is happening to you, but I sort of understand. My dad lives far away now, and I hardly ever get to see him. I miss him." She paused, then continued. "But there's something that helped me, that maybe will help you too."

Mia looked at Ashley, listening carefully.

Ashley spoke the words slowly. "If something happens to your daddy, you will still have a heavenly Father. He will take care of both you and me."

Tears streamed down Mia's face again. "It's what Daddy has been trying to tell me—that God will be with me."

In that moment Ashley knew without doubt that her words had not been her own. Reaching out, she hugged Mia again.

Oh, Lord, how did you manage to do that? Ashley thought. *What if I had sneaked out instead of talking to Mia? And how did you manage to help me too?*

More to Explore: John 14:1–6

Girl Talk: Have you ever noticed some unusual timing in your own life? Perhaps someone said something at just the right time. What happened?

God Talk: "Jesus, you know I find it hard to talk with someone who's facing something really difficult. Thanks for helping me with the questions to ask, the words to say, and the hugs to give. Thanks even more for being the biggest Hugger there is because of the way you love every one of us. Amen."

From *Girl Talk* by Lois Walfrid Johnson

166

"We can rejoice, too, when we run into problems and trials, for we know that they are good for us—they help us learn to endure. And endurance develops strength of character in us."

—Romans 5:3–4 (NLT)

God Uses Problems to Perfect You

We can have joy even in the middle of problems and pain. We aren't happy *because* we have problems, but because we know the suffering has a purpose. Part of God's purpose is to produce character in his children. However, the problems themselves don't build character. *Responding correctly* to problems is what develops a godly character.

Beth and Rosa both had mean stepfathers. Rosa refused to do things he asked, got into yelling matches, and ended up running away from home. Beth's stepfather was just as difficult to get along with, but she chose to respond to her situation differently. Beth decided to be quiet, but pray for her stepfather's heart to be softened. It didn't happen overnight—it took endurance on Beth's part—but within a year she and her stepfather were spending time together fishing. Two situations—two very different responses—and two very different outcomes.

We start out as spiritual babies, and we need to grow up. If we always got everything we wanted, when we wanted it, we'd be spoiled and remain babies. So the next time you face a problem, be determined to learn from it.

More To Explore: Matthew 5:10–12

Girl Talk: Think of a problem you are facing now, whether big or small. How would God say to respond?

God Talk: "Lord, I want to do what you would do when a problem comes my way. Help me to remember you are testing me to make my faith grow. Amen."

From *Girlz Rock* by Kristi Holl

"I am convinced that neither death nor life, neither angels nor demons, nor any powers . . . will be able to separate us from the love of God."

—Romans 8:38–39

Never-Ending, Never-Failing

Everybody's different. You've noticed that, right? So each person's plan is obviously different from all others too. But there are some parts of God's vision that apply to all of us, and we already know what they are.

Part One is this: nothing will come between you and God. Once you've accepted that God IS your life, you can't take that away. It would be like trying to un-ring a bell. You can make bad choices, ignore your parents, pick the wrong friends, and God will still love you. Everybody else might give up on you, but God won't.

Can you do anything you want and get away with it? Uh, no. There are always consequences for breaking God's rules. He is a parent, after all. But those consequences do NOT include him telling you to get lost. He'll love you anyway and do everything possible to get you back on track.

So why not save yourself the trouble and do it God's way to begin with? It's a whole lot easier to get the plan and go with it if you follow what you know: God loves you and only wants good for you. Stick with him.

More To Explore: 1 John 4:16

Girl Talk: Do you feel loved by God? Think about the people who love you best in the world and then imagine love a thousand times greater! Wow!

God Talk: "God, you love me so much that I can't even fathom it. Thank you that nothing can separate your love from me."

From *That Is So Me* by Nancy Rue

168

"No, dear brothers and sisters, I am still not all I should be, but I am focusing all my energies on this one thing: Forgetting the past and looking forward to what lies ahead."

—Philippians 3:13 (NLT)

Bury the Past

Nobody's perfect, and Paul admits that. But he's not wasting any time on regrets and guilt over his past failures. He wisely concentrates all his attention and energy on making a total change in his priorities. He clings to what is truly valuable, both here on earth and for eternity.

You may have things you want to forget too. Maybe you totally blew your speech in reading class. Or you tripped in the bleachers and fell on top of a crush-worthy boy. Or maybe a memory that tortures you is more serious. Perhaps you let somebody down in a big way or have really hurt someone.

We all make mistakes and do things we aren't proud of later. Even after we ask God's forgiveness, the guilty feeling can linger. But you can't change the past or control it in any way. Do keep the lessons you learned, but forget the incidents and the emotions attached to them.

Concentrate your energy and thoughts on what lies ahead. You'll see improvement over past failures, but even more important, you'll look forward to the truly priceless victory over death and an eternity with Christ.

More To Explore: Luke 9:62 and Acts 9:1–31

Girl Talk: Do you think about past mistakes and worry over them? Are you stuck in the past?

God Talk: "Lord, help me to quit fretting about things in the past. I want to look to the future. I give my concerns to you right now, in Jesus' name. Amen."

From *No Boys Allowed* by Kristi Holl

"When you ask, you must believe and not doubt, because the one who doubts is like a wave of the sea, blown and tossed by the wind. That person should not expect to receive anything from the Lord."

—James 1:6–7

Riding the Waves

We can always go to God for wisdom. But when you pray, you must believe in your heart that God hears you and will answer you. People who can't make up their minds—believing one minute, then doubting the next—are as unstable as the rolling waves of the sea.

Do you doubt God when a fearful thought crosses your mind? To know if you're really "double-minded," check what's coming out of your mouth. Do you sound like this? "I just know God heard my prayer. I'll be on the lookout for my answer ... Boy, I don't know. It's taking a long time to get my prayer answered. I don't think God heard me ..." THAT'S doubt.

The one who gets her prayers answered, the Bible says, is the one who prays in faith. Even when nothing seems to be happening, the words coming out of her mouth are still filled with faith: "I know God heard me. I know my answer is on its way. God's timing is perfect." That's what faith is—believing even before circumstances match up.

More To Explore: Ephesians 4:14–15 and Matthew 21:22

Girl Talk: Do you ask God for help and leave your troubles in his hands? Or do you ask for help, but do your own thing anyway because you think it's better?

God Talk: "Lord, I know I don't always wait for your answer. Please help me to have patience and to trust that you will come through for me. Amen."

From *Girlz Rock* by Kristi Holl

170

"I am bringing my righteousness near, it is not far away; and my salvation will not be delayed."

—Isaiah 46:13

Saved!

You remember Isaiah, don't you? The prophet God sent to talk to the people of Jerusalem when they were at their worst?

Seriously, those people were a mess. God said they were so stubborn that it was like the muscles in their necks were iron and their foreheads bronze. They absolutely refused to listen to God and obey him, which put them so far from him they were barely in the same universe. And yet God still said, "I am going to save you. I'm going to bring peace and justice, and nobody can put you down any more."

"What's the deal?" you may ask. "They didn't deserve to be saved!"

That's just the point. God doesn't save us from our own bad behavior and stubborn thoughts and downright yuckiness because we deserve it. He saves us because he loves us and just wants us with him. All we have to do is trust him. It's that simple.

The guy writing the psalm above was running from people who were seriously out to get him. He knew the only one who could save him, even if he died, was God. If he could trust that, surely we can too.

More To Explore: John 3:16–17

Girl Talk: When you think of God saving you, what is the first thing that comes into your mind?

God Talk: "Jesus, thank you for dying on the cross and saving me from my sins. I don't deserve your amazing love, but you love me so much anyway! Amen."

From *That Is So Me* by Nancy Rue

"When Joseph came to his brothers, they stripped him of his robe . . . and threw him into the cistern."

—Genesis 37:23–24

In the Pits

When Joseph's father gave Joseph a beautifully colored robe, Joseph's brothers were so jealous that they ripped it off and threw him into a deep, empty well. Later, they sold Joseph as a slave!

Bella also felt other people's jealousy. She had taken voice lessons for years, and she had the best voice in the seventh-grade choir. Although no one was surprised when she won the lead in the spring musical, several girls were angry about it. During one of the rehearsals, a coil of rope was left where Bella would be sure to trip over it. She did—and sprained her ankle so badly that she had to quit the show.

What happened to Bella—and to Joseph—was totally unfair. They may have both asked, "God, why did you let this happen to me?" "Why?" is a question that God often doesn't answer, at least not right away. He asks us to trust him instead, even when bad things happen.

We don't live in heaven yet. Our world isn't perfect, and neither are people. Sometimes awful things happen. But through it all, always remember: God loves you, and you can trust him. If you're patient, he will bring amazingly good things out of any situation.

More To Explore: Romans 8:28

Girl Talk: Describe the last time you asked God why something happened. Do you trust that God will take care of you no matter what?

God Talk: "Lord, I don't understand why some things happen. Help me to remember that trusting you is the most important thing. Amen."

From *Shine On, Girl!* by Kristi Holl

172

"Remember that the temptations that come into your life are no different from what others experience. And God is faithful. He will keep the temptation from becoming so strong that you can't stand up against it. When you are tempted, he will show you a way out so that you will not give in to it."

—1 Corinthians 10:13 (NLT)

Stand Strong

We all want to have—or do—something that we know we should avoid. Everyone experiences temptation of one kind or another, and the temptation itself is NOT a sin. God is always there for you. Turn to him, and ask for help. God will always show you a way out.

Sometimes you need to get away from the temptation. If you're tempted to buy too much candy, leave the store. If you're tempted to take money, remember these words and get away: "The love of money is a root of all kinds of evil, for which some have strayed from the faith in their greediness ... But you, O man of God, flee these things and pursue righteousness, godliness, faith, love, patience, gentleness" (1 Timothy 6:10–11 NKJV). No matter what test you face, God will be faithful in each and every one. He'll show you a way out. So stand strong in the Lord!

More To Explore: Luke 22:31–32 and Ephesians 6:12–13

Girl Talk: What are some things that tempt you? What do you do when they are staring you in the face? What do you think God wants you to do?

God Talk: "Lord, when I see ______, I feel really tempted. I know I shouldn't do it, but it is hard to resist. Help me to resist these temptations and rely on you for all my needs. Amen."

From *Girlz Rock* by Kristi Holl

"Moses said to God, 'Who am I, that I should go to Pharaoh and bring the Israelites out of Egypt?' "

—Exodus 3:11

I Will Be With You

Talk about scary. Moses was minding his own business just tending his father-in-law's flock of sheep when suddenly a bush burst into flames but didn't burn up. In fact, it talked—and told Moses it was God.

But the truly terrifying part was when God said to Moses, "Now, go. I am sending you to Pharaoh to bring my people the Israelites out of Egypt" (Exodus 3:10). The Pharaoh was powerful enough to have anybody—or everybody—snuffed out if he got ticked off enough. When God told Moses to go to the palace and say, "All right, Pharaoh, give 'em up, let's go," it was enough to make Moses say, "Me? You want *me* to do what?"

The first thing we human beings do when asked to do the seemingly impossible is say, "I can't. You don't understand: I'm not the one for the job." We might get away with that with just plain people, but not with God. He simply says, as he did to Moses, "I will be with you" (Exodus 3:12). So what does God expect? He expects us to believe that he knows who the right person is for the job. He is, after all, God.

More To Explore: Job 42:4

Girl Talk: Have you ever been asked to do something that seemed impossible?

God Talk: "Jesus, even when the job seems too big for me, I know that you are with me. Help me to trust you when the path looks tough. Amen."

From *That Is So Me* by Nancy Rue

174

"Ever since I went to Pharaoh to speak in your name, he has brought trouble on this people, and you have not rescued your people at all."

—Exodus 5:23

A Lot to Ask

God reassured Moses, right there in the burning bush, that he would be with him when he went to the Pharaoh. But even after he gave Moses clear instructions and promised him it was all going to turn out okay—Moses still wasn't convinced.

After all, he wasn't the sharpest tack in the box when it came to public speaking. It was all he could do to say, "Pardon your servant, Lord. Please send someone else" (Exodus 4:13). So God told Moses he could take his brother Aaron with him, who could wow people with his words. When Moses and Aaron went to Pharaoh, though, he pretty much laughed in their faces and made the Israelites work even harder. Some of them went to Moses and Aaron and told them to back off—they were better off before they started making noises with the Pharaoh. Moses went to God and said, "What are you *doing*? Why aren't you working with me here?"

God said Moses had to trust that this was the way to do it. God makes the same thing clear to us. He expects us to speak his Word and trust that he knows what he's doing, even when it doesn't seem like it.

More To Explore: Psalm 37:5

Girl Talk: What was a time when you didn't understand what God was doing?

God Talk: "God, I know that sometimes the things you want me to do will be hard. Help me to trust you always. Amen."

From *That Is So Me* by Nancy Rue

"Didn't we say to you in Egypt, 'Leave us alone; let us serve the Egyptians'? It would have been better for us to serve the Egyptians than to die in the desert!"

—Exodus 14:12

The Big Finish

Just as he promised, God turned Pharaoh's heart, and he let the Israelites go. And then he complicated things. He told Moses to lead them around in circles so Pharaoh would think he could come after them and take them back. That's exactly what happened.

What in the world was God thinking? That he really wanted a big finish to this thing, so the Israelites would see how powerful he was, how much he loved them, and how much he wanted to do for them.

This time Moses knew what God expected of him, and he said to the frightened people, "Do not be afraid. Stand firm and you will see the deliverance the Lord will bring you today" (Exodus 14:13). Then God gave Moses the power to part the Red Sea so they could walk across on dry land, and then drowned the Egyptians when they tried it. Now *that* was dramatic.

God expects you to keep following him, no matter how bad things look. If you don't, you might miss the big finish!

More To Explore: 1 Chronicles 29:11

Girl Talk: Have you ever persevered through something tough and then seen a spectacular ending that made all the troubles worth it?

God Talk: "Jesus, help me to stand firm through trials. I know in the end there will be a grand finale, even if I don't get to see it this side of heaven. Amen."

From *That Is So Me* by Nancy Rue

176

"We boast about your perseverance and faith in all the persecutions and trials you are enduring."

—2 Thessalonians 1:4

The Tough Get Going

Even when severely tested, believers should be faithful. Keep your trust in God firm.

You've looked forward to middle school for two years. In middle school, you can be on a gymnastics team. But from the first day of practice, you're so disappointed. The coach criticizes you constantly, even though you know you're better than anyone else who tried out. A few weeks into practice, you see the coach give one of the girls a big hug, and you ask a team member about it. "You mean Rachel? That's Coach's kid. He's determined that she's going to be a gold medal winner or something." Now you understand the persecution you've been receiving. Coach wants his own daughter to be the best. You pray about it, and you decide to stay on the team. You'll just dig in and work hard, keeping your eye on your long-term Olympic goal.

There's an old saying: "When the going gets tough, the tough get going." That means persevering through trials and mistreatment. "We can rejoice, too, when we run into problems and trials, for we know that they are good for us—they help us learn to endure. And endurance develops strength of character in us" (Romans 5:3–4 NLT). So be tough—and get going!

More To Explore: James 5:11

Girl Talk: Have you ever been severely tested? How did you react to the tough situation?

God Talk: "Lord, I want to stay close to you, no matter what is happening in my life. Help me keep a good attitude throughout any trial I encounter. Amen."

From *Shine On, Girl!* by Kristi Holl

"But I have stilled and quieted myself, just as a small child is quiet with its mother. Yes, like a small child is my soul within me."

—Psalm 131:2 NLT

Chillaxing

Take it easy," Justine's mom said when Justine lost her purse at the mall. But that's the last thing Justine could do. *My whole life's in that bag*, she thought. *My school pass, my brand new raspberry lip gloss. OH NO, and my phone!*

Justine borrowed her mom's cell and ran off to retrace her steps, while at the same time, yakitty-yaking with her BFF about how this was such a disaster, and how she'd just die if she didn't get the bag back. She was so frazzled, she forgot half the stores she'd been in and was going around in circles. Finally, she slumped down on a bench and cried.

When something difficult, terrible, or awful happens, do you totally freak? Do you get unhinged? Yeah, we all do. It's, like, our minds take off in a million different directions. We get so upset—we're useless.

The Bible has a simple, but effective, eight-word remedy for this: "Be still, and know that I am God" (Psalm 46:10). See, we can't accomplish anything if we're in a state of emergency. So the first thing we need to do is stop, get quiet and calm, and let go of our need to do something immediately to solve the problem. That's the "be still" part.

The second part is the "knowing," and that's easier because we already "know" God. We know he's loving and kind. We know he's more powerful than any problem we have. We know he has come through for us in the past. We know the Word says he works everything out for our good if we love him (Romans 8:28 TLB), and that his power works best when we're weak (2 Corinthians 12:9 NLT).

So putting those two elements together—being still and knowing God—can help us simmer down, get a grip, and remind ourselves to trust more and panic less. "Be silent before the Lord," the Word advises, " . . . for he is springing into action from his holy dwelling" (Zechariah 2:13 NLT).

That's God's job — to spring into action. Our job is to stay calm, remember he can handle anything, then step out of the way, and let him.

P.S. Justine's bag was turned in to security by a girl who left this note: "I'd have been so bummed if I lost my bag. Was so happy to be able to return yours." Did the Holy Spirit nudge her? You think?

More To Explore: 2 Chronicles 20:17; Psalm 16:10

Girl Talk: Have you ever tried to "be still" before God? Try it now.

God Talk: "Heavenly Father, please help me to always remember you're *in* control and have everything *under* control. Amen."

From *Whatever: Livin' the True, Noble, Totally Excellent Life* by Allia Zobel Nolan

"When his master saw that the Lord was with him and that the Lord gave him success in everything he did, Joseph found favor in his eyes and became his attendant."

—Genesis 39:3–4

Irresistible Love

After his brothers did him dirty, Joseph could have given up and become a little street kid, thinking God had abandoned him. But Joseph stayed focused on God as his guide, and it paid off.

Look at *how* it paid off. Potiphar—the pharaoh's guy who bought Joseph from the Ishmaelites his brothers sold him to (whew!)—saw that Joseph was totally connected to God. He figured if God was good to Joseph, he was going to be good to him too. He put him in charge of his whole household and trusted him to take care of everything he owned, which was a lot of stuff. God blessed Potiphar's house and family and fields too.

That's how it works with God. If other people see God in your life because you're following him as your guide, they can't help being affected as well. That girl in your class might not know she likes you because you're a God-follower, but when she comes to your house and sees how lovingly your family members treat each other (most of the time!), she may go home and be nicer to her brother or mother. God loves to spread the blessings around—through you.

More To Explore: 1 Timothy 4:12

Girl Talk: Who is someone you know who could use an example of God's goodness in their life?

God Talk: "God, help me to be an example of your love and goodness to others, just like Joseph was. I want to spread those blessings around. Amen."

From *That Is So Me* by Nancy Rue

179

"I assure you, even if you had faith as small as a mustard seed you could say to this mountain, 'Move from here to there,' and it would move. Nothing would be impossible."

—Matthew 17:20 (NLT)

Mountain-Moving Faith

Jesus promises that you can do mighty things, even if your trust in him is as tiny as a mustard seed—smaller than an ant! You can say to some problem that appears huge, "Move from here to there," and it will move.

Do you have a mountain in your life, one that is an obstacle to you? A mountain of family problems, or money problems? Maybe it's how you feel about your physical appearance. Maybe it's your difficulty studying and remembering your school work. God is in the mountain-moving business. Our part is to believe—to have faith—that he can do it.

When you trust, sometimes he suddenly takes care of the problem for you; he may remove a person from your life or give you an after-school job out of the blue. Or he sends a person to help you who knows just what to do. Often, God personally shows you, step by step, the things you can do to solve the problem. They're usually things you had never considered—and wouldn't have thought of on your own.

Faith is like a muscle. It only gets stronger by using it. Put your faith in God today, and watch that mountain start to move!

More To Explore: Mark 9:23

Girl Talk: Do you believe God can move mountains? Do you have a mountain that needs moving?

God Talk: "Lord, I want to have mountain-moving faith. Help me to trust in you at all times. Amen."

From *No Boys Allowed* by Kristi Holl

"Trust in the Lord with all your heart and lean not on your own understanding; in all your ways submit to him, and he will make your paths straight."

—Proverbs 3:5–6

Naomi's Journey Home

Naomi and her husband, Elimelech, were Israelites born and raised in the Promised Land. When a famine hit and there wasn't enough food for everyone, Naomi, her husband, and their two boys moved from Bethlehem to Moab.

Later, Elimelech died and left Naomi with two sons to care for. Her sons grew up and married Moabite women. And then after ten years of living in Moab, both of Naomi's sons died.

Naomi had lost everything that was important to her. She was a foreigner in Moab, and two daughters-in-law were all she had left. Naomi was homesick. The famine had ended in Israel, so she decided to return to her birthplace of Bethlehem in the land of Judah. Naomi's daughters-in-law loved her and wanted to go with her, but Naomi took a deep breath and told them to stay in their homeland. But her daughter-in-law Ruth clung to Naomi.

With tears in her eyes, Ruth looked at Naomi and said, "Where you go, I will go, and where you stay, I will stay. Your people will be my people and your God, my God."

That said, Ruth followed Naomi to Bethlehem. As Naomi and Ruth arrived, the women in Bethlehem hurried toward them. "Naomi, is it really you?

"Don't call me Naomi," she told them. "Call me Mara, because the Almighty has made my life bitter. I went away full, but the Lord has brought me back empty."

At the time, Naomi was too sad to see past her suffering. God was faithful to Naomi and would soon fill her life with blessings and joy. But Naomi couldn't see it yet. All she knew was that she had come home empty. You can read more about her happy ending in the book of Ruth.

We all face hard things. Maybe you've already had some tough times. They can be as simple as failing a test or as complicated as living with a chronic illness like diabetes. Or maybe, like Naomi, someone you love has died—a parent, a brother or sister, a grandparent, a friend, or a favorite teacher.

You can choose to turn your pain or grief over to God. You can trust him to provide what you need to get through it. God is always good. He's faithful to walk through tough times with you and to help you get through them.

More To Explore: Hebrews 12:14–15

Girl Talk: Do you know what it feels like to be bitter towards God?

God Talk: "Dear heavenly Father, I confess I can't always see your purpose for me. Help me in difficult times to remember how much you love me. Please guide me as you guided Naomi. Amen."

From *Real Girls of the Bible* by Mona Hodgson

"Take no part in the worthless deeds of evil and darkness; instead, rebuke and expose them."

—Ephesians 5:11 (NLT)

No Way!

You're shocked when your best friend admits she stole the semester test from the math teacher's desk and copied the answers before returning the test. Your friend offers the answers to you for free, although she plans to sell the answers to others in the class. "You can't do that!" you protest. "You know that's wrong!" Your friend laughs and says, "You're such a goody-goody. If you want a lower grade on the test, that's fine by me!" You desperately wish you'd never discovered her plan. But you *do* know. So now what should you do with the information?

You're right in deciding not to participate in the stolen test answers. Followers of Jesus should have no part in such activities, but are called to rebuke a person involved in something wrong. We should also make those actions public. You're sure your friend will hate you if you tell the teacher, but reporting the scheme seems like the right thing to do. You arrive at school early the next morning and tell the math teacher about your friend's plan. You wonder if your friend will know you blew the whistle. Maybe—but you feel at peace about your decision.

More to Explore: Romans 13:12 and Proverbs 4:14–15

Girl Talk: If you know kids are breaking the rules, is it ever okay to ignore it and walk away? What other things could you do?

God Talk: "Lord, I'm afraid to speak up when I see people doing wrong things. I'm afraid of what they'll say. Give me courage to say the words. Amen."

From *Chick Chat* by Kristi Holl

182

"Take my yoke upon you and learn from me, for I am gentle and humble in heart, and you will find rest for your souls. For my yoke is easy and my burden is light."

—Matthew 11:29–30

Yoked with Jesus

A yoke is a connection between two things so they move together. Oxen and horses are often yoked so they can pull a heavy load together. Jesus wants you to take his yoke—to be connected to him so you can move in sync with him. His yoke is light and easy to carry. His yoke is good—not hard, harsh, sharp, or heavy.

What exactly does "putting on Jesus' yoke" look like? It means being obedient to his words. Keeping his commands brings joy, but sometimes we think, *It's too hard to keep God's commandments. I just can't do it!* You're right—you can't do it, at least not by yourself. The Holy Spirit will help you, though, and give you the strength to do what's right. When you stop struggling in the yoke, forward movement can be easy! "This is love for God: to keep his commands. And his commands are not burdensome" (1 John 5:3). Settle Jesus' yoke on your own shoulders—and experience a deep, refreshing rest.

More To Explore: Philippians 4:13

Girl Talk: In what ways lately have you and Jesus been pulling together? In what areas are you struggling alone?

God Talk: "Lord, I know that I sometimes struggle against you. Please give me the help and strength I need, so that we can pull in the yoke together. Thank you for being on my team. Amen."

From *Shine On, Girl!* by Kristi Holl

"Do not merely listen to the word, and so deceive yourselves. Do what it says."

—James 1:22

Don't Fool Yourself

When bad things happen, we often pray more and eagerly search our Bibles for answers. That's exactly the right thing to do, but we might not like what we find. The bully on the bus who trips you? The Word says you are to pray for those who persecute you and pick on you, but not take revenge. How about the classmate who makes nasty remarks or teases you with unkind names? The Bible says we are to speak the truth IN LOVE to this person, not call her names back. Don't fool yourself into thinking that you're behaving like a Christian just by reading the Bible. You must also do what it says. Pray for that bully. Deal with that nasty classmate, but use kind words.

Don't be someone God says this about: "I called you so often, but you didn't come. I reached out to you, but you paid no attention. You ignored my advice and rejected the correction I offered" (Proverbs 1:24–25 NLT). Instead, be determined to put into practice what you read. You won't do it perfectly, and that's okay. But as best you can, carry out what you believe God is telling you to do in a situation. Then see what marvelous changes God makes in your life.

More To Explore: Matthew 7:21 and James 2:14–20

Girl Talk: When faced with a tough situation, do you turn to God? Do you read the Bible and do what it says?

God Talk: "Lord, thank you for giving me your Word. Help me to read it and obey, instead of what I want to do. Amen."

From *Girlz Rock* by Kristi Holl

184

"God tested Abraham's faith and obedience."
—Genesis 22:1 (NLT)

This Is Only a Test

Sometimes God tests us to strengthen our faith or prove our loyalty. Only a test will reveal if we truly mean what we say. Abraham had already passed many tests, but none as big as when God asked him to sacrifice his only son, Isaac. God needed to see if Abraham would be obedient no matter what God asked him to do.

Do you face a test today? What can you learn from this lesson that might help you in the weeks and years to come? Think of one test you're facing—a grumpy teacher, a difficult parent, an annoying little sister? How might God use that test to prepare you for tomorrow?

"The refining pot is for silver and the furnace for gold, but the Lord tests the hearts" (Proverbs 17:3 NKJV). Silver and gold are made pure in the fire. Heat removes the worthless material (the impurities). People are refined in God's fire of testing for the same reason. When your next test comes, pray and ask for God's help, then pass the test with flying colors!

More To Explore: Exodus 16:4

Girl Talk: Do you think God is testing you on something? How do you think he wants you to respond?

God Talk: "Lord, I want to pass any test that you give me. Help me to please you. Amen."

From *Shine On, Girl!* by Kristi Holl

"So we say with confidence, 'The Lord is my helper; I will not be afraid. What can mere mortals do to me?' "

—Hebrews 13:6

God Is on Your Side

Bullies are a nasty reality of life sometimes. A bully may be a bossy older brother who dominates the house when your parents are at work. It can be a cruel teacher or coach who discourages with his comments. A brutal kid on the school bus or playground may threaten you with physical harm.

We may think bullies are a modern thing. We might even think that God doesn't understand our situation. But see David's words in the Psalms (don't his words sound like today?): "In God (I will praise His word), in God I have put my trust; I will not fear. What can flesh do to me? All day they twist my words; all their thoughts are against me for evil. They gather together, they hide, they mark my steps, when they lie in wait for my life" (Psalm 56:4–6 NKJV). Threatening bullies have been around for thousands of years!

You may be powerless to deal with them on your own, but with God on your side, the Bible says you don't have to be afraid. So pray. Believe God will help you. Watch for it. And say boldly, "I will not fear!"

More To Explore: Deuteronomy 33:27 and Psalm 56:11

Girl Talk: Do you ever feel bullied by others? Have you ever asked God to deliver you from them?

God Talk: "Lord, sometimes other people are trying to scare me. You are my rock and my refuge. Please deliver me from their words and actions. Amen."

From *Girlz Rock* by Kristi Holl

186

"She made a vow, saying, 'Lord Almighty, if you will only look on your servant's misery and remember me, and not forget your servant but give her a son, then I will give him to the Lord for all the days of his life.' "

—1 Samuel 1:11

On Your Knees

How do you get what you want? Stomp your feet? Grab for it? Steal it? Hello! When you want something, you ask for it!

But if what you want is not a physical thing, it's hard to know who to ask to provide it for you. The only one you can ask for such things and expect results is, of course, God. That's what our Hannah did. Remember her? The woman in the Bible who wanted a baby? Stricken with sadness and shame, she went, to God and cried, "Please, Father, all I want is a son!" And then, Hannah went a step further. She said if God would bless her with a baby boy, she would give him back to God, to work for him his whole life.

Wow! That tells us something about Hannah. She didn't just want a baby, so she could be like all the other cool moms. She wanted offspring, so they could serve the God she loved. Sounds like if you want to be transformed, you have to be pretty unselfish. Don't worry. You have it in you, just like Hannah.

More To Explore: James 4:3

Girl Talk: What have you asked God for recently?

God Talk: "God, thank you that I can come to you on my knees when I want something. Help me to be unselfish in my requests, like Hannah. Amen."

From *That Is So Me* by Nancy Rue

"Where there is no vision, the people perish."
—Proverbs 29:18 (KJV)

I Have a Dream!

People need to have a vision, or goals, for their future. Without God-given goals to guide them, people get off track and totally lose direction for their lives.

Madison had a big vision. From the time she took her first dance lesson at the age of three, she wanted to be a famous ballerina. For nine years, she studied and danced. She performed in musicals, at first in the background, but more and more often in lead parts. Then disaster struck. A drunk driver hit her mom's car and smashed in the passenger side. After three different surgeries, Madison's shattered leg was put back together. She barely limped—but she'd never dance again. Madison sank into depression. Her lifetime goal was gone. Exhausted, she prayed for help daily, but saw no immediate change in her circumstances. However, God's ears were open to her prayers. (See 1 Peter 3:12.)

The next time Madison was at the hospital for physical therapy, she watched a small girl who was learning to walk again. She clapped when the seven-year-old took her first shaky steps. Right then, a new vision was born inside Madison. She'd found a new dream—becoming a physical therapist and helping others walk again. Her depression lifted, and her life was again filled with purpose.

More To Explore: Ezekiel 12:23

Girl Talk: Have you had to change any goals or dreams? Have you asked God what his goals are for you?

God Talk: "Lord, you know I would love to ______. Please show me whether this is your plan for me or not. I want to do what you have in mind for me. Amen."

From *Shine On, Girl!* by Kristi Holl

188

"When a man is gloomy, everything seems to go wrong; when he is cheerful, everything seems right!"

—Proverbs 15:15 (TLB)

Change Your Thoughts ... Change Your Day

My hair looks like I combed it with a rake, you think, and that starts the ball rolling.

This dress is ridiculous, and I won't get a new one now that Dad lost his job.

I look like a troll today. Why do I have to be so ugly?

Negative thoughts can hold you captive and multiply like ants at a picnic. But if you take control, put your hope in God and his Word, you can turn things around and have a great day, no matter *what's* going on.

When King David was "down in the dumps," he got out of his bad moods by thinking about all the good things God had done for him. When he finished, the Bible says, he was "whistling, laughing, and jumping for joy" (Psalm 9:2 MSG). "You have done so much for me, O Lord," David wrote. "No wonder I am glad! I sing for joy" (Psalm 92:4 TLB).

David had the right idea. You can't stay in a stinky mood long if you think about how wonderful God is; how many times he has answered your urgent prayers, forgiven you for your mistakes, and gotten you out of really bad scrapes. And like David, remembering instances of God's goodness will surely make you think, *Wow, am I blessed*, instead of, *Boy, I'm depressed.*

Bad hair? The Bible says, "Don't be concerned about the outward beauty that depends on fancy hairstyles... You should be known for the beauty that comes from within" (1 Peter 3:4 NLT). So fix your hair and forget about it. Then maybe work on your inner self by praying for sick kids who've lost their hair.

No money for new duds? The Bible says, "And why worry about your clothes? Look at the field lilies! They don't worry about theirs. Yet King Solomon in all his glory was not clothed as beautifully as they" (Matthew 6:29 TLB). So maybe you should thank God for the clothes you do have, then use your creativity to combine an outfit in a new and different way.

Not feeling pretty? The Bible says we are "amazingly and miraculously made" (Psalm 139:13 GWT). So if God made you wonderful, maybe you should take his Word and stop thinking you're not. Oh, and here's a tip: a girl can look twice as awesome when she smiles. So why not put on one VBG (Very Big Grin) right now.

More To Explore: Psalm 43:5

Girl Talk: When do you get stuck in negative thinking? Look through the Bible for words that will help you turn those thoughts around.

God Talk: "Lord, I can get in a bad mood so easily. Help me to realize just how wonderful my life really is because you're my Savior and you love me. Amen."

From *Whatever: Livin' the True, Noble, Totally Excellent Life* by Allia Zobel Nolan

189

"Blessed is the one you discipline, Lord, the one you teach from your law; you grant them relief from days of trouble, till a pit is dug for the wicked."

—Psalm 94:12–13

How to Stay Calm, No Matter What

Some problems are over quickly, but some seem to drag on and on. Maybe your mom has a serious illness that requires constant medical attention. Or you have an older brother who gets in scrapes with the police and embarrasses you at school and church. Maybe you're teased about your weight, but getting in shape is taking forever.

Wouldn't you *love* to have the power to stay calm, no matter what happened? You can have this power! But before the power comes, God uses the events and people in our lives to build our spiritual character. He may teach you about the power of prayer during your mom's illness. He may teach you about self-discipline in food and exercise as you get in shape.

Why is God's discipline good? (It sure doesn't FEEL good sometimes!) This is what David said about it: "I used to wander off until you disciplined me; but now I closely follow your word. You are good and do only good; teach me your principles" (Psalm 119:67–68 NLT).

More To Explore: Job 5:17 and Psalm 119:71

Girl Talk: When you face problems, do you want them over right now? Have you ever thought that God gives you problems because he loves you?

God Talk: "Lord, it's hard to wait for my problems to be over. Help me to remember how deep your love is for me. You send trials my way in order for me to grow. Amen."

From *Girlz Rock* by Kristi Holl

190

"My soul is weary with sorrow; strengthen me according to your word."

—Psalm 119:28

Soothe Your Sorrows

Sarah envied her friends whose problems consisted of things like finding money for shopping or having a bad hair day. But ever since her mom got cancer, Sarah had been focused on only one thing. She helped out at home after school and on weekends, because her mom was exhausted from the cancer treatments. One night, Sarah cooked supper and folded laundry while trying to memorize facts for her social studies test. Suddenly, she was overcome with weariness. Her fears and grief weighed so heavily on her heart. Leaning on the kitchen counter, Sarah fought the tears that were always near the surface. "Oh, God, help me," she prayed.

That night Sarah crawled into bed with her Bible. She read some verses her pastor had shown her. "I pray that out of [God's] glorious riches he may strengthen you with power through his Spirit in your inner being" (Ephesians 3:16). Sarah read it out loud three times, then turned to the next one: "I can do all this through [God] who gives me strength" (Philippians 4:13). She turned off her light and repeated the verse, over and over. Slowly her mind shifted from her mom's cancer to God's power. Finally, a sense of calm settled over her, the weariness lifted, and she drifted into a peaceful sleep.

More To Explore: Isaiah 40:31

Girl Talk: What circumstances make you feel weary and worn out in your mind and emotions? How can God's Word help you transform those feelings?

God Talk: "Lord, sometimes I feel overwhelmed. Thank you for all the help and encouragement in your Word. Amen."

From *Chick Chat* by Kristi Holl

191

"In the course of time Hannah became pregnant and gave birth to a son."

—1 Samuel 1:20

Share It, Don't Stuff It!

Have you noticed that when you ask God for something, he doesn't just swoop down his almighty hand and make it happen? Most of the time, he uses other people, and that was the case for Hannah too.

While she was weeping and praying in the Lord's house, a priest named Eli saw her. At first, he accused her of being drunk, because her lips were moving but no sound was coming out. As if this poor woman didn't have enough problems! But Hannah stood up for herself and told him that she had been praying out of "great anguish and grief" (verse 16). That must have really gotten to Eli, because he told her to go in peace, that God would grant her what she had asked of him.

Now, it was God who answered Hannah's prayer—she did have the son she so longed for. But Eli went to God for her too, because Hannah was honest about her feelings. She didn't pretend it was okay to be childless. She didn't hide the grief that was tearing her apart. God doesn't want us to put a happy face on something that aches inside us. Our feelings are there for a reason. Sharing them with people who love God too is the first step toward healing.

More To Explore: Ecclesiastes 4:9

Girl Talk: Has God ever answered your prayer by sending a person to help you?

God Talk: "Jesus, thank you for sending people into my life to help me when I need it. Use me to be an answer to other people's prayers too. Amen."

From *That Is So Me* by Nancy Rue

192

"These trials are only to test your faith, to show that it is strong and pure. It is being tested as fire tests and purifies gold—and your faith is far more precious to God than mere gold."

—1 Peter 1:7 (NLT)

Tested by Fire

Storms of life *will* come. But Jesus is with us, alongside us, to encourage us not to faint or give up. A test in life is like a test at school. If you look at your math test, try a couple of problems, and then quit because it's too hard, you'll fail the test. On the other hand, studying and preparing yourself will help you pass the test.

The same applies to the tests you'll encounter in life, whether they are health tests, friendship tests, schoolwork tests, or family tests. If you quit when things get hard, you'll fail the test. God will pick you up and dust you off—but you'll have to repeat the test. Studying for the tests of life—reading and thinking deeply about what God's Word says to do—will help you pass your tests and come out much stronger.

More To Explore: 1 Peter 4:12–13 and Job 23:10–12

Girl Talk: When you have a test at school, how hard do you study? Do you think you are as well prepared for trials that life will send you?

God Talk: "Lord, I know there will be trials in my life. Please help me to be prepared for them. I want to read the Bible more and talk with you. Amen."

From *Girlz Rock* by Kristi Holl

"It is better to take refuge in the Lord than to trust in humans."
—Psalm 118:8

Whom Can You Trust?

Kelsey had a rotten day at school. She flunked a math test, twisted her ankle in gym, and the boy she liked asked the new girl to the after-game dance. Kelsey wanted to crawl into a hole and disappear. Thank heavens for her best friend, Shayna. Shayna always called right after supper. Kelsey couldn't wait to pour out her heart and get some much-needed comfort. But seven o'clock passed, then eight, then nine. It was nearly ten before Shayna called, and then only to say that she'd gone shopping and to a movie with her mom, and she just got home, and she couldn't talk! In tears, Kelsey curled up on her bed. How could Shayna have let her down like that? Crying, Kelsey did what would have helped in the first place. She poured out her hurt to God. "Trust in him at all times, you people; pour out your hearts to him, for God is our refuge" (Psalm 62:8).

People can't always be there for us, even when they want to be. Most friends do the best they can, but it's a mistake to put our wholehearted trust in them. Instead, put that trust in the Lord. Only God is perfect and will never let you down. So take the pressure off your friends. Lean hard on the Lord instead.

More to Explore: Jeremiah 17:5, 7

Girl Talk: Who is the person you trust the most? How can you build up your trust in God?

God Talk: "Lord, thank you for showing me that you alone deserve my total trust. Help my faith in you to grow. Amen."

From *Chick Chat* by Kristi Holl

"For I am the Lord your God who takes hold of your right hand and says to you, Do not fear; I will help you."

—Isaiah 41:13

Are You a Quitter?

For three days, Jessica had looked forward to this moment. Standing on the corral fence, she watched as Sarah slipped a bridle over her pony's head.

"Reggie's a good pony," she said. "I've been riding him for three years."

Jessica glanced at two larger horses drinking water at a trough. They seemed so tall that she was glad to start out on a pony. Yet she felt sure she could handle any horse well.

"Let me give you a lift," Sarah offered. Jessica put one foot in Sarah's clasped hands and swung up over Reggie's bare back. "Lay your rein on the right side of his neck, and he'll turn left," Sarah told her. "Lay your rein on the left side, and he'll go right."

Moments later, Jessica was off. As she and Reggie started down the drive, she felt excited, then sure of herself. *I knew I could handle it!* Soon, they reached a place where the road ran close to the pasture. As Jessica passed by, the other horses ran straight for the fence. Without warning, Reggie plunged away from them. As he went right, Jessica went left. With a jolt she landed in the middle of the road.

"Ouch!" she groaned. Too stunned to move, she felt shaken in every bone of her body.

"Are you okay?" Sarah called as she ran to help.

"Stupid horse!" answered Jessica. "I won't try that again."

But Sarah had a different idea. "You need to get back on."

"Are you kidding?" Jessica asked.

"You don't have to be afraid," Sarah said. "Reggie has never thrown me. He was frightened by the horses coming at him."

"But he's your pony. Reggie likes you."

"So, are you a quitter? If you don't get back on now, you'll be too afraid to try again. Besides, Reggie has to know you're boss, or he'll think he can get by with throwing people."

"Well—" Slowly Jessica stood up. "Maybe you're right. The longer I think about it, the more scared I get."

Sarah led Reggie to a stump. "This time, I'll ride with you. You first. I'll hold him."

A moment later, they were off. Soon, Jessica's fear disappeared. She even started to feel excited. After a while, Sarah slid off.

By the end of the afternoon, Jessica felt like a seasoned rider. She even knew how to make Reggie mind. *What if I had missed this?* she asked herself. *What if I hadn't tried again?*

More to Explore: 1 Samuel 2:2

Girl Talk: Have there been times when you felt that God wanted you to keep trying, even though it was hard?

God Talk: "Jesus, you know how scared I get about doing something new. Show me if I'm uneasy because you want to protect me. If, instead, you want me to learn something, help me to keep trying. Amen."

From *Girl Talk* by Lois Walfrid Johnson

"I prayed to the Lord, and he answered me, freeing me from all my fears."

—Psalm 34:4 (NLT)

I Will Not Fear

When you're afraid, turn to God and pray. Have confidence in the Lord, and put your faith in him. You can count on him for help. If you concentrate on how much the Lord can be trusted, your fears will slip away.

Sometimes, believers brood about their fears. They forget the most important solution—connecting with God through prayer. Talk to the Lord. Tell him your worries and concerns. Thank him that he has everything under control—even the things that look out of control to you. Sometimes fears can make you feel lonely and cut off from God. What if you've prayed, but you feel like your prayers aren't reaching heaven? Our emotions are poor judges of the truth. You may not feel God's help, but keep on praying. Freedom from your fears will come. "In sudden fear I had cried out, 'I have been cut off from the Lord!' But you heard my cry for mercy and answered my call for help" (Psalm 31:22 NLT).

More To Explore: 2 Chronicles 20:3

Girl Talk: How often do you pray when afraid? What do you rely on to help you through fear?

God Talk: "Lord, I know you can take away all my fears. Please help me to hold on to you and wait for your help. Amen."

From *Shine On, Girl!* by Kristi Holl

196

"Come to Me, all you who labor and are heavy-laden and overburdened, and I will cause you to rest. [I will ease and relieve and refresh your souls.]"

—Matthew 11:28 (AMP)

Rested and Refreshed

Annette came home from school with a headache, afraid that she hadn't done well on her social studies test. Her legs hurt from running a mile in gym class. She fixed her little brother a snack and was ready to collapse when the phone rang. "I'll be late tonight, honey," her mom said. "Can you fix spaghetti and have it ready by six?" Annette hung up and leaned against the table. She felt overburdened.

Some days we feel so overworked, overtired, and overburdened that we can't take it anymore. Then what should we do? We can come to Jesus in prayer, being honest with him about how exhausted we are. That can be physical tiredness, but it can also be mental or emotional exhaustion. Our tired emotions might be overworked from dealing with some upsetting event. Our minds might be exhausted from too much mental work like studying. From ALL these things, Jesus wants to give you rest.

Are you overtired? Then take five or ten minutes, close your eyes, and breathe deeply. Ask Jesus to refresh your mind, body, and emotions. Soak it up. Take your time. Ahhhh...

More To Explore: Isaiah 61:3 and Matthew 11:29–30

Girl Talk: Have you felt really tired this past week? Why do you think you were so worn down? Did you know you can rest in Jesus?

God Talk: "Lord, I'm so tired. My body and mind need to be refreshed. Please give me rest. Please help me stay rested by staying close to you. Amen."

From *Girlz Rock* by Kristi Holl

Jesus said to [Satan], "Away from me, Satan! For it is written: 'Worship the Lord your God, and serve him only.'"

—Matthew 4:10

Eve's Too-Late Discovery

Talk about a great beginning! After God formed Eve, the first woman, she lived in a beautiful garden full of flowering plants and tons of trees that produced yummy fruit. Eve and her husband Adam could pick fruit from any tree except the one in the middle of the garden. God had told them not to eat the fruit of that tree.

All was well between Eve and God. Until one day.

While Eve strolled the gorgeous garden, a serpent slithered out on a branch and spoke to her. "Did God really say you couldn't eat from every tree in the garden?"

"We may eat fruit from the trees," Eve said, "but God said not to eat fruit from the tree in the middle of the garden. He said if we touched it, we'd die."

"That's silly. You won't die," the serpent sneered. "God doesn't want you to eat it because when you do, your eyes will open and you'll be like him."

Eve stared at the smooth and shiny fruit on the tree in the middle of the garden. Tempted, she picked the fruit and ate some. Then she gave it to her husband, Adam, who also bit into it.

Satan, the crafty con, had disguised himself as a serpent to tempt Eve. And his half-truth worked. According to Satan, Eve would be like God when she ate the fruit. She wasn't all-powerful like God, but she did learn the difference between good and evil. She and Adam realized they were naked, and they felt guilty for what they had done. Later when they heard the Lord strolling in the garden, they ducked behind a tree and hid from him.

God knew what Eve and her husband had done and why they'd hidden from him. Because God loved them, he showed them grace and used animal skins to make better clothes for them. But Eve still suffered the consequences of her sin. No more strolls in the beautiful garden with God. She and her husband had to leave the garden, and life became hard.

Are you ever tempted to listen to the wrong people? Kids at school, friends in the neighborhood, or even a brother or sister can make bad things look pretty good to us.

When you're tempted, you can remember Eve's story. You can choose to listen to God and trust his love for you. When you do make a bad choice and mess up, you can go to God, confess your sin to him, and accept his gracious forgiveness.

More To Explore: James 4:7

Girl Talk: Have you ever been tempted to do something that you knew was wrong?

God Talk: "Father God, help me to recognize temptation for what it is and help me to refuse to go against you and your Word. In Jesus' name, amen."

From *Real Girls of the Bible* by Mona Hodgson

"Do not merely look out for your own personal interests, but also for the interests of others."

—Philippians 2:4 (NASB)

But What About Me?

Do you know people who only talk about themselves? When you eat a meal with them, the entire time they chatter on about *their* problems, *their* activities, *their* feelings, and *their* life. How much more fun is it to be with a girlfriend who also asks about your interests?

Besides being interested in other people and their lives, it's important to look out for them as well as yourself. In a crowded lunch room or school bus, don't just look for an empty seat for yourself; look for one for your friend as well. Instead of being "me-minded," train yourself to be "others-minded." Romans 12:15 (NKJV) says that we should "rejoice with those who rejoice, and weep with those who weep." Is your friend thrilled about her A on the science test? Then be happy with her. Is she sad because her grandma died? Then be sensitive to that and tone down your stream of chatter. "But what about me?" you ask. You want "give and take" in your friendships. But you'll notice a wonderful thing that happens. While you're busy meeting a friend's need, God will meet yours.

More To Explore: 1 Corinthians 10:23–24 and Galatians 6:1–2

Girl Talk: Do you tend to always talk about yourself? Do you focus on others' needs, not just your own?

God Talk: "Lord, I want to listen to others better and not just focus on myself. Please show me ways to help my friends and family. Amen."

From *No Boys Allowed* by Kristi Holl

199

"I call to God, and the LORD saves me. Evening, morning and noon I cry out in distress, and he hears my voice."

—Psalm 55:16–17

God Is Always There

When Lauren woke up and rolled over, the pain in her shoulder reminded her of her bike accident and broken collarbone. "God, I know I shouldn't complain," she whispered, "but I really hate wearing this brace! It's ugly, and I can't run now, and it hurts worse than the doctor said it would. Help me!" Did God hear her cry? Absolutely. When Lauren lay quietly, other things came to her mind: how lucky she was not to be killed when the car hit her, how blessed she was to have friends who carried her books, and how fortunate she was to live in a country where doctors were available to set bones. By the time she was done praying—which is both talking *and* listening to God—Lauren's feelings were the opposite.

We can trust that God hears us when we cry out to him. We can trust him to handle the concerns we face each day, and to identify every worry and care that troubles us. By giving up "ownership" of our worries, we transfer the problem to God to solve. "Give all your worries and cares to God, for he cares about what happens to you" (1 Peter 5:7 NLT).

More To Explore: Psalm 5:2–3 and Micah 7:7

Girl Talk: When you have troubles, do you dwell on them? Or do you count your blessings?

God Talk: "Lord, I know things won't be perfect for me. When I am in pain or have problems, help me to come to you and give you my fears. Amen."

From *Girlz Rock* by Kristi Holl

"Cease striving and know that I am God."

—Psalm 46:10 (NASB)

Keep Calm

When times are frightening and our world is falling apart, the Lord tells us to calm down. We are to stop spending so much energy on figuring out what to do. He says to be silent, to be still. Remember that he is almighty God, and he has everything under control.

When you're upset or angry or in pain, it takes faith to be quiet and concentrate instead on God's power to save you. Stretch your faith muscle, and think on the good things of God and how he's solved your problems in the past. "Meditate within your heart on your bed, and be still" (Psalm 4:4 NKJV).

Part of being still and knowing that he is God is trusting in a good outcome. If God is permitting problems or a crisis into our lives, he has a purpose. And if we trust him through it, he will make it all work out for our good. "We know that in all things God works for the good of those who love him, who have been called according to his purpose" (Romans 8:28).

The next time a problem hits you, *stop.* Don't wear yourself out running around. Get quiet instead. Let God speak to you and help you.

More To Explore: Job 37:14

Girl Talk: When you're upset, how do you act? Do you panic and have outbursts, or do you talk with God?

God Talk: "Lord, I sometimes panic when things go wrong. I want to be calm. Please help me go to you first for help and patience. Thank you for your perfect example. Amen."

From *Girlz Rock* by Kristi Holl

201

"Truthful lips endure forever, but a lying tongue lasts only a moment."

—Proverbs 12:19

True or False?

Nobody likes to be lied about. It hurts—a lot! Maybe you overhear your friend say you got your new skirt at Goodwill, when she knows it was a gift from your favorite aunt. Or a jealous girl tells others that you cheated to get that "A" on your English test, when you studied hard for three solid hours for that grade. What do you do? Do speak up—calmly—and tell the truth of the matter. But keep it short and simple, then drop it or change the subject. Don't gossip or run the other person down, no matter how tempting the idea is. We don't like to admit it sometimes, but we want the other person to hurt as badly as we do or be just as embarrassed. They deserve it, right? Maybe, but resist that temptation.

Someone's lie may be believed for a short while, but in time (often by your pure speech and behavior), the lies will be shown for what they are. Determine to be a girl known for telling the truth—make that your reputation—and your words will stand the test of time.

More To Explore: Acts 5

Girl Talk: Do you think little white lies are okay? If so, when does a white lie become a beige lie and a gray lie and then a full-blown black lie?

God Talk: "Lord, it is really tough to be truthful all the time, but I want to be. Please help me tell the truth—at all times—in every situation. Amen."

From *No Boys Allowed* by Kristi Holl

"Trust in the LORD with all your heart; do not depend on your own understanding."

—Proverbs 3:5 (NLT)

Battling Bewilderment

Life can be confusing. Sometimes we just don't know what to do. Learn to lean on, trust in, and be confident in the Lord. Trust him with your whole heart and mind. Don't depend on figuring things out yourself.

Do you ever wonder what God is doing in your life? You've prayed about the things that worry you, or the situations causing you distress, but nothing seems to be happening. As believers, we have the privilege of staying peaceful in the middle of trying times. We can trust in God even when we don't understand what has already happened or what is going to happen in the future. We can "rest in the Lord, and wait patiently for Him" (Psalm 37:7 NKJV).

Sometimes tragedies strike. Baby brother catches a virus that attacks his lungs, and he ends up in the hospital. A tornado flattens our house. Our parents get a divorce. We are shocked and bewildered. What do we do now? Remember: *nothing* that has happened took God by surprise. He knew it was coming, he has a plan, and he'll take care of you. You don't have to figure everything out! "Trust in Him at all times, you people; pour out your heart before Him; God is a refuge for us" (Psalm 62:8 NKJV).

More To Explore: Proverbs 3:7; 28:26

Girl Talk: Do you ever feel confused when making a big decision? Do you worry over it or ask God about it?

God Talk: "Lord, I feel really confused about ______. I don't know what to do. Please guide me and show me the way to go. Amen."

From *Girlz Rock* by Kristi Holl

203

"He reached down from on high and took hold of me; he drew me out of deep waters. He rescued me from my powerful enemy, from my foes, who were too strong for me."

—Psalm 18:16–17

Call 9–1–1!

Maybe you aren't facing any enemies at school or in your neighborhood. Your enemy lives in your house. You were happy when your mom remarried, and you loved your stepdad. But with the remarriage came your older stepbrother, who seems to hate the new family. He takes his anger out on you.

But you know about God's rescuing David from his enemies. And you know that "God doesn't show partiality" (Acts 10:34 NLT). If God would rescue David, he would rescue you. You pray to be protected from your stepbrother and to have a safe home. One afternoon, your stepdad arrives home unexpectedly from work and sees his son attack you. He steps in immediately. In the end, your stepbrother moves to his mom's house in another state, and peace settles over your home.

There are many millions of people on this earth. Why would God take time to rescue you? "He led me to a place of safety; he rescued me because he delights in me" (Psalm 18:19 NLT). He saves you because he loves you.

More To Explore: Psalms 144:7; 40:1–3

Girl Talk: Can you describe a time when you felt that you needed rescuing? How did you solve the problem?

God Talk: "Lord, I feel scared when I think about ______. Please help calm my fears and rescue me from this situation. Amen."

From *Shine On, Girl!* by Kristi Holl

"My enemies will turn back when I call for help. By this I will know that God is for me."

—Psalm 56:9

You Can Do It!

One of the "muscles" God gives you is strength when you're in trouble. And who can get in more trouble than you? It might not be the principal's-office kind, but if you are a girl between 8 and 12, there are dilemmas in your life. This psalmist has nothing on you.

"*My adversaries pursue me all day long*" (verse 2). Heard any gossip this week? Any rumors?

"*In their pride many are attacking me*" (verse 2). Anybody jealous right now? Seen any fights over who said what to whom?

"*All day long they twist my words*" (verse 5). Have there been any meetings in the girls' restroom about what she said, how she said it, and what she meant?

"*They conspire, they lurk, they watch my steps*" (verse 6). Has anybody criticized anybody this week? Told on anybody? Jumped at the chance to tease?

A girl has to be strong to get through all that. You are. You just have to go where that strength comes from. "In God I trust," you have to say, "and am not afraid. What can man (or girl!) do to me?" (verse 11).

More To Explore: Isaiah 41:10

Girl Talk: How's your Trust Muscle doing? Is it in need of a workout?

God Talk: "God, thank you that you give me the strength to overcome gossip and hurtful words. Give me the courage to do the right thing. Amen."

From *That Is So Me* by Nancy Rue

205

"In peace I will lie down and sleep, for you alone, Lord, make me dwell in safety."

—Psalm 4:8

Ahhh ... Sleep

Samantha never worried during the day. She was too busy with school, soccer, babysitting, and her friends. But once she crawled into bed, fears invaded her mind. What would she do about the money she owed her best friend? When would she finish her history project? Why did her grandmother look so frail these days? Worries swirled around her mind, stealing her sleep.

Samantha was certainly *not* lying down and sleeping peacefully. But she remembered one great secret: prayer will push out worry. So Samantha took each situation, one by one, and prayed for God's help and intervention. Step-by-step, she gave her worries to him, and at last she fell into a peaceful sleep.

Your safety and success don't depend on your worrying and planning. The Lord is your security. "Do not be anxious about anything, but in every situation, by prayer and petition, with thanksgiving, present your requests to God. And the peace of God, which transcends all understanding, will guard your hearts and your minds in Christ Jesus" (Philippians 4:6–7).

So tonight, pray and give God your worries. Then snuggle down and sleep, trusting him to take care of you.

More to Explore: Psalm 3:5

Girl Talk: Do you ever worry yourself to sleep? Does that help solve your problems? What can you do instead?

God Talk: "Lord, please take care of me and all my concerns. Thank you for restful sleep. Amen."

From *Chick Chat* by Kristi Holl

"My command is this: Love each other as I have loved you."
—John 15:12

Say "I Love You" in a Million Ways

Jesus commands us to love each other. A command is an order, not just a nice-sounding suggestion. We are to love each other in the same way Jesus loved his disciples: in words and in actions.

Is it hard for you to say "I love you"? It can be. With family members, getting mushy can be downright awkward and embarrassing if you're not used to it. With friends, it can be considered "uncool" to say the words. But try saying them anyway: *I love you, I care about you, You mean a lot to me* . . . however you want to say it. Tell people how much you care about them—in spoken words, in little notes, in handmade cards—but tell them.

Don't stop there though. Words without similar actions are meaningless. If your friend says, "I really care about you," but she's always too busy to talk or listen to you, then her words will mean very little to you. So add actions to your words. Help your mom put away groceries. Help your dad with yard work. Pick some wildflowers for your sister's desk. Actions sometimes DO speak louder than words.

More To Explore: John 13:34–35 and 1 Peter 3:8

Girl Talk: How often do you tell your friends and family that you care about them? How do you show it?

God Talk: "Father, help me to show my family and friends that I love them. Teach me to love like you, Lord. Amen."

From *No Boys Allowed* by Kristi Holl

207

"In all these things we are more than conquerors through him who loved us."

—Romans 8:37

On to Victory!

No matter what kind of trouble or challenge you face right now, overwhelming victory is yours through Christ. Not just enough victory to survive or get by. No! A *super* strong victory, through Jesus, who loves and lives in you.

The key to having victory in our lives—instead of becoming victims of others or bad circumstances—is Jesus. It is only through him that success is ours. As you lean on him and trust him to give you whatever you need, you will learn by experience that you CAN do all things through Christ, who gives you the strength (Philippians 4:13). No matter what you face, you are *still* more than a conqueror.

God is all-powerful—more than enough for any trouble or circumstance—and his Spirit lives in us. "I will ask the Father, and He will give you another Helper, that He may be with you forever" (John 14:16 NASB). The Holy Spirit in us is our helper. As you spend time with God and talk to him and share your fears, you'll draw strength from him. Instead of focusing on the problem, keep your attention on Jesus, the problem solver.

Then be ready for a sweeping victory!

More To Explore: Deuteronomy 20:4

Girl Talk: Are you going through a tough situation right now? In the past? Did you handle it alone? How could you handle it better with God's help?

God Talk: "Lord, I'm really worried about ________. I don't know what to do, but I know you will get me through this. Please help me to stay calm and trust in you. Amen."

From *Girlz Rock* by Kristi Holl

"Because he turned his ear to me, I will call on him as long as I live."

—Psalm 116:2

The School of Life

Think about the things you've learned in school lately: how to do long division, how to multiply fractions, how to write a paragraph that actually makes sense. Now think about other skills you've mastered: riding a two-wheeler, ice skating, making a killer milkshake. Once you learn how to do those things, you don't have to keep going back to whoever taught you and say, "Could you show me that again?"

But when it comes to getting along with people, controlling some of your own little urges, or figuring out the next right thing to do, you never just "get it" once and for all. Learning those things is part of the long journey you'll take all your life, because the kinds of situations you have to deal with change as you get older. For instance, you learned that pitching a fit wasn't going to get you your way when you were two. (Okay, maybe three . . . or four . . .) Now you have to learn how to compromise so everyone gets a little bit of satisfaction. Later you'll learn what things NOT to compromise on.

The harder life gets—and it will—the more help you'll need from God. Keep getting closer now, so turning to him for guidance will be as natural as pitching that fit used to be.

More To Explore: Proverbs 9:9

Girl Talk: What's one thing you are learning right now about how to be a better example of God's love?

God Talk: "Jesus, help me to turn to you first when I hit a bump in the school of life. Keep teaching me new ways to love you and love others. Amen."

From *That Is So Me* by Nancy Rue

209

"Be on your guard; stand firm in the faith; be courageous; be strong. Do everything in love."

—1 Corinthians 16:13–14

On Guard!

Life can throw some frightening things at you—totally out of the blue. Be ready, and stand true to what you believe. Be strong and brave in the faith God has given you. Everything you do must be done with love.

Rosa knew about frightening things. Her mom remarried three years after Rosa's dad left them. Rosa grew to love her stepdad and stepsister. Just when they seemed like a real family, crisis struck again. Rosa's mom was diagnosed with a disease that would eventually confine her to a wheelchair. Rosa's own faith wavered, but in the coming weeks, she learned about courage and trust from watching her parents. They stood true to what they believed: that God was good ALL the time, that he had everything under control, and that they could trust him. No matter what.

God wouldn't command you to do something unless he was willing to help you do it. During a crisis or difficult time, simply "standing firm" doesn't sound like much to accomplish, but it is. Say over and over—out loud—"God loves me, and I can trust him." Do it as long as it takes to build your faith up.

More To Explore: Colossians 4:2

Girl Talk: Did you ever think standing still and strong could be so tiring and disheartening? Who can you ask for support as you stand strong?

God Talk: "Lord, I want to be strong for you. Please give me the strength to do what is right and not budge. Amen."

From *Shine On, Girl!* by Kristi Holl

"God is our refuge and strength, an ever-present help in trouble. Therefore we will not fear."

—Psalm 46:1–2

Safety in the Storms

If you fall into the deep end of the pool but can't swim, a lifeguard will rescue you. Usually we need rescuing from things less obvious than drowning. You might have two papers to type, and your computer breaks. Or perhaps you agreed to be the hostess for your class barbecue, but now it's raining, and you have no place to put fifty classmates. Help! Or, more seriously, maybe you or someone you know is being abused at home. In all these cases, someone must come to your rescue. It's okay to ask a trusted adult for help—especially if someone is being abused.

How do we make God our shelter from storms and the strength we need to get through these situations? By prayer and faith. Sometimes the rescue comes immediately. Other times it takes a while. Sometimes the answer from God is to take action. Other times the answer is to keep reading your Bible. But the help WILL come. God has promised it. Stand firm until the answer comes, and "imitate those who through faith and patience inherit the promises" (Hebrews 6:12 NKJV). Because of that assurance, take courage. Help is on the way!

More To Explore: Psalm 62:7–8 and Psalm 13:5

Girl Talk: Have you ever asked God to rescue you? How did he answer you?

God Talk: "Lord, I need your help every day. Thank you for always being here for me. I know I can always call on you. Amen."

From *No Boys Allowed* by Kristi Holl

211

"Plans fail for lack of counsel, but with many advisers they succeed."

—Proverbs 15:22

Seek Advice

It's good to carefully plan projects, but those plans often don't work out if you fail to ask advice during the planning stage. If you listen to many advisers, your projects are more likely to succeed.

Suppose you and your best friend are tired of having no privacy from your younger brothers and sisters. You decide to build a tree house where you can be left alone. Your dad offers to help with the tree house plans, but you say you don't need help. You and your friend already know exactly the kind of tree house you want. You work till sundown two nights in a row to build your creation. Unfortunately, you've built the little house on a dying branch. The limb breaks during the night, and in the morning you find the tree house on the ground, smashed to pieces.

Pride and overconfidence can keep us from asking for advice. That's usually a mistake! No one is smart enough to do everything on her own. The right counsel can make the difference between success and failure, between victory and defeat. Listen to wise people, learn from their experience, and succeed!

More to Explore: Proverbs 19:20

Girl Talk: When you have a problem, do you ask for advice? How do you choose the best people to ask? Do you then listen to their advice?

God Talk: "Lord, thank you for giving me people who care about me. Help me to listen to wise advice. Amen."

From *Chick Chat* by Kristi Holl

"The Lord is close to the brokenhearted and saves those who are crushed in spirit."

—Psalm 34:18

Whispers of Love

Do you remember the last time you were brokenhearted? It hurt, didn't it, when your best friend dumped you? Or your grandpa died. Or your dad didn't get home for your birthday. It actually feels like your chest has been split in two, especially when you cry, as most of us do when our spirits are crushed by some hurtful life-thing.

And yet, "the Lord is close to the brokenhearted" (Psalm 34:18). Even before you start to cry, even before you realize how hurt you are, God is already there with the heavenly tissue, the almighty hug. And when you throw yourself down on your bed or throw tennis balls against the fence, you can feel God whispering that he's so sorry you're in pain. He doesn't let you skip the tears and the hurting chest and the heaviness of a broken heart. But he does let you rely on him to lead you through your feelings and gives you space to feel them. That's especially important if other people tell you not to cry.

Best of all: he will heal your broken heart. God eases into the raw places and not only makes you feel better, he makes you stronger.

More To Explore: Psalm 147:3

Girl Talk: Have you ever felt whispers of God's love in the midst of a sad situation?

God Talk: "Lord, you are capable of healing every broken heart. Please heal the splinters of pain that are inside mine. Amen."

From *That Is So Me* by Nancy Rue

213

"Blessed is the man who trusts in the Lord, and whose hope is the Lord."

—Jeremiah 17:7 (NKJV)

Lean on the Lord

Trust can be hard. Do you have trouble trusting other people? Have people mistreated you, or let you down, or broken their promises to you? Maybe they overlooked you when you needed attention. How did that make you feel? Being mistreated and ignored can make us overly sensitive later in life. If you feel destroyed emotionally when your friend doesn't compliment you on your new dress, her opinion is too important. If you're depressed for weeks when someone doesn't invite you to a party, your hope is in the wrong place. You're using other people's reactions to you to define who you are. If you look to others to let you know if you're "okay" or "acceptable," you will constantly need to be working for their love and approval.

It's time to shift that trust to God. If we trust in him, we won't be let down. Even the most loving parents or devoted friends will let us down sometimes. They're human, not perfect. But believers can trust God for their self-esteem. We can count on him to see us through any pain or difficulty we're in. "The Lord God, my God, is with you. He will not fail you nor forsake you" (1 Chronicles 28:20 NASB).

More To Explore: Psalm 32:10

Girl Talk: When you do something, do you think about what your friends will say? How often do you think about what God will say?

God Talk: "Lord, I know I put too much importance on what others think of me. Help me to think only of what you think of me. Amen."

From *Girlz Rock* by Kristi Holl

"The Lord is my light and my salvation—whom shall I fear? The Lord is the stronghold of my life—of whom shall I be afraid?"

—Psalm 27:1

Fight Fear—and Win!

Fears come in all shapes and sizes. You may be afraid of the water, but you are required to take swimming lessons at school. You may be moving, and you're afraid to go to the new school. You may live in an area where tornadoes or hurricanes are frequent. You may be afraid that you'll never have a close friend who really, really cares about you. God never commands us to do something that he won't give us the power to do. You can count on that. If he tells you to have courage, to be brave, then he will give you the strength and power to do it.

It's normal to feel fear. Most of the great men and women of the Bible felt horrible fear at times. God simply says that when you feel the fear, don't run. Don't flinch from doing what is right. Step out, and God will meet you there. And when the challenge is over, you'll realize God was with you—walking you through it step by step—all the way. You will feel much less fear the next time you face that situation.

More To Explore: Isaiah 43:1–2

Girl Talk: Imagine something you want to do, but are scared to try. Can you see yourself doing it with God's help?

God Talk: "God, sometimes I feel really scared about ________. I know you are there with me all the time. Please help me to put my trust in you and leave my fear behind! Amen."

From *No Boys Allowed* by Kristi Holl

215

"I will know that you stand firm in the one Spirit . . . without being frightened in any way by those who oppose you. This is a sign to them that they will be destroyed, but that you will be saved—and that by God."

—Philippians 1:27–28

Fearless!

Don't be frightened or feel threatened by your enemies. Your calm fearlessness will prove to them—it will be a sign—that you will overcome. Your peaceful courage is evidence that you are going to be saved, even by God himself.

Because you were homeschooled, most of your friends are from church or other homeschool families. When you start middle school in fifth grade, you're shocked and hurt by the kids who make fun of you. They ridicule your longer skirts, your "What Would Jesus Do?" bracelet, and the kittens on your notebook cover. They call you a baby—and worse. You grow to fear going to school.

"Listen to me, you who know right from wrong and cherish my law in your hearts. Do not be afraid of people's scorn or their slanderous talk" (Isaiah 51:7 NLT). This promise is given to those who follow God's laws and value his Word. If you're doing this—if you're following Jesus to the best of your ability—then you don't need to fear people's threats. Be calm and courageous!

More To Explore: Hebrews 13:6

Girl Talk: How do others treat you? Are you afraid of anyone at school? What can you remind yourself of when others taunt or threaten you?

God Talk: "Lord, sometimes I'm scared of others and what they could do. Please give me your courage. I know you will take care of me. Amen."

From *Shine On, Girl!* by Kristi Holl

"I was overcome by distress and sorrow. Then I called on the name of the Lord."

—Psalm 116:3–4

The Great Comforter

When was the last time you cried? Last month? Last week? This morning? The world can be a sad place with plenty of room for tears. Sometimes it can be so sad you feel "overcome."

Nobody feels strong in that kind of sorrow, not even big hulky men. But God sees us as strong when we go to him and say, "Help!—I can't stand this." That's when our Trust Muscle starts to flex—the tears slow down, and we come out from under the covers. We decide maybe we might like an order of fries after all. That's God at work, making us strong.

That doesn't mean it's wrong to get upset and grieve. We need to do that in order to work through our feelings. You just don't have to stay that way. Yes, cry. No, don't be hopeless. Yes, curl up with your teddy bear for a while. No, don't turn down an offer for a hug. Crying, hugging, thinking it over—all those things are God coming to the rescue, pumping up your Trust Muscle, making you stronger for next time sorrow hits. It will, but don't be afraid of it. There's nothing you and God together can't handle.

More To Explore: Psalm 20:5

Girl Talk: Think about the last time you were really sad. What made you feel stronger once you got past the tears you had to cry? See if you can find God in that. He's in there.

God Talk: "Jesus, sometimes I feel really sad. Thank you that you bring comfort to me, even in my tears. Amen."

From *That Is So Me* by Nancy Rue

217

"Consider it pure joy, my brothers and sisters, whenever you face trials of many kinds, because you know that the testing of your faith produces perseverance."

—James 1:2–3

God Uses Problems to Inspect You

It's easy to believe we trust God, and to look like our faith is strong, when we don't have any problems. But problems are what tests our faith, to reveal what's really inside us. People are like tea bags. If you want to know what's inside, drop them into hot water! Your faith is like that. When faced with a problem—an angry stepdad, a sprained ankle before the track meet, money shortages—how's your faith? Are you still confident that God will meet all your needs? Do you wait patiently for God's answers and help?

Until you've seen God supply your needs and help you through a few problems, it can be extremely hard to view problems as opportunities for joy. But "blessed is the one who perseveres under trial because, having stood the test, that person will receive the crown of life that the Lord has promised to those who love him" (James 1:12). Once your faith has endured a few tests, you will view problems differently. You will know a blessing waits for you after you face the trial successfully.

More To Explore: Romans 8:17–18 and 1 Peter 4:13

Girl Talk: Have you ever thought of problems as a chance to grow? Do you stay close to God during trials?

God Talk: "Lord, I am learning that trials are a chance to grow in my faith. Please help me to remember that. Thank you for always being with me. Amen."

From *Girlz Rock* by Kristi Holl

"So we don't look at the troubles we can see right now; rather, we look forward to what we have not yet seen. For the troubles we see will soon be over, but the joys to come will last forever."

—2 Corinthians 4:18 (NLT)

Joy Forever

Everything in this world is temporary, both the things you love and the things you hate. Problems with your parents and at school will pass away. It's the same for the good things: your solo in band, your cool wardrobe, and that new mountain bike. Even the things we like are temporary, but heaven will provide such fabulous attractions that these good earthly things will hardly seem worth noticing.

If you've accepted Jesus as your Savior, your real home is already reserved for you in heaven. How should you live on earth now? "Therefore we are always confident and know that as long as we are at home in the body we are away from the Lord. For we live by faith, not by sight" (2 Corinthians 5:6–7). In other words, we walk by faith in our heavenly future.

Try it! Fill your mind with the joy to come that will last forever.

More To Explore: Romans 8:24–25 and Hebrews 11:1

Girl Talk: Are you relying on God's will, not your own, for your decisions? Is it hard to go by faith instead of what you can actually see?

God Talk: "Lord, it's easier to do what I want and not wait for you. Help me to wait for your answers and to faithfully do what you want. Thank you for always being there for me. Amen."

From *No Boys Allowed* by Kristi Holl

219

"Because he himself suffered when he was tempted, he is able to help those who are being tempted."

—Hebrews 2:18

Hold Fast

All this talk about God saving us now as well as later makes it sound like once you believe in Jesus Christ, your life is going to be Disney World. Have you noticed that it doesn't exactly work that way?

There you are, trying to be all good for God, and kids say you're a geek because you don't watch MTV, or your coach won't let you play because you can't come to a Sunday morning practice. That doesn't feel like salvation—that feels like suffering!

And then there's the temptation thing. You believe in our Lord and you vow to do the right thing—and then up pops the opportunity to make an A+ on the test, if you'll just glance at the answer sheet the teacher left on her desk. *If I'm saved*, you may wonder, *why am I still tempted?*

Being tempted happens to all human beings, even to Jesus when he was in human form. That makes Jesus the perfect one to turn to when *you* get the urge to mess things up. Jesus says, "Been there, but didn't do that. I can help you resist temptation just like I did." Now that's what you call a rescue.

More To Explore: 1 Corinthians 10:13

Girl Talk: What is a temptation you're struggling to resist?

God Talk: "Jesus, you were tempted when you lived on the earth, so you know what it's like. Help me to resist the temptation to do or say things I know are wrong. Amen."

From *That Is So Me* by Nancy Rue

"There is a time for everything, and a season for every activity under the heavens."

—Ecclesiastes 3:1

Growing and Changing

Things change. People change, families change, bodies change, activities change—everything is changing all the time. Sometimes we want to speed up change, especially if we're waiting for something we want. Sometimes our desire is to slow change or even stop it, especially when something bad is happening. But there is a right and proper time for everything.

If you're in the middle of changes—either wanted or unwanted—remember that things are *not* spinning out of control. God is the Master of all the times and seasons of your life. "Blessed be the name of God forever and ever, for wisdom and might are His. And He changes the times and the seasons" (Daniel 2:20–21 NKJV). God loves you, and you can trust him to bring about changes at exactly the right and proper time. Learn to say, "But as for me, I trust in You, O Lord; I say, 'You are my God.' My times are in Your hand" (Psalm 31:14–15 NKJV).

Yes, changes can be annoying, even scary. Learn to relax and let them happen naturally. There's a time for every purpose under heaven.

More to Explore: Ecclesiastes 3:17

Girl Talk: What changes are you going through right now? Which changes do you wish were happening—but haven't yet?

God Talk: "Lord, I need to relax and stop fighting change. Help me to trust that you have everything under control. Amen."

From *Chick Chat* by Kristi Holl

221

"I am the good shepherd. The good shepherd lays down his life for the sheep."

—John 10:11

"Ewe" Are Loved

Today, Jesus talks about what happens after the sheep pass through the gate and go outside.

- A shepherd didn't "drive" his sheep. He went on ahead and the sheep followed his voice.
- He would lead them to pastures where they could totally pig out and have everything they needed.
- Sometimes wild animals got to the sheep. There were cliffs and ledges they could fall off of. Sometimes they just got separated from the flock and were lost and scared. The shepherd would do anything to rescue a sheep, even if it meant giving up his own life.
- It works the same way with the God Jesus came to show us. He doesn't force anybody to go with him. He goes out ahead and those who know him follow him.
- If they follow him, they'll have everything they need.
- There will still be dangers. Sometimes people fall into bad stuff. Sometimes they just wander away from God, but he will do whatever it takes to get them back.

That's a shepherd worth following.

More To Explore: Isaiah 40:11

Girl Talk: Imagine yourself as a white, fluffy, little lamb with Jesus as your shepherd. Do you feel safe?

God Talk: "God, you love me and take care of me like a shepherd takes care of his sheep. Thank you for always guiding and protecting me. Amen."

From *That Is So Me* by Nancy Rue

"The strong spirit of a man sustains him in bodily pain or trouble, but a weak and broken spirit who can raise up or bear?"
—Proverbs 18:14 (AMP)

Strength Training for Your Spirit

Everyone will experience sickness or trouble sometimes, but if your spirit is strong, you can face it and survive. But someone with a weak or wounded spirit finds it nearly impossible to bear up under anything.

Haven't you noticed this difference in yourself? On Monday, when you're confident inside and someone calls you a stupid name, you shrug it off. You know that the problem is with the other person, not you. But if it happens again on Wednesday, when you feel weaker inside, the same remark makes you cry. Sometimes you know the cause of feeling "down" (a bad grade, overhearing a fight between your parents, the flu), but some days there seems to be no reason. When your spirit is weak, it's hard to overcome or endure anything with the right attitude.

So what can you do? First, you must learn to encourage yourself. There won't always be someone around to do it for you. David learned this too and wrote, "Why, my soul, are you downcast? Why so disturbed within me? Put your hope in God, for I will yet praise him, my Savior and my God" (Psalm 42:11).

More To Explore: Psalm 51:10–12 and 1 Peter 1:3–7

Girl Talk: Are there days when your spirit feels stronger and more confident? Or weaker and easily hurt? Do you ask God for help?

God Talk: "Lord, sometimes my spirit gets hurt so easily. Please help me to rely on you, not on others. I want my hope to stay in you! Amen."

From *Girlz Rock* by Kristi Holl

223

"Help me, Lord my God; save me according to your unfailing love. Let them know that it is your hand, that you, Lord, have done it."

—Psalm 109:26–27

Who Did It?

When you need help, cry out to God. He loves you more than you could ever measure. God will rescue you in such a way that it's clear to others who did it.

Your family is having some tough times since your dad lost his job. It's hard just paying the rent and buying groceries. When the overnight class trip to the state park is announced, your heart sinks. The whole trip costs "only" $65, but you know it might as well be a million. You can't ask your parents for it. Instead, you pray: "Lord, you know I'd love to go on this trip with my class. Could you show me a way? Please give me money for the trip."

You know that if God wants you to go, he can make a way. Even so, when the answer comes, it astounds you. Your painting for the local art show wins first place, and someone offers to buy it—for $75! When your friends say, "Man, are you lucky!" you don't just smile and agree. "It isn't luck," you say. "I prayed for money to go on the trip, and God did it for me." You give God the credit.

More To Explore: Genesis 21:1–6

Girl Talk: Describe an impossible situation that worked out just in time. Who or what did you give the credit to?

God Talk: "Lord, I know nothing is impossible with you. Please help me with ______. I know if you want it, it will happen. Thank you. Amen."

From *Shine On, Girl!* by Kristi Holl

"She thought, 'If I just touch his clothes, I will be healed.'"
—Mark 5:28

Everybody Matters

I don't want to bother God with that. He has all those really sick, hurting people to take care of."

Has that thought every flickered through your mind? Did you decide not to pray about something because it wasn't as bad as what your friend was going through with her parents getting a divorce?

That may be how the lady felt in this story in Mark 5:25–34. She'd been bleeding for twelve years, which is probably longer than you've even been alive. She went to one doctor after another, but none of them could help. Since she was bleeding, she was considered unclean, so nobody wanted to hang out with her, much less take care of her.

But she didn't think she was as bad off as the guy who got to Jesus before she did. His little daughter was dying. She had so much faith, though, that she figured if she could just touch a corner of Jesus' robe, she'd be healed, which turned out to be true. Her bleeding stopped immediately.

The cool thing about God is that Jesus stopped and told her that her healing was going to last forever. We not only get better when we turn to God, we also know it's for real. Like the bleeding lady, we can go in peace.

More To Explore: Matthew 6:26

Girl Talk: Have you ever decided not to pray about something because you thought that God wouldn't care?

God Talk: "Jesus, thank you that you care about everything, even the little things. And thank you that when you heal me, I can trust that it's for real. Amen."

From *That Is So Me* by Nancy Rue

225

"I have told you these things, so that in me you may have peace. In this world you will have trouble. But take heart! I have overcome the world."

—John 16:33

Nothing Is Too Big for God

Are you facing trouble right now? Trouble with a bully? Trouble with your family? You see no way out. The Israelites felt the same way when the armies of Egypt chased them and the Red Sea blocked their escape route. They cried out to their leader, Moses, saying "What have you done to us by bringing us out of Egypt?" Moses replied, "Do not be afraid. Stand firm and you will see the deliverance the Lord will bring you today." God parted the Red Sea. The Israelites walked through on dry ground, and the sea closed again to swallow up the Egyptian armies (Exodus 14).

Like the Israelites, if you've accepted Jesus as your Savior, you're one of God's chosen people. He'll help you overcome your problem too—and totally defeat it. When facing a difficult situation, ask God to make a way through it for you. He will. You may have to step out and do something scary, just as the Israelites did when walking between high walls of water on each side. But no matter what your trouble, "in all these things we are more than conquerors through him who loved us" (Romans 8:37).

More To Explore: Exodus 14

Girl Talk: Have you ever had a situation where you felt there was no way out? How did you deal with it?

God Talk: "Lord, I'm really scared about ______. Please help me get through this. I want to be courageous for you. Amen."

From *No Boys Allowed* by Kristi Holl

Making Choices that Inspire Inner Beauty and Outward Faith

If you're like me, you've probably discovered something. Sometimes new beginnings are fun and sometimes they're scary. What makes the difference?

Take the first day of a new year in a school where you know most of the students. It's fun to be with your friends again. But what if you're starting at a school where you don't know anyone? Are you wondering whether even one person will talk with you?

But think about this — the beauty of knowing someone who promises he will be with you always. Day or night, 24/7, no matter what is happening. That's the Jesus I know, because I've asked him to be the most important person in my life.

When Jesus died on the cross, he gave his life for me — for you — so that we can ask forgiveness and receive it. When we ask him to be our Savior and the Lord of our life, he answers, "Yes, yes, yes! That's why I died for *you*."

Jesus also gives us the privilege of learning to know him better. That doesn't mean he always gives me what I want. Or that what I want always comes the moment I ask for it. It means that if I allow him to help me, he's there for me — always listening — always watching over me. **The beauty of believing in a faithful Jesus means that every day I have the privilege of getting to know him better.**

Because that means so much to me, I use a Bible reading program with suggested chapters for each day. I also keep a journal to record the questions I have and the thoughts I receive in answer to my questions. Before I start reading, I pray, "Lord, what do you want me to know about ...?" and finish the sentence.

Then I watch to see what verse or verses seem to jump off the page or seem lit by a holy spotlight.

As I write down those words, I call it *finding the promise.* Next, I *lay hold of the promise I've received.* I tell the Lord, "Thank you! That's for me! It fits what I'm asking you about." Then I *pray the promise*, repeating the words I've read, because I believe it's what the Lord is saying to me.

In the hours or days that follow, I often return to that promise, repeating it as the Lord's guidance, comfort, and help for me. I *stand or kneel on that promise.*

In John 8:47, we read that the person who belongs to God hears what God says. That's the Beauty of Believing—to hear what he wants to say to us. It's allowing him to help us in every part of our lives.

Now think again about starting a new school where you don't know anyone. **Think about what it would mean to have Jesus walk with you into every situation**. Maybe *you'll* be the one who talks to someone and makes a great new friend!

—Lois Walfrid Johnson

"All Scripture is inspired by God and is useful to teach us what is true and to make us realize what is wrong in our lives. It straightens us out and teaches us to do what is right."

—2 Timothy 3:16 (NLT)

Instruction Book

God's Word, from beginning to end, is true. The Bible is our instruction manual. It teaches us how to live godly, successful lives. It is also useful to correct us when we take a wrong path.

Emily received a cell phone for her birthday, but she was soon so frustrated that she was ready to toss it in her desk drawer and leave it. She couldn't program her friends' phone numbers into it. She couldn't figure out how to text-message. It was supposed to have a choice of twenty different rings, but she couldn't get it to play the tune she wanted. Frustrated, she went to find her dad. "This thing doesn't work," Emily said. Her dad took the phone and pressed a few buttons. "Looks okay. Did you read the instruction book?" he asked.

In the same way that Emily needed to read the instruction manual for her cell phone, we need to read God's Word, our instructions for living. The Bible isn't just to carry to church on Sunday morning. In it, we have God's blueprint for our lives. It has the answer to every need we might have. But we need to read and study it.

More to Explore: Proverbs 6:23

Girl Talk: When you have a question about life or a problem to solve, whom do you ask for help? Do you go to God's Word for answers?

God Talk: "Lord, thank you for giving us your Word. Give me a real desire to read and obey it. Amen."

From *Chick Chat* by Kristi Holl

227

"'My thoughts are completely different from yours,' says the Lord. 'And my ways are far beyond anything you could imagine. For just as the heavens are higher than the earth, so are my ways higher than your ways and my thoughts higher than your thoughts.'"

—Isaiah 55:8–9 (NKJV)

Heavenly Thoughts

We will never completely understand God, because he thinks and acts beyond anything we can imagine in our limited, human minds. God and humans see things and people so differently. Just as heaven is beyond our understanding, God's ways are higher in quality than ours.

For example, you may have difficulty forgiving people, and you still remember what they did to you. God, on the other hand, forgives and forgets, removing your sin far from you. Sometimes we consider ourselves very "spiritual" when we manage not yelling at someone. However, God says our thoughts must be right too, and that hating someone is like murder in our hearts. God's thoughts about events in your life are different than yours too. You might pray to remain in your hometown, but your dad gets transferred to another state anyway.

Strive to know God better through prayer and Bible study, but know that you'll never totally understand him or his ways. That's okay. That's why he's God!

More to Explore: Psalm 92:5 and Romans 11:33–35

Girl Talk: Are you facing a difficult situation right now? Are you blaming God for it, or do you trust him to see you through it?

God Talk: "Thank you, Lord, for everything you do for me. Please help me make it through this difficult situation. I know that you know what is best for me. Please help me to see it too. Amen."

From *No Boys Allowed* by Kristi Holl

"When he, the Spirit of truth, comes, he will guide you into all the truth."

—John 16:13

Saved by the Holy Spirit

One of the jobs of the Holy Spirit is to guide us. We often need help in making decisions or choosing the right path to take. The Holy Spirit (also called the Helper) wants to guide you. When you ask others for advice, they give you conflicting opinions about what to do. The Holy Spirit, however, knows the whole truth about the situation—all sides of it—and wants to help you make the *best* decision.

No one learns to hear from the Holy Spirit overnight. It takes time—and learning from your mistakes. But the following things can help you "tune-up" your hearing:

- Have regular prayer time with God. Don't just talk to him. Sit and listen too.
- Be willing to do God's will, even if it's different from what you want.
- Realize you will probably receive guidance one step at a time, rather than a detailed plan or map. As you take each step of obedience, the Holy Spirit will reveal the next step.
- Have an attitude of gratitude.
- Feed your mind on God's Word.
- Don't do anything unless you have peace in your heart about it. Pay attention to the little warning signs that the Holy Spirit sends your way. Stop and wait until you have peace.

Cooperate with the Holy Spirit, and get ready for an exciting adventure as he guides you into all truth.

More to Explore: 1 John 4:6

Girl Talk: Do you want help with decisions but aren't sure where to turn? Do you ask God for help but aren't sure he's answering? He is! You can trust that he hears and he cares.

God Talk: "Lord, sometimes I need help, and I'm confused. I know you have the answers, if I will just listen. Please help me to be patient and wait for your answer. Amen."

From *Girlz Rock* by Kristi Holl

229

"As your words are taught, they give light; even the simple can understand them."

—Psalm 119:130 (NLT)

Turn On the Light!

You're home alone when the electricity is knocked out during a lightning storm. Heart pounding, you crouch in total darkness for a moment. Then you remember the emergency supply of candles and matches in the kitchen drawer. Hands waving in front of you, you grope your way toward the kitchen. You bang your shins on the corner of an end table, hit your hip on the door frame, and slip on the rug in front of the kitchen sink. You're so grateful when you find the candles and matches. After striking a match, you light several candles and place them around the house. The light pushes back the darkness, showing you where to walk and how to avoid painful encounters.

God's Word is like that. As the principles are studied and put into practice, they give us light to live by. The Bible shows us how to be healthy, how to prosper, how to grow in love for others, and how to avoid dangerous situations. "Your word is a lamp for my feet, a light on my path" (Psalm 119:105).

Is there an area of your life where you're stumbling in darkness? Then open God's Word, read and study, and be amazed at the light God shines on your problem.

More to Explore: 1 Peter 2:9

Girl Talk: When you receive the light of God's Word, do you absorb it (and keep it hidden)? Or do you reflect it (and share the light with others)?

God Talk: "Lord, thank you for giving us your Word. Help me to understand it. Amen."

From *Chick Chat* by Kristi Holl

"I am the gate for the sheep."

—John 10:7

Follow the True Shepherd

Let's clear up the sheep-pens-gates thing.

Sheep were quite valuable, so sheep owners built pens for them with walls to keep them from wandering away. There was only one opening, and that had a gate. Anybody entering any other way, like by climbing over the fence, was obviously up to no good (John 10:1).

Several shepherds kept their sheep in the same pen and hired one watchman to guard them. When a shepherd came in and called to his own flock, they knew who he was. The other sheep, who didn't belong to him, would just go on doing whatever it is sheep do.

So Jesus is the way for God to come in and call to us. We belong to him. We recognize his voice in the Gospels. The gate swings open and you can follow wherever Jesus leads you in your life.

Just watch out for people who try to get you to follow them instead of Jesus. Just keep your eyes on that gate. Jesus is right there calling your name—way louder than those other voices. Follow his.

More to Explore: Psalm 100:3

Girl Talk: What "thieves and robbers" might be trying to climb over your wall?

God Talk: "Jesus, thank you that you are a good shepherd. Help me to stay focused on you, so that I can hear you calling my name. Amen."

From *That Is So Me* by Nancy Rue

"The suffering you sent was good for me, for it taught me to pay attention to your principles."

—Psalm 119:71 (NLT)

God Uses Problems to Connect You

Anna refused to wear her helmet, then she received a concussion when her bike skidded in gravel and she crashed. Sarah refused to go to bed on time and talked on the phone till midnight on school nights, then she was sick and missed an outing to the water park. Kate went to the mall when she was supposed to be studying, resulting in her having no money for things she needed—and failing several tests. Each girl had plenty of problems and pain to work through, but (in the end) Anna began wearing her helmet, Sarah started getting enough sleep, and Kate studied during the school week instead of shopping. Their problems were blessings in disguise.

Some lessons we learn only through pain and failure. When you were very young, your parents probably told you not to touch the hot stove, but you *learned* not to do it by being burned once. Sometimes, unfortunately, we only learn the true value of something—health, money, a friendship—by losing it, at least long enough to feel some pain.

When you next face a problem, pray and ask God if he is trying to teach you something. Listen for his answer. Then obey yourself right out of the problem!

More to Explore: Psalm 94:12

Girl Talk: Think back to a time when you made a wrong choice. What were the consequences? Do you think God was teaching you something?

God Talk: "Lord, I sometimes make sinful choices and unwise choices. Please help me to see what I did wrong, so that I don't do it again. I want to learn and grow. Amen."

From *Girlz Rock* by Kristi Holl

232

"You are the light of the world."

—Matthew 5:14

Shine On!

Are you ever afraid of the dark? Just about everybody is at some point—usually when there's a storm going on outside, or something makes a weird noise, or you wake up from a freaky dream. Darkness can be frightening, especially when it's that inside blackness you feel when you're sad or confused or hurt. You just want somebody to turn on a light, right?

Jesus knew about that, and at one point (John 8:12), he called himself the light of the world. All people had to do was turn to him and he would chase away the sadness and fear and confusion. In today's verse, he said we, too, are the light of the world. He expects us to carry on the work he started, rather than keeping the message of his love and forgiveness to ourselves.

If Jesus were to use a modern-day metaphor, he might say, "Don't put your flashlight under your sweatshirt, so nobody else can see the path in the dark." What would happen if you did that? You wouldn't be able to see *your* way either. If you whipped out that flashlight and sent its beam out, all of you could see where to go.

You see God so much better when you share him. You are, after all, the light the world needs.

More to Explore: Philippians 2:14–16

Girl Talk: How do you think you shine? In what ways are you a light to people who need to see?

God Talk: "God, you are a brilliant light for me when I'm frightened or sad or confused. Help me to shine your light for others who also need to see. Amen."

From *That Is So Me* by Nancy Rue

"The Spirit of the Lord will rest on him — the Spirit of wisdom and of understanding, the Spirit of counsel and of might, the Spirit of the knowledge and fear of the Lord — and he will delight in the fear of the Lord. He will not judge by what he sees with his eyes, or decide by what he hears with his ears."

— Isaiah 11:2–3

Go with Your Gut

If you're a follower of Jesus, you have the Holy Spirit living inside you. The Holy Spirit will give you understanding and knowledge of situations to guide you. You can't always make wise decisions based on what you see or hear.

Olivia was thrilled when Courtney invited her to her party on Saturday. Olivia and her friends spent one whole afternoon deciding what they'd wear. However, for no reason that Olivia could see, she started having funny, sick feelings in the pit of her stomach. She prayed about it, but the feeling only grew worse as the day of the party drew near. At the last minute, she decided to skip it. On Monday — after hearing about the alcohol at the party and some property that had been destroyed — she silently thanked God for warning her to skip the party.

If you don't have peace about a person, a situation, or an activity, pay attention! Then obey those "funny feelings" and avoid trouble. Trust the Holy Spirit's guidance, and let him keep you safe.

More to Explore: John 14:17

Girl Talk: Can you think of some past times where you ended up in a bad situation? Before you went, did you have a "funny feeling" about that person or activity?

God Talk: "Lord, I need to listen to you when you try to warn me about things. Thank you for protecting me. Amen."

From *Chick Chat* by Kristi Holl

234

"Do not be yoked together with unbelievers. For what do righteousness and wickedness have in common? Or what fellowship can light have with darkness?"

—2 Corinthians 6:14

Learning to Love

Book in hand, Brittany flopped down on her bed and rolled onto her stomach. Riley slouched deeper in a comfy chair nearby. It was fun being together again. When they were younger, they had gone to the same school and had been close friends. Then, two years ago, the boundary lines changed, putting them in different schools, even though they still lived near each other.

Now, Riley leaned forward. "Is that your sister's book about dating?"

Brittany flipped pages. "Yup. Here's where we left off." She began reading aloud. "*Love isn't something that just happens. You choose whom you love or don't love.*"

Riley stopped her. "Just a minute. What does that mean?"

"Let me finish," Brittany kept reading. "*Some people say, 'I fell in love. I just couldn't help myself. But—'*"

Again Riley interrupted. "That's true. I *do* fall in love. If I like a boy, I like him. And right now I like Todd. What's so bad about that?"

"What's *good* about it?" Brittany's blue eyes met Riley's brown ones. Brittany had never liked Todd because of the way he acted. More than once, the two girls had talked about how he treated others.

Brittany went back to the book. "*Some people say, 'I fell in love. I just couldn't help myself.' But early in every relationship there's a moment of choice, whether we think about it or not. We decide, 'I'm not interested in that boy as more than just a friend.' Or we tell ourselves, 'I like that boy. I hope he becomes my boyfriend.'*"

"That's true," Riley said. "I decide, all right. When I meet a boy, I know real soon if he's the one for me. I don't know why my mom won't let me start dating."

"But you're missing the whole point of the book," Brittany said. "We can know a lot of people and be nice to them. But the book says there are times when we should choose *not* to date someone—especially someone we feel romantic about. We can wind up getting hurt. Not all guys treat girls well."

Brittany is right. Love is a choice, whether you decide to love your little sister even when she's annoying or be kind to a friend even after she has hurt you. Love isn't just a feeling. If you do decide to love a special guy someday, make sure he's one who loves the Lord.

More to Explore: 1 Corinthians 13:4–7

Girl Talk: What is a time when you decided to love someone even though you didn't feel like it?

God Talk: "Dear God, it seems a long way off, but someday I might find a guy I want to marry. If that happens, help me to choose a man who loves you with all his heart. Amen."

From *Girl Talk* by Lois Walfrid Johnson

235

"But the seed falling on good soil refers to someone who hears the word and understands it."

—Matthew 13:23

Plant, Grow, Bloom!

This whole metaphor about the seeds was so complicated, even the disciples were confused. Read about it in Matthew 13:3–8, and maybe you'll see why. Because Jesus wanted them—and you—to really get it, he told them what it meant in Matthew 13:18–23.

Some people, he said, hear the message of God's love and forgiveness, but they don't really take it in, so the first time they're tempted to do something wrong, they forget all about God. That's like the seed that falls on a path and gets trampled. Others take in the message with joy and go with it for a while, but then some big bad thing happens, and they turn away, because God "failed" them. That's like the seed that falls among rocks. Still others hear it and talk about it and almost look like they get it, but they don't really live it. Their faith gets choked out by worrying. That's the seed that lands in the weeds.

But there are those people, Jesus said, who hear the message, understand it, and live it, so that they produce all kinds of good things for God. They're like the seed that falls into good, well-prepared soil. Jesus said to get your soil ready. He wants your heart to be a good place for the message to grow.

More to Explore: Psalm 1:1–3

Girl Talk: What are you doing to make your life fertile soil for the Word of Jesus to take root?

God Talk: "Jesus, I want your Word to grow in my heart. Make my heart good soil, with no weeds or rocks. Amen."

From *That Is So Me* by Nancy Rue

"But if from there you seek the Lord your God, you will find him if you seek him with all your heart and with all your soul."
—Deuteronomy 4:29

Totally Involved

Cara's feelings about a boy in her neighborhood had her totally confused. Rumors said Troy was a little wild, and her parents didn't trust him after witnessing an angry explosion. Yet, he was funny, and he liked Cara. Just being near him made it hard for Cara to breathe. She wondered how God felt about her hanging with him. She prayed about Troy once in a while, but her feelings remained confused. Why didn't God answer her?

For one thing, Cara treated God like a vending machine. She tossed in her quarter (a minute of her time) and expected an answer to fall into her hand. She wasn't seeking God with her whole heart and mind. One day, after fighting with her mom about Troy, Cara shut herself in her room and got serious. She opened her Bible, prayed, read, and prayed some more. Lying on her bed, she waited and listened. By the end of the morning, she had her answer. It wasn't what she'd hoped for, but she felt God was impressing on her to avoid Troy.

God is there for you at all times. Seek him with your whole heart and an open mind, and you *will* find him.

More to Explore: 2 Chronicles 31:21

Girl Talk: How is your relationship with God? Is he like a casual acquaintance? A good friend? A loving father? How much time do you spend with him?

God Talk: "Lord, sometimes I rush through my time with you. Show me how to seek you with my whole heart. Amen."

From *Chick Chat* by Kristi Holl

237

"Now the one who has fashioned us for this very purpose is God, who has given us the Spirit as a deposit, guaranteeing what is to come."

—2 Corinthians 5:5

Spirit Talk

How way cool would it be if whenever you had to confess something to your parents, you had a friend murmuring the right words in your ear? And would it not be totally awesome if the very minute you started to do something wrong, this same friend froze you in place so you couldn't mess up?

The Holy Spirit is just such a friend. It's the Spirit that guides our thinking and gives us our words and influences our actions. Part of God's plan for everybody, including you, is that you don't have to figure out everything on your own.

The Spirit has already been working in you for some time. That day you almost laughed at the kid who stutters, and then you suddenly told everybody to leave him alone; that night you nearly lied to your mom about your report card, and then blurted out the truth; that morning you woke up deciding to get ready without being nagged are all evidence that God's Holy Spirit was working in you, showing you how great life can be if you just let him have his way with you.

More to Explore: John 14:26

Girl Talk: Have you ever felt a little nudge to do the right thing, even when you wanted to do the complete opposite?

God Talk: "Jesus, teach me how to listen for your Spirit. Thank you that I get to have such a friend with me all the time. Amen."

From *That Is So Me* by Nancy Rue

"Those who led the way rebuked him and told him to be quiet . . . [but] Jesus stopped and ordered the man to be brought to him."

—Luke 18:39–40

Don't Hush Up—Speak Up!

Why is it that sometimes—a lot of times!—when you speak up about something that's bugging you, people shush you? Seriously, you're on a car trip and you say, "I'm hungry," or "I have to go to the bathroom," or you just want to know, "Are we there yet?" and your parents jump all over you.

The blind man in the Bible story must have felt that way. He was sitting by the roadside when Jesus passed by, and he realized he might actually have a chance to see again and not have to beg for food and money. So he called out, "Jesus, Son of David, have mercy on me!" And what did the people in the crowd with Jesus do? They "rebuked" him. They told him, sharply, to back off. Jesus, they said, didn't have time to listen to him.

Hello! Healing people was what Jesus *did*! He ordered the man to be brought to him and healed him on the spot.

If you have something important to say, especially if you want to be "healed" of something—whether it's cluelessness in math or loneliness for your always-working dad—speak up to God, and don't shrink if people tell you to hush up. God wants to hear you.

More to Explore: Mark 11:24

Girl Talk: What do you need from God right now? Tell him about it!

God Talk: "Jesus, thank you that you always hear my prayer requests, no matter how big or small they are. I love you. Amen."

From *That Is So Me* by Nancy Rue

239

"Keep this Book of the Law always on your lips; meditate on it day and night, so that you may be careful to do everything written in it. Then you will be prosperous and successful."

—Joshua 1:8

Formula for Success

Keep reading and talking about God's Word. Think with careful attention on all that is written in it. That way you'll be able to do the things it teaches. If you do, your days will be marked by peace and good fortune and success. That's God's formula.

What's success? You want to have good relationships at home and at school. You want to succeed in your school work. You desire good outcomes on your soccer team or with your piano lessons. Success doesn't mean lots of money and cool clothes.

So if you're NOT being prosperous and successful, if your days are full of turmoil instead of peace—apply God's formula for success. Go to God's Word and find the answer to your problem. God's Word is jam-packed with words of wisdom on how to have a successful life. Study it carefully, do what you see written there, and look out! The blessings of peace, joy, success, and loving relationships will overflow.

More to Explore: Proverbs 11:12

Girl Talk: Are you getting into the Bible each day? Reading a chapter each day is a great way to learn what God wants for you. Just dive in, and God will speak to you.

God Talk: "Lord, I know you gave us the Bible to guide our lives. Please help me to learn what I need to learn. Help me to understand what you are saying to me through your Word. Amen."

From *No Boys Allowed* by Kristi Holl

"Speak, for your servant is listening."

—1 Samuel 3:10

Big Plans for Little People

What if God had something in mind for you from the time you were born—even before? What if you started to train for it right after you stopped drinking out of a baby bottle?

That's what happened to Samuel. Before he was even born, his mother promised that he would be brought up in the temple by Eli. Right after he was weaned, she took him to Eli, and he had to start early learning about the duties of a priest.

But God had something even bigger in mind for Samuel. He revealed to him, in person, what was going to happen to Eli's sons. It was a huge thing, a thing Samuel then had to tell Eli, a thing that made him very sad. Eli had let God down by not disciplining his sons for the wrong they'd done in the temple, and God wasn't going to let that go.

Big hard stuff for Samuel, and yet he did it. He was only about twelve years old when God began this work in him. As he grew up, everybody realized that Samuel was a prophet, a person God revealed himself to.

More to Explore: Jeremiah 1:4–5

Girl Talk: What do you think God has in mind for your life? It's ok if you don't have any idea yet.

God Talk: "God, even before I was born, you knew me and loved me. Thank you that you have a plan for my life. Give me the strength to do whatever it is you want me to do—now and in the future. Amen."

From *That Is So Me* by Nancy Rue

241

" 'My thoughts are not your thoughts, neither are your ways my ways,' declares the Lord. 'As the heavens are higher than the earth, so are my ways higher than your ways and my thoughts than your thoughts.' "

—Isaiah 55:8–9

Sarah's Big Surprise

Sarai, later called Sarah, was a princess. Her name even meant "princess." But Sarai's castle was a tent pitched here and there from Canaan to Mesopotamia.

Sarai knew the Lord had promised her husband Abram he'd be the father of a great nation and many generations would come from him. She also knew in order for God to make a great nation from their children, she'd have to have babies who would grow up and have babies. But their cradle was empty. And in that day, if a woman couldn't have children, people thought God had cursed her. That she'd done something to make God mad at her.

Ten years had passed since God's promise to give Sarai and Abram children. She was seventy-five years old. She wasn't getting any younger, and she still hadn't had a baby. Sarai doubted that God's promise would ever come true. But God still had his own plan. The Lord came to Abram again. He changed Abram's name to Abraham and Sarai's name to Sarah.

"I'll bless Sarah and give you a son by her," God said, "She'll be the mother of nations. Kings will come from her."

Sarah laughed at the thought that she, a ninety-year-old woman, could be having a baby. But nothing gets in the way of God's plan. When Sarah gave birth to a son, they named him Isaac. The name *Isaac* means "laughter." Sarah said, "God has brought me laughter, and everyone who hears about this will laugh with me. Who would've thought I'd nurse a child at my age?"

Sarah learned that God uses a different clock than we do. God keeps his promises, but he does it in his perfect time. And

God's perfect time for something to happen isn't usually soon enough for us.

Have you ever prayed and prayed and waited and waited for something? Have you ever lost your patience with God? Maybe you prayed for a new brother or sister. Or you asked God to help you pass a math test you studied for. Maybe you prayed for your parents to get back together. Sometimes God says no. Sometimes he says yes. Other times he'll tell you to wait. Waiting is hard. But God always knows what's best.

More to Explore: Psalm 27:14

Girl Talk: Have you ever asked God for something and then had to wait a long time for it to happen?

God Talk: "Jesus, please help me remember that your way is best. Help me wait for you with patience and peace. Amen."

From *Real Girls of the Bible* by Mona Hodgson

"Keep my Sabbath days of rest."

—Leviticus 19:30 (NLT)

Take a Break!

Early in Old Testament times, God gave his people the Ten Commandments, or rules for living. One commandment said to rest one day out of every seven. Most believers choose Sunday as their day of rest. It is time to be spent in God's house with other believers, as well as resting time away from work.

Jesus was also concerned about the apostles getting too tired. Once, they were so busy that they weren't taking time to rest. "Because so many people were coming and going that they did not even have a chance to eat, he said to them, 'Come with me by yourselves to a quiet place and get some rest'" (Mark 6:31). Someone once joked, "Seven days without rest makes one weak." However, it's true. You can't be strong and exhausted at the same time. So follow God's plan, and rest one day a week. If you do, you'll enjoy the other six much more!

More To Explore: Exodus 20:8 and Leviticus 26:2

Girl Talk: Make a list of all your activities during one week. Do you have enough time to rest? If not, pray about which activities to cut back on.

God Talk: "Lord, thank you for giving us a day of rest. Please help me make the best use of my time so that I can actually take a day to rest. Thank you for always wanting what is best for me. Amen."

From *Shine On, Girl!* By Kristi Holl

"Great peace have those who love your law, and nothing can make them stumble."

—Psalm 119:165

Chill

When Jacki moved with her family from a city in the East to a small Midwestern town, she immediately checked out the Dance Club. Jacki had ten years' experience in ballet and had performed in the *Nutcracker Suite* many times. By the time she moved, rehearsals had already begun for the Christmas performance. Jacki observed that none of the girls in lead parts were half as talented as she was. Jacki joined the group that danced in the background, but she burned with jealousy over the "star" part. Finally, Jacki could stand it no longer. She talked to the dance instructor. "I don't mean to brag or anything, but I could do a much better job in the lead." Several girls overheard her, and Jacki feared she'd made a few enemies. Sure enough, girls started avoiding her.

If Jacki had loved God's Word and made it a part of her life—and her actions—she could have avoided stumbling into the "jealousy" and "arrogance" traps. She could have been at peace if she'd acted according to the Scripture: "Love is patient, love is kind and is not jealous; love does not brag and is not arrogant" (1 Corinthians 13:4 NASB).

There's no need to stumble through life, falling down constantly and having to pick yourself up. Instead, learn to love God's laws—and live in peace.

More to Explore: Romans 15:13

Girl Talk: Are there areas in your life where you stumble? What verses in the Bible could you apply to bring peace to the situations?

God Talk: "Lord, I don't want to make trouble for myself. Teach me to love your laws. Amen."

From *Chick Chat* by Kristi Holl

"Oh, how I love your law! I meditate on it all day long."
—Psalm 119:97

Go Ahead—Soak It Up!

Do you ever soak in a tub full of bubbles? It's soothing, peaceful, and totally relaxing—pure heaven. So is soaking in God's Word. When we love something, we love to think about it. If you love a person, it's the natural thing to do to think about him or her. And if you love God's Word, his letters to us in the Bible, you'll spend time thinking about it. You'll ponder how to apply the words to your life.

When you soak in the tub, your skin wrinkles like a prune. That's changing from the outside in. When you soak in God's Word, he changes you from the inside out. Meditating on Scripture verses can replace stress with peace; sickness with healing; anger with compassion; hate with love; worry with faith; and weariness with energy. That's a lasting kind of makeover. If you have a special need right now—peace, rest, strength to persist—find a verse that specifically addresses that subject. Memorize it, or at least carry around the verse on a card. Then, at free moments during the day, read and think about the verse, especially how you could apply it to your life and situation.

More to Explore: Deuteronomy 6:6–9 and Psalm 1:2

Girl Talk: Use the concordance at the back of your Bible or an online source to find a verse you want to memorize. Write it down, and read it several times today.

God Talk: "Lord, thank you for giving me the Bible to answer my questions. Help me to look to your Word whenever I have a need. Amen."

From *No Boys Allowed* by Kristi Holl

"Listen to me, O my people, while I give you stern warnings. O Israel, if you would only listen! . . . But no, my people wouldn't listen."

—Psalm 81:8, 11 (NLT)

Are You Listening?

God wants his followers to listen to him. He gives serious warnings to us when we are taking a wrong path and headed in a bad direction. Like a frustrated parent, he too often sees his people refuse to listen to his warnings.

You may have a talent for hearing only what you want to hear. When you're on the phone with a friend, you can easily tune out your mother's call to help cook supper or your dad's warning to finish your homework and get to bed. Maybe you don't want to be disturbed, or you just don't like what they're saying. Many times, we ignore our heavenly Father the same way.

We are told that the whole Bible is useful for straightening us out and teaching us to live our lives rightly (see 2 Timothy 3:16). Through the Bible, the Lord warns us of pitfalls and steers us in the right direction. God also sees our hard times and wants to comfort us. God is still speaking to us through his Word. Are you listening?

More to Explore: Isaiah 1:19–20

Girl Talk: Do you listen to what God has to say in the Bible? If not, why not? If you do pay attention, what do you do with the instructions and warnings?

God Talk: "Lord, I need to listen to you better. Help me make the changes that need to be made in my life. Amen."

From *Chick Chat* by Kristi Holl

246

"I am the vine; you are the branches. If you remain in me and I in you, you will bear much fruit; apart from me you can do nothing."

—John 15:5

Stay Connected

Have you ever planted a garden? If you cut the branches from the vine for any reason, the branches soon wither and die. Your connection to God is just like the relationship between a branch and the vine it's growing out of.

Today, make that flow through Jesus Christ uninterrupted. By saying he is the vine and you are a branch, Jesus stressed the need for you to stay connected to him. Branches are cut off vines for many reasons. Environmental issues like wind and cold; hungry wild animals; and bugs and insects worming their way through all pose threats to branches on a vine.

You, too, face cold situations sometimes. Your circumstances might make you feel like a wild beast is trying to eat you up! Little by little, worries seem to sneak into your heart, like a pesky inchworm. These all threaten to cut you off from Jesus Christ, the vine.

One of the ways branches are protected is by covering or wrapping them. You can cover yourself too! Ban these branch cutters from your life by praying. Spend time sharing your thoughts with him, and listening for his voice to speak to you.

More To Explore: John 15

Girl Talk: What things threaten to cut you off from God?

God Talk: "Father God, thank you for helping me stay connected to you today. I understand that I can do nothing without your help. Amen."

From *My Beautiful Daughter* by Tasha Douglas

"None of you should look out just for your own good. You should also look out for the good of others."

—Philippians 2:4 (NIrV)

It's Not Fair!

Lexy was angry when she came to the supper table. What made it even worse was that she was angry about being angry. Recently, Dad had come home from his tour of duty with the military, and Lexy didn't like the way she felt.

I should be happy, she thought. *I should be glad Dad is home.* But she had mixed-up feelings about all that was going on.

Partway through the meal, she started in. She complained about the things her older sister Brianna got to do that Lexy didn't. She whined that her little brother Ethan always got special treatment. Her parents listened. They told her that they treated each of their kids differently because each of their kids needed different things. Lexy wasn't sure she believed them.

After dinner, Brianna and Ethan left the table, and the kitchen suddenly grew quiet. Lexy sat with elbows on the table, feeling ignored.

"I've been thinking." Dad broke into her thoughts. "When I was away, I kept thinking about what I'd like to do with each of you when I got home."

Lexy stood up. *Sure. Take Ethan to the circus. Take Brianna to—*

"When it was really hot—it felt like 300 degrees at least—I remembered how you love ice cream. You and I are the only ones who can eat a whole La La Palooza. Eight scoops of Bridgeman's ice cream smothered in a double serving of butterscotch, pineapple, and strawberry toppings; nuts; cherries; and a sliced banana!"

Lexy looked at Dad. He was right. Scoop after scoop of ice cream. Eating a whole La La Palooza was absolutely the only thing she could do better than both Brianna and Ethan.

Lexy giggled. "Eat it all and you get a medal!"

"Last time you and I went to Bridgeman's was just before I shipped out," Dad said. "You and I sat and ate and talked. We talked about all the ways you were going to grow up when I was gone."

Tears welled up in Lexy's eyes. It had been one of the most special times of her life.

"Want to go now?" Dad asked. "Just you and me? You can tell me all the good things that have happened to you this year. No Ethan to interrupt. No Brianna with a phone growing out of her ear. How about it?"

Lexy smiled. "I'd like that," she said. In that moment, she knew. *Dad really does think about what's best for each of us.* And she felt loved right down to her toes.

More to Explore: Colossians 3:14

Girl Talk: What can you do to make sure that everyone in your family feels like an important part?

God Talk: "Jesus, please show me what special thing I can do to show love to each member of my family. Amen."

From *Girl Talk* by Lois Walfrid Johnson

"He calls his own sheep by name and leads them out."
—John 10:3

Jesus Calling

For the first few days of school, you might wear a nametag until the teacher learns who everybody is. Don't you love it, though, the first time she calls you by your name, without having to look at your tag? She took the time to learn your name. It's cool.

The bigger the class, the longer it takes. And in middle school, when a teacher has more than one class, it could be a week or two. Think about God, with the billions of people on the earth he has to teach—not to mention all the ones who have lived before now. He knows every one of them by name. Not just "Shelby," "Meg," "Bethany." He knows middle names, last names, nicknames—without nametags or a seating chart.

Imagine God calling your name right out loud. If it feels so good when a human teacher knows who you are, how would it feel to hear your name coming out of that almighty mouth?

That's how important you are to God—enough for him to know your one-of-a-kind name and call you by it so he can lead you into the life he has planned for you—the life with your name on it.

Listen. He's calling.

More to Explore: John 10:14–15

Girl Talk: How does it feel to know that God knows everything about you—even the yucky stuff—and still loves you more than you can imagine?

God Talk: "Jesus, thank you that you care about me so much. It's hard for me to wrap my head around sometimes. Help me to hear your voice when you call my name."

From *That Is So Me* by Nancy Rue

"Your word is a lamp for my feet, a light on my path."
—Psalm 119:105

Illuminating Your Life

We're all on a journey through life. It can be dark and confusing at times. But God's Word—the principles and commandments in it—lights the way. It makes the narrow path visible, so we don't have to stumble and fall. Lamps and lights also serve as warning signals, like when a bridge is out. In the same manner, God's Word acts as a signal, warning us away from trouble.

Maybe you can't find a specific Bible verse to cover your situation. If not, pray and ask God for his advice. He promises to give it to you. James 1:5 (NLT) says, "If you need wisdom—if you want to know what God wants you to do—ask him, and he will gladly tell you. He will not resent your asking." Sometimes you can sense the answer right away, and sometimes you have to wait for a while before you know what to do. But God *will* answer. "You will light my lamp; the Lord my God will enlighten my darkness" (Psalm 18:28 NKJV).

Put an end to the darkness on your path through life. Turn on the Light!

More to Explore: Job 29:2–3

Girl Talk: When you have a problem, do you do what *you* want to do? Or do you ask God what *he* wants you to do?

God Talk: "Lord, I don't always wait for you to tell me what to do. Help me to stop and pray about my problems before I do anything. I know what you want for me is best. Thank you. Amen."

From *Girlz Rock* by Kristi Holl

"You do not have because you do not ask God."

—James 4:2

Asking and Receiving

People try to get their needs met in many ways. They might work hard for something. They might steal it. They may be jealous, so they fight for something that belongs to someone else. But none of these ways work. They still don't have what they want or need. Earlier, Jesus told his followers, "Until now you have asked for nothing in My name; ask and you will receive, so that your joy may be made full" (John 16:24 NASB). But often, people don't ask God, and so they don't receive what they need.

Wishing isn't praying. Hoping isn't praying. Asking God to meet your needs is praying. Some people complain that God isn't answering their prayers, but they haven't actually asked God for anything! Couldn't God read your mind and give you what you need anyway? Yes—and sometimes he does. But he wants us to ask and receive. He wants us to talk to him about everything—including making a new friend and buying some jeans that fit. And his promise? "And my God will meet all your needs according to the riches of his glory in Christ Jesus" (Philippians 4:19).

Do you "have not" because you "ask not"? Then talk to God right now. He wants to meet your needs.

More to Explore: Luke 11:9–10

Girl Talk: How much time do you spend wishing and hoping for something? How much time do you spend asking God for what you need?

God Talk: "Lord, help me remember to ask you for everything. Thank you for providing the things I need. Amen."

From *Chick Chat* by Kristi Holl

251

"Do not rely on mediums and psychics, for you will be defiled by them. I, the Lord, am your God."

—Leviticus 19:31 (NLT)

Who Ya Gonna Call?

A Ouija board, palm reading, horoscopes, fortune tellers—just a harmless way to have fun at birthday parties and sleepovers? No way! God's Word specifically warns us against trusting anyone who claims to contact the dead, tell the future, or see into the spiritual realm for information not available to the rest of us. Why the warning? You will be wrongly directed by them. If you want wisdom and insight for making decisions, go to the Lord instead, who is your God.

God understands that you need help. You want to make choices that will have a positive effect on your future. But don't go to psychics and fortune tellers. Go directly to God instead. "If you need wisdom—if you want to know what God wants you to do—ask him, and he will gladly tell you. He will not resent your asking" (James 1:5 NLT).

If you want true help for your future, go to the Bible for answers, and pray directly to God. You can't go wrong there!

More to Explore: Leviticus 20:6

Girl Talk: Ever read horoscopes in a magazine or wanted to call a psychic hotline? Do you know that God has all of the answers and wisdom you'll ever need?

God Talk: "Lord, I trust you for direction in my life. I know I don't need to consult anyone else. I just want to follow you. Amen."

From *No Boys Allowed* by Kristi Holl

"Here is my servant, whom I uphold, my chosen one in whom I delight; I will put my Spirit on him, and he will bring justice to the nations."

—Isaiah 42:1

Sensing God's Smile

It feels so good when a person you look up to is proud of you. You probably sit up taller and get a big ol' grin on your face. And best of all, you want to do even better.

What if GOD said that about you? He actually does sometimes. Can't you feel God's pleasure when you help your little brother with his homework, even though he has recently flushed yours down the toilet? Don't you experience God's pride when you refuse to spread that rumor that would really get you some attention? God loves it when we do it his way. He delights in us.

We're all constantly doing things that disappoint him. But being the great Maker of Promises, God promised us that he would send someone in whom he delighted every minute of every day. Someone who could show us how to be better in the delighting-God department, so that the world we live in would be more fair.

God announced that this someone was here in a loud, clear voice when Jesus was baptized. He said from heaven, "This is my Son, whom I love; with him I am well pleased" (Matthew 3:17). Jesus is here, showing us how to please God too.

More to Explore: Jeremiah 9:23–24

Girl Talk: What little things have you done recently that made God smile?

God Talk: "Jesus, thank you that you set such an awesome example for me. Help me to become more like you. Amen."

From *That Is So Me* by Nancy Rue

253

"Friendship with the Lord is reserved for those who fear him. With them he shares the secrets of his covenant."

—Psalm 25:14 (NLT)

God's Friend

You probably have one or two very good friends. They get to be your friends, because they show respect to you. They respect your opinion, your time, your property, and your feelings. Because they treat you this way, you trust them and share many secrets with them—secrets you don't share with just anyone. You have no desire to share special things with people who make fun of your opinions or ignore your feelings.

God reveals special things to us too—if we respect him and obey his Word. If we are already doing what his Word says, we are his friends. And when we need special information (like "Should I go to this party?" or "Should I try out for the swim team?"), he will give it to us. Jesus told his disciples the same thing: "I no longer call you servants, because a servant does not know his master's business. Instead, I have called you friends, for everything that I learned from my Father I have made known to you" (John 15:15).

What could be more exciting than being friends with God and having him tell you secrets about himself, your life, and his many promises?

More to Explore: John 14:21

Girl Talk: What kinds of friends do you like best? What kind of friend are you? Are you friends with God?

God Talk: "Lord, thank you for wanting to be my friend. I'm glad that we can share secrets with each other. Amen."

From *Chick Chat* by Kristi Holl

254

"Let the peace (soul harmony which comes) from Christ rule (act as umpire continually) in your hearts [deciding and settling with finality all questions that arise in your minds]."
—Colossians 3:15 (AMP)

Wait and Listen

Let's say you need to make a decision. You want to go out for volleyball, your mom suggests that you sign up for flute lessons, and your dad thinks you might start an after-school babysitting business instead. It's your choice. You wish you could do all three, but there isn't enough time. You have to choose, but you're so confused!

Don't blindly push ahead with a plan until you feel at peace. Sit or lie down at night, be still, and pray about your situation. Is there any anxiety in your heart? Do you think of reasons this might be a bad idea? Does your conscience warn you that there's something wrong in your plan of action? If you sense any of these things, stop. Don't make that decision yet. It might not be God's will, or it just might not be the right time yet. "Trust in the Lord with all your heart; do not depend on your own understanding. Seek his will in all you do, and he will direct your paths" (Proverbs 3:5–6 NLT). Wait for God to guide you where it's safe to follow.

More To Explore: James 1:5

Girl Talk: Do you have a question for God right now? What would you like to know? Ask him for help, then be quiet and wait for an answer. He will tell you!

God Talk: "Lord, please help me be quiet and wait for your guidance. I want to be certain I'm doing your will. Amen."

From *Shine On, Girl!* by Kristi Holl

255

"The Lord appeared to us in the past, saying: 'I have loved you with an everlasting love; I have drawn you with unfailing kindness.'"

—Jeremiah 31:3

Never-Ending Love

Our limited human minds find it hard to grasp how much God loves us. His love continues forever and can be counted on in all our times of need. Think about the person you love most in the world. Then multiply the love you feel for this person a thousand times. That's only a tiny drop of the love—the everlasting love—that God feels toward you.

Every day for a month, take a few minutes to think about how much God loves you. Say it out loud: "God loves *me*. The all-knowing, all-powerful, all-loving God of the universe loves *me*!" See how that changes your feelings during the month. We would live much differently if we truly understood how much God loves us. He wants only the best for us—all the time. God wanted us so much that he pulled us to him. Jesus said, "No one can come to me unless the Father who sent me draws them" (John 6:44). People do not come to Christ strictly because of their own ideas or decisions. It is God pulling them to him. He loves you and wants you that much!

More to Explore: Psalm 103:17 and Titus 3:3–6

Girl Talk: Do you feel that God really loves you? How do you think he shows his love to you each day?

God Talk: "Lord, it's hard to believe that you love me so much, but I am so grateful to have your love. Help me to show love to others the way you show your love for me. Amen."

From *Girlz Rock* by Kristi Holl

"Everyone who hears these words of mine and puts them into practice is like a wise man who built his house on the rock."
—Matthew 7:24

Solid Rock

They had some pretty big rainstorms in the land where Jesus lived. You may have seen some like them, where the rain comes down in sheets and washes away big chunks of dirt and sand. You might even have heard about mudslides, where whole houses tumble down a mountain when the big rains come.

Then, as now, it was best to build a house on a strong foundation—like rock. It wasn't going to move and it wasn't going to wash away. God is described as a rock sometimes, because he doesn't move away, and he's always there for protection. It also makes sense, then, to build your *life* on rock, the God-rock.

That means making your decisions based on God's ways. Think about God's love in the way you treat other people. Move forward with God's promises in your mind. If you do that, you won't be "washed away" when the "rains" come. There's no time like now to find that rock and start building.

More to Explore: 1 Peter 2:4–6

Girl Talk: Listen to your life. Is it raining anywhere? Those rainy places will tell you where you need the God-rock. Get there, before the storm breaks.

God Talk: "God, I want to build my life on your foundation. Show me how to hold tight to you so that I can withstand the rains of life. Amen."

From *That Is So Me* by Nancy Rue

257

"One day Jesus was praying in a certain place. When he finished, one of his disciples said to him, 'Lord, teach us to pray.'"

—Luke 11:1

Learning to Pray

Jesus had the habit of prayer, of talking to his Father, praising him and asking him for things. After one of these prayer times, a disciple asked Jesus to teach them how to pray too.

Morgan's Sunday school teacher challenged the whole class to pray at least ten minutes every day that week. But each time Morgan sat down with her timer to pray, her mind went blank. She felt guilty, but she couldn't think of anything to say. Her mom gave her a seven-minute formula for prayer, but Morgan felt silly using it. She didn't have any success with prayer as long as she tried to copy someone else's prayer method.

Don't try to imitate someone else's prayer life. We're all different, and our prayer lives will be different. Our life circumstances are different too. Your grandmother who lives alone might pray two hours every morning. You'd have to get up at 4:00 a.m. to do that and still get to school on time. Don't compare your prayer times to anyone else's. Instead, talk to God. Ask him to teach you how to pray, how much to pray, what to pray for, and how to listen for his answers.

Don't be shy about asking God for help with your prayer life. He's willing to help you with anything. "Let us come boldly to the throne of our gracious God. There we will receive his mercy, and we will find grace to help us when we need it" (Hebrews 4:16 NLT).

If you need help with your prayer life, be honest with God. Begin by saying, "Lord, teach me to pray."

More to Explore: Psalm 19:14 and Romans 8:26

Girl Talk: How often do you pray? Do you know what to say, or do you find yourself stumbling along? Have you asked God for help?

God Talk: "Lord, I feel so lucky to be able to talk to you whenever I need to. I'm not always sure what to say. Please help me find the words. I want a better prayer life with you. Thank you for always being there. Amen."

From *Girlz Rock* by Kristi Holl

258

"And so I tell you, keep on asking, and you will be given what you ask for. Keep on looking, and you will find. Keep on knocking, and the door will be opened."

—Luke 11:9 (NLT)

Seek and Find

Have you ever been on a scavenger hunt? The list of items to find is long, and sometimes you look a long time before you find an item. Prayer can be like that. God promises that if we keep on asking, we'll be given what we need. If we keep searching for answers, we'll find them.

Can you ask for and receive *anything* you desire? Probably not. No matter how many times you ask your parents for a car of your own, you won't get one until you're old enough to drive safely. That's because they love you and want to protect you. God, your heavenly Father, is the same.

As you look for God's answers, one of two things will happen. God may give you what you asked for, or he may change your desire *as you spend time with him.* You may lose your desire for what you've been praying for. God will change your desire to match what he wants to give you—something much better than what you asked for in the first place.

More to Explore: 1 John 3:21–22

Girl Talk: Do you ask God for what you need? How confident are you that God will answer your prayers?

God Talk: "Lord, I know I need to ask you for what I need. Help me to see what you want me to see. Show me the doors you want me to knock on. Amen."

From *No Boys Allowed* by Kristi Holl

"Test them all; hold on to what is good."

—1 Thessalonians 5:21

Testing! Testing!

You honestly want to do what God wants, but sometimes you have trouble recognizing his voice. Is it God or just your own ideas? You can't test those voices until you know God better. You may think of him as an angry judge—until you read: "Therefore, there is now no condemnation for those who are in Christ Jesus" (Romans 8:1). You're not sure you can count on God—until you read: "And surely I am with you always, to the very end of the age" (Matthew 28:20). The better you get to know God, the easier it is to recognize his still, small voice. Consistent reading and study of the Bible will renew *your* mind. Knowing God's truth will help you recognize the lies you'll hear in the world. It's like learning anything new. Before you could add, if someone had claimed that two plus two equaled five, you probably would have believed her. You wouldn't know any different. But once you learned your addition tables, if someone told you that two plus two equaled five, you'd spot the lie. You'd know the truth by then—that two plus two equals four.

In the same way, you can spot the lies of the world by filling your mind more and more with God's truth. Test everything. Compare what you hear to the Word of God.

More to Explore: Acts 17:11

Girl Talk: Do you believe everything you hear? How can you use the Bible to discover whether people are telling the truth?

God Talk: "Lord, thank you for the Bible that teaches me the truth. Help me to go to it for answers first. Amen."

From *Chick Chat* by Kristi Holl

"You are the salt of the earth."

—Matthew 5:13

Staying Salty

When somebody says, "Please pass the salt," you know that person wants a little more flavor on her hamburger or her French fries. Back in Jesus' day, salt was also used for preserving food, the way we put ours in the refrigerator to keep it from going bad. Salt was valuable because without it, supper would be a rotten affair.

When Jesus said, "You are the salt of the earth," he meant that you are important. You can give life "flavor," make it fun and interesting, show people love, be who you are. And you can also keep the good things going. By being honest and compassionate and brave, you preserve those values the way salt preserves beef jerky.

"But if the salt loses its saltiness," Jesus said, "how can it be made salty again?" In his day, the salt used in Israel was from the Dead Sea and was full of impure stuff that caused it to lose some of its flavor. The people then would have understood that Jesus was saying, "Don't be sinful and impure, or you can't be what you were put here to be—a giver of life and a saver of goodness."

More to Explore: 1 Peter 2:12

Girl Talk: Do any of your friends need a little "salt" in their lives? How can you give them a taste of God?

God Talk: "Jesus, please use me to help others and to bring your 'salt' to the world. I want to keep the good things going and preserve all the values that you love."

From *That Is So Me* by Nancy Rue

"Jesus said to her, 'I am the resurrection and the life. The one who believes in me will live, even though they die; and whoever lives by believing in me will never die. Do you believe this?'"
—John 11:25–26

The Name Game

Has anyone ever called you something besides your given name? If it was a negative term, you know how much it hurts. That's because to Father God, your name represents your character, saying something to the world about who you are.

God has many names. And each one tells you something about God's nature too. But if you call God by one name in particular, you'll really get to know God in a special way. Today, think about that first name God used to help you understand that trusting God is all you need: *I Am*.

Can you imagine asking someone their name and they answer with, "I am"? What would you think of them? Maybe you'd be tapping your foot, waiting for them to finish their sentence thinking, okay, so you are ...? Thankfully, Jesus Christ clarified the fuzziness of Father God's "I Am" statement.

Jesus spoke the words "I AM" frequently as he shared his life with his followers. His words make it clear that Jesus is the one who leads daughters to Father God, and that God is the source of everything you need today and always.

More To Explore: John 8:12; John 10:9; John 15:5

Girl Talk: Do you know what your name means?

God Talk: "Father God, thank you for revealing yourself to me through your many names. I'm depending on you to be all that I need today as I follow your son Jesus Christ, whose name is above any other."

From *My Beautiful Daughter* by Tasha Douglas

262

"And pray in the Spirit on all occasions with all kinds of prayers and requests."

— Ephesians 6:18

Say a Little Prayer

Pray on ALL occasions? When you're lonely? When you're at a party? When you wake up in the night? When you jog? When you eat? Yep — all those times, and more. God's interested in every detail of your life and loves you to share it with him. Don't you just love it when your best girlfriend calls to talk? You eagerly tell each other every tiny detail about your activities of the day. God feels the same way when we frequently take time out to talk to him.

Sometimes we don't pray much, because we get too busy with things we need to do. We might only pray when we're in trouble or upset. We do pray more when in desperate need of guidance or comfort. But sometimes we don't pray because we don't know what to say. We are to "pray in the Spirit" — and it is the Holy Spirit who helps us to pray. "The Spirit helps us in our weakness. We do not know what we ought to pray for, but the Spirit himself intercedes for us through wordless groans" (Romans 8:26).

Go ahead. Close this book and take a few minutes to tell God about your day. He's waiting to listen, and he's all ears.

More to Explore: Romans 12:12 NLT

Girl Talk: How often do you pray to God? What do you tell him about?

God Talk: "Lord, I'm glad I can talk to you whenever I need to. Thank you for always being available. Help me to remember to talk to you all the time. Amen."

From *No Boys Allowed* by Kristi Holl

"Yet faith comes from listening to this message of good news — the Good News about Christ."

— Romans 10:17 (NLT)

Walking by Faith

Dawn's faith was tested when her parents divorced, and she moved from a small town to a big city. From a sprawling house on a quiet street, she moved into a noisy fourth-floor apartment. In her small school, she'd been in musical groups and always had a part in the spring play. At her huge new school, she felt like a drop of water in the ocean — invisible and swallowed up. And yet, Dawn faced each day expecting something good to happen. She trusted that God had everything under control and would bring good out of it.

Where did she get such faith in the face of so many unwelcome changes? The Word of God. She repeated these verses every day: "'For I know the plans I have for you,' declares the Lord, 'plans to prosper you and not to harm you, plans to give you hope and a future'" (Jeremiah 29:11); and "we know that in all things God works for the good of those who love him, who have been called according to his purpose" (Romans 8:28). Why does speaking God's Word have such power? "For the word of God is alive and active. Sharper than any double-edged sword, it penetrates even to dividing soul and spirit, joints and marrow" (Hebrews 4:12).

More to Explore: Romans 1:16

Girl Talk: What things do you have strong faith about? In what areas of your life is your faith weak?

God Talk: "Lord, thank you for your Word and its power to make my faith stronger. Help my faith in you to grow. Amen."

From *Chick Chat* by Kristi Holl

"In the same way, let your light shine before others, that they may see your good deeds and glorify your Father in heaven."
—Matthew 5:16

Twinkling Like a Star

What do you think of when you hear the word "star"? After the ones in the sky, you probably go to "TV star," "movie star," "rock star." We name them after those twinkly heavenly bodies because they are somehow "above" ordinary people, and they seem to shine more. They have talent or beauty or knock-out personalities that make the rest of us want to bask in their "light."

Jesus said *all* of us need to let our lights shine. We're supposed to use our talents, share the beautiful parts of ourselves, make people happy. But there's a difference between that kind of light and the light movie and rock stars send out. The shining Jesus wants us to do is not for the praise and the fame and the adoring fans. It's for *God's* glory. He wants us to do shining things—like love and be generous and make sacrifices—so that God will get the praise and the fame and the adoring fans.

More to Explore: Ephesians 5:8

Girl Talk: Think about your talents. Come on, you have tons. Can you make a baby laugh when nobody else can? Make a killer tuna fish sandwich? Whatever those lights are, think of how you can shine them in a way that shows God to someone.

God Talk: "Jesus, you gave me an inner light like a star! Help me to shine that light into the world. And let people see that my light comes straight from you."

From *That Is So Me* by Nancy Rue

"The person who rests in the shadow of the Most High God will be kept safe by the Mighty One. I will say about the Lord, 'He is my place of safety. He is like a fort to me. He is my God. I trust in him.'"

—Psalm 91:1–2 (NIrV)

How's My Mom?

As Mom and Maddie and two-year-old Rachel walked the short distance home from church, Maddie noticed the shadow in Mom's eyes. Since Dad stopped living with them, Maddie had seen that shadow of unhappiness often. That evening, Mom started drinking again.

Maddie pretended that she didn't see what was happening. Yet as she watched TV, she kept count of the glasses, and her uneasiness grew. Sometimes when Mom drank, she just got sad and talked strange. Other times she acted mean.

In her funny toddler way, Rachel went over to Mom and held up her sippy cup. Mom pushed the cup aside. Rachel tried again.

"Don't bother me!" snapped Mom, shoving the little girl away.

Rachel yowled. Maddie jumped up and pulled her into the kitchen. After filling her bottle, she took Rachel to the bedroom, changed her clothes, and put her to bed.

Feeling as though a giant hand twisted her insides, Maddie crept into her own bed. For a long time she lay there, afraid to fall asleep. Eyes full of tears, Maddie wondered as she had a hundred times, *What did I do wrong? Where are you, God? I'm so scared.*

The next day, as Maddie was returning home from school, she heard Rachel crying from the sidewalk. Bounding up the porch steps, Maddie tried to open the front door. It was locked. Peering in the window, Maddie saw Mom sprawled on the sofa, sound asleep. A bottle lay on the floor beside her.

Maddie felt sick. She ran around the house to the backyard and saw Rachel's playpen in full sunlight.

When Rachel saw Maddie, the little girl held up her arms and whimpered. Maddie picked her up and hugged her. When she saw Rachel's sunburned arms and face, Maddie broke into sobs. *Oh, God, what should I do?* This time her cry for help was a prayer.

In that moment she remembered Pastor Evenson at church.

Could I talk to him? Maddie wondered.

Staggering under Rachel's weight, Maddie stood up and started walking to church.

If you have hard things in your life, Jesus understands when you hurt. He wants you to ask him for help. He wants to heal you. But you also need to talk with people you trust.

More to Explore: John 14:1

Girl Talk: Are you facing tough situations in your life that require backup?

God Talk: "Thank you, Lord, for caring about what happens to me. If I'm ever in trouble, remind me that I can always ask you for help. Help me to also talk to the right grown-up. Amen."

From *Girl Talk* by Lois Walfrid Johnson

"The Lord came and stood there, calling as at the other times, 'Samuel! Samuel!' Then Samuel said, 'Speak, for your servant is listening.'"

—1 Samuel 3:10

Who's That?

Monica felt a nudge, almost a gentle whisper inside, when she first met the girl in the apartment next door. Monica hoped they could be friends and walk to school together, since they were in the same grade. However, her internal alarm whispered, "Don't trust her." The following week Monica overheard the girl lie to her mother about where she'd been. Later, after the girl visited Monica's apartment, some money was missing from her room. Was the funny feeling in her stomach the Lord trying to warn Monica about her new friend?

We must be alert and notice when God is trying to get our attention. Remember when God talked to Moses out of the burning bush? Moses could have been so self-focused that he never noticed the bush off to the side. But Moses was paying attention. "So when the Lord saw that he turned aside to look, God called to him from the midst of the bush and said, 'Moses, Moses!' And he said, 'Here I am'" (Exodus 3:4 NKJV).

Invite God to speak to you. Like Moses, pay attention to your surroundings. Like Samuel, perk up your ears and say, "Talk to me, Lord. I'm listening."

More to Explore: Genesis 22:11

Girl Talk: Does God speak to you? How do you experience his voice? How can you know it's him?

God Talk: "Lord, I can't run my life without you. I need to hear from you every day. Please teach me how to hear you even better. Amen."

From *Chick Chat* by Kristi Holl

267

"Blessed are the peacemakers, for they will be called children of God."

—Matthew 5:9

Give Peace a Chance

Don't you love it when the whole family gets together for Christmas or Thanksgiving or just a big ol' reunion? It's so cool to sit at the table and look around and realize you're part of something special that nobody can take away from you. Nobody can gossip you out of *that* circle.

You're also part of God's family, an even bigger group which frankly doesn't always get along. If you really want to make God the Father happy, try teaching other members of God's family how to cooperate rather than fight. Help your brothers and sisters negotiate who gets the remote without drawing blood. Bring your girlfriends together to talk things out instead of joining in the drama. Stop the squabbling on the soccer team and convince the players to focus on teamwork.

In the middle of that, you're going to see who you are. While you're making peace, you'll see that you're strong and brave and loving and righteous. You've become God's Go-To Girl, the one he can count on. Talk about a blessing, huh?

More to Explore: Hebrews 12:14

Girl Talk: How can you be a peacemaker at home? How can you be a peacemaker with your friends?

God Talk: "God, when my friends aren't getting along or when my siblings are picking a fight, give me the courage to make peace. Thank you that I get to be part of your great big family. Amen."

From *That Is So Me* by Nancy Rue

❀

Believing ... It Transforms You

Feeling chubby? Bad hair day? Nothing to wear? Join the club. We're never satisfied with the way we look. We're always trying to change how we appear on the outside. And there's no shortage of companies offering all sorts of expensive things that (they say) can help. But if we want to revamp how we look on the inside, there's only one thing we need to do: believe.

Crack open the Bible, and you'll find oodles of stories about people who've changed radically because they believe. I love the one about Dismas*, the "penitent thief."

Dismas lived during the time of Jesus. He was a liar and a murderer. But most of all, he was a thief. Now in Dismas' line of work, there wasn't much time for believing. Then, too, if there really were a God, Dismas always reasoned, he most certainly wouldn't have anything to do with a low life like him.

In his travels, though, Dismas heard rumors of some Hebrew, a guy called Jesus, who was supposed to be the Savior of the world. But guys like him came and went. Dismas wasn't impressed.

Until he saw Jesus, battered and bloody, on the cross next to his. Dismas knew he, himself, deserved punishment. He'd been caught stealing, and had the lives of others on his hands. And Gestas**, a notorious thief to the left of Jesus, finally got what he deserved. But what had Jesus done to warrant such a death?

At first, like Gestas, Dismas ridiculed Jesus. If he truly was the Savior, why not save himself and Dismas too? But then, Jesus

---

* The Bible doesn't name the thief to Jesus' right. However, the Gospel of Nicodemus gives him this name.

** The Gospel of Nicodemus names the thief to Jesus' left as Gestas.

locked eyes with him and something powerful passed between them. It was as though Jesus looked past the wasted life, the evil crimes, the bitter callousness and offered a clean start, beginning right then, a hope of forgiveness, love, and peace.

Transfixed by the love he saw in Jesus' eyes, Dismas chose to believe.

"Jesus," he said so sincerely tears mixed with his sweat and ran down his face. "Remember me when you come into your kingdom."

"This very day," Jesus answered, "you will be with me in paradise."

And there, on the cross, Dismas was instantly changed—from a ruthless criminal into a saved soul. It's a great example of the transformative beauty of believing.

Now, we don't have to wait until the end of our lives to choose Jesus. We can experience him right here, right now, right this minute. What's more, we can revel in the knowledge that Jesus loved us first. He loved us when we were sinners, and even in our darkest hour, he will always extend forgiveness, love, and peace. Jesus offers us all this, as he did Dismas, if we but do one thing: believe.

—Allia Zobel Nolan

268

"Make every effort to keep the unity of the Spirit through the bond of peace."

— Ephesians 4:3

Powerful Peace

Have an intense desire to be united to fellow believers. Pursue harmony with others enthusiastically. Peace is powerful. It will keep you stuck together with Holy Spirit Super-Glue! Don't let the devil or another person divide you from other followers. Guard your peace and stay together.

Keeping peace and harmony among believers was the apostle Paul's desire too. He wrote, "I appeal to you, brothers and sisters, in the name of our Lord Jesus Christ, that all of you agree with one another in what you say and that there be no divisions among you, but that you be perfectly united in mind and thought" (1 Corinthians 1:10). The devil will work overtime to disturb and disrupt this peace, however. He will set you up to get you upset with others. Why? Because Satan knows how powerful people are when they are united in peace. Most things that happen are not worth losing your peace over — nor your power. So stay glued together!

More To Explore: Romans 14:17 – 19

Girl Talk: In what areas of your life do you sense that you're losing your peace? Ask God for help in keeping your peace and staying united with other Christians.

God Talk: "Lord, sometimes it's so hard to live peacefully with everyone. Give me your strength to do this. Amen."

From *Shine On, Girl!* by Kristi Holl

269

"A wise man will hear and increase learning, and a man of understanding will attain wise counsel."

—Proverbs 1:5 (NKJV)

Anybody Listening?

When you're excited to share something with your family or best friend, do you do all the talking? Do you "tune out" anything others might say because you're so focused on your own speech? Then you are missing an opportunity to grow and learn. When a teacher or parent tries to correct you about something, do you pay attention and consider what is said? Or are you content to simply appear as if you're listening, while you wait for them to finish and go away? Proverbs says you should do the opposite of tuning others out. You'd be much smarter, in fact, to seek out sensible people and ask for guidance.

Don't let your pride trick you into thinking you already know everything. Assume that you don't, and be open to learning from other (hopefully wiser) people in your life. Do two things. First, listen when others share their thoughts with you. Since you already know what YOU know, you won't learn anything by doing all the talking. Learning only increases when you *listen*. Second, if you have a decision to make, seek out sensible, godly people and ask their advice.

Want to put yourself on the fast track to learning? Zip your lip, sharpen your ears, and become wise!

More to Explore: Proverbs 12:1

Girl Talk: When you listen to others, are you really listening to them or thinking about what you will say next?

God Talk: "Lord, thank you for always being a good listener. Help me to be a better listener. Thank you. Amen."

From *No Boys Allowed* by Kristi Holl

"A gossip betrays a confidence; so avoid anyone who talks too much."

—Proverbs 20:19

Loose Lips

Never choose a gossip for a friend. Such a person tells secrets. Don't hang around with someone who reveals private information that should not be passed on.

Sadly, there are people who pretend to be your friends, using smooth talk and flattery to persuade you to reveal your secrets. They like to be "in the know" and enjoy being the first one to spread a story. Gossip creates harsh disagreements that often force a group of friends to split and take sides. This is *not* the kind of people you want for friends. "Watch out for those who cause divisions ... Keep away from them" (Romans 16:17).

What kind of people should you surround yourself with? "A gossip betrays a confidence, but a trustworthy person keeps a secret" (Proverbs 11:13). How can you know who's trustworthy? Test her. Tell her a small secret and wait. Does she keep it to herself? If so, try revealing something more personal. Again, wait a week or two. Does your secret get spread around? Trust and reveal more a little bit at a time. There are trustworthy people you can have for friends. Search for them, but avoid the gossips.

More to Explore: Proverbs 26:20–22

Girl Talk: Are you a gossip? Do you give in to the temptation to tell secrets about other people?

God Talk: "Lord, I don't want to gossip. Take control of what I say and keep my lips sealed." (See Psalm 141:3 NLT.)

From *Chick Chat* by Kristi Holl

271

"A friend loves at all times."

—Proverbs 17:17

Ruth's Family Ties

Ruth was a Moabite woman who married into an Israelite family. When her husband died, Ruth decided to follow her mother-in-law, Naomi, to Israel. Ruth wanted to care for Naomi, who had lost her husband and two sons. Naomi had no one else to care for her, and she wanted to return to her homeland.

Ruth loved Naomi with a love so deep that it led Ruth away from all she'd known and into a foreign land—into a land whose people didn't get along with her people. She chose Naomi's God over the false gods of the Moabites. She chose to serve Naomi even though Naomi had nothing to offer her.

Ruth and Naomi arrived in Bethlehem when the barley fields were golden and ready for harvest. According to the law and custom in Judah at that time, the poor could glean or gather for themselves whatever the harvesters missed. Though Ruth was a woman alone and a foreigner, she stepped out in faith to provide for her mother-in-law.

Boaz, the owner of the field, showed up while Ruth gleaned. He turned to the foreman of his harvesters and asked, "Whose young woman is that?"

The foreman said, "She is the Moabitess who came home with Naomi."

Boaz then spoke to Ruth. "Don't glean in any other field. Follow my servant girls. You will be safe here. And whenever you're thirsty, get a drink from the water jars."

He spoke with kindness and care. Ruth bowed. "Why are you being so kind to a foreigner?"

Boaz said, "I've been told about all you've done for your mother-in-law since the death of your husband. How you left your father and mother and your homeland and came to live with a people you didn't know. May the Lord, the God of Israel, bless you."

That day Ruth carried an unusually large amount of barley home to Naomi.

"Where did you glean today?" Naomi asked. "Blessed be the man who noticed you."

"On the fields of Boaz," Ruth said.

"Boaz is my close relative. He's one of our kinsman-redeemers." Naomi realized then that the Lord hadn't stopped caring for her. The exact field Ruth gleaned from that day belonged to her husband's relative Boaz. And before long, Boaz agreed to marry Ruth.

God blessed Ruth for her faithfulness to God and to Naomi. Ruth discovered God's loyal and loving nature. God gave Ruth a new people, a new home, a new husband, and a son to carry on Naomi's family name.

Like Ruth, you can be a loving friend to your family members. Are you getting to know stepsisters or stepbrothers? Do you have a grandparent living in your home? Or maybe your situation involves a parent who doesn't know Jesus. Can you think of ways to show them the loyal and loving nature of God?

More to Explore: Ruth 1:3–4:22

Girl Talk: What specific thing can you do—today—to be a loving sister, daughter, or friend?

God Talk: "Thank you, Lord, for my family. Help me to be a good sister, daughter, granddaughter, and friend to them. Amen."

From *Real Girls of the Bible* by Mona Hodgson

"Never criticize or condemn—or it will all come back on you. Go easy on others; then they will do the same for you."

—Luke 6:37 (TLB)

Cutting Down

No one enjoys being around someone who is a faultfinder. Don't be a girl who puts others under a microscope, searching for flaws and defects to point out to others. If you judge others, expect the same thing to happen to you.

Maybe you think the girl who sits next to you in band smells odd, and she squeaks like a hyperactive mouse. After band, your best friend pinches her nose and points to Miss Mouse as she leaves. What should you do? Join in and make fun of her? Share the weird things Mouse did during the hour? It's tempting, even though James 4:11 (NKJV) says, "Do not speak evil of one another." Why do we like to do it then? Usually to feel better about ourselves. Cutting someone down makes us feel more important, but it's an unloving thing to do. Don't do it, no matter how tempting. Instead, examine your *own* behavior and learn to accept others, warts and all. Then you'll be in the happy position of having others do that for you.

More to Explore: Romans 2:1

Girl Talk: Have you judged or criticized anyone at school or in your family? Has someone judged or criticized you? How did it make you feel?

God Talk: "Lord, I don't want to be a faultfinder. Please help me talk about others the way I want them to talk about me. Amen."

From *Chick Chat* by Kristi Holl

"Oh, why didn't I listen to my teachers? Why didn't I pay attention to those who gave me instruction? I have come to the brink of utter ruin, and now I must face public disgrace."
—Proverbs 5:13–14 (NLT)

Hearing Impaired

Someone at the end of his life spoke these words. When it was too late, he realized that the teachers in his youth had tried to help him learn valuable lessons for life. But he didn't pay attention and had come to ruin.

You have teachers at home (your parents and grandparents), at school (your instructors), and at church (Sunday school teachers, pastors, and youth leaders). They're all trying to help you learn valuable things so your life will be successful. Sometimes we feel these people are too old and too "out of it" to be able to teach us what we need to know. They didn't grow up in our world, so how can they know what things to teach us?

Because some things never change. Principles for building loving relationships, gaining financial success through hard work, and taking care of our bodies don't change. Those principles are found in the Bible, and the Word of God is the same forever.

More to Explore: Proverbs 15:32 and Jeremiah 3:25

Girl Talk: Do you listen when your parents have something to talk about with you? Do you thank your parents for guiding you?

God Talk: "Lord, I know you gave me my mom and dad and others to help guide me in your ways. Please help me to remember that they love me and want what's best for me. Thank you. Amen."

From *Girlz Rock* by Kristi Holl

274

"Blessed are you among women, and blessed is the child you will bear! But why am I so favored, that the mother of my Lord should come to me?"

—Luke 1:42–43

Let's Celebrate—Together!

Half the fun in having something good happen to you is sharing the joy with someone who's excited for you. God set it up that way. We see it in the Bible, when two women received fabulous news.

First there was Elizabeth, who was "very old" (Luke 1:7) and still didn't have any children. When an angel came to her husband, Zechariah, and told him Elizabeth was going to have a son, Elizabeth was one happy lady.

Six months later, her relative Mary also had a visit from an angel, telling her that she too was going to have a baby. Mary wasn't as excited as Elizabeth at first. She wasn't even married yet. But the angel assured her that this was a good thing, that this baby was the Messiah himself, the Son of God.

Mary hurried to Elizabeth's house, but she didn't even have to tell Elizabeth what was going on. John leaped inside Elizabeth's belly, and she was filled with God's Spirit. Next to Mary and Joseph, she was the first one to believe that Jesus was God's Son, before he was even born. That must have been reassuring to Mary. That's the kind of friends God made us to be.

More to Explore: Psalm 51:8

Girl Talk: Have you ever been really, truly joyful when a friend of yours received good news? How did you show it?

God Talk: "God, give me a spirit of joy so that I can be happy for my friends when they receive good news. Then we can praise you together! Amen."

From *That's So Me* by Nancy Rue

"Do not consider how handsome or tall he is. I have not chosen him. I do not look at the things people look at. Man looks at how someone appears on the outside. But I look at what is in the heart."

—1 Samuel 16:7 (NIrV)

You're My Friend, Kate

Kate looked down at her skirt. No matter which way she twisted it, she just couldn't make it fit right. Even worse, the material was starting to fade from the many times it had been washed.

Across the locker room, her friend Libby stood in front of a mirror. As Kate watched, Libby carefully brushed her long hair until it hung smoothly down her back. But it wasn't Libby's silky auburn hair that made Kate feel out of it. It was her awesome top and jeans, dangly earrings, and sandals.

Kate was quiet as she and Libby walked home from school. Though they'd been best friends for years, something was changing.

Libby broke the silence. "Kate, is something wrong?"

Kate shook her head. She didn't want to admit how she felt.

"You'd tell me if something was wrong, right?" Libby said.

Kate started kicking a stone along the edge of the street. *I'd like to bring back the old days*, she thought. *Sometimes I feel so far away from Libby.* Yet she felt embarrassed to say anything.

"Remember how we always shared secrets?" asked Libby.

Kate smiled, but the ache didn't leave her heart. *I'm afraid to tell her*, she thought. *Maybe she won't like me anymore.*

But Libby knew her too well. "Spit it out, Kate," she said.

Finally Kate spoke. "Sometimes I don't feel like your friend anymore. We used to be alike, and now we're different."

"What do you mean?" asked Libby.

Kate could barely get the words out. "Our clothes," she said.

"Ohhh." Understanding came into Libby's eyes. "And that's why you've been acting strange lately?"

Kate nodded.

"But clothes shouldn't make any difference between us!"

Kate choked on the words, hardly able to speak. "My clothes are so *old*. But you have a whole closet full of wonderful, beautiful tops. The latest style in jeans. Jeweled flip-flops."

For a long moment, Libby was silent. When she spoke, she sounded as if she'd been thinking hard. "Kate, what if you had a bunch of nice clothes and I didn't? How would you treat me?"

The question surprised Kate. Her gaze met Libby's. "It wouldn't make any difference."

Libby smiled. "I know," she said. "And I've got an idea."

Kate looked at her and waited, afraid to hope.

More to Explore: 2 Corinthians 4:16 and Matthew 6:25–34

Girl Talk: Are there times when you feel embarrassed because your clothes aren't the same as those worn by other kids?

God Talk: "God, protect me from thinking I'm worth something only if I have clothes like everyone else. I want to please you with the way I am in my heart. Amen."

From *Girl Talk* by Lois Wilfred Johnson

"For lack of guidance a nation falls, but victory is won through many advisers."

—Proverbs 11:14

Listen Up!

One day, you notice a dark spot on your shoulder. You scrub till the skin is raw, but the spot remains. You forget about it, but a month later, you notice it again. It seems darker—and bigger. Then one day, you read an article in a teen magazine about skin cancer. It says to watch out for moles that darken or grow. You go to talk to your mom. "Look at this," you say, peeling off the Band-Aid. After consulting a dermatologist (skin doctor), you have the suspicious mole removed. It isn't skin cancer—not yet. But getting advice from your mom and the skin doctor may have saved your life. Ignoring the problem could have been deadly.

When you have a problem, it's good to share it with trusted others, like a parent, teacher, counselor, youth pastor, or doctor. Confiding in your best friend is fine, but your friend may not know what to do either. "Plans fail for lack of counsel, but with many advisers they succeed" (Proverbs 15:22). It can be scary to share your problem with an adult, but it's even scarier keeping it to yourself and not knowing what to do. People care about you and want to help. Let them!

More To Explore: Proverbs 24:6

Girl Talk: Is there anything you are worried about right now? Can you name one or two adults you trust who could help you out? God is always there for guidance too!

God Talk: "Lord, I'm worried about ______. Please help me know who I should talk with about this. I don't want to worry about it anymore. Amen."

From *Shine On, Girl!* by Kristi Holl

277

"God, for whom and through whom everything was made, chose to bring many children into glory ... So now Jesus and the ones he makes holy have the same Father. That is why Jesus is not ashamed to call them his brothers and sisters."

—Hebrews 2:10–12 (NLT)

Family Ties

Nobody wants other people to see them as weak. But a refusal to acknowledge your own limitations is an attitude of pride. Having a proud heart means that you believe you can do everything for yourself, without the help of anyone else. Girls who are proud miss out on the beauty of believing, because instead of trusting God, they trust in themselves.

Father God goes against such proud people. But, faithgirl, when you bow your head and admit to God that you need his help, he gives you the special ability to accomplish everything he wants you to do. As a beautiful daughter of Father God, you have an entire family to help you along your journey of life. Ups and downs. Triumphs and tragedies. Blessings and tough breaks. Your family in Christ will be there for you, but only if you let them. As God connects you to the family of faith, be grateful! Starting today, look out for brothers and sisters in Father God's family.

More To Explore: Romans 12:4–6

Girl Talk: Do you know what gifts God gave you? Read 1 Corinthians 12. As you consider the gifts listed in the passage, ask God to show you what he gave you to honor him.

God Talk: "Father, thank you for adopting me into your family! Teach me to rely only on you to accomplish my part in your plan."

From *My Beautiful Daughter* by Tasha Douglas

"If someone is caught in a sin, you who live by the Spirit should restore that person gently."

—Galatians 6:1

Support Each Other

Alyssa was shocked when she heard that Taylor, a girl in her youth group, was caught drinking with some older kids. When she spotted Taylor at school, Taylor turned red and walked the other way. Taylor skipped youth group Wednesday night, and Alyssa wished she could do something. Finally, she decided to stop at Taylor's house on the way home. She had no idea what to say, but she wanted Taylor to know they wanted her back in youth group, no matter what. When Taylor opened the door, she blinked in surprise, then hung her head. "We missed you at group," Alyssa said. "Can we talk?" Taylor looked up, tears in her eyes. "Sure. Come on in."

If you're a follower of Jesus, you will have the same desire he does: "I will seek what was lost and bring back what was driven away, bind up the broken and strengthen what was sick" (Ezekiel 34:16 NKJV). We all fail, and we all make mistakes. Instead of judging another believer, talk with her gently. Help her back on the right path. That's love in action.

More to Explore: Matthew 9:13

Girl Talk: Do you know a believer who is caught in some behavior that's wrong? How can you help? Are *you* caught in such behavior?

God Talk: "Lord, help me to not become prideful when someone else is caught doing something wrong. I want to have love for that person instead. Amen."

From *Chick Chat* by Kristi Holl

279

"The beginning of strife is as when water first trickles [from a crack in a dam]; therefore stop contention before it becomes worse and quarreling breaks out."

—Proverbs 17:14 (AMP)

Don't Burst the Dam!

Have you ever seen a dam in a river or a lake? Usually made from cement, a dam holds the water back. But a tiny crack in the dam, if left unrepaired, can get bigger fast.

Rebecca had the same fight with her mom every Saturday morning. Rebecca thought her room looked comfortable. Her mom called it a pigpen. On her way out the door to her job, Rebecca's mom always stopped by her room and said, "Young lady, when I get home today, this room had better be spotless." Rebecca always demanded, "What's wrong with it?" Her mom yelled, "Dirty clothes on the floor. Empty soda cans. Moldy food. Get this mess clean, or you're grounded!" Rebecca's shouts of "That's not fair!" followed her mom as she left for work.

A person who quarrels invites many problems into her life (see Proverbs 17:19). Next Saturday, what could Rebecca do differently? Instead of snarling, "What's wrong with my room?" Rebecca could simply say, "Okay, I'll clean it." Simple. Easy. Stops the leak in the dam immediately. No quarrel.

Some people insist on having the last word in a disagreement. Actually, a person who can bite her tongue and be silent in order to stop a fight is highly respected.

More to Explore: Proverbs 26:21

Girl Talk: What kinds of quarrels do you get pulled into? What can you do to end them?

God Talk: "Lord, I want to end fights before they start. Please show me how. Amen."

From *Chick Chat* by Kristi Holl

"Two are better than one, because they have a good return for their labor: If either of them falls down, one can help the other up."

—Ecclesiastes 4:9–10

Reaching Goals: Get Support

Some goals, especially small ones that can be done today or very soon, you can do alone. But large goals are easier to reach if you get help and support from others. Two working together are better than each person working alone.

Suppose your goal is to train your singing voice so you can sing solos at church or school someday. You can work alone, but how much better to ask for the support and help of your family, your music teacher at school, or your youth leader.

Way back in Genesis 2:18, God said it wasn't good for a man (or a girl) to be alone. He knows we do better with help, so don't be ashamed or shy about asking for support. Even Jesus sent his disciples out two by two when it was time for them to minister (Mark 6:7). You'll be able to achieve your goals much easier (and have encouragement on the days you want to quit) if you enlist help from other people. So look for help in reaching your goals, and be sure to help *others* reach theirs!

More to Explore: Exodus 4:10–16 and Numbers 11:10–17

Girl Talk: Is there something you are working toward right now? Who do you think can help you achieve your goal?

God Talk: "Lord, I thank you for giving me such big dreams. Please help me find the right people to help me. Amen."

From *Girlz Rock* by Kristi Holl

281

"There is one body and one Spirit—just as you were called to one hope when you were called—one Lord, one faith, one baptism; one God and Father of all, who is over all and through all and in all."

—Ephesians 4:4–6

Many Parts, One Whole

"You're so much alike!"

Ever heard that said about you and your best friend—or even your whole group of best buds? It's neat, actually, to be identified as a group. Even though you're each unique, it gives you a close feeling to know you're connected by what you have in common.

The whole community of God is like that. Each person is created as a special individual, and yet we're all part of one thing:

- One Body—the body of Christ, which is the whole Christian church.
- One Spirit—the Holy Spirit of God which fills us all and guides us along.
- One Hope—that Jesus will return and set everything right, once and for all—no more pain and sorrow and disappointment.
- One Faith—our belief that Jesus died so that we can live forever with God.
- One Baptism—that sacrament that says we've committed ourselves to living as Jesus taught us and that we'll someday be in heaven with God.
- One God and Father of All—which requires no explanation!

That's what makes us a family. That's what we belong to.

More to Explore: Romans 12:5

Girl Talk: Tell as many members of God's community as you can that you are glad to be in the same family. Hugs are optional, but encouraged!

God Talk: "Wow, Jesus! It's incredible that I get to be a part of your community, one that stretches from my own neighborhood to the other side of the world. Thank you! Amen."

From *That's So Me* by Nancy Rue

"Always think about what is true. Think about what is noble, right and pure. Think about what is lovely and worthy of respect. If anything is excellent or worthy of praise, think about those kinds of things."

—Philippians 4:8 (NIrV)

Shae's Gift

On the bus ride to her friend's house, Shae took a good look at Zoe. *Something's wrong*, she decided. *Zoe is changing.*

The change bothered Shae. Since third grade, the two had been good friends. Even on that first day of school, they had ridden the bus together. But now, Shae didn't understand what was happening. When Zoe laughed, it didn't reach her eyes. Instead, the laugh that was once full of fun had a hard ring to it.

Just thinking about it, Shae twisted a strand of her long blonde hair. What made Zoe seem so hard? So turned off to the things she used to like?

When their bus squealed to a stop, Shae and Zoe climbed down and walked to the house. In the kitchen, they found Zoe's dad sitting at the table.

"Hi, Zoe. Hi, Shae. Have a good day?"

Zoe shrugged.

"How did your test go?" her dad asked.

"Same as always." Zoe's dark eyes were angry. Turning her back to her dad, she seemed to say, *What's it to you?*

Without another word, Zoe headed down the steps to her bedroom in the basement. Shae accepted a bowl of munchies from Zoe's dad and then followed her friend.

When Shae entered the room, Zoe handed her an MP3 player. "Listen up! You'll like it!"

Shae slipped the headphones in her ears. At first, the song sounded fun and catchy. Then Shae began hearing the words. There were swear words, but even worse were the things the singer was saying about girls. It was insulting. Looking at the picture of the singer on the screen, Shae felt uneasy. After a minute, she turned down the volume and shut off the player.

Is this the singer's way of selling lots of CDs?

Of one thing Shae felt sure. The music would negatively affect a girl who listened. That was exactly what she had seen in her friend.

Removing the headphones, Shae leaned forward, tucked her face into her hands, and started praying. After a moment, she looked up and cleared her throat.

"Zoe, we've been good friends for a long time. Remember what we promised each other? That we'd always tell each other stuff, even if it's hard?"

When Zoe met her eyes and nodded, Shae began. "Do you know what the words of these songs really say?"

More to Explore: Psalm 119:9

Girl Talk: What kind of music or movies are you putting in your head?

God Talk: "Protect me, Jesus, from harmful thoughts that would enter my mind through what I see, hear, and read. Help me to focus only on thoughts that are true, noble, and right. Amen."

From *Girl Talk* by Lois Wilfred Johnson

283

"If you spend yourselves in behalf of the hungry and satisfy the needs of the oppressed, then your light will rise in the darkness, and your night will become like the noonday."
—Isaiah 58:10

A Miracle for Dorcas

Dorcas liked to sew, but she didn't have a fancy sewing machine with a buttonholer or a sleeve attachment. She sewed by hand in her home in Joppa, the main seaport of Judea, about thirty-five miles northwest of Jerusalem.

Dorcas was a disciple and belonged to one of the first Christian congregations. And one of her favorite ways to serve Jesus was to serve the poor in her community. The Bible says Dorcas always did good and helped the poor. Not just on Sundays or at Christmas time or when her church or the post office had a food drive. Sewing clothes for the needy was one way Dorcas helped.

When Dorcas became ill and died, many widows and others mourned her death. They washed her body and placed it in an upstairs room in her house along the Mediterranean Sea.

Two men from Dorcas' hometown went over to Lydda where the apostle Peter was preaching. They told Peter to come to Joppa at once. When Peter arrived at Dorcas' house, they took him upstairs to her room. The crying widows surrounded Peter, showing him the robes and other clothes Dorcas had made for the poor.

Peter sent them all out of the room. He knelt on the floor and prayed. Then he said, "Tabitha, get up."

Dorcas, whose name translated to *Tabitha* in Aramaic, opened her eyes. She saw Peter and sat up. She'd been dead, and now she was alive again.

Peter held Dorcas' hand and helped her to her feet. Then he called the believers and widows in to see Dorcas alive again. The miracle became known all over Joppa and many people believed in the Lord.

God gave Dorcas more time on earth to praise his name. More time to use her heart and her hands to serve God and the poor in her community.

Like Dorcas, you can allow God to use your gifts, abilities, and talents to serve the poor and needy in the world. You can share your time and talent to let them know God loves them and cares about them. How will you show God's love?

More to Explore: Acts 9:36 – 43

Girl Talk: What can you do to serve the poor in your community?

God Talk: "Lord, you see the needs of all people all around the world. Your heart breaks for them. Please show me the things that break your heart and give me a heart to serve the needy. Amen."

From *Real Girls of the Bible* by Mona Hodgson

"Be kind and compassionate to one another, forgiving each other, just as in Christ God forgave you."

—Ephesians 4:32

Sharing the Love

Kayla's Sunday school teacher said, "Your life may be the only Bible your friends read. Are they learning anything about God by watching you?" Kayla knew she didn't do any really bad stuff—no drinking, no drugs, no smoking, no swearing. But did her unbelieving friends learn anything about God's love by being around her? From that day on, Kayla determined that her life and her actions would demonstrate God to her friends. She made a list of things she could do to show God's love, forgiveness, and compassion in some form each day to a friend. Sometimes she gave a compliment or a word of encouragement. Sometimes she helped a friend carry something or gave a hand with homework. Sometimes it was forgiving a friend instead of being mad.

If your friends never read the Bible, would they still learn through your actions that "love is patient, love is kind" (1 Corinthians 13:4)? Give to others what God has so freely given to you. He's devoted to your well-being, he forgives instead of getting revenge, he's sympathetic to your problems, he's patient, and he's kind. Let God have control of your life so you can love others the way he loves you!

More To Explore: Romans 12:10

Girl Talk: Think about your circle of friends. To whom can you reach out and show God's love? Write down a few things to try this coming week.

God Talk: "Lord, please help me to show my friends your love. Thank you for your love and forgiveness to me and everyone. Amen."

From *Shine On, Girl!* by Kristi Holl

"Now there are different kinds of spiritual gifts, but it is the same Holy Spirit who is the source of them all. There are different kinds of service in the church, but it is the same Lord we are serving. There are different ways God works in our lives, but it is the same God who does the work through all of us."

—1 Corinthians 12:4–6 (NLT)

No Cookie-Cutter Christians

Believers are not cut out with cookie cutters. God made us individuals, with different gifts to share with one another. Although our gifts are different, they all come from one source: the Holy Spirit. God works in our lives very differently, but it is still the same God working in each of us.

Not everyone is a performer, nor wants to be. Does that mean you have no gifts? Not at all! "God has given each of us the ability to do certain things well ... If your gift is that of serving others, serve them well ... If your gift is to encourage others, do it! If you have money, share it generously ... And if you have a gift for showing kindness to others, do it gladly" (Romans 12:6–8 NLT). Serving, sharing, encouraging, showing kindness—these are things we can all do.

You are unique. Share your unique gifts, and watch God use you to be a blessing to others.

More to Explore: 1 Corinthians 12:7–11

Girl Talk: Think of a few talents you have. Are you hiding them or using them? Are you using them to be in the spotlight or for God's purpose?

God Talk: "Lord, I know you have given me many talents. Help me to realize what they are and to use them for your glory. Amen."

From *No Boys Allowed* by Kristi Holl

286

"Be humble and gentle. Be patient with each other, making allowance for each other's faults because of your love."
—Ephesians 4:2 (NLT)

God's Kind of Allowance

Kelsey heard an inspiring sermon about loving others the way Jesus loved her. All aglow with warm feelings, she was determined to show God's love to each person she met. Before the day was over, she realized she didn't always want to love others. She loved helping people who were nice to her, like her mom and older sister. It irritated her to be gentle or humble with her older brother, who thought he ruled the world and everyone in it. She was patient with her elderly neighbor. But tolerating her best friend's bad memory when she forgot to pick up Kelsey for the movie was something else. Slowly it dawned on Kelsey that we are told to love others—*period*. Having warm, fuzzy feelings has nothing to do with it.

What are some actions you can take to love others better? For one thing, don't give up on people when they mess up. Make allowances instead. Also, come alongside people in trouble and help them through it. Everyone has a crisis from time to time. A loving person helps shoulder the load until the crisis passes. Remember how much God loves you—then share that love with others.

More To Explore: Romans 15:1

Girl Talk: Is there anyone whose behavior is irritating you right now? How can you show love to that individual instead of impatience?

God Talk: "Lord, I know I need to love everyone, but I'm having a hard time with ______. Please give me the right words as I try to show this person love. Thank you. Amen."

From *Shine On, Girl!* by Kristi Holl

"Think of ways to encourage one another to outbursts of love and good deeds."

—Hebrews 10:24 (NLT)

Be a Spirit Lifter

To encourage means to inspire someone with courage and hope, to raise their confidence and lift their spirits. It means to think of ways to contribute to someone else's growth or progress. We are to spur each other on to perform good efforts and generous expressions of love.

Do you know anyone who needs some encouragement? Do you have a friend whose family is going through a divorce? A sister who didn't make the cut on the basketball team? How could you convince your friends or family members to be of service (along with you) to build up this person's spirits?

Don't just feel sorry for someone. Instead, do something positive. Right now, you might be thinking, "But who's going to encourage *me*?" Unfortunately, many believers feel like they can't help someone else if they're feeling down in the dumps themselves. Not true! In fact, that's one of the nice things about lifting someone else's spirits. While you are busy encouraging people and getting your friends to help, your *own* joy will go through the roof!

More to Explore: Galatians 5:13–15

Girl Talk: Do you know someone who could use some encouragement? How could you help them?

God Talk: "Lord, I want to help others. Help me to find ways to encourage others and give them joy. I want to be like you. Thank you. Amen."

From *No Boys Allowed* by Kristi Holl

"When [Jesus] saw the crowds, he had compassion on them, because they were harassed and helpless, like sheep without a shepherd."

—Matthew 9:36

Lost Sheep

Megan was chatting with her best friend, Nora, when she noticed a girl on crutches approaching the school. The girl caught her crutch on a chunk of protruding cement and dropped her books. Nora laughed and grabbed Megan's arm. "Did you hear how that happened? She sprained her ankle trying to skateboard with some little kids. What a loser." Megan hesitated, then shook off her friend's hand and hurried to help the girl pick up her books. She carried her bag into the school for her.

As believers, we must not be critical of someone else's struggles. God wants to use you to help others. If you're critical instead of kind, you're useless. We are called to love one another. The only time you are to ever look *down* upon someone is when you're bending over to help them *up*. Look around you today with a loving, compassionate eye. Who could use your help?

More to Explore: Titus 3:14

Girl Talk: When your classmates have trouble or sickness or problems, how do you respond? Do you gossip about them? Or do you try to help them?

God Talk: "Lord, I don't want to criticize someone for having a problem. Show me how I can help instead. Amen."

From *Chick Chat* by Kristi Holl

"If anyone obeys his word, love for God is truly made complete in them. This is how we know we are in him: Whoever claims to live in him must live as Jesus did."

—1 John 2:5–6

False Claims

You remember the summer you accepted Jesus as your savior in vacation Bible school, along with your two best friends. You attended Sunday school together for years. But now that you're in middle school, you find excuses not to go. You stop reading your Bible. You want to see movies that your new friends see, so you begin sneaking out and lying about where you go. Your parents don't trust the kids you now want to hang out with, so you lie about that too. If anyone pins you down about your relationship with Jesus, you always say, "Oh, yeah, I'm a Christian." But you know your behavior says otherwise.

Many inside and outside the church claim to love God. But do they pass the test? Be sure that if you say you're a follower of Jesus that you actually have the desire to follow him and grow in your relationship with him. And choose your friends accordingly. You can't—and shouldn't—judge whether someone is saved or not, but a person's lifestyle can be one good indication. Choose friends whose actions match what they say they believe.

More To Explore: John 15:4–5

Girl Talk: Think of your actions the last few weeks. Would God say that you obey him? Why or why not?

God Talk: "Lord, my actions don't always match what I say I believe. I want to follow you every day, not rely on myself or others. Please help me do that. Amen."

From *Shine On, Girl!* by Kristi Holl

290

"On the evening of that first day of the week, when the disciples were together . . ."

—John 20:19

Stuck Like Glue

Can you even imagine how close the disciples must have been? They spent three years traveling around as a group. They saw amazing things together that other people might not even believe. They even had to go into hiding together after their Lord was killed, so they wouldn't be put to death themselves.

They had their issues as a group. Jesus was always breaking up arguments over who was his favorite and who was going to sit next to him in heaven. But when Jesus was crucified and they were left alone, they stuck together, just like he told them to. It might have been safer for them to separate and run in different directions, but he'd said for them to love each other, lay down their lives for each other, and that's what they were doing when he returned and appeared to them.

As members of his community, God gives all of us the courage to stick together for him. You can keep your friends going when other kids tease them. You know you have a place to go when the world says you're a geek. God gives you that place among the other members of his community. Stick together.

More to Explore: Colossians 3:17

Girl Talk: Do you have a group of Christian friends you can count on when times get tough?

God Talk: "Jesus, help my friends and me to become better and better friends every day. Help us to love each other and stick tight when someone needs help. Amen."

From *That's So Me* by Nancy Rue

"Our purpose is to please God, not people. He is the one who examines the motives of our hearts. Never once did we try to win you with flattery, as you very well know. And God is our witness that we were not just pretending to be your friends so you would give us money!"

—1 Thessalonians 2:4–5 (NLT)

Honor Your Friendships

When someone who rarely speaks to you suddenly gushes with praise about your "ultracool outfit" or your "brilliant science project" or "your totally fabulous hair," don't you smell something fishy? Most of us have a good nose for false praise and flattery. Our first thought is: *Okay, what do you want from me?* Have you caught *yourself* doing the same thing with friends sometimes? Do you give honest praise? Or do you flatter someone so she'll invite you to her pizza party, let you borrow her cool sweater, or give you a ride to the game?

Paul says in this verse that personal profit was never his aim in treating his friends well: "nor did we put on a mask to cover up greed" (1 Thessalonians 2:5). Don't wear a phony mask with your friends. Don't try to hide the reasons for things you say and do. Be honest with your praise, but watch your reasons for it. Do it out of love, not to get something in return.

More to Explore: James 4:4

Girl Talk: Look at your friendships. Are you friends because you honestly like them or because of what they can give you?

God Talk: "Lord, I sometimes think too selfishly. Help me to be honest with everyone I meet, including you. Thank you for your loving care. Amen."

From *Girlz Rock* by Kristi Holl

292

"Do not withhold good from those to whom it is due, when it is in your power to act. Do not say to your neighbor, 'Come back tomorrow and I'll give it to you'—when you already have it with you."

—Proverbs 3:27–28

Be Generous

Rachel was awakened in the night by fire engines. Sirens screamed and lights flashed. Within an hour, a neighbor's house had burned to the ground. Everyone got out safely—a mother and four small children—but they lost everything. The next day, her parents collected things for the family. Rachel was glad to help her mom pack up sheets and towels and canned goods for the neighbors. But when her mom suggested she add a few stuffed bears from her collection, Rachel paused. "Well, okay, I'll sort through them this weekend and decide which ones to give away." Her mom replied, "Those children have nothing left—no toys or clothes or beds. I think if they had teddy bears to hold tonight, it might help them." Rachel stared at the floor. "I hadn't thought of that. I'll get the bears now."

It's good to feel compassion for people, but that feeling needs to be followed by action. "Suppose a brother or a sister is without clothes and daily food. If one of you says to them, 'Go in peace; keep warm and well fed,' but does nothing about their physical needs, what good is it?" (James 2:15–16).

More to Explore: Galatians 6:10

Girl Talk: Have you helped someone else by giving them something of yours? Who could use your help today?

God Talk: "Lord, I need to be more sensitive. Help me to notice people in need and then to help them generously. Amen."

From *Chick Chat* by Kristi Holl

"Wisdom will save you from the ways of wicked men, from men whose words are perverse."

—Proverbs 2:12

Choosing Friends Wisely

You and your neighbor may have been best friends since kindergarten, but lately something has changed. Your neighbor has begun lying to her parents about where she goes after school. She also seems to enjoy stirring up trouble in your group of friends by spreading rumors and making people mad at each other. These days, you're also embarrassed by your friend's filthy language. The last straw comes when you get detention one day. Your friend breaks a rule at school, and because you happen to be with her, the teacher assumes you're guilty too. Your friend doesn't mind detention—in fact, she seems proud of it. You hate it, though.

You need to make a choice soon. Your reputation at school has been damaged, and your feelings have been hurt by the gossip. Frankly, you're tired of having her for a friend. She's changed too much. Even though your neighbor's been a good friend for years, she isn't the kind of friend God would choose for you now. She enjoys breaking rules and proclaims it to everyone. You may have to make a very difficult decision: not to hang with her anymore. Use wisdom and find friends whose values more closely match yours.

More to Explore: Proverbs 4:14–16 and 2 Corinthians 6:17

Girl Talk: How do you choose your friends? To you, what are the qualities of a good friend?

God Talk: "Lord, I want to make wise choices about friends. Bring friends you choose into my life. Thank you for keeping me safe when I follow you. Amen."

From *Chick Chat* by Kristi Holl

294

"Resist him, standing firm in the faith, because you know that the family of believers throughout the world is undergoing the same kind of sufferings."

—1 Peter 5:9

In It Together

Abby felt alone though. She felt like her parents just wouldn't let her grow up, and it was embarrassing. She couldn't see the videos other kids saw. Her parents pulled her out of movies shown at school that they considered inappropriate. Her classmates made fun of her for it. Her mom had to okay Abby's clothes before she bought them. That meant popular short-shorts, tight tees, and tiny bathing suits all were left behind in the dressing room. Abby felt like such a baby. She finally let out her frustration in youth group one night. To her amazement, six other girls said they had the exact same frustration! Whether the girls liked it or not, they had godly parents who watched over them. This sometimes brought unfair suffering when the girls got ridiculed at school. When that happens to you, what should be your reaction? "When you do good and suffer, if you take it patiently, this is commendable before God" (1 Peter 2:20 NKJV).

No one enjoys being called a baby. Even so, thank the Lord if you have parents willing to help you lead a godly life in an ungodly world. They care about you so much!

More To Explore: 1 Peter 2:21–23

Girl Talk: When you feel alone, do you share your feelings with anyone, or do you keep things bottled up? What are some ways you can reach out and share your feelings?

God Talk: "Lord, I know I'm not the only one who suffers trials. Please help me remember that I am not alone. Amen."

From *Shine On, Girl!* by Kristi Holl

"The second is this: 'Love your neighbor as yourself.' There is no commandment greater than these."

—Mark 12:31

A Look in the Mirror

Brynn hated using the mirror in the school bathroom. The light gave her skin a funny color and every spot and blemish showed.

She was so busy looking at herself that she barely noticed the girl who had come in. A strange movement in the mirror caught her attention. *What's she doing?* The girl wore a cute hat that fit close around her head. When she twisted it in place, Brynn saw under the brim.

Did I imagine it? she wondered. Then she knew she hadn't. The girl was bald!

Just then, Brynn realized she'd been caught staring. Red crept into her face. *There I go again—forgetting how someone else might feel.*

Picking up her books, Brynn turned to leave, but something clicked in her mind. *The girl with cancer.* She had just changed her schedule to come into two of Brynn's classes.

Everyone had been talking about the girl and how she was taking chemo. Someone said she had lost all her hair. The rumor must be true.

As Brynn turned back, she looked in the mirror in time to see a tear roll down the girl's cheek. Other tears followed. The silent weeping made Brynn feel miserable. *Should I say something? Or pretend I don't notice?*

For a moment, Brynn stood there, trying to decide. The girl acted as if she didn't see her. At last Brynn spoke. "I'm Brynn. What's your name?"

The girl's lips quivered. "Yolanda. Yolanda Garcia." Leaning down, she turned on a faucet and splashed cold water on her face. "I'll be all right," she mumbled.

But Brynn felt sure Yolanda was just trying to be brave. "I don't know what's wrong, but can I help?"

Yoland turned to face her. "Help? I wish you could." If the words hadn't sounded so hopeless, Brynn would have thought the girl was bitter. Instead, she seemed ready to give up.

"What's wrong?" Brynn asked.

As if unable to stand up anymore, Yolanda braced herself against the sink. Brynn waited while Yolanda drew a ragged breath. "Some boys found out—" she struggled to speak. "They found out I've lost my hair. When I walk through the hall, they come up behind me and pull off my hat."

"Oh no!" Yolanda's pain pierced Brynn's heart. "Can I help?"

It's easy to feel sorry for someone. It's a lot harder to put yourself in their shoes and try to find a way to help. That takes courage.

More to Explore: 1 Corinthians 16:14

Girl Talk: Have you ever seen a girl who looked upset, but you didn't say anything because you were afraid to ask what was wrong? Next time that happens, see if you can lend a helping hand!

God Talk: "Jesus, it's so easy to be selfish and think only about myself. Sometimes I need your help and sometimes I need to see what is happening to the people around me. Help me love them with your love and find practical and creative ways to help. Amen!"

From *Girl Talk* by Lois Walfrid Johnson

"Those who love to talk will experience the consequences, for the tongue can kill or nourish life."

—Proverbs 18:21 (NLT)

Power-Packed Words

Nothing's more fun than a gab session after school over a soda, or on the phone late at night. Let's face it. Girls love to talk. A lot! There's nothing wrong with that, but pay attention to what you say. If your friend tells you about her science fair idea, you can say, "Fabulous idea. How'd you ever think of something that cool?" Or you can say, "At least ten people in class will do that project. It's soooo lame." Guess which words bring life and joy to your friend and which ones kill her idea?

Before speaking, pause a moment and consider the effect of your words. How do you think the person receiving them will feel? Sometimes we get so busy sounding clever and making snappy wisecracks that we forget the pain our remarks can cause someone else. And there are consequences for that. Friendships don't last long when you dish out a steady diet of negative comments, criticism, and (not so funny) put-downs. Use your words to nurture the people in your life. Be uplifting and spread a little joy around. Then sit back and watch it all come back to you, many times over!

More to Explore: Proverbs 10:19–21 and Ecclesiastes 10:12–14

Girl Talk: Do you use your words as weapons, or do you use your words to uplift others?

God Talk: "Lord, I realize that all words have power. I want my words to have a positive effect and lift up others. Help me to choose my words wisely. Amen."

From *No Boys Allowed* by Kristi Holl

297

"Do not be misled: 'Bad company corrupts good character.'"
—1 Corinthians 15:33

Don't Lose Yourself

Don't be fooled into thinking that it doesn't matter what kind of friends you have. Hanging out with immoral and dishonest friends can change you! They can ruin your good habits, morals, and godly character.

Sometimes believers think that they can hang out with dishonest or immoral friends because Jesus did it. After all, he hung out with thieving tax collectors and prostitutes. Shouldn't we do the same thing so that we can be good witnesses to them? Yes and no. There is a difference between talking with "bad company" and choosing them for your closest friends.

Consider this example. When you mix a glass of pure, clean water with a glass of dirty water, it all becomes dirty and cloudy. The dirt spreads—not the purity. If you're healthy when you sit next to a very sick person, you can catch his flu, but he won't catch your health. In the same way, bad company is "catching."

Do be friendly with everyone, but choose moral girls with good character for your closest friends. Then you can build one another up and grow in godly character together.

More to Explore: Proverbs 13:20

Girl Talk: Who are your closest friends? How do they behave? How do you behave when you are with them?

God Talk: "Lord, I want to make good choices when making friends. Help me to find those who have good character and who want to get closer to you. Thank you. Amen."

From *Girlz Rock* by Kristi Holl

"Jonathan said to David, 'Whatever you want me to do, I'll do for you.'"

—1 Samuel 20:4

Soul Sisters

Have you ever been friends with somebody that it didn't make sense for you to be friends with—but you just loved each other? Your mother and hers did NOT care for each other, but you two really hit it off.

That's the way it was with Jonathan and David. Jonathan's father was King Saul. God had already said David was going to replace Saul, and Saul wasn't having it. He was out to get David, and David was running scared. But David and Jonathan were best friends. It was Jonathan David went to and said, "How have I wronged your father, that he is trying to kill me?" (1 Samuel 20:1).

You'd think Jonathan would have been torn between his best bud and his dad, but Jonathan immediately said, "Never! You are not going to die!" Then he offered to do anything to help David escape Saul's wrath.

Jonathan wasn't being loyal to his blood family. His loyalty was to God's family. How did he know which to choose? How do *we* know? God puts it in us to be able to decide on his side. As members of that family, the love is deep inside us. Like Jonathan, we only have to listen to it.

More to Explore: 1 Samuel 18:3

Girl Talk: Have you ever had a friend you loved as much as your own soul—like Jonathon loved David?

God Talk: "Jesus, help me remember that everyone who believes in you is a family member. I want to look out for them just like I would look out for my brother or sister. Amen."

From *That's So Me* by Nancy Rue

299

"Don't be stuck-up. Make friends with nobodies; don't be the great somebody."

—Romans 12:16 (MSG)

A Humble Heart

Adele's fingers flew across the keypad as she excitedly texted all her friends: "I'm a Brown Belt! Yay!!" When she bumped into Paige, the new girl, she even told her.

"Wow," Paige said. "That's awesome! Congrats!"

Now Paige, a karate expert with dozens of trophies to her name, could have spoiled Adele's day with one sentence: "Been there, done that, black belt, five-time champion." Instead, she did a self-effacing and praiseworthy thing: she shared in Adele's joy and kept her own achievements to herself.

Seems Paige not only knows karate, she also knows how to be humble. And today, it's hard to find girls who are. That's because the world encourages a "look-what-I've-done-I'm-better-than-you" attitude, and a lot of girls are buying into it. They spend gazillions of hours on social media playing the one-upmanship game and bragging about themselves.

The Bible says when our hearts become proud, we're so full of ourselves, there's no room for the Lord (Psalm 10:4). And that's exactly what happens. Instead of thanking God ten times to Sunday for his abundant grace, proud girls start believing that they—not God—are responsible for the good stuff that comes their way. The result? Unlike Paige, they look down on everyone and act like total divas.

More To Explore: Luke 14:7–14

Girl Talk: Do you ever feel the need to brag about your talents? What's something small you could do to be more humble?

God Talk: "Heavenly Father, help me to remember to be humble, and put you first, others second, and myself last. Amen."

From *Shine On, Girl!* by Kristi Holl

"Make my joy complete by being like-minded, having the same love, being one in spirit and of one mind."

—Philippians 2:2

United as One

Emily's family endured several shocks in the course of a month. Her dad's company went bankrupt, and he lost his job. When he couldn't find another one that paid as well, they sold their large home with a pool and moved into a tiny house. Then her mom discovered she was expecting another baby. Emily was in turmoil—until one evening they had a family roundtable discussion about their situation. "Loving God comes first," her dad said, "and then loving each other. If we pull together, we can make this work." The discussion that followed brought out different ideas for making money, cutting costs, and helping care for the baby when it arrived. There were many different ideas—but the family was like-minded about their purpose: loving God and loving one another.

Unity should exist among Christians. This doesn't mean thinking exactly alike on everything. It means having the common goal of working together and serving one another. Being unified comes with a great reward: God's presence in your life. "Be of good comfort, be of one mind, live in peace; and the God of love and peace will be with you" (2 Corinthians 13:11 NKJV). United we stand!

More To Explore: Romans 12:16–18

Girl Talk: Do you think your church family provides a united front? How can you improve on working together, both at church and at home?

God Talk: "Lord, I want to work better with my family. As much as depends on me, help me live with them in peace and find ways to love them and serve them. Amen."

From *Shine On, Girl!* by Kristi Holl

301

"The way of fools seems right to them, but the wise listen to advice."

—Proverbs 12:15

Lend Me Your Ear

At lunchtime, Kylie was falsely accused by a teacher of leaving a pool of spilled milk on the floor. She hadn't done it, and she fumed as she cleaned up the mess. As she stewed, she mentally rehearsed what she intended to say to that lunchroom monitor. After all, she had to defend herself. She only planned to tell the truth. That teacher had no right to accuse her! Kylie's best friend tried to talk her out of having that heated confrontation, but Kylie wouldn't listen. After all, she was 100 percent right. What could be wrong with telling off that mean teacher?

The Bible warns about the consequences we'll receive if we refuse to be guided by others' godly opinions. "Where there is no guidance the people fall, but in abundance of counselors there is victory" (Proverbs 11:14 NASB). Why is it so important to listen to others? Because we are so easily fooled into thinking we're doing the right thing. We can be very sincere in our beliefs—but still be sincerely wrong. "There is a way that appears to be right, but in the end it leads to death" (Proverbs 16:25).

Be smart. Get advice from trusted people before making your decisions.

More to Explore: Proverbs 15:22

Girl Talk: Do you have a problem that you wish you could share with someone? Do you have a trusted adult to confide in: a teacher, pastor, counselor, parent, or grandparent?

God Talk: "Lord, sometimes I try to figure everything out by myself. It's scary to talk about my problems. Please give me courage to ask for advice. Amen."

From *Chick Chat* by Kristi Holl

"Greater love has no one than this, than to lay down one's life for his friends."

—John 15:13 (NKJV)

Best Friends Forever

The greatest sacrifice of all time was Jesus' dying on the cross to make it possible for us to go to heaven: He himself did nothing wrong, yet he died so that we might live. Jesus said that his followers were to love each other in the same way—ready to make sacrifices.

You probably will never have a chance to sacrifice your life for a friend in some dangerous, life-or-death situation. You may never be called on to rescue a drowning person or hunt in a blizzard for a lost child. However, you can make other sacrifices for your friends. What can you give up? Time. Energy. Sometimes money. You can give a friend time to listen to her problems when you'd rather go shopping or watch TV. You can help when a friend is loaded down with work or needs assistance on a project. And you can pray for them.

Proverbs 17:17 says, "A friend loves at all times." That's more than when it's just fun or convenient. While few of us will ever be called on to give up our lives for a friend, we can daily think of others and make the sacrifices that we can.

More to Explore: Romans 5:6–8

Girl Talk: Have you ever sacrificed something for a friend? How did that make you feel? How did your friend feel?

God Talk: "Lord, I thank you for giving up your life for me. Help me find ways to help my friends and family and to help with a willing heart. Thank you for your wonderful example. Amen."

From *No Boys Allowed* by Kristi Holl

303

"They devoted themselves to the apostles' teaching and to fellowship."

—Acts 2:42

A Family of Believers

In the days soon after Jesus went back up into heaven and the disciples began to gather followers for him, anybody who gave his or her life to Jesus REALLY did. They sold all their stuff and put all the money together to make sure everybody had enough. They met every day and ate together and celebrated God with every meal. These were not just go-to-church-on-Sunday people. It worked, because "the Lord added to their number daily those who were being saved" (Acts 2:47).

God still wants us to have that kind of family feel with our fellow believers. We're made to come together in groups and eat and share and praise together—otherwise, why would there even be churches, and church camps, and youth groups? Yes, we all need time alone to pray and listen to God, the way Jesus did. But just as much, we're created to bow our heads together, to hold hands as we go to God, to sing in choirs, and to serve each other communion.

When you worship with a community, you can't help but have a sense that you belong there. That's because it's all about God—God bringing us into his family like one big reunion.

More to Explore: Matthew 18:20

Girl Talk: Do you have a church you love? If so, look around for girls who might feel left out there. Make sure they get to experience that big family love too.

God Talk: "God, thank you that I get to be part of a big family of believers. Help me to always be willing to invite others into that family. Amen."

From *That's So Me* by Nancy Rue

"All of you, be like-minded, be sympathetic, love one another, be compassionate and humble."

—1 Peter 3:8

Caring for One Another

Sarah had a kind and generous heart by nature, and she didn't understand why other kids had trouble getting along—until Tiffany moved to town. Tiffany was in Sarah's grade at school, and she attended youth group and Bible study every week. But she didn't just participate like everyone else. She blew into the room, like a gust of wind that unsettled everything. She was loud, thought she knew it all, and was determined to change everything so it was done "right." Bossy and opinionated—that described Tiffany perfectly, Sarah thought. Sarah would have preferred avoiding Tiffany altogether, but she knew Jesus wanted her to be kind and loving toward Tiffany. *Help me, Lord*, Sarah prayed as she acted in kind ways. Over several months, Sarah's heart slowly lined up with her loving actions. In the end, Tiffany became Sarah's close friend.

Being kind and loving toward one another isn't just a good idea. It's a commandment from God, and it applies whether we feel like being compassionate or not. Show love and kindness to others—it will come back to you multiplied many times over!

More To Explore: Luke 10:30–35

Girl Talk: Are there any people in your life you have a hard time getting along with? Why do you think they are the way they are? Think of one way to care for them today.

God Talk: "Lord, I know you want me to do my part to live in peace with everyone. Sometimes I have a hard time with ______. Please help me be more kind and loving toward this person. Thank you. Amen."

From *Shine On, Girl!* by Kristi Holl

305

"A good man brings good things out of the good stored up in him, and an evil man brings evil things out of the evil stored up in him."

—Matthew 12:35

Treasure Hunt

You can't tell by studying a person's looks if she is good or bad. Watch the person's actions instead. Someone with a good heart will say and do kind things. But watch out for the person with an evil heart!

Where our hearts go, our lives will follow. If you store up good things in your heart, good things will come out of you. That includes godly words and kind actions. If you store up evil things, then that's what will come out of you. There's an easy way to discover the condition of your heart (or someone else's). Just check out your daily actions. Whatever appears on the outside, first took place on the inside.

If someone gave your heart a checkup, what kind of treasure would they find? Be sure you're filling your heart with God's Word. Then you'll have treasure that you (and others around you) will cherish.

More to Explore: Psalm 37:30–31

Girl Talk: Do you know what is stored in your heart? How can you tell? Take time to examine your heart. Is it taking you where you want to go?

God Talk: "Lord, help me be more careful about what gets stored in my heart. I only want good things coming out of me. Amen."

From *Chick Chat* by Kristi Holl

"Meanwhile, Zacchaeus stood there and said to the Lord, 'I will give half my wealth to the poor, Lord, and if I have overcharged people on their taxes, I will give them back four times as much!' "

—Luke 19:8 (NLT)

From Taker to Giver

When Zacchaeus met Jesus, it changed him from a cheating tax collector into a generous giver. He was sorry for his selfishness and proved it by giving half his money to the poor. He even went to those he'd cheated and paid them back four times more than he'd stolen from them. Zacchaeus became a radical giver!

How much do you enjoy being around the girl at school who constantly lets you pay for the movie rentals and soda every week, while she keeps her money for her own shopping trips? Self-centered takers are no fun to be around. It's normal to want to see that our needs get met, but we need to look out for the needs of others too.

Make a change in your thinking. Look at the people in your life and ask yourself, "What can I give *you* or do for *you*?" Become a radical giver. Besides helping others, joy will flood your own heart.

More to Explore: Acts 20:35 and Deuteronomy 15:7–11

Girl Talk: What do you have that you could give to others? Is it hard for you to give, without expecting anything in return?

God Talk: "Lord, I thank you for all you give to me. I want to give to others, without thinking of myself. Thank you for helping me give with a loving heart. Amen."

From *No Boys Allowed* by Kristi Holl

307

"There is a path before each person that seems right, but it ends in death."

—Proverbs 14:12 (NLT)

What Now?

Each person makes many choices every day. *Should I do this or that? Should I go here or there?* The path that seems right to us can end in disaster. By ourselves, we just aren't smart enough to figure things out!

So how can you know if you're on a wrong path—when it appears okay? First, check it out with God's Word. There may be guidelines or a commandment concerning your situation. What about the times there isn't a specific Scripture to go by? (There are no verses telling which brand of running shoes to buy or which band instrument to play.) In those cases, find a trustworthy, godly person and ask for advice. Don't rely on your own understanding. Let God lead you.

More To Explore: Proverbs 1:7

Girl Talk: Can you think of two or three godly people you can turn to for advice? What qualities do they have? Keep them in mind when questions pop up.

God Talk: "Lord, I want to make sure I'm taking the right path. Please help me make the right choices and ask the right people. Amen."

From *Shine On, Girl!* by Kristi Holl

"So let's not grow tired of doing what is good. At just the right time we will reap a harvest of blessing if we don't give up."
—Galatians 6:9 (NLT)

Hanging in There

Natasha and Janice had signed up to be vacation Bible school volunteers. But halfway through the session, the newness wore off, and Janice decided it was way too much work. Besides, she had volunteered for a week, and that was enough. So she told the VBS director she was burnt out. Then she quit.

Natasha hung in for the entire three weeks, honoring her commitment, and when VBS ended, she felt a sense of real accomplishment. And what's more, on the last day, the class thanked her with a hand-painted card.

See, doing good isn't only admirable—it's one of our jobs as Christians. God wants us to be his helpers. He wants to accomplish his will through us. He wants to be able to say, like the master in Jesus' parable, "Well done, my good and faithful servant" (Matthew 25:21 NLT). But to do that, we have to stay the course—continue doing good—not for a day or even a year but until God's work is completed. And that won't be until Jesus comes again. When he does, girls who've remained faithful because of the "strength and energy that God supplies" (1 Peter 4:11 NLT) will get paid in full.

More to Explore: 1 Kings 19:1–18

Girl Talk: What can you do to regain your commitment to do good when you grow tired or frustrated?

God Talk: "Jesus, when I get tired or bored of doing good, remind me to look to you for strength. Amen."

From *Whatever: Livin' the True, Noble, Totally Excellent Life*
by Allia Zobel Nolan

Section VI — The Beauty of Believing

* ❀ *

"I know what it is to be in need, and I know what it is to have plenty. I have learned the secret of being content in any and every situation, whether well fed or hungry, whether living in plenty or in want."

—Philippians 4:12

Happy No Matter What

Michelle had plenty of clothes, but she wanted to buy expensive clothes with the "right" labels. She lived in a nice house, but she wanted a fancier one, so she could throw lavish parties for her friends. She wasn't happy with what she had. Then, one weekend, her youth group did an activity called "24 Hours in a Box." On a cold night, the group spent the night outside in the parking lot, sleeping in cardboard boxes like the homeless people downtown. After a sleepless night, Michelle realized she lived in a palace compared to some people. The next day, she thanked God again and again for a warm house, hot water for a shower, and enough food to eat.

"If only I had ..." (prettier looks, more athletic skill, better grades, a fancier house, a cell phone or iPod, brand-name clothes). We need to remember that circumstances are not the problem if we're not content. Learn to be happy with your life at this very minute—even if you're working to make it better.

More to Explore: 2 Corinthians 12:7–10

Girl Talk: What things do you feel you need in order to be content with your life? Can you learn to be truly happy with less?

God Talk: "Lord, I want to be content. Help me to focus on all the things you've already provided for me instead of wishing for more. Amen."

From *Chick Chat* by Kristi Holl

310

"Don't be concerned about the outward beauty that depends on fancy hairstyles, expensive jewelry, or beautiful clothes. You should be known for the beauty that comes from within, the unfading beauty of a gentle and quiet spirit, which is so precious to God."

—1 Peter 3:3–5 (NLT)

Unfading Beauty

Our current culture places all its importance on outer beauty. Beauty is a billion dollar business, including plastic surgery, exercise equipment, and designer clothing. From the movies to magazines, our world screams that outer beauty is all that matters. Not true! We all know girls who are gorgeous, but when they open their mouths, nasty things spew out. Suddenly, they lose their beauty. If you're unhappy, lonely, insecure, and crabby, a total body makeover won't change a thing. The beauty has to start in your heart.

How do you acquire this kind of beauty that is so precious to God? By spending time alone with him. Talk to him. Read his Word. The neat thing about inner beauty is its ability to transform how you look on the outside. Some of the most beautiful women in history didn't have good facial features or fancy clothes. They had an inner peace and a loving spirit that radiated, making them beautiful on the outside as well.

More to Explore: 1 Timothy 2:9–10

Girl Talk: How much time do you spend looking in the mirror and trying to improve your outer beauty? How much time do you spend in God's Word, improving your inner beauty?

God Talk: "Lord, I care too much about how I look on the outside. Please help me focus on my spirit, to make it more loving and peaceful. Amen."

From *No Boys Allowed* by Kristi Holl

"The people brought children to Jesus, hoping he might touch them. The disciples shooed them off. But Jesus was irate and let them know it: 'Don't push these children away. Don't ever get between them and me. These children are at the very center of life in the kingdom. Mark this: Unless you accept God's kingdom in the simplicity of a child, you'll never get in.' Then, gathering the children up in his arms, he laid his hands of blessing on them."

—Mark 10:13–16 (MSG)

Kingdom Kids

Have you ever spent time with little kids? They might irritate you sometimes, but you can learn a lot by observing them! The simple, unwavering trust in the heart of a child is something Father God really loves. The beauty of believing with childlike faith means you give attention to your heavenly Father's presence. Simply put, faithgirlz love spending time with Father God! One of the best things about being with God is that he lifts you up higher. In the presence of God, you're like a small toddler on the shoulders of her father, seeing things the way he does.

Maybe you didn't earn the grade you wanted on that test. Perhaps Mom won't let you watch that movie. When you're unable to see the good in a situation, Father God can. Today, no matter what comes your way, ask your heavenly Father to pick you up and put you on his shoulders, so you can see things the way God does.

More To Explore: Isaiah 55:8–9 NIV

Girl Talk: What do you think Father God is like?

God Talk: "Father, thank you for teaching me to trust you with simple faith. I will love you Lord, with all of my heart, soul, strength, and mind, just as you have said. It is my honor to make pursuing you my number one goal. I adore you, Father!"

From *My Beautiful Daughter* by Tasha Douglas

312

"Unto You, O my Strength, I will sing praises; for God is my Defense, my Fortress, and High Tower, the God Who shows me mercy and steadfast love."

—Psalm 59:17 (AMP)

Praise the Lord!

We worship and thank God for many different things. He is our strength when we're weak and our protection when we're attacked. He's our fortress to hide in when we're afraid, our mercy when we make mistakes, and our love when we are lonely.

As you sit by the stream, a deep peace flows through you. How much you have to be thankful for! You can hardly believe the changes since last year. Your dad's serious illness is over, and the boy who was picking on you at school has moved away. Your parents have gone to counseling and worked hard, and now there's laughter back in your home. Now that you can concentrate again, your grades have risen. God has healed your family from so many frightening things. You can only sit by the stream and murmur, "Thank you, God. Thank you. Thank you!" over and over.

Praise God at all times. We can praise him in the storm as his strength brings us through, and we can praise him when the sun shines again. Take time—right now—to thank God for his many blessings.

More To Explore: Psalm 59:9–10

Girl Talk: Can you list five things—both happy things and hard things—that you can thank God for right now? Then thank the Lord and praise his name!

God Talk: "Lord, help me always remember to thank you for all you have done. Thank you for ________. I want to praise your name. You are an awesome God! Amen."

From *Shine On, Girl!* by Kristi Holl

"I praise you, Father, Lord of heaven and earth, because you have hidden these things from the wise and learned, and revealed them to little children."

—Luke 10:21

You're In!

One of the clearest ways God shows us that we are worthy of love without having to DO or BE anything is through Jesus. When our Lord picked his disciples, he wasn't like a team captain on the playground, calling out the names of the best players to be on his side. Jesus selected the most motley crew you could dream up—a big ol' fisherman, who was always losing his temper; a tax collector people couldn't stand (ask your parents about the IRS and you'll understand); a whole bunch of guys who had to have everything explained to them, like, twenty times.

In this verse, Jesus even says they're "little children," not all smart and educated, just open to learning, willing to obey, eager to please. Little kids don't try to be that way—they simply are. Jesus praised God for them. He praises God for you. And he reveals himself to you. So don't worry. You've already been picked for the team. You don't have to stand there pretending you don't care while everybody else lines up behind the captains. You're in, and you always have been.

More To Explore: Luke 24:25

Girl Talk: Have you ever felt like the disciples—foolish, unworthy, or just plain confused?

God Talk: "God, thank you that you don't require perfection. Thank you that it doesn't matter how small or unimportant I am—you still want to use me! Amen."

From *That Is So Me* by Nancy Rue

314

"Cultivate inner beauty, the gentle, gracious kind that God delights in."

—1 Peter 3:4 (MSG)

God Knows You Inside Out

Brittany dressed in the latest fashions, had her hair fixed like her favorite movie star's, and had a sharp, clever remark for everyone. It really irritated her that her neighbor, Paige (who was plain and ordinary-looking), had more friends. Brittany's own sister had the nerve to say she wished Brittany was more like Paige! But why? Brittany had no idea.

It's all about beauty. We have an outer life that everyone can see. What others think of us is determined by our outer life. But we have an inner life too, which God sees. Our reputation with God is based on our heart, or inner life. We tend to give 90 percent of our attention to our outer life, and very little to our inner life. But God doesn't watch just our actions. He examines the attitudes, motives, and desires of our heart. All these things are important to him—and to others.

The inner person is who we *really* are. So cultivate true inner beauty. Before long, that inner beauty will also be seen and appreciated on the outside.

More to Explore: Luke 16:15

Girl Talk: Does the way you act match how you feel on the inside? Would you be embarrassed if others could see the real you?

God Talk: "Lord, my heart doesn't always match what I say and do. Thank you for helping me get rid of the bad attitudes in my heart. Amen."

From *Girlz Rock* by Kristi Holl

"They were all trying to frighten us, thinking, 'Their hands will get too weak for the work, and it will not be completed.' But I prayed, 'Now strengthen my hands.'"

—Nehemiah 6:9

Down in the Dumps

You may be surrounded by people who say, "You can't do that! You're weak! You'll never succeed!" If you listen to such voices, discouragement will set in. Don't pay any attention to them. Instead, pray. Ask God to give you strength to keep pressing on toward the finish line.

Sometimes the people who discourage you are rivals. It might be the girl who warms the bench but wants your spot on the volleyball team. It might be the classmate who is competing with you for the lead in a school play. But sometimes those who make discouraging remarks are members of your own family—or a close friend. That's harder to bear. Once in a while, someone who loves you might try to discourage you, because they're afraid you're trying something too difficult. No matter where a negative remark comes from, you don't have to accept it. Just say to yourself, *No, thank you! I'm not interested in any discouragement today!* and stay enthusiastic instead.

The next time you're working to achieve something, turn a deaf ear to people who try to discourage you. Instead, call on the Lord for *his* encouragement.

More To Explore: Isaiah 35:3–4

Girl Talk: Do people make discouraging remarks to you? Do you make them to others—or do you try to encourage people?

God Talk: "Lord, I want to ignore people's negative remarks. Help me to listen only to you. Amen."

From *Shine On, Girl!* by Kristi Holl

"For we are God's handiwork."

—Ephesians 2:10

Work of Art

Each person is "God's workmanship." It means you're a masterpiece, a work of art! So learn to see yourself the way God sees you.

You may not feel like a work of art—no way! In fact, you may hate walking by mirrors, whether at home, at school, or when shopping. All you notice are your dorky glasses, or your zitty forehead, or your skinny figure. Although you are, in fact, an attractive young girl, you're so focused on the traits you dislike that you can't see anything else. You need to remember you're God's work of art. He created you just the way you are with a special plan in mind for your life.

Don't say negative things about yourself, like "I hate my nose" or "I'm too short" or "My stomach's fat." Don't downgrade yourself. Instead, say out loud every day, "I accept myself. God created me, and I'm his work of art. He has a wonderful future planned for me." Say this often enough, and you will gradually accept yourself as God's masterpiece. Why is this so important? If we don't accept ourselves, we'll find it hard—if not impossible—to accept others.

So smile. Really big. Remember—you're a work of art!

More to Explore: Isaiah 60:21

Girl Talk: How do you feel about your looks? Do you like how God has made you? Are there things you'd like to change?

God Talk: "Lord, I want to accept myself the way you made me. Help me to believe that I am truly your masterpiece. Amen."

From *Chick Chat* by Kristi Holl

"Rejoice in the Lord always. I will say it again: Rejoice!"
—Philippians 4:4

Miriam's Journey

Remember Miriam? She helped to save her brother from the cruel Egyptian pharaoh. When Pharaoh declared that all Hebrew baby boys were to be killed, Miriam watched her mother place her baby brother Moses in a basket in the Nile River, hoping that he would float to somewhere safer. Miriam followed the basket. When Pharaoh's daughter found it, Miriam boldly stepped out of the reeds and said to the pharaoh's daughter, "Do you want me to get one of the Hebrew women to nurse the baby for you?"

Pharaoh's daughter paid Miriam's mother to take baby Moses home and care for him until he was old enough to live in the palace. Because Miriam spoke up, with God's help, she was able to save her baby brother.

Years later, after ten terrible plagues, Pharaoh allowed Moses and Aaron to lead the Israelites out of Egypt to the land God had promised them. But before they got very far, Pharaoh changed his mind. He wanted the Israelites back in slavery. His army chased Moses, Miriam, and their people to the Red Sea.

But just when the Israelites reached the water's edge, something amazing happened. God separated the waters, and Miriam, Moses, and the Israelites crossed the sea on dry land.

Pharaoh's army followed them. But when all the Israelites were safe on the other side of the Red Sea, God let the water go. The waves rolled in on Pharaoh's men. Moses, Aaron, Miriam, and their people were safe.

Because Miriam followed God's guidance when Moses was a baby, Moses survived to lead his people out of slavery. Even though our actions—like Miriam's—may seem small to us now, they can have big consequences in the future.

Do you know what Miriam did next? She became a worship leader. Miriam praised God with her tambourine. And all the women followed her, playing instruments and dancing for God while Miriam sang a chorus:

"Sing to the Lord,
for he is highly exalted.
The horse and its rider
he has hurled into the sea."

As a young girl, Miriam learned that God is faithful and just. She learned to trust God and to praise him. God is faithful to you too. Like Miriam, you can pay attention to God's work in your life and worship him. Think about all the times he's helped you, taken care of you, and blessed you. You can show your friends and family and the other people in your life how to be thankful and praise God.

More To Explore: Read Miriam's story in Exodus 2:1–8; 14:5–15:21.

Girl Talk: What is one way you can worship God today?

God Talk: "Dear heavenly Father, you are so good to me. Thank you for your goodness, Lord. Please help me to develop a thankful heart. I want to praise you more. For Jesus' sake, amen."

From *Real Girls of the Bible* by Mona Hodgson

"Trust God from the bottom of your heart. Don't try to figure out everything on your own. Listen for God's voice in everything you do, everywhere you go. He's the one who will keep you on track."

—Proverbs 3:5–6 (MSG)

Your Constant Guide

If you hike through the wilderness in a national park, you can hire a guide. He'll keep you on safe paths, away from bears and poisonous snakes. He'll show you the clean streams for drinking water and lead you by the prettiest scenery. Or you can go out on your own. Your chances of snake bite, bear attack, polluted water, and falling off a cliff increase immediately.

Your life is like a path through that wilderness, and God is your committed guide. The hike may still be strenuous, but you'll have a safer and much more enjoyable experience. Coming up with your own plan and ignoring God and his Word can put you in the way of many dangers and unnecessary tough times. Avoid being a know-it-all. "Don't be impressed with your own wisdom. Instead, fear the Lord and turn your back on evil" (Proverbs 3:7 NLT).

Trust God and keep on a well-guided path that will lead to inner beauty and outward faith.

More to Explore: Psalm 37:3–6 and Proverbs 28:26

Girl Talk: Do you ever feel lost? Do you ever strike out on your own, with no guidance? Have you ever asked God for help?

God Talk: "Father, I know I go off on my own sometimes. Help me to trust in you and follow your will for my life. I love you, Lord. Amen."

From *No Boys Allowed* by Kristi Holl

"Pleasant words are like honey. They are sweet to the spirit and bring healing to the body."

—Proverbs 16:24 (NIrV)

Wedding in the Family

With a final look in the mirror, Kallie pushed aside a strand of her brown hair. Then she lined up at the back of the church with her sisters Alyssa and Morgan.

As the shortest bridesmaid, Kallie would lead the others down the aisle. She was the youngest of four sisters and often felt like a tagalong. Too old to be a flower girl, but much younger than her sisters, Kallie was almost surprised when her sister Caryn asked her to be in her wedding.

Just then, Alyssa leaned forward to tell Kallie that she looked great. But Kallie felt sure she was kidding. "Hey, don't make fun of me!" she whispered. "I wish I looked as awesome as you."

Alyssa shook her head, but before she could answer, the signal came.

Remembering to walk slowly, Kallie started down the aisle. When she reached the steps, she managed to get up them without tripping on her long dress. Then she turned and looked toward the back of the church.

Next came Alyssa and Morgan. Then Caryn started forward. With her long white dress, her dark skin and eyes looked especially beautiful. Caryn seemed to shimmer all the way down the aisle. *I've never seen her so beautiful!* thought Kallie.

At the wedding reception, Gran found her. "Kallie, your hair is lovely that way!"

"Oh, Gran, I just couldn't get it the way I wanted!"

"You couldn't possibly improve on how it is," answered Gran. "And you held your long skirt just right as you went up the steps."

"Didn't I look clumsy? I was sure I did."

"Best of all, the way you stood at the altar, quietly listening, was respectful and nice."

Kallie sighed. "I wanted to itch every minute. I felt like scratching my back. Alyssa and Morgan look so much nicer than I do."

Gran's smile faded. Her voice was gentle, yet firm. "Kallie, I gave you three compliments. What do you want to do about it?"

Gran moved away, and Kallie felt uneasy. *What was she telling me?*

As Kallie watched, Gran walked over to Alyssa and her boyfriend, Jamal. Looking at Alyssa, then at Gran, Jamal grinned. Kallie heard the low rumble of his voice.

"How about this awesome girl? I found a really good one, don't you think, Gran?"

Alyssa blushed but smiled up at him. "Thanks, Jamal. I'm glad you like the way I am."

Jamal's slow smile reached his eyes. In that moment, something clicked in Kallie's mind. *So that's what Gran meant!*

More to Explore: Proverbs 31:26

Girl Talk: Think of a time when someone complimented you. How did you feel about what that person said? What would be a good way to answer that compliment?

God Talk: "Thank you, Jesus, that compliments are special gifts. Help me know what to say when people compliment me. And help me encourage others with honest compliments that make them feel special. Amen."

From *Girl Talk* by Lois Walfrid Johnson

320

"Being confident of this very thing, that He who has begun a good work in you will complete it until the day of Jesus Christ."
—Philippians 1:6 (NKJV)

Confidence in ME?

Be very sure—be confident—that God lives in you. He is working in you to mature you, and he will keep working until you're finally finished—complete and perfect. You are a child of God. To feel better about yourself, be sure to do the following things:

- Never speak negatively about yourself.
- Think about and speak positive things about yourself.
- Never compare yourself with others.
- Find something you like to do—something you're good at—and practice it over and over.
- You and God together determine your worth; don't let someone else do it.
- Stay close to God, your true source of confidence.

God is living and working in you every minute of your life. You can be confident of that!

More to Explore: Philippians 2:13

Girl Talk: Do you ever feel like your confidence is missing? Do you realize how much God loves you? What is one thing you can do to feel more confident today?

God Talk: "Lord, when things don't go right, I can feel down really easily. Please help me to remember that all I need is you. Thank you for your confidence in me that never ends. I love you! Amen."

From *Girlz Rock* by Kristi Holl

"Don't copy the behavior and customs of this world, but let God transform you into a new person by changing the way you think. Then you will know what God wants you to do, and you will know how good and pleasing and perfect his will really is."
—Romans 12:2 (NLT)

Brand-New

The world is full of evil practices, violence, and dishonesty. Don't copy the ways of the world! Instead, let God change you from the inside out into a new person by changing your thinking. This changing—or transforming—isn't a one-time event. It's a process that takes time, much like the process of a caterpillar changing into a butterfly. After the transformation has taken place, you—like the butterfly—will see the wonderful plan God has for your life.

God wants you to have a joyful, abundant life, but you need to grow daily closer to him. God gave you a new spirit, not a new brain. Your mind still has its old sinful patterns. It needs to be transformed by reading God's Word and thinking about how to apply it in your everyday life. In time, you'll experience "love, joy, peace, forbearance, kindness, goodness, faithfulness, gentleness and self-control" (Galatians 5:22–23).

More to Explore: 1 John 2:15

Girl Talk: Are there areas of your mind that need changing? What can you do to start the process?

God Talk: "Lord, I want to be more like you. Show me what my part is—and help me to do it. Amen."

From *Chick Chat* by Kristi Holl

322

"Call to me and I will answer you and tell you great and unsearchable things you do not know."

—Jeremiah 33:3

Anna's Call to Prayer

Anna didn't always do what everyone else did. Every country and generation has its own customs. During that time, it was the custom that a Jewish widow without children would move back into her parents' house until another man wanted to marry her. But that's not what Anna did.

Anna was married only seven years when her husband died. Instead of doing what others would've done, she moved into the temple in Jerusalem. The Bible says Anna never left the temple. She worshiped God night and day, fasting and praying. Anna was a prophetess.

Made of white marble and decorated in gold, the temple was more like a city than a church. Huge walls surrounded the area, which was about the size of twelve soccer fields. Watchtowers stood at the corners of the wall. Jews and Gentiles came to the temple to pray, to offer sacrifices, to pay their temple tax, and to discuss religious issues with rabbis. This was where Anna lived and served God.

When Anna's husband died and left her alone, Anna became a woman who talked about the coming Messiah and then about Jesus, the Messiah, to all who would listen. She was a woman who talked to God night and day. Anna lived a life of prayer in an active relationship with God.

Mary and Joseph took baby Jesus to Jerusalem to present him to the Lord. It was written in the Law that every firstborn male was to be consecrated to God. Anna was an old lady when Joseph and Mary showed up at Herod's Temple.

"Jesus." Anna's lips trembled with joy as she spoke his name. This was the Messiah she'd been waiting for. Praying for. Talking about. Anna gazed into the tender eyes of the one who came to save her, her people, and the world from sin.

We're never too young or too old to thank God for his goodness and speak to others about Jesus, God's holy Son.

Whether bad things happen—like your best friend moves away or your parents get divorced, or good things happen—like you win the state spelling bee or your family takes a dream vacation, you can live like Anna did. You don't have to live in a church or in a temple, but you can be a girl who prays night and day. You can tell the people around you about Jesus who is Savior to all who believe in him.

More To Explore: 1 Thessalonians 5:17

Girl Talk: What is one way you can worship God today?

God Talk: "Lord God, I'm so glad I can talk to you and that you listen to me. Please teach me how to pray more for other people. In Jesus' name, amen."

From *Real Girls of the Bible* by Mona Hodgson

323

"Give thanks to the Lord, for he is good; his love endures forever."

—1 Chronicles 16:34

Fill It Up

After you've run four times around the track during gym class, your fuel tank is low. You feel shaky, so you know you need an energy bar or drink. Inside, you also have a "love tank" that gets empty. God fills it whenever you spend time with him, reading his Word or just talking to him and letting him love you. But when it goes too long between God visits, your love tank gets close to empty. You won't get the shakes, but symptoms might include being impatient, rude, jealous, or just totally stressed.

Good news! God's love is everlasting—it never runs out. Even better news—it's always available to us, just for the asking. It doesn't matter what time of the day or night it is. It doesn't matter where you are. It doesn't matter if you're alone or in a crowd. When you realize that your love tank is getting low, stop. Get alone if you can, or just close your eyes. Take several deep, deep breaths. Then thank God for being such a good God and for his love, which never runs out.

More to Explore: 2 Chronicles 5:13

Girl Talk: Do you ever feel your "love tank" getting low? How do you usually fill yourself up again? Do you go to God?

God Talk: "Thank you for your love, Lord. Please help me remember that you are with me always. Fill me up with your love every day. Thank you. Amen."

From *No Boys Allowed* by Kristi Holl

"You [God] created my inmost being . . . all the days ordained for me were written in your book before one of them came to be."

—Psalm 139:13, 16

Uniquely You

Have you ever known identical twins? At first, it was probably hard to tell which one was which, until you got to know them. Then it was like, duh, anybody could tell them apart. One was super-quiet, the other would talk your ear off. One could run like a track star, the other could always be found curled up with a copy of *Anne of Green Gables*. Two people might look exactly alike, but each one is totally different on the inside.

So not only are you worth creating on the outside in all of your one-of-a-kindness—you were custom-designed, tailor-made, handcrafted on the inside too. That's because you were set up for a purpose nobody else has. Doesn't it make sense that God gave you the right personality to carry it out? And that personality is different from anyone else you might want to copy. Why miss out on what God has in store for you while you're trying to get in on his plan for somebody else? Your plans are the best—for YOU—and so is your personality. You're so worth it.

More To Explore: Ephesians 2:10

Girl Talk: What makes you unique? How does your uniqueness help you serve God and others?

God Talk: "Jesus, thank you for creating me just the way I am! Thank you that you have a unique plan for my life—and for everyone else's too. Amen."

From *That Is So Me* by Nancy Rue

325

" . . . so that you may surely learn to sense what is vital, and approve and prize what is excellent and of real value."

—Philippians 1:10 (AMP)

True Value

When Jessica moved to a new town and started middle school, she studied the various groups of girls. Who would be her new friends? She liked both Grace and Elizabeth—they were fun and kind and friendly—but they definitely weren't "cool." On the other hand, Brit and Kayla were obviously the most popular girls. Boys swarmed around them. They invited Jessica to sit at their lunch table, and, at first, Jessica was thrilled to be singled out. But the filthy language she heard there—and the nasty backbiting of other students—made her feel dirty. Jessica had a choice to make. Would she choose friends of excellent moral value with high standards? Or would she settle for friends with glitz but no character?

How can you learn to prize what God values? Read God's Word and let it change your thinking. "Do not conform to the pattern of this world, but be transformed by the renewing of your mind. Then you will be able to test and approve what God's will is—his good, pleasing and perfect will" (Romans 12:2). Choosing what God values will place you in the center of his will—and there's no better place on earth to be!

More To Explore: 1 Thessalonians 5:21

Girl Talk: What do you suppose God thinks about the decisions you make and the people you hang out with?

God Talk: "Lord, I don't always make the best choice with my time. In everything I do, I want you to be proud of me. Please help me make the right decisions. Amen."

From *Shine On, Girl!* by Kristi Holl

"Stern discipline awaits anyone who leaves the path; the one who hates correction will die."

—Proverbs 15:10

Big Price to Pay!

There will be serious correction for the person who gives up living God's way. The person who hates to be disciplined or scolded for wrongdoing will die. It may be a physical death, a moral death, or a spiritual death.

Sometimes we don't like to think of God as someone who disciplines us when we rebel and go our own way. "That's not loving!" some people declare. Actually, the opposite is true. God disciplines us *because* he loves us, just as an earthly father corrects his kids to help them live a better life. If God didn't love us, he'd let us rebel and do nothing about it. But he knows that the consequences of living a life without him will kill us. The Lord will do what's necessary to convince you to get back on a path toward life. That's because he loves you so much.

More To Explore: Hebrews 12:11

Girl Talk: Has God had to discipline you in the past year? Did you get the message and turn back to him or is he still trying to get your attention?

God Talk: "Lord, I don't like being disciplined, but I know it's because you love me. Please help me listen to you and correct my ways. I want to follow you more closely. Amen."

From *Shine On, Girl!* by Kristi Holl

327

"No matter what happens, always be thankful, for this is God's will for you who belong to Christ Jesus."

—1 Thessalonians 5:18 (NLT)

Attitude? Gratitude!

Life happens when you've made other plans. But no matter what happens, God intends that we who belong to Christ should be grateful. Events are important, but God is even more interested in your attitude when things happen. Will your attitude be one of gratitude?

It's a cinch to be thankful on days the sun shines, our hair behaves perfectly, there's no school, and we're going shopping. Anyone in the world can be grateful on days like that. But can you be grateful no matter what happens? Like when your little sister pesters you, or it rains on the day of your birthday picnic? Believe it or not, *yes*, you can even be thankful then.

As David wrote, "I will praise the Lord at all times. I will constantly speak his praises" (Psalm 34:1 NLT). Develop a thankful heart, one that looks every day for things to be grateful for. Then you'll find it much easier to be thankful when things happen that you don't like and didn't want. A heart full of gratitude to God is a joyful heart, no matter what happens.

More to Explore: Ephesians 5:20

Girl Talk: Do you have a grateful heart? If not, do you desire to have a thankful heart?

God Talk: "Lord, please develop a thankful heart within me. I praise you right now for all of the blessings in my life. I love you. Amen."

From *No Boys Allowed* by Kristi Holl

"I keep my eyes always on the Lord. With him at my right hand, I will not be shaken."

—Psalm 16:8

A Healer for Jairus' Daughter

Jairus, a synagogue ruler, had a sick daughter. As a synagogue ruler, he was a powerful man, but he was powerless to heal his sick daughter.

Jairus heard Jesus had the power to work miracles, and Jesus was coming to their town. While his daughter lay at home dying, Jairus left to find Jesus. When he did find Jesus, Jairus hurried into the crowd, fell at Jesus' feet, and begged Jesus to come to his house and heal his daughter.

The Bible doesn't describe Jairus' daughter's illness, but she must have been very ill when her father left to find Jesus. While Jesus stopped to speak to a woman in the crowd, someone came from Jairus' house and told him, "Your daughter is dead. Don't bother the teacher anymore."

Jesus heard and said to Jairus, "Don't be afraid. Believe, and she'll be healed."

When Jesus arrived at the house, mourners cried for Jairus' daughter. Jesus only let Peter, John, James, and the girl's father and mother inside the room with him. Perhaps because he knew they were the only people who believed he could heal her. Meanwhile, the mourners continued to wail and Jesus said, "Stop wailing. She's not dead. She's asleep."

The mourners laughed at him. They believed the girl was permanently dead because they didn't believe Jesus could bring her back to life.

Jesus reached out and held the girl's hand. "My child," he said, "get up."

Immediately, her spirit returned to her body. Having received her miracle, the girl stood up and walked around. Do you know what Jesus did next? He told her parents to give her something to eat. Jesus made sure all of her needs were met.

Jesus wants us to trust him to do the same for us. You can give your health and your very life to Jesus. And like Jairus' daughter, you can accept Jesus' gift of grace. Maybe your heart has been broken by the loss of a friend who moved away or by the rejection of someone you love. Maybe you need to accept Jesus' hand and let him help you up, out of sadness, grief, or anger.

Or maybe, like Jairus' daughter, you've seen Jesus work a miracle in your life or in the life of a family member. Have you thanked Jesus for his presence in your life?

More To Explore: Mark 5:21–24, 35–43

Girl Talk: How have you seen the healing hand of God in your life or in the lives of those around you?

God Talk: "Dear God, you are my provider. You know my needs. And I'm so glad you take care of me and will never leave me. Thank you. Amen."

From *Real Girls of the Bible* by Mona Hodgson

"I praise you because I am fearfully and wonderfully made; your works are wonderful, I know that full well."

—Psalm 139:14

No Trash Here

Does God make junk? Seriously. Is there anything tacky about a box turtle? Anything fake about a velvety red rose? Anything boring in a sunset over the water?

Since God created you, obviously you aren't junk either. In fact, you are, as David puts it in the Psalm for today, "fearfully and wonderfully made." Fearfully, by the way, doesn't mean Godzilla. It means "awesome"—you were made to be awesome. God knit you together that way, with love in every stitch. He thought of you, and you *became*.

You are the result of God's precious thought, which means several things for you:

- You are beautiful. Maybe not modeling agency beautiful, but gorgeous in your own way. Believe it.
- You have a responsibility to find your true beauty. That doesn't mean plastering on what everybody else says is "beauty." It's about discovering your best qualities.
- God wants you to show that beauty in everything you do. Just let what is beautiful within you shine to every person you meet.

Doing that involves a journey. It's the one God wants you to take. It's the reason he made you—fearfully and wonderfully.

More To Explore: 1 Samuel 16:7

Girl Talk: In what ways are you beautiful? Yes, you!

God Talk: "God, thank you that I am fearfully and wonderfully made. Help me to see the beauty in myself and discover the beauty in others. Amen."

From *That Is So Me* by Nancy Rue

330

"Then I said to them, 'You see the trouble we are in: Jerusalem lies in ruins, and its gates have been burned with fire. Come, let us rebuild the wall of Jerusalem, and we will no longer be in disgrace."

—Nehemiah 2:17

Fight Discouragement!

We too often have to rebuild. What if, after your parents' divorce, your dad moves five states away? After that, you see him only in the summer. Discouragement sets in, and you quietly give up. Why try to have a relationship with your dad when he lives so far away? You confide in your best friend that you plan to skip your next summer visit—and why. Yes, your friend agrees, the relationship with your dad has broken down. It's sad, but it doesn't have to stay that way. "Come on. You can rebuild," your friend says. Together with your friend, you brainstorm some ways to heal the relationship with your dad.

It's easy to be down when you see things in ruins, whether it's your messy room or failing grades. Disappointments happen to everyone. But discouragement—when we lose confidence in ourselves, God, or others—*is a choice.* We can choose to be discouraged. Or we can do what Nehemiah did. We can study the situation and decide to rebuild.

More to Explore: Isaiah 35:3–4

Girl Talk: Are there things in your life that look ruined? In what ways can you begin to rebuild?

God Talk: "Lord, I choose not to be discouraged. Help me fix the broken things in my life. Thank you! Amen."

From *Chick Chat* by Kristi Holl

"Don't be afraid. Stand firm. You will see how the Lord will save you today. Do you see those Egyptians? You will never see them again. The Lord will fight for you. Just be still."

—Exodus 14:13–14 (NIrV)

I Dare You

Emma yawned and looked up at the hands of the clock. With a new boy in school, it had been an exciting day. Yet now, time seemed to have stopped.

Annabelle, the most popular girl in the room, had asked Emma to walk home with her from school. Lily, the second most popular girl, was coming along. Sure, it was longer to walk the way they chose, but it would be worth it.

At last, the moment came. Surrounded by a hundred other kids, they pushed their way out the school door and started down the street. Soon, they left the others behind.

Annabelle giggled. "Don't you like the new boy? I just love Aiden's brown eyes. And his muscles—*wow!*" She tossed her head, and her blond hair swung around her shoulders. "Did you see the way Aiden watches me? I'm sure he likes me."

Sure that clouds had moved across the sun, Emma glanced up. But nothing had changed. Twice Aiden had spoken to her that morning. When they traded test papers, he grinned at the funny mark Emma used for corrections. He liked the cartoon she drew at the bottom. She had wondered, *Could he really like me?* But now Annabelle said—

Just then, Annabelle opened her book bag. "Look! I've got half a pack of cigarettes my mom left out. Let's cut down this street, and no one will see us."

Emma stopped in her tracks. "No, I don't think so."

"Oh, come on," Annabelle said. "I've smoked before. It's not a big deal."

"I've tried it too," Lily joined in. "It won't hurt you."

"Sorry," Emma said. "I know people who can't stop smoking. I don't want to start."

"Are you kidding?" Annabelle asked. "You'll never be popular that way!"

"You're just a chicken," Lily said. "I dare you to give it a try."

Emma cringed. Her mixed-up feelings seemed like a waterfall tumbling over rocks. "I *like* you!" she wanted to cry out. "I don't want you dying of lung cancer the way my uncle did!" But the words stuck in her throat.

She wondered if Annabelle and Lily could see that her face felt hot with embarrassment. *Is this what it means to be popular?*

More to Explore: Isaiah 53:5

Girl Talk: Is it important to be popular with everyone? Do you think God sometimes wants us to be *unpopular*?

God Talk: "When I'm tempted to do wrong, help me to say no, Jesus, even if I'm scared. Thank you that even though you often weren't popular when you lived on earth, you have become the most important person who ever lived."

From *Girl Talk* by Lois Walfrid Johnson

"You made all the delicate, inner parts of my body and knit me together in my mother's womb. Thank you for making me so wonderfully complex! Your workmanship is marvelous—and how well I know it."

—Psalm 139:13–14 (NLT)

An Inside Job

Imagine God carefully forming you inside your mother's body, putting together all your miniature inward parts. He created each tiny organ, bone, and muscle, then linked them together in a pattern that created you. What a miracle!

If this is true, then why do girls worry about being too fat or too thin? We fall into the deadly trap of comparing ourselves to others, then envying how they look. Your body image (or how you see yourself) may not be based on the facts. You can feel too skinny, yet look beautiful to everyone else. Most important, you always look beautiful to God! He carefully molded you to look *exactly* like you do.

It's fine to want to appear your best. Wash your hair often, press your wrinkled blouse, and wear clothing styles that flatter you. But don't forget—while people notice the outside of you, God studies your heart. If you really want to change how you feel about your looks, start on the inside. See yourself through God's eyes, the one who so carefully made you and loves you.

More to Explore: 1 Peter 3:3–4

Girl Talk: How often do you worry about your appearance? Can you give this worry to God? Do you believe he cares?

God Talk: "Lord, I know you created every part of me, and you don't make mistakes. Help me to be content with every aspect of who I am. Thank you for loving me. Amen."

From *No Boys Allowed* by Kristi Holl

333

"God said to Moses, "I AM WHO I AM. This is what you are to say to the Israelites: 'I AM has sent me to you.'"

—Exodus 3:14

The Great I AM

God appeared to Moses as a burning bush and said outright that he was the God of his fathers, Abraham, Isaac, and Jacob. And what did Moses do? He "hid his face, because he was afraid to look at God" (Exodus 3:6).

Once he did believe he was seeing God, Moses was scared nobody would believe him. People, he knew, would ask him what God's name was. What was he supposed to tell them? That's when God revealed something huge about himself, not just to Moses, but to us. He said, "I am who I am."

God is. He just is, and that's all he needs to be. He requires no explanation. When Moses accepted that, God told him who he was—the leader and freer of the Israelites. If you can say, "God IS, and I believe he is exactly who he is," then God will show you that you too are just who you are. He'll help you understand that there is no need to try to be what someone else tells you that you should be. In time, he'll show you what your purpose is, that thing that shows you all that you are. For now, just relax into the knowledge that who you are is exactly who you need to be.

More To Explore: John 8:58

Girl Talk: Think about who God is. Make a list of all his incredible qualities.

God Talk: "God, thank you for who you are. And thank you that I am free to be me. Amen."

From *That Is So Me* by Nancy Rue

"Don't take pride in following a particular leader. Everything belongs to you."

—1 Corinthians 3:21 (NLT)

The Real "In" Group

Most classes have a few girls who have decided they are the "popular" group. They will claim to have inside information that others don't have, or act as if they are more special than anyone else. Don't fall for that! Don't let your feelings about yourself be determined by what group you belong to or who accepts or rejects you. You already belong to the coolest group you could join: Father, Son, and Holy Spirit!

God designed you to have friendships that are rewarding, with give-and-take sharing. Centering your life on someone who demands to be the focus will throw your friendship out of balance. But if you belong to Christ (have accepted him as your Savior), then you're a daughter of the King. You are as worthy as anyone else on earth—anyone! So don't brag about being part of So-and-So's group, or follow the "popular girls" because they have more of what the world offers. Your worth comes from belonging to Christ—not to a particular friend or group.

More to Explore: 1 Corinthians 3:3–6

Girl Talk: Do you rely on friends for self-esteem or on God? You may rely on both, but always remember that God's opinion of you matters the most.

God Talk: "Lord, I sometimes worry too much about what others think of me. Please help me remember that you are the one I need to please. In you, I have all the love and respect I will ever need! Amen."

From *Girlz Rock* by Kristi Holl

"The Lord is gracious and righteous; our God is full of compassion."
—Psalm 116:5

A Cure for the Woman in the Crowd

Imagine not being able to be with your family or friends because you're considered unclean. You're an outcast. Not because of anything you've done, but because of an inner wound you have no control over. That's what life was like for the woman who was "subject to bleeding," also called the "woman in the crowd."

This woman had been subject to bleeding for twelve years. No doctor could heal her. Any attempts to cure her only made the problem worse. She must have been anemic and weak. And according to Jewish law at the time, she was ceremonially unclean, which meant everyone avoided her. They believed if they touched her or anything she touched, they too would become unclean. No one wanted anything to do with her. With no money to live on, no strength to keep going, and no friends to encourage her, she was desperate for healing.

Then one day, as she hovered at the edge of a crowd at the lake, she saw Jesus. She had heard about Jesus, and she believed if she could just touch his cloak, she'd be healed. Jesus was her only hope. Ignoring her pride, fear, and embarrassment, she pressed into the crushing crowd.

Her fingers brushed the fabric of Jesus' cloak, and in that instant, her bleeding stopped. She knew she'd been freed of her suffering. Then she slipped back into the crowd.

But Jesus turned and asked, "Who touched my clothes?"

The disciples must've thought Jesus was joking. Peter said, "You see all these people crowded against you. Lots of people touched your clothes."

"Someone touched me. I know power went out from me." Jesus kept looking around. Because he was God, Jesus certainly knew who had touched him and why. Still, he wanted her to come forward and tell her story. The woman stepped out of the crowd, fell at Jesus' feet, and told him of her illness and his healing touch.

"Daughter," Jesus said, "your faith has healed you. Go in peace, free from your suffering."

In Greek, the word for *healed* also means "saved." Because of her faith in Jesus, he healed her from her physical illness and saved her spiritual being too.

Faith requires risk. The woman in the crowd knew that. She risked being discovered and rejected, but her faith was greater than her fear. Like her, you can humble yourself and reach out to Jesus.

More To Explore: Luke 8:43–48

Girl Talk: Do you trust Jesus enough to turn to him for healing—in your heart or in your body?

God Talk: "Father God, you're a loving and caring God. Thank you for loving me. I want to show the people around me your great compassion. Please help me do that, Lord. In Jesus' name, amen."

From *Real Girls of the Bible* by Mona Hodgson

336

"For God has not given us a spirit of fear, but of power and of love and of a sound mind."

—2 Timothy 1:7 (NKJV)

What Are You Thinking?

It's common to fear trying new activities, going new places, making decisions, and giving a performance. But you don't have to be afraid! God hasn't given you that fear. Instead, he's given you courage and power for using your abilities, love, and good judgment. You can be levelheaded, with your thoughts and feelings under control.

So how do we get over this fear? "You should not be like cowering, fearful slaves. You should behave instead like God's very own children, adopted into his family—calling him 'Father, dear Father'" (Romans 8:15 NLT). Instead of shrinking back in fear, call on your Father for help. He wants to give you a sound mind. Ask him for that, then step out in faith. Take that test. Try out for that musical. Enjoy living a life free from fear.

Self-control is a fruit of the Spirit. And that includes controlling your mind.

More to Explore: Psalm 34:4–8

Girl Talk: Do you feel you make decisions confidently or out of fear of something else? Have you talked to God about it?

God Talk: "Lord, I am tired of making choices out of fear. Please help me rely on you and make confident choices. Thank you for being with me through every choice. Amen."

From *No Boys Allowed* by Kristi Holl

"My mind and my body may grow weak, but God is my strength; he is all I ever need."

—Psalm 73:26 (TEV)

Got God? Got Everything

It just doesn't seem right. Everywhere we look, girls are practically getting away with murder. They cheat and get good marks. They're snotty to teachers and never get punished. They're stuck-up, yet still popular.

What's wrong with this picture? You gotta wonder.

Back in David's time, a man named Asaph (a talented music director in the temple) was way bummed about this. So he wrote up his experience in a psalm (73). Asaph believed that God is good, and yet he admits that for a time, he "nearly" lost faith in how God operates. Simply put, he complains: "God, these wicked guys don't follow your rules and they prosper. Me? I behave, but have nothing to show for it. What good is being good? Phooey!" (Psalm 73:4–14 TLB, paraphrased).

Now, Asaph felt that way because he did something we all do sometimes: He took his eyes off God and put them on himself. And the more he thought about what he perceived was his unfair treatment, the more jealous and disgusted he became. He felt confused, but didn't know what to do. "I tried to think this problem through," he wrote in the Psalm, "but it was too difficult for me, until I went to your Temple. Then I understood what will happen to the wicked. You will put them in slippery places, and make them fall to destruction!" (Psalm 73:16–18 TEV).

Returning to God's house snapped Asaph out of his self-pity. Away from worldly distractions, he was better able to reconnect with the Lord and receive the grace to refocus on the truth he knew from the start: God is good.

We can almost see him smacking his palm to his forehead, thinking, *What a dummy I've been. I might not have as many riches as the wicked, but I'm way better off because of what I* do *have: the Lord.*

And "since I have you," Asaph thought in this "ah-ha" moment, *"what else could I want on earth?"* (Psalm 73:25 TLB).

After that, Asaph admitted he'd been wrong to complain, and marveled that even then, God still loved and guided him. With that, came joy and praise. " ... as for me," he writes in the psalm's last lines, "how wonderful to be near God, to find protection with the Sovereign Lord, and to proclaim all that he has done!" (Psalm 73:28 TLB).

Lesson learned: Wealth and success can be here today and gone tomorrow. But when you've got God, you have everything.

More To Explore: Philippians 4:11 – 12

Girl Talk: Feeling whiny? Read the rest of Psalm 73.

God Talk: "Heavenly Father, when I see others who do wrong and seem to get away with it, help me remember Asaph. Amen."

From *Whatever: Livin' the True, Noble, Totally Excellent Life*
by Allia Zobel Nolan

"See, I am doing a new thing! Now it springs up; do you not perceive it?"

—Isaiah 43:19

It's a Brand-New Day!

Suppose your friends are all on the volleyball team, but you want to join the school's new video production team. It sounds exciting—but it meets after school when the volleyball team practices. It takes courage for you to tell your friends you're dropping volleyball this year to join the video production team. You know you'll miss your friends after school. Yet, the new project excites you, and you hope you'll make even more friends as you work to produce the school's daily news reports. It's up to you to branch out and try new things. "Each of you must take responsibility for doing the creative best you can with your own life" (Galatians 6:5 MSG).

God is always in the process of doing new things in your life. He wants you to think creatively and use your imagination to experiment with fresh ideas. We must be willing to take some risks (and even fail a few times) on the way to success.

Don't be afraid to try new things: new activities, new attitudes, and new relationships. Branch out and see what wonderful things God has in store for you!

More to Explore: Isaiah 42:9

Girl Talk: Are you stuck in routines that never change? What new hobby or activity could you try this week? What person at school could you talk to for the first time?

God Talk: "Lord, you are so creative. I know you want to do many new things in my life, both now and as I grow up. Give me courage to take some risks. Amen."

From *Chick Chat* by Kristi Holl

339

"Don't worry about anything; instead, pray about everything."
—Philippians 4:6 (NLT)

Don't Worry Away: Pray

As believers, we are not to be anxious or upset, troubled or uneasy in our minds. How? Pray about everything, and turn the situations over to God for help. Easier said than done, right? Well, try these ways to tame that worry habit:

- Separate "bad" worry from real concern. Decide if you can do anything about the situation. If so, write down a plan to handle it.
- Don't worry alone. Talk to a friend, parent, teacher, youth leader, or counselor. By talking it out, you may discover solutions on your own that you couldn't see before.
- Take care of your body. We are more likely to worry when we're too tired, aren't eating healthy meals, and don't get enough exercise.
- Control your imagination. Don't get caught up in imagining all kinds of horrible "what-ifs." Our imaginations can take us from mild worry to a full-blown anxiety attack if we don't choose more realistic thoughts.
- Trust God. Whatever situation you're facing, invite God into the middle of it.

Worry is a bad habit, but trusting God can become a habit too. So tame that worry habit, and live a life filled with peace.

More to Explore: Psalm 55:22

Girl Talk: When you have a worry, what do you tend to do? Does worry take over your life, or do you give it to God and get on with living?

God Talk: "Lord, there's always something I can worry about. Please help me to come to you first, giving you all my worries. Thank you for always taking care of me. Amen."

From *Girlz Rock* by Kristi Holl

"Strive for full restoration, encourage one another, be of one mind, live in peace. And the God of love and peace will be with you."

—2 Corinthians 13:11

Living in Peace

Do you ever aim for perfection? Do you try to achieve a perfect math score? Do you attempt the perfect batch of chocolate chip cookies or the perfect swan dive? We aim for perfection—for excellence—many times in our lives. As we keep trying, we keep improving and getting closer to our goals. But only God is actually perfect, or ever will be. He is happy with us if we keep growing and trying to do better. It's like shooting a bow and arrow. You're aiming for a perfect bull's-eye, but you're pleased as your arrows get closer and closer.

Even more important than tests and sports is how we live with people. Will we ever live perfectly with our friends and family members? No, but we can head in that direction. Don't dish out that put-down you usually snap at your brother. Don't bicker about whose turn it is to empty the dishwasher or fold laundry. Don't be touchy when your best friend doesn't give you her undivided attention at the ball game. God is the source of the love and peace you need, and he wants to help you live in harmony with others.

More to Explore: Romans 12:14–18

Girl Talk: In the past day or so, have you helped at home with a loving heart or a resentful attitude? Could you do better next time?

God Talk: "Lord, I know I have a hard time getting along with my family and friends sometimes. Please help me to help others willingly and with joy. Amen."

From *No Boys Allowed* by Kristi Holl

341

"God created mankind in his own image, in the image of God he created him; male and female he created them."

—Genesis 1:27

Creature Care

Finally, on the sixth day, God made people. He simply spoke, and there they were, male and female, as beautiful and balanced and perfect as everything else he created. The Scripture says God made humans in his own image. We're not sure if we look like God, but we know it means every human being is worthy of honor and respect.

Since we're made in God's image, we have the same responsibility God has—to take care of the world. We must be pretty awesome if God trusts us to care for the creatures he so carefully thought up and crafted and put in his handmade world. So hug your Bible and thank God for both the job and the instructions for how to do it. Then hug your dog, cat, bird, or snake if you have one. You might just wave at your fish. They can be hard to hold onto.

And choose one of these to do.

- Feed the family pet(s) tonight.
- Provide for a wild animal (bird feeder or bread for the ducks in the pond).
- Volunteer to do something for a neighbor's pet—like hang out with a dog that's tied up in a backyard.

More To Explore: Genesis 1:26

Girl Talk: What things do you do to care for the planet—or your own backyard?

God Talk: "God, thank you for this beautiful world I get to live in! Help me to take care of it, so that in the future others can enjoy it just as much as I do. Amen."

From *That Is So Me* by Nancy Rue

"But the fruit of the Spirit is love, joy, peace, forbearance, kindness, goodness, faithfulness, gentleness and self-control."
—Galatians 5:22–23

Me Thinketh Some Fruit Stinketh!

Roadside fruit stands in the summertime are the result of healthy trees, cared for, pruned, and sprayed by gardeners. The fruit of the Spirit (love, joy, peace, patience, kindness, goodness, faithfulness, gentleness, and self-control) is the result of a healthy human spirit cared for by the Holy Spirit.

Does your "tree" produce rotten fruit sometimes instead? When your little brother makes you late for school, do you call him names? After school, do you devour the entire contents of the cookie jar? A short temper, a mean mouth, and a lack of self-control are NOT fruits of the Spirit.

Fruit doesn't appear overnight. You don't plant a skinny young tree and find ripe pears on it the next day. Fruit appears slowly. It's true of the fruit of the Spirit too. Do we produce this fruit all by ourselves? No. Jesus says, "Yes, I am the vine; you are the branches. Those who remain in me, and I in them, will produce much fruit. For apart from me you can do nothing" (John 15:5 NLT). Jesus living in you, through the power of the Holy Spirit, "grows" the fruit. Your part? Just hanging out on the vine!

More to Explore: Matthew 12:33

Girl Talk: How is your fruit? Is it fresh or does it reek? What one fruit do you think you need help with the most?

God Talk: "Lord, I really want to grow in the fruit of the Spirit. Help me to be more like you. Amen."

From *No Boys Allowed* by Kristi Holl

343

"I — yes, I alone — am the one who blots out your sins for my own sake and will never think of them again."

— Isaiah 43:25 (NLT)

Gone and Forgotten

Nicole forgot her math book and ran back to the classroom after school to get it. No one was there. Crossing the room, she spotted a wadded-up twenty-dollar bill and picked it up. It must have fallen out of someone's pocket, Nicole reasoned. There was no way to tell who the money belonged to. "Finders, keepers," she muttered, stuffing it in her pants pocket.

Halfway home, Nicole began to feel guilty. She knew she should have turned the money in to the office or left it on the teacher's desk. It wasn't "finders, keepers." It was stealing. "Lord, I'm sorry," she prayed. Nicole headed back to the school, where she turned the money into the principal's office. She still felt guilty, though, until she read Jeremiah 31:34 (NLT): "And I will forgive their wickedness and will never again remember their sins." Nicole decided that if God could forgive and forget her wrongdoings, then she would shake off that feeling and forget it too.

God isn't waiting to punish you the minute you do something wrong. When you confess, God forgives your sins completely. It's over and done with. God chooses to wipe it from his memory — and you can forget it too.

More to Explore: Joel 2:13 – 14

Girl Talk: Have you done something this week that you feel guilty about? Is there something you can do about it — right now?

God Talk: "Lord, I choose to do wrong things every day. Please forgive me for ____________. Thank you for forgiving and forgetting. Amen."

From *Chick Chat* by Kristi Holl

"This means that anyone who belongs to Christ has become a new person. The old life is gone; a new life has begun!"
—2 Corinthians 5:17 (NLT)

The New You

Have you ever watched one of those home makeover shows? Maybe you've even had your own facial or makeover at a party. Guess what, faithgirl? God is an extreme makeover artist; and your makeover into the image of Jesus Christ is a special piece of God's ultimate work of art. Because the makeover process can get embarrassing, Father God begins discreetly! Before you're ready for the public, Father God prepares you in private. If you've ever seen a makeover, you know this is the loving thing to do. Makeovers get messy and ugly before they get pretty. Father God is not out to shame you in front of everybody else.

A beauty queen in the Bible named Esther had a fabulous (and long!) makeover in private too, before she went public. "Before a young woman's turn came to go in to King Xerxes, she had to complete twelve months of beauty treatments prescribed for the women, six months with oil of myrrh and six with perfumes and cosmetics" (Esther 2:12).

The Holy Spirit knows exactly what Jesus looks like, and is skilled at creating that same look in you. Today, remember God is preparing you for your destiny.

More To Explore: Ephesians 2:10 NIV

Girl Talk: Dig a little deeper. Can you find the purpose of myrrh as a beauty treatment?

God Talk: "Father, thank you for choosing to make me over! I am grateful for the work of your Holy Spirit within me. I'm excited about being made over into the image of God! Amen."

From *My Beautiful Daughter* by Tasha Douglas

345

"Cast all your anxiety on him because he cares for you."
—1 Peter 5:7

Cast Away Your Cares

Nobody likes to carry anxiety on her shoulders. You know, that gut-twisting feeling inside when you think your clothes look weird, or you dread being called on in class when you don't know the answer. Most girls feel anxious when doing something different, like meeting new people or trying to ice skate for the first time. But anxiety can also attack when you're reading a book or watching a movie and something reminds you of a bad time in your past. Everyone has anxious thoughts. The good news is that you don't have to keep them!

You can cast your cares and worries on the Lord, because he's concerned for you and wants to help you. But you have to mean it. None of this wishy-washy "giving your worries to God" and grabbing them back a minute later. CAST your anxieties on him—throw them with great force, so they stay put. Get rid of them! Believe that he has every situation under control, that he sees your need and is willing to meet it. Don't carry your anxieties and worries a minute longer. Wind up, take aim, and throw those cares away!

More to Explore: 1 Peter 5:10

Girl Talk: Do you focus on the bad stuff that comes your way, or do you look to the future for good things to come?

God Talk: "Lord, you know all my worries and fears. I give them to you, each and every one. Thank you for caring about my every thought and feeling. Amen."

From *No Boys Allowed* by Kristi Holl

"Then Jesus cried out, 'Whoever believes in me does not believe in me only, but in the one who sent me. The one who looks at me is seeing the one who sent me.'"

—John 12:44–45

Seeing the Father

Has anyone ever told you that you look like one of your parents? Maybe you've heard that you have your father's nose, or you walk like your mother. This is because you inherited your physical attributes from your parents. A chemical in your body, called DNA, determines how you look. You resemble your parents because you have the same DNA they do.

There's a special son who looks just like his father too. That son is Jesus Christ. Just as your parents passed down their DNA to you, Father God passed down his DNA to his unique son, Jesus Christ. Jesus Christ has the exact nature and character of Father God. Jesus even told his first followers that "anyone who has seen me has seen the Father" (John 14:9).

Though God the Father is invisible, Jesus Christ the son is visible. By looking at Jesus, you can see exactly what God the Father is like. But not only does Jesus look like the Father, he is actually one with the Father. That's why Jesus could say: if you've seen me, then you've seen the Father. Today, as you consider what Father God is like, discover him by learning about Jesus Christ.

More to Explore: Matthew 11:29

Girl Talk: What do you think Father God is like?

God Talk: "Father God, thank you for your son Jesus Christ. In looking at him, I see you. Amen."

From *My Beautiful Daughter* by Tasha Douglas

347

"All have sinned and fall short of the glory of God, and all are justified freely by his grace through the redemption that came by Christ Jesus."

—Romans 3:23–24

A Forgiven Woman's Fragrant Faith

Luke tells the story of a woman who was known for her sin, but he doesn't give her name or identify her sins. It doesn't seem to matter for the sake of the story—just that she had done something everyone else thought was pretty bad.

A Pharisee named Simon invited Jesus to dinner. He had heard about Jesus, because Jesus had been preaching in Judea and the surrounding areas. While Jesus reclined at the Pharisee's table with his feet out behind him, the woman known for her sin showed up with an alabaster jar. She had probably heard Jesus talk about how, through grace, one could be forgiven and lead a new life.

The woman stood at Jesus' feet and wept, her tears cleaning his dusty feet. After she wiped his feet dry with her hair, she kissed them, and then broke open an alabaster jar and poured perfume on Jesus' feet.

The Pharisee Simon was someone who loved the law and was proud of his good works. He thought to himself that if Jesus were a prophet, he wouldn't have let this unclean woman touch him. He must have had a disapproving look on his face, because Jesus said, "Simon, I have something to tell you."

"Tell me, teacher," the Pharisee said.

"Two men owed money to a certain moneylender. One owed him five hundred denarii, and the other fifty. Neither of them had the money to pay him back, so he canceled the debts of both. Now which of them will love him more?"

Simon said, "I suppose the one who had the bigger debt canceled."

"You're right," Jesus said. "Do you see this woman? I came

into your house. You didn't give me any water for my feet, but she wet my feet with her tears and wiped them with her hair. You didn't give me a kiss, but this woman hasn't stopped kissing my feet. You didn't put oil on my head, but she poured perfume on my feet. Her many sins have been forgiven — for she loved much. But he who has been forgiven little loves little."

Then Jesus spoke to the woman. "Your sins are forgiven," he said. "Your faith has saved you; go in peace."

God knows you better than anyone else and still loves you and forgives. Others may reject you for what you do or don't do, but Jesus forgives you. And because of his love and forgiveness, you can live in peace with God. That's grace.

More To Explore: Luke 7:36 – 50

Girl Talk: Think about the last time someone forgave you for hurting them. How did that feel?

God Talk: "Dear God, thank you for sending your perfect Son, Jesus, to die for my sins. Every day, help me see my sins and confess them to you and accept your great forgiveness. Amen."

From *Real Girls of the Bible* by Mona Hodgson

348

"The Lord himself goes before you and will be with you; he will never leave you nor forsake you. Do not be afraid; do not be discouraged."

—Deuteronomy 31:8

No Fear Here!

What a comfort to know that we are never alone, that in every scary situation the Lord himself goes before us to mark out a safe path, then walks us through it. We don't need to let discouragement stop us, and we never need to turn and run in fear.

Fears come in all shapes and sizes. You might experience fear of the dark, ferocious dogs, or crashing thunderstorms. Most people fear performances, whether it's a dance recital or giving a book report in class. Maybe your fears are even bigger, like fear of parents divorcing or fear that a sick grandparent won't recover. Will God be there through it all? Absolutely!

Whatever your fear, the answer is the same. "For He Himself has said, 'I will never leave you nor forsake you.' So we may boldly say: 'The Lord is my helper; I will not fear. What can man do to me?'" (Hebrews 13:5–6 NKJV).

More to Explore: 1 Chronicles 28:20

Girl Talk: What sort of things make you feel afraid? Have you asked God to free you from those fears?

God Talk: "Lord, I'm afraid of ____________________, and I want to be free from that fear. I give it to you. Thank you for never leaving my side. Amen."

From *No Boys Allowed* by Kristi Holl

"The law of the Lord is perfect, refreshing the soul. The statutes of the Lord are trustworthy, making wise the simple . . . They are more precious than gold, than much pure gold."

—Psalm 19:7, 10

Pure Gold

We all have things we consider valuable. One girl might value her big house with a swimming pool, while another girl might value straight A's or a spot on the swim team. David (who wrote many of the psalms) thought God's Word, the Bible, was the most valuable thing—even more valuable than gold! We also must learn to value God's Word above everything else we have.

How do you treat something that is valuable to you? You look at it. You spend time with it. You don't forget about it, but instead often put it first before everything else. We must treat God's Word that way. "And you must commit yourselves wholeheartedly to these commands I am giving you today . . . Talk about them when you are at home and when you are away on a journey, when you are lying down and when you are getting up again" (Deuteronomy 6:6–7 NLT). As we place a high value on God's Word, we'll see God change our lives in brand-new ways.

More to Explore: Joshua 1:8

Girl Talk: What do you value the most? How much time do you spend in this activity? How much time do you spend in God's Word?

God Talk: "Lord, you are the most important person in my life. Help me to put you first every day. Amen."

From *Chick Chat* by Kristi Holl

350

"Woe to you when everyone speaks well of you, for that is how their ancestors treated the false prophets."

—Luke 6:26

You're So Worth It

How about a round of "Have You Ever?"

Have you ever:

- worn an outfit like everybody else had and felt totally self-conscious the entire time?
- been at a party where you felt like an alien?
- not been able to think of anything to say when somebody you really wanted to be friends with started talking to you?
- snubbed somebody you liked, because you were with girls who probably wouldn't accept her?
- pretended to be fine when you weren't, so nobody would know what you were really feeling?
- not raised your hand in class, even when you knew the answer, because other kids might think you were a know-it-all or not cool?

We've all done things like that, because we're not totally sure we're "worth it" when we're just being real. Here's the deal: you were worth creating, even if somebody else doesn't think so. So drive right through the roadblocks that keep you from being the real you. You are perfect just the way you are—good enough, unique enough, you enough. God wouldn't have made you any other way.

More To Explore: Psalm 103:11

Girl Talk: What roadblocks do you need to drive through? Ask God to help you knock them down.

God Talk: "God, help me to see myself as you see me—beautiful, loved, special, and so worth creating. I love you. Amen."

From *That Is So Me* by Nancy Rue

"But let all who take refuge in you be glad; let them ever sing for joy."

—Psalm 5:11

Count It All Joy

A refuge is a safe place, protected from attack or violent storms. It's a place you can run to, and you'll be safe as long as you stay there. God is our refuge too. When you're going through tough times, when you're afraid, he's the best place to go for shelter. Not only will you be safe, but you'll be so relieved that you'll sing for joy!

We don't always run to God for help or shelter when we're going through trouble. You might eat a candy bar when upset, or go shopping, or zone out with a gripping movie. Will that help? Not really. You might forget your troubles for a short time, but you won't feel happy or cheerful for long. That only comes—and stays—when you seek shelter from your dangers or hardships by going to God, in his Word and in prayer.

Sometimes, before you actually feel the joy, you have to praise and worship God by faith. In other words, you praise him when you don't really feel like it. But if you do this, if you choose to be cheerful, your joy will bubble to the surface. Don't be surprised if you even burst into song!

More to Explore: Romans 15:13

Girl Talk: Do you feel joyful most of the time? Would your friends consider you joyful, or maybe grouchy?

God Talk: "Lord, I want to be joyful, no matter what bad stuff comes my way. Please fill me with your never-ending joy so that others will be drawn to that joy in me. Amen."

From *No Boys Allowed* by Kristi Holl

"I have learned to be content whatever the circumstances."
—Philippians 4:11

Crafting a Content Heart

Learn to be satisfied with how things are, no matter what is happening in your life. Whether you have too little, just enough, or more than enough, be stable and unchanging in your moods. Learn to get along happily, whether you have much or little.

Amber found it easier to be content with her life when her dad still had his high-paying job. When he was laid off, and Amber had much less, a discontented spirit set in. Over several months, though, Amber learned to be content. She learned to enjoy videos and popcorn at home with her family instead of going into the city to a show. In fact, she had to admit that she enjoyed her family a lot more every day, now that her dad was home in the evenings.

If you have asked God for something that is going to be good for you, he will give you what you asked for. But rest in the knowledge that if it's not right, God will do something far better than you asked for. Trust him completely to handle the situation. A contented heart—free from anxious thoughts and worries—is a priceless possession.

More to Explore: Hebrews 13:5 and Matthew 6:31–34

Girl Talk: Do you ever feel content? Do you worry about how much you do or don't have? Have you asked God to give you contentment?

God Talk: "Lord, I tend to think a lot about what I want but don't have. Please help me to be content with what I have. I know you will give me everything I need. Thank you. Amen."

From *Girlz Rock* by Kristi Holl

"We all, like sheep, have gone astray, each of us has turned to our own way; and the Lord has laid on him the iniquity of us all."

—Isaiah 53:6

Baa, Baa, Black Sheep

Sheep aren't very smart. They wander off, get lost, and fall off cliffs. They require constant watching. Each of us has drifted away like a silly sheep. We have left God's well-marked paths to follow our own wrong ways.

Maybe you were raised in a Christian home, went to church faithfully, and were homeschooled until sixth grade. Then you go to public school. You expect the kids to make fun of you, but instead they invite you to games, parties, and movies. You know your parents wouldn't approve of the movies you're seeing, but you don't want to look judgmental. Like a wandering sheep, you stray off a godly path. At one party, when someone produces some pills and other drugs, you nearly fall off the cliff. You come to your senses, though, and call your dad to pick you up.

When you arrive home, your dad leans over and hugs you hard. "I'm so glad you called," he says. If *you've* wandered off the right path, it's never too late to go home. Even if you do not have an earthly father like this one, your heavenly Father always welcomes you back home.

More To Explore: Matthew 18:12–14

Girl Talk: Have you ever wandered away from what you know is right? What happened? How can you get back on the path?

God Talk: "Lord, even though I know the right things to do, I don't always do them. I know you are always there welcoming me back. Please keep me near you. Amen."

From *Shine On, Girl!* by Kristi Holl

354

"'Come, follow me,' Jesus said, 'and I will send you out to fish for people.'"

—Matthew 4:19

Go Fish!

When Jesus started his preaching ministry, he began to gather followers. These people (disciples) would first hear his teaching. Then afterwards, they could teach and preach to others, telling about the things they had seen Jesus do. Jesus still calls us to follow him and learn from him, and then lead others to Christ.

You know many people—at school, in your neighborhood, maybe even in your own home—who don't know Jesus as their Savior. How can you introduce these people to Jesus? "Let your light shine before men in such a way that they may see your good works, and glorify your Father who is in heaven." (Matthew 5:16 NASB)

In other words, let your good efforts shine out in such a way that others will know your faith in God is real. Letting your light shine can be as simple as putting a smile on your face, saying a kind word to someone, or giving a sincere compliment. How you *live* is just as important as what you *say* to others about Jesus. It's like the bait when you go fishing—it's attractive and makes people come closer.

More to Explore: Luke 5:10–11

Girl Talk: What can you do today to "let your light shine"? Do you have someone in mind to talk to about Jesus?

God Talk: "Father, I want to lead others to you, but I'm afraid. Please give me courage and strength to do what you want me to do. Amen."

From *No Boys Allowed* by Kristi Holl

"Jesus answered, 'I am the way and the truth and the life. No one comes to the Father except through me.'"

—John 14:6

Living Water for the Samaritan Woman

There was a woman who lived in Sychar, a small village in Samaria. Because she needed water, this Samaritan woman trekked to Jacob's well. People usually drew water at the end of the day. But not her. She carried her jar to the well around noon, probably because she wanted to avoid the stares and gossip of other women.

Still, when she arrived at the well, she wasn't alone. Jesus was resting on the ground nearby while his disciples went into town to get food. The woman noticed that he was a Jew. In those days Jews and Samaritans did not get along.

"Will you give me a drink?" Jesus asked.

"You're a Jew and I'm a Samaritan woman," she said. "How can you ask me for a drink?"

"If you knew the gift of God and who asks you for a drink," Jesus said, "you would've asked him and he would've given you living water."

"Sir, you have nothing to draw with, and the well is deep. Where can you get this living water?"

Jesus said, "Everyone who drinks this water will thirst again, but whoever drinks the water I give him will never thirst. The water I give him will become in him a spring of water welling up to eternal life."

Jesus wasn't talking about plain old well water. He was talking about salvation and eternal life with God. Jesus was the living water. He was the only one who could satisfy the deep thirst in the Samaritan woman's soul.

"Sir," she said, "give me this water so I won't get thirsty and have to keep coming here to draw water."

Then Jesus revealed that he knew all about her life—that

she had had five husbands, and the man she was then living with was not her husband. He told her that he was the Messiah.

Jesus knew the Samaritan woman needed more than just water from the well that day. He knew she needed forgiveness for her sins. And he knew she needed to know that God loved her that much.

God knows your needs too, even before you do. And he doesn't decide your importance because of your color, your ethnic background, the money in your piggy bank, how often you attend church, or the good things you do. He looks into your heart. And like the Samaritan woman at the well, if you put your faith in Jesus, your thirst will be quenched by living water.

More To Explore: John 4:1 – 42

Girl Talk: How do you think the Samaritan woman felt when Jesus chose her to carry the news that he was the Messiah back to her town?

God Talk: "Jesus, thank you for your living water. Thank you that you died so that I can have eternal life. Amen."

From *Real Girls of the Bible* by Mona Hodgson

"I write these things to you who believe in the name of the Son of God so that you may know that you have eternal life."

—1 John 5:13

Going My Way?

One summer when Melissa was ten years old, she'd prayed and asked for forgiveness during Bible school. Later, her sixth-grade teacher challenged her faith. He claimed that if God loved everyone equally, then everyone was a child of God and would go to heaven. Melissa knew he was wrong, but she couldn't put the reason into words. But that night, when digging into her Bible for answers, she found a familiar verse: "But as many as received Him, to *them* He gave the right to become children of God, to those who believe in His name" (John 1:12 NKJV, emphasis added).

Her uncle said that all the world's religions were the same, that they were just different ways to get to heaven. Again, Melissa went back to God's Word for answers. "Salvation is found in no one else, for there is no other name under heaven given to mankind by which we must be saved" (Acts 4:12). And "Jesus answered, 'I am the way and the truth and the life. No one comes to the Father except through me'" (John 14:6). Melissa nodded. The Bible was clear. Salvation can be found only through Jesus.

For Melissa, that finally settled it. God said it—and she believed it.

More to Explore: Romans 8:16

Girl Talk: Do you know *why* you believe what you believe?

God Talk: "Lord, I want to know your Word better. Thank you that we can be *sure* we have eternal life. Amen."

From *Chick Chat* by Kristi Holl

357

"We know and rely on the love God has for us. God is love. Whoever lives in love lives in God, and God in him."

—1 John 4:16

Living to Love

Love is more than an emotion we feel toward another person or some kind act we do. To truly love is to have God work through our lives. If you're a believer, then God lives in you. And God *is* Love. So God is patient, God is kind, he does not brag, he endures things, he believes all things, he is full of hope, and God never fails. (See 1 Corinthians 13:4–8.) As we ask him to work in us and love others through us, we will begin to see the very same characteristics become true in our lives. God is Love, and that's why "love never fails" (1 Corinthians 13:8 NKJV).

First John 3:16 (NLT) says, "We know what real love is because Christ gave up his life for us. And so we also ought to give up our lives for our Christian friends." You may never have to physically die for anyone, but loving others will cause other things in you to die. You may have to die to selfishness, a short temper, or backbiting—any habit that prevents you from truly loving others.

God lives in you. Lean on that love, and spread it to others!

More to Explore: Psalm 36:7–9 and 1 John 3:24

Girl Talk: How hard (or easy) is it for you to be loving? Do you have bad habits that need to die?

God Talk: "Lord, I know that you are love. Help me to be more loving, just as you love me. Thank you for your perfect example. Amen."

From *Girlz Rock* by Kristi Holl

"He created them male and female and blessed them."

—Genesis 5:2

Beautifully Blessed

When somebody sneezes, you say, "God bless you." When you sit down to eat a meal, someone asks the blessing. If you live in the South, whenever anybody does anything nice, somebody else is sure to say, "Bless your heart."

We bless all over the place, most of the time without even thinking about it. But when someone is blessed by God, that means:

- she will grow to be fabulous.
- she can influence others in major ways.
- people will listen to her.
- she has a responsibility to care for the world and for the life she's been given.

From the beginning, God has blessed each newborn baby in that way. You, then, can grow and be even more awesome than you are now. You can show God to other people, so their lives can be amazing too. You can do that, because you know it's your job. You can, because you are blessed.

Not everybody takes that blessing seriously. Some people don't even know about it. But it's who you are in God's eyes.

So go, Blessed One. Grow and be fabulous. Change lives. Speak out. Care for the world. It's what you were made to do.

More To Explore: Numbers 6:24–26

Girl Talk: Pull out a piece of paper. Make a list of all the ways you have been blessed.

God Talk: "God, thank you for your love. Thank you for your blessings. Help me to always remember how much you care for me. Amen."

From *That Is So Me* by Nancy Rue

359

"Don't worry about anything; instead, pray about everything. Tell God what you need, and thank him for all he has done."
—Philippians 4:6 (NLT)

All AND Nothing

Don't be worried, concerned, anxious, troubled, or uneasy about *anything*; instead, talk to God about *everything*. Tell God what you need—he wants you to—but don't forget to thank him for what he has already done for you. If you do, you will develop a grateful heart.

You will find dozens of opportunities to worry every day, if you choose to. You may have personal troubles: your upcoming test, a sick parent, someone mad at you at school. You may worry about the state of the world: tragedies seen on TV, or a parent overseas in the military. Just remember: every opportunity to worry is also a chance to involve God in the matter. Since he's all-powerful, what better person to be involved?

Worry about nothing. Pray about everything. Like learning any new habit, it takes more effort at first. But if you do this each time a worry invades your mind, it will soon be an automatic response. You'll turn immediately to God, give him the concern, and thank him for however he is going to work it out.

More to Explore: Matthew 6:25

Girl Talk: Is there something you worry about on a regular basis? Do you see why it doesn't help you to dwell on it?

God Talk: "Lord, I know I shouldn't worry, but it comes back again and again. I want to give this issue to you and not think about it again. Thank you for giving me peace. Amen."

From *No Boys Allowed* by Kristi Holl

"For God is not a God of disorder but of peace."
—1 Corinthians 14:33

Settle Down!

Maybe you need God's special peace. You pace back and forth across the living room, muttering under your breath. You can't believe it. Both your best friends have been chosen for pep squad, but not you! Your cheers at tryouts were just as good as theirs! Why weren't you chosen? Weren't you pretty enough? Did you look awkward or stupid? The more you fume, the worse you feel. Not being chosen for pep squad is disappointing—but you're allowing yourself to get emotionally troubled by keeping your mind stirred up. Two hours later, when you have a headache and an upset stomach, you decide to get a grip. You pour your heart out to God, giving him your frustration and disappointment—and fear that your friends will now leave you behind. You let it go and allow Jesus' peace to fill your heart, calm your emotions, and settle your thoughts.

Yes, it's disappointing. But tryouts are over, and you still have all the good things in your life that you had before. God is in control, and he knows more about the situation than you do. Remember, "the Lord will give strength to His people; the Lord will bless His people with peace" (Psalm 29:11 NKJV).

More To Explore: Colossians 3:15

Girl Talk: Have you had any disappointments lately? How did you deal with them? Have you tried asking Jesus to give you his peace?

God Talk: "Lord, I know things won't always go my way. Please give me your peace about each situation. Thank you for always being with me. Amen."

From *Shine On, Girl!* by Kristi Holl

361

"Your approval or disapproval means nothing to me, because I know you don't have God's love within you."

—John 5:41–42 (NLT)

People Pleasing

Jesus was often criticized, but the approval of people meant nothing to him. His unwavering confidence in God's approval set him free from human opinion. It can also free you from the trap of "people pleasing."

Nicole's youth group at church was having a lock-in Friday night. Nicole had a starring role in the evening's opening skit, and she looked forward to it. That is, until Kaylie invited her to a skating party for the same night. Kaylie was the most popular girl in Nicole's grade and rarely spoke to Nicole. Now she'd been invited to a party with Kaylie's friends! Nicole desperately wanted to go. What would Kaylie think of her if she turned down a party invitation to go to church?

Jesus had some hard words of warning on this subject: "No wonder you can't believe! For you gladly honor each other, but you don't care about the honor that comes from God alone" (John 5:44 NLT). If you live to earn the rewards that come from pleasing people, you create a trap for yourself. If, instead, you concentrate on receiving *God's* approval, you can live free from the trap of human opinion.

More to Explore: 1 Thessalonians 2:6

Girl Talk: When you have to make a decision, whose approval matters the most to you? Your own? A friend's? Your parents'? God's?

God Talk: "Lord, help me look to you for my approval. If my actions and attitudes please you, that's all that matters. Amen."

From *Chick Chat* by Kristi Holl

"'For I know the plans I have for you,'" declares the Lord, '"plans to prosper you and not to harm you, plans to give you hope and a future.'"

—Jeremiah 29:11

Dream a Big Dream

God has a plan for your life, and it's a good plan to help you grow stronger and be successful. We sometimes fear God's plan will hurt us or keep us from having something we truly desire. But we can have hope for the future. God has promised he will meet our needs and give us each what is best.

All girls dream about the future. Maybe you dream of breaking your school's hurdles record or getting the lead in the fall musical. Maybe your career goals include a scholarship to a music school or becoming a scientist to cure cancer. Whatever your dreams are, they may not just be *your* ideas. God may have placed them in your heart.

Because God also gave us free will, begin taking little steps toward reaching your dreams and goals. First, talk to God about them. Ask him to change anything about your goals that he wants to change. Then, break your future goals into smaller steps you can begin now. Study. Practice. Learn. Reach for excellence. Then you will be ready to fulfill God's plans to prosper you in the wonderful future that lies ahead.

More to Explore: Psalm 139:17

Girl Talk: Do you trust God with your dreams? How would you feel if he told you that his dreams for you were different than yours?

God Talk: "Lord, I trust you with my dreams. I know you have a great future for me, and I'm excited about it! Amen."

From *No Boys Allowed* by Kristi Holl

363

"How can a young person stay on the path of purity? By living according to your word."

—Psalm 119:9

Wash Me

Have you ever seen a newborn baby? It is a grimy sight at first! You arrived here looking just like that too. The truth is, newborns need help getting cleaned up. And that first bath starts a practice of regular washing that keeps a child healthy and clean for the rest of his or her life.

As you grow older, someone teaches you what to do, and you're able to wash yourself off regularly, keeping yourself clean on your own. And even though you know what to do now, sometimes the mess gets so big, you need help getting cleaned up. The beauty of believing is like that too!

Just like that newborn baby, when you're first born into God's family, all the grubbiness of your life before clings to you. Messy birth is part of being born into the family of Father God. Yet, God never intends to leave you icky! It pleases God to wash you clean when dirty situations start to pollute your life. When you're not in the best of moods, your parents don't seem to understand, or if your friends start treating you unkindly, your Father in heaven will wash you clean.

More To Explore: Psalm 51:5 NIV

Girl Talk: Are you facing any messy situations in your life that you want God to help you clean up?

God Talk: "Father God, open my heart to receive your grace to remove the impure things contaminating my life. I want to be clean in your presence, Father God. I'm depending on you to wash me up and keep me clean today!"

From *My Beautiful Daughter* by Tasha Douglas

"Let us run with perseverance the race marked out for us."
—Hebrews 12:1

Sticking to It

The Christian life is a long-distance race rather than a short sprint. It takes a combination of patience, endurance, and persistent determination to finish the race.

Lauren was a long-distance runner on the school track team. She dreamed of running a marathon someday. Her main event in the spring was the 1600 meter run; she also ran cross-country in the fall. Lauren ran on the days she didn't want to, the days it rained, the days her shins hurt, and the days she had plans with her friends. In the races themselves, she regulated her speed carefully to avoid tiring too soon. She saved enough energy for the "kick," a sprint for the finish line on the last lap. But to Lauren, the best thing about racing was Leah. Leah cheered her on, waited at the end of the runs with water and a shoulder to lean on, and picked Lauren up a few times when she fell.

In the race of life, God understands that we will stumble and fall sometimes. We don't need to run the race perfectly—or alone. Jesus makes sure we never run solo. He goes ahead of us to clear a path and behind us to pick us up when we fall. He runs beside us to encourage us.

More to Explore: Matthew 24:13

Girl Talk: What in your life do you need endurance for? Where do you find it?

God Talk: "Lord, I want to finish my race with flying colors. Thank you for running it with me. Amen."

From *Chick Chat* by Kristi Holl

"Go into all the world and preach the gospel to all creation."
—Mark 16:15

Preach It, Sister!

There it was, the disciples' job description. And yours.

"But how am I supposed to do that?" you may be asking. "I'm just a kid!"

Here's the deal. Right now you're in Phase One of that job. You're learning the Good News so that, when you're a more mature Christian, you'll be ready to spread the Word in whatever way God wants you to. But you don't have to wait until you know it all (because nobody ever totally does). Right now you can show Christ to the people in your little piece of the world by doing and being all that you've learned about in this book. If someone asks why you're so happy or where you get the courage to stand up to people or how you always seem to know the right thing to do, you can tell them it's all about your relationship with God.

That's the preaching part. As for the go into all the world part, remember that the world is made up of millions of classrooms, soccer fields, households, church halls, school buses, dance studios, and backyards. As you go into the ones in your world, spread the word by what you say and do and are. Even a kid can do that.

More To Explore: Matthew 28:18–20

Girl Talk: What corners of the world do you enter each week?

God Talk: "Jesus, I want to show you love in everything I do and every place I go. Give me the courage to share your Good News. Amen."

From *That Is So Me* by Nancy Rue